"You can't refuse me."

"You shall just have to learn to love idleness and leisure, my dear. I assure you it has its merits. But first, I do believe we should correct one deficiency before the adventure begins in earnest."

Rosamunde stared back at him mutely.

"Kissing. The deficiency in kisses. You know, the thing that separates us from the beasts."

"I had thought that was reason or compassion."

Luc ignored her. "Good. I didn't hear a 'no.'"

"But this is impossible. I'm in mourning."

He defused her with a steady look.

"And besides, perhaps I don't even like you."

"Me? You don't like, me?" he raised his quizzing glass to his eye.

Her eyes sparkled with laughter.

Other AVON ROMANCES

Sophia Nash

A Dangerous Beauty

AVON BOOKS
An Imprint of HarperCollinsPublishers

This is a work of fiction. Names, characters, places, and incidents are products of the author's imagination or are used fictitiously and are not to be construed as real. Any resemblance to actual events, locales, organizations, or persons, living or dead, is entirely coincidental.

AVON BOOKS
An Imprint of HarperCollins*Publishers*
10 East 53rd Street
New York, New York 10022-5299

Copyright © 2007 by Sophia Nash
ISBN: 978-0-06-123136-0
ISBN-10: 0-06-123136-3
www.avonromance.com

First Avon Books paperback printing: June 2007

Avon Trademark Reg. U.S. Pat. Off. and in Other Countries,
Marca Registrada, Hecho en U.S.A.
HarperCollins® is a registered trademark of HarperCollins Publishers.

Printed in the U.S.A.

10 9 8 7 6 5 4 3 2 1

To Madeleine

Acknowledgments

My greatest thanks go to agent extraordinaire Helen Breitwieser at Cornerstone Literary for her belief in this book and her professional guidance, and to Avon Executive Editor Lyssa Keusch for her enthusiasm and unerring critical eye. I owe you. Oh, how I owe you both.

My appreciation also goes to the following people for their advice and friendship: Kathryn Caskie, Alicia Rasley, Cybil Solyn, Judi McCoy, Tim Bentler-Jungr, Mary Jo Putney, Kathleen Gilles Seidel, Jean Gordon, Kim Pawell, Annie Abaziou, Lanette Scherr, Lurdes Abruscato, Karen Anders, Deborah Barnhardt, Louise Bergin, Jeanne Adams, Leah Grant, Meredith Bond, Sherry Buerkle, Diane Perkins, Pam Poulsen, Denise McInerney, Lisa Gosselin, Christina and Philippe Gérard, Laurie and Eddie Garrick, Peter and Alexandra Nash, and Bunny and Kim Nash.

And finally, as always, endless gratitude to my family for their steadfast support and encouragement.

Author's Note

Each chapter of *A Dangerous Beauty* begins with an epigraph from *The Devil's Dictionary*, a wickedly jaundiced tome by Ambrose Bierce (1842–1914), whose work inspired me. Though some Regency purists might question the use of quotations from a gentleman who neither lived during the (1811–1820) Regency period nor resided anywhere remotely near England (San Francisco, California), I hope readers will overlook these liberties and take pleasure in Bierce's great wit.

While the epigraphs are direct quotations from Bierce's *The Devil's Dictionary*, the definitions created for the fictitious *Lucifer's Lexicon* in *A Dangerous Beauty* are products of my own imagination. In addition, this novel is a work of fiction. The story of the hero, Luc St. Aubyn, is not in any way based on the life of Ambrose Bierce.

Finally, readers who are curious about the mysterious illness in the story might be interested to know that it is grounded in reality. Known as *ciguatera* today, it is food poisoning caused by the consumption of warm-water marine finfish such as groupers, jacks, snapper and mackerel, some of which have accumulated naturally occurring toxins through their diet. Manifestations of ciguatera in humans involve sometimes serious combinations of gastrointestinal, neurological, and cardiovascular disorders.

Booklovers and wordsmiths who would like to learn more about the story behind the story may visit http://www.sophianash.com.

A Dangerous Beauty

Chapter 1

Expectation, n. *The state or condition of mind which is preceded by hope and followed by despair.*

—The Devil's Dictionary, A. Bierce

It was said Rosamunde Isabella Maria Solange Magred Edwina Langdon was given so many names because she was the last child the seventh Earl and Countess of Twenlyne would ever have. But that was only half the truth.

The earl and his wife had carefully chosen names each time the countess had found herself with child. But while there had been great joy with the arrival of each of their first four children—all boys—there had been little surprise. For the last one hundred years the earldom had provided England with enough strapping males to make up a small regiment, but nary a single female.

All the present countess's sons looked like her—

1

blond hair, brown eyes and a fine sprinkling of freckles on their upturned noses. And the earl was proud of his towheaded sons.

But he wanted a daughter. A daughter whose miniature he would carry in his pocket like his contemporaries. A daughter who would giggle and primp and twirl him about her jam-smeared little fingers. A daughter who would give him headaches and the ultimate heartache when she found another man who could make her eyes sparkle just a little brighter than they did for him.

And so, when the countess bore her fifth offspring—a daughter—after a long and painful breech delivery, the proud papa bestowed on this magical child the long string of feminine names he and the countess had chosen during her previous lying-ins. That they were the jumble of French, English, Spanish, Italian and Welsh names of each of the prior Countesses of Twenlyne was no coincidence.

In the rosy glow of the first morning after her birth, the earl hugged this miraculous girl child to his breast and reverently stroked her raven-black curls so like his own. From the glazed window, a shaft of sunlight bathed her slate-blue baby eyes as he gazed adoringly at her.

"You'll not have to put up with that ordinary color for long, my darling. I shall eat crow if they don't change into the proper Welsh Langdon colors by next midsummer's eve." And for the merest moment the earl felt his heart squeeze in recognition. Staring into her intelligent eyes, which were certain to turn into the smoky aquamarine shade of generations of Langdons, it was as if he had always known her. Their souls were destined to become entwined.

The entire household, in fact the entire county, celebrated the earl's happiness while the temporarily neglected sons only grumbled a little.

There was no question the frail countess would recover, for she knew her duty as a mother. And so she did. The earl refused to let doctors dampen his good spirits when his wife became with child soon after Rosamunde's birth.

The countess submitted to her discomfort with customary quiet grace, but it was not to be. She was delivered of another daughter, this one christened with her mother's name only, for there were no other ancestral names left to parcel out. Black-haired, brown-eyed Sylvia Langdon came into creation the same day the countess had nothing more to give this world and so passed on to the next.

If everyone held their breath when the countess died of childbed fever, it was for naught. For the earl, who had loved his wife quite devotedly, transferred that love to his children and never sought a new countess. In his mind, there were too many gothic stories about second wives who evolved into evil stepmothers.

And so, the reclusive earl chose to bury his heart in his love of the land and his children. His progeny gloried in his undivided attention during wild gallops and long nature walks amid the mystical circular stones abounding in the Cornish landscape of their home, Edgecumbe. Theirs was a working estate and the children were brought up to love country life—indeed, to know nothing of town.

It was heaven.

If the siblings noticed their father had a special place in his heart for Rosamunde, they tried to ignore it. The thing was, she was hard not to like. While she could pretend to be a proper, quiet young lady when forced into the role, there was no one who had a greater penchant for adventure—something guaranteed to endear her to her toad-loving, accident-prone brothers. She was always ready to race headlong into any escapade. If it included climbing trees, racing horses or lethal weapons, *all the better*.

And while her brothers might have been continually put out by her uncanny ability to outride them, outswim them, and even best them at every skill involving a target, well, it was something they tried to hide behind young male cockiness. Her generous nature, the only trait she had inherited from her English mother, was a useful balm in tending to bruised brotherly pride. That and her beautiful voice. For while all the siblings were musical by nature, especially Phinn and Sylvia, only Rosamunde could sing.

And oh how she could sing. Almost every evening they gathered in the music room, her father on the pianoforte, Sylvia with her harp and her brothers on various instruments, while Rosamunde sang Welsh songs of love and loss.

There was really but one fault she possessed. The earl called it "bloody pigheadedness" and refused to recognize he had inherited it himself from generations of strong-willed, hot-tempered blue bloods whose clashing characters boiled down to the same overriding element—passion. The cool British traits had melted away in the face of the overpowering heat of more unsteady temperaments. But this trait had benefits. When a Langdon loved, there was nothing insipid about it.

As her long, lanky coltlike limbs grew toward womanhood, Rosamunde began to wish she could trade in her sporting prowess for the cool serenity her younger sister Sylvia possessed in ample quantity. But Rosamunde was plagued with a face that revealed her every emotion.

The first cloud appeared on her horizon when she turned fifteen. Rosamunde learned there was more to boys than their rude noises and lilting taunts. This discovery came in the form of a particularly handsome example of the species, Lord Sumner, the eldest son of the Duke of Helston, whose family had taken up residence at Amberley, a long vacant castle in the neighborhood. Only the younger son of the family was absent, apparently gone to war.

At a supper dance in the village assembly rooms, Rosamunde set eyes on the duke's heir. And it was here for the first time that she failed, utterly and completely, at something. No matter how much she tried to capture his interest, the twenty-six-year-old gentleman was blind to her yet enraptured by several other girls, most notably Augustine Phelps, the reigning beauty of the county.

But Rosamunde had set her cap on him and, well,

there was that issue of her stubbornness to contend with, tinged with the elemental female desire to lead the male species down the right path . . . toward their destiny. Even if it meant kicking and screaming—*their* kicking and screaming.

Rosamunde flopped onto the chaise longue in her bedchamber for a coze with her sister after a particularly exhausting morning following the hounds, and a late breakfast at the Duke of Helston's estate.

"Sylvia, it's positively unnerving"—she tossed her unpinned riding hat with the dashing pheasant feathers onto the bed—"the way he looks at me, or more to the point, the way he looks right through me as if I don't exist."

Sylvia jumped toward the bed and removed the hat. "You know hats on beds foretell disaster."

"I seem to earn a measure of bad luck wherever I go." She shrugged her shoulders ruefully. "Oh Sylvia, I need your help. What am I to do? You're so much better at this sort of thing than I."

"That's not—"

"I heard Auggie whisper I look like a witch, what with this hair and figure."

Sylvia sighed. "Well, *our* hair is unfortunate. But everything else that wicked girl says is ridiculous. There's a reason Father calls you his dangerous beauty and I'd give anything for your height."

"She called you 'the dearest angel from heaven.'"

Sylvia tried to hide a smile.

"Now you'll tell me that perhaps she isn't *so* wicked after all."

Sylvia's face lit up with merriment before both girls dissolved into laughter.

Rosamunde wiped her eyes. "Well, at least Henry finally spoke to me at the breakfast."

"So it's Henry now?" Her sister's eyes were as round and dark as well-worn half pennies. "What did he say?"

"He slapped me on the back and congratulated me for jumping that deep ditch at Penhallow. Then our brother ruined the moment."

"Which one?"

"Phinn. He drew next to us and said I looked like a spotted hen, with mud splattered on my face. Of course I had no idea," Rosamunde said.

"Oh *Edwina*." It was her sibling's favorite nickname for her—all because she liked that one the least of her plethora of names. The picture of the countess Edwina in the portrait gallery always seemed to stare at her in an accusatory fashion as if Rosamunde had misbehaved recently and escaped unscathed, and the countess was annoyed she was stuck within the confines of a frame and unable to do anything about it.

"And then Fitz and Miles *and* James turned to look at me and started laughing. And worst of all, Phinn intercepted Henry's handkerchief with one of his own. I was so close to having a little memento to place under my pillow at night." She sighed dramatically. "I know I'm being ridiculous. Come on, it's hotter than Hades. Let's go swimming."

And that is how the season went. Much plotting and few results. All the while, Rosamunde's fifteen-year-old, childish emotions warred with her emerging womanhood.

The next year was worse, as the duke's family chose to summer in Brighton under the splendid onion-domed Pavilion as favored guests of the Prince Regent.

But the following June, Rosamunde got the seventeenth-birthday present of her dreams—the return of the Helston clan, specifically the duke's heir.

Little did she know, her dreams—and the attainment of such—might just prove to be the opposite. Personally, her sister swore afterward, it was the accumulation of more than a decade and a half of ignoring the power of superstition. Everyone knew there was more magic in Cornwall than there were saints in heaven.

Rosamunde's desire to see Lord Sumner that dangerous hot season was unrelenting in its intensity. Yet each time she found herself near him, she became tongue-tied and could not stop herself from acting like a smiling simpleton. Her nervousness around him infuriated her. There was something about his light brown hair falling into his eyes and his smile that left her heart racing and her prayers filled with requests for forgiveness. All of her brothers noticed it and teased her relentlessly, as any normal sibling would.

The morning before the duke's family was to repair to town, Rosamunde put on a good face and laughed off her dejection. Determined to move her thoughts from Lord Sumner, she boldly chose to ride her father's new four-year-old iron-gray stallion to the beachhead.

Rosamunde lowered her body to the horse's white-peppered mane, urging the already excited animal to new speeds. She galloped Domino toward the tall sea grasses on the nearby cliffs of Perran Sands and was exhilarated by the sense of freedom.

Lord Sumner. Who needed him? What was he, compared to her family and the beauty that surrounded her, especially on the back of a powerful horse with a mind to explore the stark splendor of the land?

Overlooking the wind-whipped sea from a magnificent promontory point, she suddenly noticed another rider near the cliffs in the distance. A man astride a massive chestnut with four white socks. She sucked in her breath. *Lord Sumner.*

Just when she had determined to forget him. Not that it meant a thing to him. Why, he barely knew she existed.

"Hey ho," he called, riding up. "Lady Rosamunde? What a great surprise. I thought ladies were still abed at this wickedly early hour." His horse crow-hopped near hers.

Her heart beat so strongly she felt sure he could see it through her riding habit. She swallowed her nervousness and reminded herself she didn't care anymore. "I am not a lady, sir."

He chuckled.

She felt the heat of a blush and was mortified. She never blushed. "What I mean is that I am not that sort of lady."

"Clearly not. Good God, is that a stallion?"

"Why, yes."

"Amazing. Boots here is ready for a bit of a run to

earn his oats. Shall we have a go at it, then? A race down to the end of the beach?" He laughed and the sun struck his hair in a way that revealed the gold in his brown locks.

She nodded, unable to say a word. And with a shout they were off.

The powerful hindquarters of Lord Sumner's gelding pumped into the sandy soil but were hampered by the gentleman's weight. The horses pounded along the path parallel to the cliff side by side at times, clearing low-lying coops and field markers with inches to spare. When Rosamunde's mount nosed ahead as they wound down toward the beach below, she knowingly violated the cardinal rule of courtship . . . marriage-minded females should never tamper with male prowess.

Shooting past the outcropping of rocks at the end of the crescent of sand, she turned to see Lord Sumner right behind.

"Lady Rosamunde"—he dipped his head in an exaggerated fashion—"I concede defeat." Oh, he was so dashing, even with his ruddy complexion. "But we never did specify a prize to the winner, did we, Scamp?"

Scamp? With that one silly word, her dreams shriveled yet again. "Why, I'll have you know I'm seven and ten, sir. And taller than most ladies by a full hand at least. I'm no scamp."

Lord Sumner pursed his lips in silent laughter and dismounted, his boots making deep impressions in the sand. He looped his arm through his horse's reins and crossed to help her dismount. His superior height compounded her annoyance at his benevolent smile.

He tilted his head and a wave of amusement passed over his expression. "Perhaps. But don't you think *scamp* refers to sensibility rather than age?"

His deep baritone voice did queer things to her insides.

"Your sister and Augustine—*Miss Phelps*—for example, don't have a scampish bone in their bodies despite their tender years."

He was so close to her, the closest he'd ever been, and it—specifically, the mysterious, masculine look in his eye—was scrambling her wits. She longed to grasp his neck and tug him down to her, her—well, to be honest, she just wasn't sure. She knew the mechanics of kissing, but wondered how they wouldn't end up bumping noses. Would he twist his face left or right? Or maybe straight on?

"Well then, madam,"—his dazzling smile was entrancing—"what shall be your prize?"

His lips were a mere few inches from her own. She gazed into the depths of his eyes and swallowed painfully. "A—a kiss," she whispered. Oh God, what had she said? She closed her eyes in embarrassment. She hadn't really just suggested he kiss her? She reopened her eyes, sure to see him laughing at her.

But he wasn't. His eyebrows rose and a flush of scarlet stained his cheeks. It seemed he leaned toward her slightly, so she met him more than halfway. Placing her arms around his neck, she pecked him quickly on the lips.

"Why, how very generous of you, Lady Rosamunde. Not that I'm not delighted to accommodate—but surely"—he tugged at his neckcloth—"Surely you must know that . . . well, my heart is otherwise en—"

Her heart fell to the pit of her stomach and she whirled away from him, willing herself not to hear another word. She threw herself into the saddle without later knowing how she managed it without his help. But she had to get away—as far and as fast as possible—to lick her wounds in private.

Henry—Lord Sumner to her forevermore—was in love with someone else. He thought her a mere child to be amused. She would never, ever be so embarrassed again in her entire life.

Or so she thought.

She rode along the cliff paths from the edges of the duke's property toward her beloved Edgecumbe feeling sorry for herself and then thoroughly disgusted by her self-pity.

For goodness sake, hadn't she watched her handsome brothers make complete fools of themselves over this jumped-up notion of love? It was supposed to be a strong, mutually held sentiment that made one a better person, not a blithering idiot, when it knocked on one's heart. But surely, her feelings were much stronger than her silly brothers' sensibilities. Surely, she hadn't made such a cake of herself.

In her heart, she knew she had.

She had been more foolish than the lot of them.

She could only take comfort in knowing that she would at least be able to play the wise older sister when Sylvia came to cry on her shoulder with natterings of love.

The fields were at their most bountiful, the harvest process just begun. Rosamunde crossed into her father's lands many hours after leaving the scene of her disappointment. She turned the stallion over to the stable master, who was deep into the long process of polishing the crested family carriage.

"Why, Lady Rosamunde, you've missed all the goings-on. Your father's returned from town. And the visiting bishop and the two Miss Smithams came to call."

Rosamunde shuddered and prayed she wouldn't have to face the three biggest gossips in all of St. Ives, Penzance and Land's End combined.

Jones must have seen her expression. "Don't worry, miss, they've gone now. Back to their ministerin'." He coughed and she could swear she heard him mutter, "or tittle-tattlin' if you were to ask."

Rosamunde admired the stable master's handiwork on the carriage and beat a hasty retreat to the back entrance of her family home. Within a trice she was in front of her washstand, the tepid water soothing away the traces of tears on her dusty cheeks. She glanced at the looking glass and saw what appeared to be the loneliest, plainest girl in the world. It was not often that her desire for a mother overwhelmed her, but this was one of those times. She fingered her mourning locket engraved with a rose. She always wore it. Beneath the gold oval and a thin glass lay a lock of her mother's flaxen hair intricately woven with her own black strands. Glancing at the miniature of her mother near the washstand, Rosamunde shook her head. She looked nothing like her.

She knew she must speak to her father. He was the only one who understood her, and would know what she should do to stop making such a fool of herself. Maybe he would suggest a grand tour or her first trip to London. Then she would be able to store away this ridiculous obsession and return to some semblance of normalcy. At least she wouldn't have to worry about losing her heart again. It was lost somewhere on Perran Sands.

The sounds of clinking harnesses and carriage wheels on pea gravel drifted in from the window. Curiosity got the better of her and she adopted the pose every female knows from birth, falling into the shadows to peek through the curtains.

The Helston bronze-and-silver crest were emblazoned on the doors of a black town carriage with a Salisbury boot. No less than four outriders flanked the elegant carriage, the riders' dark purple livery and tall powdered wigs bespoke of elegance wasted this far south of London. They must be deadly hot inside. Why hadn't they taken an open landau instead of this boxed-up funereal equipage?

A small, hard ball of ill ease formed in Rosamunde's stomach. What was going on? The duke's family had never condescended to visit before. Her father had even joked that apparently an earl wasn't high enough in the instep for the Helston duchy. Her curl of fear blossomed into glacial foreboding as the duke, a large man, jumped from the conveyance without bothering to wait for the step to be lowered. His heir emerged and stood deferentially behind his father like a well-trained king's page.

So focused was she on Lord Sumner and his father that she almost failed to note the small withered hand that appeared at the shadowed doorway of the carriage. The haughty duke looked down at it and barked some sort of order. Rosamunde stiffened. One of the duke's servants closed the carriage door, forcing the lady within to remain ensconced.

Rosamunde had never felt cowardly in her life. But the urge to run away was upon her and it was as primal as the desire an animal has to escape a well-oiled trap. For a quarter hour she paced, disordered thoughts jangling through her mind.

A sharp rap on the door followed by the footman's message that her father required her presence in the library erased her plans of escape. She would never disobey her father.

While she knew the servants wouldn't openly stare at any member of the family, she felt the weight of every maid and footman's gaze on her back as she passed them. This was ridiculous. She had nothing to fear. She calmly smoothed the wrinkles from her favorite dark blue velvet riding habit and knocked once on the library's carved oak door.

Four pairs of eyes trained their attention on her as she crossed the length of the room, her short riding boots' heels clicking loudly on the intricate parquet floor. The duke, Lord Sumner and Phinnius framed her father, who bore the blackest expression Rosamunde had ever seen on his erstwhile handsome, kindly face. Lord Sumner was pale and refused to meet her gaze.

She pushed back her shoulders. She hadn't done anything atrocious enough to merit this. Lord Sumner would never have revealed the embarrassment of that kiss. It was just her father's expression—it made her feel guilty even when there was really nothing to confess. Well, maybe he was justifiably annoyed about her taking the stal—

"I never thought I would see the day when a child of mine would bring such dishonor to our family," her father said quietly.

"I'm so sorry, Father," she started. "I won't ever take out Domino without your permission a—"

"Domino? You rode my stallion?" Her father covered his face with his hands and dragged them down his visage, leaving angry red marks. "Who cares about Domino?" His voice was dangerously calm.

"Wha—" Rosamunde began.

"Don't say another word," her father interrupted. "You're to listen and only respond 'yes' at the obvious places."

"I really don't think—" said Phinnius.

"You're not here to think, Phinn. As my heir, you're here to witness a change to our family," her father responded.

Rosamunde felt a weight drop in her stomach and she stood stock-still. The Duke of Helston's face wore an impressive mask of stone, and his son appeared on the verge of tears. What, dear God, was going on?

The duke gave an almost imperceptible nod toward his son. Lord Sumner turned and made two long strides to face her. He caught up her bare hand in his gloved one and held it firmly. He closed his eyes tightly for a long moment, then breathed in deeply. "Lady Rosamunde, would you make me the happiest of men by consenting to become my bride?"

Rosamunde had the strangest urge to slap him. She had never lifted a finger to a soul. Her free hand balled into a fist. He had made a mockery of her greatest desire. She scanned the deadly serious faces in the room.

"Lord Sumner, sir, you cannot be serious. You certainly don't seem happy. You look more like a man facing the gallows, if you were to ask me." She snatched her hand back. "And you scarcely know I exist. Really. I could never—"

The long squeal of chair legs dragging along the floor coincided with the sound of her father's palm slamming his desk. "I told you we did not want to hear another word from you with the exception of 'yes.' After which you shall go upstairs, have one bag packed and prepare to leave for London. I'll not have you waste another moment of His Grace's time."

The duke replaced his hard expression with one of boredom, disgust and a banked anger that made Rosamunde's nerves desert her.

"Your Grace," said her father, "I must apologize for my daughter's behavior—again."

The duke turned his cold gaze on her father. "It is rumored she is the most spoilt female in the county.

I do hope you will have her better trained before she is under my roof. There is little tolerance for coddled females there. Ah, but my son knows well how to mete out lessons in good behavior."

A chill swept through Rosamunde. The duke's pale green eyes looked like the dangerous thin ice on the pond during winter. She glanced down at his hands and they appeared peasantlike, brutish and thick-skinned. She shivered once.

"But what has happened? Why is Lord Sumner being forced to ask for my hand?" she whispered, her eyes trained on the corner of her father's desk.

His Grace banged his walking stick on the floor. "I'll tell you why, you thoughtless girl. Your chance to say 'no' was left on the beach. If you had had the sense to say 'no' then, and hadn't lured my son to that private cove, and enticed him with your wiles, then he would not be here now, forced to solicit the hand of a conniving chit. Do you think I will enjoy seeing the Helston bloodlines tainted by a—a gel of such questionable character? Do you?" His voice had grown in pitch until the last was said with a roar.

"But, noth—nothing happened. We raced, and I'm sorry if it was slightly improper. It was just a race . . ." Her voice trailed off as she watched a large vein in the center of the duke's forehead beat a wild tattoo.

"And did you not ask him to kiss you?"

She jerked her face toward Lord Sumner and saw him close his eyes and shake his head. *The coward*. What had he done? Why wasn't he coming to her defense? He didn't want her, he implicitly told her he lov—

"Well?" her father demanded. "What do you have to say for yourself, Rosamunde?"

"But, he doesn't like me—"

"Not according to the Miss Smithams and the bishop," her father interrupted.

The blood in her head rushed to the ends of her fingers and she thought she might just faint for the first time in her life.

"Are you actually suggesting you did not behave with the utmost lack of propriety whilst hiding yourselves near the beachhead?" asked the duke from behind her.

She whirled to face him. "Of course we didn't, Your Grace."

"Your impertinence is insupportable." He stepped so close to her she could smell traces of stale cheroots and overly sweet cologne.

Her father's eyes narrowed and she tasted the metallic tang of blood. She had chewed her inner cheek to ribbons.

"Then why is there sand and wrinkles on the back of your gown, and your hair tumbled down?" His Grace demanded.

Rosamunde instinctively touched the back of her head and felt the tuft of a sea oat in her hair. Bile rose in her throat.

"I've been riding along the downs, and stopped to rest a little before returning home." She brushed the back of her blue velvet riding habit. "It's just a bit of dirt from the place I chose to sit." She wasn't going to admit to crying for long minutes in a small hollow.

The duke snorted and turned to face her father. "I thought you said your daughter was a well brought up, clever thing who would be able to adjust to her new role. The chit cannot even lie intelligently."

Rosamunde turned to Lord Sumner and hoped he would see her desperation. He turned away.

"But, he—he loves another."

Lord Sumner twisted back toward her, his face contorted in agony.

"My son knows his duty. He doesn't love anyone except his father, girl. And you would do well to learn by his example." The duke sighed impatiently. "Enough of this. You should be thankful I've decided to save your reputation, if only because it's time my son takes a wife. Why, if your father were not who he is—I assure you we'd leave you to your fate. A thank-you would be in order, actually. But I see you've not learned your manners yet. Well, we shall meet at St. George's in a month's time. There your lessons will commence. I shall arrange for the archbishop—" said the duke.

"No," Rosamunde interrupted in a whisper.

"What"—the duke's mouth was an inch from her own "—did you say?" He was stooped and she could see his hands shaking with rage.

She stepped back and almost sat on her father's desk. "I said *no*. I won't marry him."

An ominous silence crawled in on hot feet.

"Your Grace," said her father. "Please excuse us. We will of course meet you as discussed. Rosamunde is most honored by your son's offer and accepts. I shall have my solicitor draw up the marriage settlements in London while you procure the special license from the archbishop. On behalf of my family, I thank you for the courtesy of your visit." Her father bowed deeply.

Rosamunde stepped forward. "But, I will not—"

Before she could utter another word, the duke struck her.

Hot pinpoints of pain echoed from the corner of her eye to the bottom of her chin. And in the instant her father did not censure the duke, Rosamunde understood the unbearable feeling of the loss of her only remaining parent's trust and love. What she felt now was true panic, the sort where horror rises up the back of one's throat and tightens like a vise. It was the horrible realization of being a pawn, unable to extricate oneself from a dark future, much like an animal caught in a poacher's snare.

She swallowed and valiantly struggled to regain her calm. Her father, when they were alone, would believe her. He would allow her to explain that this was some sort of horrid misunderstanding. And then he would disentangle her from this, this nightmare of epic proportions. Everything would be fine.

The stillness was palpable. Or maybe it simply seemed the seconds had turned into minutes. Finally, Phinnius pulled her toward the door. The last thing she saw was a glimpse of her father's face full of implacable anger and embarrassment directed toward her.

Fate had finally caught up with her.

Her sister had once asked if she felt nervous sitting on the high pedestal her father placed her on each day. Rosamunde hadn't understood what Sylvia was talking about. She did now. Her fall from grace was as hard as it was long, and the gods—or the Devil—were demanding punishment for curses due.

A nightmarish ritual ensued of daily demands and arguments by her father and silence from her. She would die before she succumbed and she knew with a heavy heart that her father was holding fast to the same course. Ten days locked in her room with only bread and water changed nothing. Then her father mysteriously unlocked her door without a word and left for London with orders for the rest of the family to join him in a fortnight. Now she was ripe for the plucking.

Little did Rosamunde know, fate would intervene again—not once but twice more in her lifetime. The next time it was in the form of a marriage-minded country squire, successful at hiding his mean-spirited ways by employing acting abilities Shakespeare would have admired. Alfred Baird's chief allure was his timing and his false sympathy.

The very day her father left for town, Mr. Baird appeared with flowers in his hands and the enticing offer of a marriage of convenience to a pillar of Cornish society on his lips. More importantly, he appeared to believe her and offered something she craved, escape and the promise to shield her from gossip.

Without anyone's knowledge or approval, Rosamunde fled with him to Scotland, married in haste, and repented not in leisure.

When her father signaled his refusal to provide

a dowry by not receiving them at Edgecumbe, the squire's artful performance ended and her life slogged forward into one long flood of sadness and pain.

Only her sister was loyal to her. Sylvia had appeared on the squire's doorstep soon after the marriage, vowing to stay with her. She took Rosamunde's side with belated vengeance. And young Rosamunde was too distraught to try and dissuade the one person who still loved her.

The squire knew all too well how to whittle her spirit, and Rosamunde soon learned the lessons the duke had threatened to teach her and more. In the privacy of their small cottage, Alfred's temperament shifted on terrifyingly trivial whims. The constant attempts to keep him in good humor always failed, which led to degrading insults and long sets of rules and duties by day and fear by night. In short, Rosamunde endured an utterly pathetic existence with no end in sight.

And perhaps worst of all, she was not allowed to sing.

She withdrew from her former life and friends, finding solace in nature and her sister. Persistent wistfulness slowly sapped away her natural exuberance, and she became a quiet coward in the real and imagined gardens of her life, doing all she could to avoid any hint of scandal. She had lost almost everything, and lived carefully so she would not lose it all.

The next time fate would intervene would be eight years later.

It would be a long wait.

Chapter 2

Brandy, n. *A cordial composed of one part thunder-and-lightning, one part remorse, two parts bloody murder, one part death-hell-and-the-grave and four parts clarified Satan. Dose, a headful* all *the time.*

— The Devil's Dictionary, A. Bierce

"**C**are for a dose of mother's milk?"

Luc St. Aubyn, the eighth Duke of Helston, glanced up from his writings, toward the entrance of his quiet lair. Only one person would dare . . .

A small clawlike hand dangled a bottle of brandy from a crack in the doorway.

"I've told you I don't imbibe before breakfast. Why are you skulking about, Ata?"

The door opened a bit wider and the tiny form of his grandmother appeared. Her face was overwhelmed by a large black lace cap, which matched the fichu above her ebony silk gown.

Luc sighed. "I hate when you walk about like that"—he gestured to her widow's weeds—"like you're in the grave already."

She smiled without showing her aged, long teeth. "But I am, dear boy, I am." The stiff crinoline under-skirt of her gown made faint crackling noises as it swung to one side when she closed the door.

Her gowns were always too long because she thought it would elongate her short stature. As far as Luc could tell, it only made her trip more often than most people.

She continued, "I have at least one limb in death's maw, anyway, as well you know."

He glanced sharply at her gnarled hand and the de-canter she gripped awkwardly. "You know I've never an appetite before noon."

She moved across the dusty Aubusson carpet, reached for a crystal goblet from a side drawer in his leather-topped desk and filled it with the amber liquid. "That's why Cook is so loyal to us. Your breakfast is always delayed, and so convenient. It never has to be heated, or chilled, or even tossed away. Better yet"—and here she lifted the glass to her lips and drank long and deep without sputtering—"it can be shared."

"Ata," he murmured, hiding a smile. "What will the servants think?"

"Do we care?"

"Apparently not."

She appeared slightly owlish, but Luc knew better. His grandmother could hold her liquor better than a twenty-five-stone sailor on home leave. In fact, he had never seen her anything but clearheaded, despite her frequent communion with Beelzebub's brew.

He pushed aside his papers, weighted by a ship's compass, and withdrew another balloon-shaped glass.

"I've always thought people who breakfast late develop greater intelligence than those who muddle with muffins at dawn," she said while pouring him a glass. "All that rubbish about early birds and worms. Why would anyone want to be compared to something that lays eggs?"

He tried to stifle a chuckle. It would only encourage her. "And they say I'm a hopeless case."

"A hopeless case? Surely not. A rogue, perhaps. Even a rake. Yes, definitely a rake. Maybe even the worst sort of rake. But then, everyone loves a rake. Idealistic young milksops need rakes to shoot in order to become heroes. And God knows the society columns need rakes and their exploits to sell newspapers. But most of all, England needs rakes to satisfy the females. For there is no kiss like one from a rake."

"Ah, the voice of experience," he said dryly.

"Maybe. Maybe not, but there's still time. I'm allowed my own little expectations of finding happiness after I see to your own—"

"Enough." He lowered his feet from the edge of his desk with a loud thud. "I'm not in the mood for your lunatic ravings of connubial bliss and the sodding importance of heirs. I'm only here because"—he scratched his head—"Well, because I refuse to disappoint both you and Madeleine at the same time."

"Good boy. I knew your lessons in deportment would serve us well in the end."

"I'll walk my sister down the church aisle, and then I'm for town."

He knew that shrewd look on his grandmother's face.

"I mean it."

Silence.

He shook his head. "I won't stay a moment longer than that. You might have talked me into reopening this monstrous, musty place for Madeleine's wedding, but that doesn't mean I must mingle with fools."

More silence.

"All right. I'll stay through the wedding breakfast." He lifted his glass, and pungent fumes wafted through the still air. "As long as you serve *my* sort of breakfast." He tipped his glass in mock salute and took a long pull of the golden liquid. The false warmth of the brandy tickled his senses and flooded his being with calm.

"Was there any doubt I would?" she responded with a musical laugh.

The sound wound around his heart and swelled his emotions. It left him with a rare magnanimous notion. "Maybe"—he pursed his lips—"I'll even stay for the next fortnight to help you prepare instead of returning to town as planned. Could use a quiet week to finish this—"

His grandmother responded more quickly than a wallflower responds to an invitation to dance. "I'll hold you to that."

"Have I ever let you down?"

She raised her penciled-in eyebrows until they almost disappeared under her fussy black lace cap.

"I resent that," he muttered.

"Did I say anything?"

He glared at her. "How many people are invited, Ata? I suppose I should know if I'm to be imprisoned for the duration."

"Not that many really. Just two or three dozen here on the estate. And perhaps there are a few more—a mere handful, really, staying at the Hearth and Horn in the village. And then I suppose there are others who have arranged lodging in the neighborhood."

"The total number is . . . ?"

"About two hundred, I would think."

"Two, blasted, hundred?" He closed his eyes and lowered his head into his hands.

She poured another glass of fire and brimstone for him. "Maybe three."

"And who are the people who have finagled an invitation to stay under this roof?"

"Well, we're a bit ill-paired. There are a few too many females, I'm afraid."

"There can never be too many females," he said wolfishly. "Perhaps this won't be so bad after all."

His grandmother took on a serious expression suddenly. It saddened him. He had forced a promise from her years ago that she wasn't to ever be distressed again—no matter how loud he barked.

"No, Luc. You're not to sniff about them."

He stiffened. For the love of . . . "Don't tell me you've invited the deserving crows? *Not the Widows*

Club? Even you know we can't have a passel of weeping nuns at Madeleine's wedding." He glanced at her somber attire. "Present company excluded, of course," he said gruffly.

Silence.

More silence.

Ata's eyes narrowed.

"So"—he forced a smile—"I see we'll be enjoying the scintillating company of the widows for the next few weeks. How charming. How utterly, bloody, charming."

"Quite." She plucked at her gown. "But, don't forget your promise. They're not to be dallied with. They've been through enough."

"Right. No dallying. No bloody dallying . . . just a bit of weak tea and conversation. But no dallying." He paused and felt one of his brows rise as he muttered, "Does that include no tarrying?"

Ata blinked.

"You know . . . tarrying along shadowy corridors, or in the gamekeeper's hut. You did mention a rake's kiss being good for England's females, didn't you?"

It seemed that his grandmother did indeed have a level to her tolerance of his bad manners and he had exceeded it. Her pained expression was proof enough.

"Oh, all right. You know, you've elevated silence to an art form. Very well. I'll pay the penance. What may I do to please you?"

"You're to come down and entertain the widows. Now. Politely."

"Now? Some of them are here? When did they arrive?"

"They've been here for two days already, Luc. You've just been oblivious to it."

"You know I prefer to take my meals in here. I have my work and all." He waved his ink-stained fingers over the scattered papers on his desk and on the floor and then stilled when he faced Ata's stony expression again. "And how would you suggest I entertain them?"

"With archery. I like to whisper to them that they can envision their dearly departed husbands at the bull's-eye. It does seem to cheer them up quite a lot."

My dear Rosamunde,

While I might be a mystery to you, as we have never met, I have heard of the ills that have befallen you and find society's reaction quite wanting. Thus I extend to you an invitation to join my private and very clandestine Widows Club, a society I formed to help deserving ladies find a happier future. We're gathered for an extended house party at Amberley—very near where you live I believe—in celebration of my granddaughter's wedding. After, I invite you and your sister to stay with me in town.

Please forgive the bluntness that comes from attaining social consequence too early in life, but it is my fondest hope you will cast off any silly, prideful notions and that your curiosity will triumph over any apprehensions you might hold regarding this request to spend a season or two with me and a few other ladies who share your circumstances.

I require only your discretion, my dear, if you choose to join my secret Widows Club. A carriage shall be sent to you upon your acceptance of this invitation.

I remain your future confidante,
Merceditas St. Aubyn
Dowager Duchess of Helston

The edges of the letter fluttered in the breeze as her sister read it. Rosamunde deposited the two heavy bandboxes she was carrying on the ground and leaned against the red oak. To calm her nerves she hummed, something Alfred had always forbidden.

The late summer sun was high in the sky and the shade was a welcome relief. Here, in the endless series of fields that resembled nothing more than a massive well-ordered patchwork quilt, Rosamunde finally let exhaustion overtake her. She rubbed the sensitive flesh of her forearms where the handles had cut into her. They had walked far enough and fast enough for the prickle of immediate fear to recede along with the slight chill in their bones. Carrying life's possessions was hot work.

Sylvia raised her large, dark eyes from the note. "I wish you had told me about this earlier."

"Dearest, it was too absurd to even consider when I received it a fortnight ago. But I found the idea gained merit with Algernon's arrival." She cursed under her breath. "I still can't believe Alfred broke his promise and left the cottage to his cousin."

"Well, I believe it," replied Sylvia. "Alfred was excellent at breaking promises."

"It's a wonder his cousin gave us a year of peace. But then, Algernon seems to take pleasure in giving a proper face to the outside world." Rosamunde looked away. "I knew if I showed you the letter before we left you might refuse."

"I should think *you* would be the one digging in your heels. I mean, really, Rosamunde, the idea of fleeing to London with so little in our pockets was ill-advised. But this . . ." She shook her head. "Please tell me we're not going to Amberley—to stay with the Duchess of *Helston*? You're mad. Why, I've heard people in the village describe the new duke as being eccentric and very ill-mannered, not at all like—like his brother."

Rosamunde looked toward a flock of sheep whose heavy coats were prime for sheering, too disheartened to face her sister's doubting expression. "We're staying at the invitation of the *dowager duchess*. And we'll probably see little of the duke. We've nothing to fear."

"Nothing to fear? Do you really think the new Duke of Helston doesn't know what happened eight years ago between his brother and our family? And even if luck is with us and he doesn't know, do you really think he'll be in the dark for long?" Sylvia whipped her head around. Long strands of her black hair caught in her face and she brushed at them. "Why, half the *ton* will be down from London for his sister's wedding. Everyone will whisper and cut you at every opportunity. And you," Sylvia paused for emphasis, "you who have avoided society for the last eight years like the plague? Does this dowager know our history?"

Rosamunde shook her head. "I don't know."

"Let's go back. He won't have missed us."

Rosamunde looked at the angle of the sun in the cerulean sky. Strange how the weather could be so beautiful on such a dark day in her life. "Oh, he'll have missed us. In fact, we had better keep walking." She took the letter from Sylvia and grasped her bandboxes again to keep going. "We'll be lucky if Algernon's hunger outpaces his desire to kill us once he learns we've gone. I'm counting on his famous appetite and Cook's popovers. She promised to stave him off as long as possible. I'm also hoping his avaricious nature will help us. The solicitor prepared all the ledgers. He will well enjoy counting his newly inherited wealth. *Again.*"

Sylvia's beautiful face was distraught.

"We haven't a choice, my love," Rosamunde continued softly as they trudged up a long hill. "I won't spend another night in that godforsaken place. I've given enough years of my life and yours for my mistakes, and I'll not do it all over again with Alfred's cousin—especially when his interest is . . . well, I'd rather not think about it."

"But we can't go to Amberley. You know we can't," her sister moaned.

"We haven't the means to go anywhere else." She paused and continued in low tones. "I wish you would reconsider and return to Edgecumbe. I beg you to go. You know I've hated the sacrifices you've made. It only makes me feel worse."

"We agreed not to reopen the subject, Rosa."

"No, *you* said you wouldn't talk about—"

Suddenly they were at the crest of the hill and before

them lay, in all its majesty, one of the most beautiful castles in southern England . . . Amberley. The warm honey-colored stone reflected the early afternoon sun. The architect had practiced care and restraint in the symmetry of the design; two great turrets flanked the impressive middle. The inhabitants clearly possessed a fine fortune given the staggering window tax they must be forced to pay. There was mullion glass upon mullion glass, the myriad panes glittering in every direction. And this was only the rear of the castle.

Stately gardens swathed the estate from end to end. Seeing the profusion of blooms, Rosamunde's eyes misted for the first time. Her own garden had been her consolation and her salvation in the end. She had been able to lose herself and her memories there and it was the only thing she would truly miss.

Her steps faltered as they wended their way through the pea-gravel footpaths toward the tiered upper levels. A group of people was gathered at one end of the property near the castle, and they appeared to be playing some sort of—

"Hallooo!"

A tiny, wizened lady dressed in the severest of mourning crossed toward them, a profusion of black lace in her wake.

Rosamunde whispered to her sister, "Well, brace yourself, dearest, this could be very embarrassing." She whipped her bags behind her and sent up a prayer.

"Heavens," the lady said breathlessly, bustling up to them. "You must be—" She let the question hang in the stillness.

"Mrs. Baird, ma'am. Rosamunde Baird, and my sister, Lady Sylvia Langdon. We're lately of Barton's Cottage." She bobbed a small curtsy. "We've come to call on Her Grace."

The older lady's eyes flashed with humor and a magnificent smile made Rosamunde blind to the lady's wrinkles. Why, she looked like a mischievous gypsy, with her dark eyes and olive complexion.

"La! You're looking at her. Delighted to make your acquaintance, my dears." She smiled shrewdly. "I'm Merceditas St. Aubyn."

Both Rosamunde and Sylvia swooped into deferential court curtsies, and Rosamunde felt the flush of embarrassment. She had already offended the one person who had offered their only chance of escape. "Your Grace," she whispered, her gaze on the ground.

"No, no, my dears, we'll have none of that here." The dowager grasped her arm and tugged her to regain her footing. "I'm delighted to have you join us." She peeked at the bandboxes. "I take it you will both honor us with a nice long visit, then?"

"If your invitation is still open, Your Grace."

"For as long as you like, Rosamunde. I may call you Rosamunde?" She linked arms with her. "I'm too old to remember titles and surnames and the like. I find multiple hyphenated names the worst sort of pretension, don't you? I do believe the gentry invented them to irritate the rest of us. You may call me Ata, as all my friends do."

"Yes, Your—Ata." Rosamunde stared at the little lady. She had never had anyone become intimate with her so quickly. In fact, never had anyone invited her to friendship other than in her girlhood.

"Come along, then. You can leave your possessions here. I'll send a footman. Now tell me, Sylvia, are you adept at archery? I have a divine bow made of—"

Rosamunde's mind blocked the banter between her sister and the duchess as they crossed the vast gardens. She still had so many questions, but was too polite to voice them. She tried to quiet her inner turmoil by breathing deeply. She should tell the duchess about her notorious history before her courage failed her.

"Your Grace, I'm sorry to interrupt, but I must tell you a little about my past before we join the others," Rosamunde said hesitantly.

"Your past? Why I refuse to dwell on sadness, my dear. Tragedy doesn't last—that's its chief charm. You're only to think of the future here. It's the primary rule of my little group." She paused and looked at her sideways. "You haven't forgotten that discretion is one of the other guiding principles, have you?"

"No, of course not," Rosamunde replied. "But, I must tell you—"

"No, you must not. Not now, we're almost upon them. I shall introduce you to the other members of the club. There are four ladies who chose to join us here. You probably haven't made their acquaintance as they are from other parts." She paused. "And there are others to meet as well."

Rosamunde inhaled sharply and wondered, not for the first time, if the new Duke of Helston was anything like his father. The former ruthless peer of the realm and his family had left Amberley soon after the scandal, never to return. Until now.

She had heard five years ago that the duchess had taken ill and preceded the old duke in death a scant month or two before the duke had suffered a fatal carriage accident. Lord Sumner—Henry—it had been a long time since she had allowed herself to think of him—had been lost at sea two years later.

It was rumored that the new duke, a former commander in the Royal Navy, had returned to London after assuming the title. Not that she knew anything more about the mysterious gentleman. Her unreliable reports came from Cook, who parceled out daily doses of weak tea and village gossip.

They approached a vibrant green lawn littered with several archery targets near a small bridge strangled by overgrown wisteria vines. A large crowd of guests, gathered to cheer on the competitors, turned their attention toward them and Rosamunde felt mortification trickle down her spine. Any hope she had held of not being recognized after her long absence from society was extinguished by the many shocked and outraged expressions of the local gentry upon her arrival.

Oh, this was every bit as ghastly as she had known it would be. The utter silence turned to sputters of disgust from those who knew her. Inquisitive strangers pressed closer. She heard again all the whispered vileness of before.

Wanton . . . slut . . . soiled goods . . . whore. The words swirled 'round and 'round her brain just as they had so long ago when she had last entered the village church.

Rosamunde forced herself to take shallow breaths. She gripped Sylvia's hand when she felt her trying to shrink away.

The tiny dowager duchess pursed her lips. "Goodness me," she bellowed, "I'm certain I misheard the most outrageous thing. Certainly none of the guests here to attend my granddaughter's wedding would ever breathe a word against one of my dearest and oldest friends." She glanced at Rosamunde and winked. "I'm certain of it."

Silence.

"I thought not. Come along Mrs. Baird, Lady Sylvia. I must introduce you to my grandson." She tilted her head toward a lone gentleman who was too distant to have witnessed Rosamunde's embarrassment.

As they walked toward him, the fickle-natured crowd turned their attention to the duke, allowing her the chance to regain a modicum of composure. She concentrated on the dark figure who wore his black hair tied in a severe queue, a fashion of the last century.

Rosamunde could only see his profile, but the tinge of gray in his sideburns proved he had passed his early thirties. He wore none of the more vivid colors of the gentlemen down from town. Clad in unrelieved black with the exception of a white shirt and cravat, he appeared in deep mourning as well.

He tossed aside a tall beaver hat, fastened an arrow in the long heartwood bow, and toed the chalk mark on the grass. The severe line of his rugged physique suggested a sort of predatory power and raw masculinity.

He squinted under the noonday sun and took aim, his arm steady and sure. But at the same moment he let fly his arrow, Rosamunde caught a feminine voice behind her tittering, "Why he's the infamous Lord Fire and Ice, don't you know."

It was clearly enough to ruin his concentration and he missed the target's center by a hand's width. He cursed under his breath and turned his black gaze to her. Did he think she had said it? A stream of pure awareness swept through her and she inhaled roughly. She could feel the blood pulsing through every vein in her body as she stood rooted to the spot.

A dangerous, shadowy expression perched above his long aristocratic nose, which showed the effects of a round or two of physical altercations. His dark complexion stood out among the rest of the crowd of standard-issue pasty-faced, blue-eyed Englishmen. And while he held not a hint of his deceased father's or his brother Henry's looks, if not for his height, he resembled the kindhearted dowager duchess more than anyone. Why then, did Rosamunde have the oddest desire to flee? *Or was it to rush toward him?*

Rosamunde clenched her hands when she became aware they were shaking. He had stared at her too long and the tension was nearly unbearable..

The low hum of conversation halted, everyone noticing his impolite glare. He handed his bow to one of the ladies and crossed the short distance to his grandmother.

"Ah, another one, or is it two?"—he leaned to catch a glimpse of Sylvia—"of our fallen doves, I see."

"Luc," his grandmother hissed. "Your metaphor is about as misplaced as your aim."

He ignored her. "Quite a little covey we have. And few dogs to enjoy the hunt." He smiled, revealing large dazzlingly white teeth, one just crooked enough to make him appear even more devilish, if that was possible.

A few titters drifted from the audience and Rosamunde felt anew the embarrassment of her situation. Why, every Cornish family of noble mien was here. And while they dared not say another word against her lest they incur the dowager's disfavor, they could and would all stare at her and remember her downfall. Eight years would seem like yesterday to the gossips, who could recite every last major scandal from the last two centuries with a clarity that would astound fusty historians.

"Ladies, I beg your forgiveness." The dowager turned to her grandson. "Luc, may I present Mrs. Baird and her sister, Lady Sylvia Langdon? My dears, Luc St. Aubyn, the Duke of Helston."

He leaned close and grasped Rosamunde's hand before bringing it to his lips. "Your servant, *madam*." His heavy lidded eyes glanced up from her hand and he murmured, "I do so hope you are the widow, as opposed to your sister?"

It was then that Rosamunde realized his eyes were not black at all, just a very deep, arresting midnight blue. But his manners—*abominable*. His grandmother was of the same mind, if her expression was any indication.

"I am, Your Grace."

He eyed her shrewdly.

"Care to join our little entertainment? The other ladies have had a turn." He dusted off the edges of his hat and donned it. "Amusing little activity, really. Provides diversion for both spectators and participants."

"Thank you, Your Grace. But,"—she glanced at the ground—"I'm in mourning and must decline your invitation."

"That shouldn't stop you. Why I'm in mourning too, Mrs. Baird," he muttered. "Mourning the loss of my solitude and freedom."

His grandmother stamped a cane perilously close to his right boot. "And I'm mourning the loss of your manners." She harrumphed. "It's unfortunate that I'm in perpetual mourning because of you."

He threw back his head and laughed before offering his arm to Rosamunde. "Come, Mrs. Baird, I invite you to explore the joys of throwing off the shackles of good manners. Let us engage in serious foul play. Devil's rules."

She cocked her head in misunderstanding. "Devil's rules?"

He placed her hand on his arm and drew Sylvia to his other side. A frisson of heat snaked through his linen shirt and coat to race through Rosamunde's arm.

"All's fair, and extra points for poor sportsmanship." He leaned forward to whisper wickedly, "Perhaps Elizabeth Ashburton will teach you a few tricks." He glanced at the demure lady who had distracted him earlier.

She was not going to play. She had taken a lifetime oath to forsake all manner of tomfoolery soon after she married, and this audacious gentleman was not going to make her break her promise to herself, even if he was their host. "Perhaps my sister shall join you."

"No, no, Mrs. Baird. You're here to have fun. Grandmamma insists upon it for her *special* friends." He looked at her knowingly. "Now then, the object of the game is to impress everyone with the beauty of one's form." He winked. "Two points if you can make someone swoon."

"I doubt I can make anyone swoon, sir." She dropped his arm when they reached the small group of archers. She was not going to let them convince her to—

"Come now, Mrs. Baird. You would deny Her Grace the pleasure of watching you enjoy yourself? Or are you the rare female who hates to exhibit herself?" He paused and examined his fingernails. "You don't look the sort, if I do say so."

"I kindly thank you for your invitation, however, ladies of a certain age, such as mine, should engage their time more usefully and leave the delights of youth to the younger set."

"Are you suggesting I am too old to—?"

An elegant lady with blonde tresses stepped forward and interrupted him. She was as delicately beautiful as a porcelain doll bedecked in pale blue lace and pearls, but her claws were as sharp as a barnyard cat's. "Why, is it . . . why, fancy that. Lady Rosamunde Langdon, or it's plain Mrs. Baird now, is it not?"

Augustine Phelps. A prime example of the many reasons Rosamunde chose to bury herself in one of the most unfashionable corners of England. She glared at her but held her tongue. Her old rival had recently affianced herself to a Hanoverian baron of questionable pedigree and unquestionable stupidity.

"How you've changed, Rosamunde. But then I suppose one can hardly be surprised."

Sylvia faded into the crowd as fast as a pickpocket on payday. Confrontation had never been her sister's forte.

Auggie took a deep breath and a joyfully evil gleam lit her eyes. "Many a lady has lost her looks after undergoing half of what you've endured . . . or rather, *earned*." The last was whispered and a giggle escaped at the end to lighten the tone.

The duke cleared his throat and turned to his grandmother. "And I always thought brides-to-be were"— he cupped his hand near his mouth to smother his voice—"innocent chicks . . . or rather *hens* as the case may be. But clearly they are buzzards in waiting. And why, I ask you? Don't they know only widows have a chance at true domestic bliss? It's the brides who have everything to fear."

Rosamunde choked on her laughter.

Augustine blanched and sputtered most endearingly. "Well," she continued, "I wouldn't count on her to join the game. She doesn't mix with—with people of our stature."

"Heaven's no, *Auggie*. We peasants know our place." Rosamunde regretted her audacious words and was shocked by her rash comment. She had thought a lifetime of repentance and withdrawal from society had ruthlessly cured her from almost every instance of impetuous behavior—until now.

Her Grace yanked her grandson's arm and he leaned down. In a very rude stage whisper, the little dowager motioned toward Augustine. "She is not one of us."

"Well, I say—" Augustine breathed, aghast.

"Yes, and altogether too much," the duke interrupted her with a glare.

Augustine Phelps, ill suited to the task of true aristocratic pretension, blushed and walked away to join the large flock of luncheon guests.

His Grace appeared completely bored by such caterwauling. He thrust a bow into Rosamunde's hands. "Your turn, Mrs. Baird. Widows first, then buzzards and everyone else—including peasants."

The satinlike finish of the hardwood caressed the palm of her hand. It had been years since she had felt the weight of a bow in her hands, and yet it felt so familiar. The almost forgotten excitement of childhood competition filled her belly along with guilt for forsaking her promise to herself. Everyone knew the path to hell was paved with . . . oh, but she would appear ungracious, she reasoned, if she refused again.

The bell signaling the start of the late picnic nuncheon clanged and the spectators' interests proved fickle. Bows and fine figures held nothing over cold lobster and warm strawberry tarts.

"Well, Mrs. Baird?" he asked, perilously close to her ear.

"I don't perform before an audience, Your Grace."

His expression was mocking when he leaned down to his petite grandmother and whispered something. Ata immediately began clapping and ordering the lingering guests to the small tents on the other side of the gardens.

"Now, Mrs. Baird, this is becoming tedious. Do let's get on with it. Your refusal to play has left me aquiver." He sighed in ennui. "I've promised to engage in one round with each of the widows and one round it will be. Then you may retire to your room for the rest of your stay if you desire. To embroider. Or whatever it is you do."

Rosamunde narrowed her eyes.

What the devil was she doing? Her stance was perfect, the arch of her back forming a graceful slope in contrast to the astonishing strength she possessed in her arms. She stood as he had always pictured Diana the Huntress, steady and sure, confidence emanating from every pore while a slight breeze teased tendrils of her raven black hair around her face. Her starkly pale complexion held not a hint of rosy glow to offset her strangely haunting eyes. Not blue, not green, but some otherworldly color between the two. He had only ever seen eyes like that in a remote corner of Wales, where it was said the sea and the sky were captured in the eyes of the natives.

But now, at the last second before she released her arrow, she closed those troubled eyes—not one but both of them. Surprisingly, her arrow missed the center by less than a foot. But still . . .

"It would help if you kept your eyes open," he drawled. "Perhaps you need an incentive? I've found prizes are remarkable at improving aim, Mrs. Baird."

"With your strange rules, Your Grace, I'm astonished you're offering advice to better my game."

"Touché." He paused. "But you've piqued my interest." He faked a polite yawn. "I long to see how well you do with your eyes open. So what shall it be? Everyone has a price, Mrs. Baird," he murmured. "Everyone."

A hint of a breeze played with a wisp of her hair, covering her lush lips for a moment. She said not a word.

"Come, come, Mrs. Baird. What is your fondest wish?"

Her eyes darted to her sister, sitting apart from the throngs of people. Lady Sylvia's lovely profile was in relief against the lush verdure of the willow tree behind her.

"Ah, selflessness is your goal. A common flaw of my grandmother's destitute widows. Too bad it's not more of a passionate turn, but then I suppose we don't know each other well enough for you to confide in me." He was determined to provoke her. He didn't know why her cool nature inflamed his outrageousness. Usually, it took more than an unusual face to roust him from his world-weariness. It had been a long time since he'd had an interest in anything except his sister, grandmother and his clandestine writing.

She raised her chin but was silent.

"A hundred pounds says you can't hit the bull's-eye

in—let's see—shall we say five tries?" He watched anger war with pride in her expression.

"A hundred pounds for *each* arrow in the center?"

Oh, she was intriguing. "Always willing to up the ante for a lady, Mrs. Baird. Let us be clear, then. We shall each have five chances. Any of yours that remain in the center, after all play, will be eligible."

"All right." Her voice might have been quietly warm and inviting, but her eyes were as cold as a kitchen maid's hands in winter.

"Don't you want to negotiate the terms should I best you, madam?"

She lifted her chin and stared at him.

"Hmmm, no help from you again, I see. I think I would fancy a bit of your embroidery should I win. It's sure to be exquisite."

Her lips twitched just the slightest bit before she assumed her stance. The line of her figure was as rock steady as before. There was a sort of animal-like sleekness to her form as she concentrated on the target. And then, with a speed that astounded, she shot five arrows in rapid succession. Only one fell short of the mark.

"A pity, Mrs. Baird." He shook his head and nudged a case open next to the bows and arrows on the ground. As he fingered the hinge, he heard rather than saw a single shocked intake of breath from her direction.

Without glancing at her, he picked up his unusual-looking ivory inlaid double-barreled long gun and tucked it to his cheek. With a single well-powdered shot, more than half the quills in the center were rendered into a tangle of broken shafts and charred feathers.

"Cheater." Her voice was so low he barely made out the word.

"Devil's rules, Mrs. Baird, devil's rules." He turned to her as he checked the smoldering flint and priming pan. "Or perhaps just bad manners. Shall I take another shot or shall you concede, then?"

She ignored him as she placed the bow she had been clenching on the stand. "I suppose your rules include reneging on debts of honor too?"

"Naturally. That is the beauty of them. They constantly evolve as necessary."

"Your logic is as sinful, I think, as you, sir."

"We understand each other perfectly, madam."

As he watched her tall form retreat toward her sister under the tree, he contemplated this thorny new dilemma. How was he to arrange a surreptitious small windfall for this, this—he could feel the blood pounding in his chest—mesmerizing witch? It had been a long time since he felt anything moving in the vicinity of his heart. Perhaps it was just the deviled eggs. They had appeared a bit questionable, sitting in the sun.

Reneging on a debt of honor, indeed. Why, even Lucifer had a code of conduct.

Chapter 3

Piano, n. *A parlor utensil for subduing the impenitent visitor. It is operated by depressing the keys of the machine and the spirits of the audience.*

—The Devil's Dictionary, A. Bierce

"Now, my dear ladies"—an immediate hush fell when Her Grace uttered the words—"we finally have a moment to ourselves. Rosamunde, would you be so kind as to pour the tea?"

The tiny dowager was uncanny in her ability to read people. Rosamunde had needed something to occupy her hands to relieve the tension. She sat stiffly on the edge of an embroidered gold settee in the music room, surrounded by Sylvia and four other ladies in varying shades of full black to palest lavender—with the notable exception of Her Grace. Today the dowager had switched from deepest mourning to, well, it could only be described as marigold yellow. She looked like a merry, petite canary. Only the tips of her tiny slippers showed. The lady simply refused to allow anything or anyone to dampen her lighthearted spirit. His Grace was just the opposite, if Rosamunde was to hazard a guess. Why, yesterday, the mysterious man had seemed to welcome disharmony. Well, she had had enough mystery and discord in her life.

As she poured, Rosamunde said not a word. It had been so long since Rosamunde had socialized with strangers she feared saying the wrong thing and so she offered nothing to the conversation. The other ladies, who had the advantage of prior acquaintance, chatted amongst themselves. She glanced sidelong at the happy faces and felt like a marauder.

"I'm not certain if all of you have had the chance to meet our newest member of the Widows Club, Mrs. Rosamunde Baird, as well as her sister, Lady Sylvia Langdon." The dowager turned to her. "Rosamunde and Sylvia, may I present a long-standing family friend, the Countess of Sheffield, Grace Sheffey, recently out of mourning, as well as Georgiana Wilde, Elizabeth Ashburton, and Sarah Winters. We will of course dispense with certain formalities since we are all sisters here."

Each lady nodded slightly as her name was mentioned.

Ata continued. "Since the weather doesn't seem to be cooperating with my plans today for a nice long march to Cudden Point, we shall have to amuse ourselves indoors. I know most of you find that revolting."

A few coughs and smiles proved the ladies were

too polite to disabuse the dowager of her notions.

"However," she continued, "before the week's end we shall go on an expedition to Godolphin Cross to explore their marvelous horse stables."

Horse stables? Why, none of these ladies looked the sort to care a fig about horseflesh. But just the thought of a sleek, equine beauty brought a shiver of excitement down Rosamunde's spine. She would, of course, tamp down her feelings and beg off somehow. Riding horses had been the first thing she had given up in the name of punishment for her impetuous behavior of so long ago.

"Well, now that's settled, shall we have some music? Rosamunde and Sylvia, do you sing or play?"

Before Rosamunde could answer, Ata continued, "Elizabeth, dear, will you favor us with a sonata, perhaps one from Mr. Mozart?" She motioned toward the pianoforte.

"Your Gr—or rather—Ata, you know I play wretchedly. Georgiana plays much better than I," Elizabeth insisted.

Well at least she was not the only one struggling to address the duchess so informally, thought Rosamunde with a smile.

"Elizabeth," said Georgiana with the beautiful eyes, "that is most unfair. You know I play wretchedly."

"Oh dear." Ata laughed. "Well there must be some—"

Rosamunde saw Ata turn her way. She raised her hands and shook her head. "I've never played the pianoforte. But"—she hesitated and looked at her sister's anxious face—"Sylvia is accomplished on the harp."

"Rosa!" Sylvia's eyes widened.

"But it's true."

"But—"

"My dear, Sylvia"—Ata's eyes had misted over—"why, the harp is my favorite."

"But Rosamunde is the one with the great gift. Her voice is . . ." Sylvia paused, unable to continue after glancing at the dowager's pleading expression. "Oh, but it's been many, many years since I've—"

"Please? I used to play long ago for hours at a time. It brought me the greatest joy."

In that moment Rosamunde noticed the old lady's hands were trembling before she quickly hid one of them, which appeared thin and wasted, beneath her shawl. Rosamunde inhaled sharply. It reminded her of the lady's hand extended from the Duke of Helston's carriage those long years ago. Her stomach churned in remembrance. Surely . . .

All eyes turned to the restrained beauty of the Countess of Sheffield when she spoke. "You would do us all a great honor by playing, Lady Sylvia."

By the look of desperation bordering on terror on the rest of the widows' faces, it was clear none of the ladies enjoyed performing.

"Well—" Sylvia began.

"Oh yes, please do," Sarah begged.

Sylvia crossed the patterned parquet floor toward the harp near the pianoforte and various other instruments. There were enough wood, bows and strings to make up a small orchestra.

Sylvia tentatively settled onto a gilded stool and

cradled the harp on her right shoulder. She posed her delicate hands on the strings and all at once achingly familiar notes of ancient Welsh music rippled through the room. It was like a warm spring rain flowing around Rosamunde, feeding the depths of her soul.

Rosamunde couldn't stop herself from humming and only wished she had the courage to stand up and sing like she used to do in her father's house.

Sylvia played for many long minutes, never missing a note, never hesitating when she moved toward the lilting conclusion. She appeared in a state of bliss, her face nuzzling the wood of the crown. Rosamunde felt the ache of tears at the back of her throat. It had been a long time since she had seen her sister so happy. Sylvia had given up so many years of her life to comfort Rosamunde in her miserable marriage. And how had she been rewarded? Alfred had forbidden any music. She should have never allowed Sylvia to live with them. She should have insisted she return home. Guilt made her hollow inside.

The harp fell silent, the last two notes ill played. There was not a sound in the room for long moments until someone cleared his throat.

Oh Lord, it was he.

The Duke of Helston stood by the door, dressed in the same austere fashion as yesterday. Rosamunde had hoped to avoid him since his outrageous ways unnerved her. There was something about the way his piercing blue eyes rested on her after his gaze swept the room, as if he knew what she was thinking and could see the chemisette under her gown. Or perhaps, even beneath her underclothes. She forced herself not to squirm.

"Lady Sylvia, you play like an angel," he drawled. "Almost as well as Grace Sheffey."

The countess burst out laughing. "Luc, you of all people know I've no talent whatsoever."

"Hmmm, perhaps I'm confusing you with Elizabeth Ashburton, then." His lips held the suggestion of a smile.

"Well, I do have a superior ear to Lizzy's," the countess confided.

"Whatever are you saying, Grace? You just told Her Grace I play better than you," Elizabeth retorted.

"Too many Graces, " His Grace muttered.

Sarah Winters, who possessed a slightly older and wiser mien, chuckled. "Perhaps we should ask you both to play a duet, then we can be the judges."

"Sarah, I believe you're forgetting your own turn," Georgiana Wilde said with a sly smile. She sat perched on the edge of her seat in a frayed gray silk gown, looking as if she knew how to fortify her defenses with a well-honed sense of humor.

They all turned to the duchess. She was staring at Sylvia, transfixed with happiness and with traces of tears on her cheeks. For once, she seemed at a total loss for words.

The duke cleared his throat again.

It brought the dowager from her reverie. "My dears, I know how much you're all loathe to play."

"That's never stopped you from forcing them to injure our eardrums in the past," His Grace murmured.

"Luc! How dare you sug—"

"I dare it because their eyes are begging me to stop this insanity and I've none of your fawning ways."

"And don't we know it," the dowager harrumphed.

His Grace ignored his grandmother. "Mrs. Baird, will you join me in the front salon? You have a visitor."

Blood pooled in Rosamunde's fingers and she felt very cold. Please let it not be Algernon Baird. She knew he would eventually find her. She had just hoped it would be later, when she was more at ease in these new surroundings. She rose unsteadily and looked at Sylvia, whose face had turned ashen.

Her Grace looked at her grandson. "Luc, you're not to leave her alone."

"Finally an order I can obey to the letter."

"Luc!"

"Your agreeable orders are so rare."

"The better for you to enjoy them when they are given," Her Grace said, annoyed.

Rosamunde, surprised anew by their banter, looked at the faces of all the people surrounding her. The Countess of Sheffield looked ready to burst out laughing. Apparently this was modus operandi at Amberley. It had been so long since she had witnessed the freedom of speaking plainly, of thinly disguising love with humor, that Rosamunde almost forgot the visitor.

The duke raised his forearm in invitation. "Mrs. Baird?"

His deep baritone voice heated her insides but it was nothing compared to feeling the coiled strength of his arm beneath hers as they removed from the music room. At the doorway, he released her briefly and she sensed the warm glide of his hand at her waist as he guided her through the narrow frame. For the first time in her life she felt petite, compared to the great stature of the gentleman next to her.

"Your Grace—"

"Oh no," he interrupted. "If I'm forced to endure season after season of weeping widows, I'll not tolerate such formality in private."

"I'm certain your grandmother suggested informality among the ladies only."

He ushered her through a long portrait gallery filled with likenesses of presumably generations of St. Aubyns—each of whom appeared more unyielding than the last. There was not a single female to be found among the austere paintings. Apparently, she thought peevishly, St. Aubyn females were considered negligible broodmares.

"Since the interview with your curious relation will require a special brand of fortitude on both our parts, I had hoped you'd become a bit more comfortable as our guest."

The mention of Algernon sent an icy tingle down her legs, but she tried to appear calm. "I suppose you may use my given name in private, then."

"Ah, fair Rosamunde." He urged her into the shadowed corridor past the portrait gallery.

"I'm anything but fair," she muttered.

He chuckled. "Better and better. I can't abide people who are fair. Can't trust them by half."

"Your character, sir, shows little variation."

His wicked smile revealed the slightly crooked tooth, and she had the urge to smile back, but did not. He was such a mystery. Humorous evil hardness prevailed one moment, and yet she wondered if there was not something much deeper, much more compassionate beneath everything.

For the moment, there was no question he was trying to divert her. And for that she was grateful, but still petrified. Algernon would force her away from here, reveal all her secrets. And she would watch the look of cynical humor drain from the duke's face, to be replaced with disgust and fury. And then she would be compelled to flee. Compelled to take her thirty-seven guineas, saved over the long years, and find a post carriage that would take her as far away as possible. She would probably have to sleep in a hedgerow and find employment. She shivered. But she would not tell Sylvia this time. Her sister would have no choice but to return to the home of their childhood, Edgecumbe.

"What are you thinking about? You look like all the demons of hell are chasing you."

They were already in front of the drawing-room door. Rosamunde looked up and he was so close she could see the comb marks in his dark hair severely pulled back in the queue.

"Rosamunde." He pulled her gently into the shadows.

She tried to hide the jolt his touch ignited. What on earth was he doing? Oh, he was probably going to try to reassure her again. But there was something about the touch of a man's hands that always made her feel confined and ill at ease. She looked at his fingers and he pointedly removed them from her arm as if he'd been burned.

"I'd not guessed you were so chickenhearted to meet this Mr. Baird." He looked down at her through half-closed eyes and she tried to steady her breathing.

"But I—"

He continued softly, "If he is anything at all like the former Mr. Baird, which is my guess after wasting time with him this morning, then you've two appealing options before you. You can either remain with us here and be hideously happy, or go with him and wish you were dancing with the devil."

"I think I should prefer singing with the angels."

"I thought you'd no musical talent, Mrs. Baird."

"So we're back to formalities, Your Grace?"

A long pause hung in the rays of light coming from a single small window in the hall. He seemed to be weighing some sort of decision.

"You've left me no choice, Rosamunde. There seems to be only one last thing to do before choosing your ghastly future."

"I find your optimistic view of life inspiring, sir."

"Perhaps I'm not always so happy. But when faced with the pleasure of a second meeting with one of the stupidest men I've yet to meet, my disposition improves greatly."

He'd taken a short step closer during the exchange and Rosamunde could only focus on his blue eyes.

"Now, as I was saying, only one thing remains . . ."

Suddenly, shockingly, he bent down and touched his lips lightly to her forehead. She felt the heat of a thousand winter night fires blaze as she held her breath in the face of such a small spark of tenderness. It was the first glimmer of true intimacy she had had in all her life.

He pulled back and looked at her for a long moment, his eyes becoming dark with mystery, and then lowered his mouth again, only this time to her own.

Every sense in her body ignited into exquisite self-consciousness. She heard a low sound, or was it a growl? Every inch of her skin turned to gooseflesh, as if she had leapt from a snowbank into a hot bath.

Her mind blurred under the onslaught. His teeth nipped at her lips and it sent a long shiver through her. His tongue gently traced the seam of her lips, and finally she understood he sought entrance, sought knowledge of her. She unclenched her jaw and relaxed only to have excitement burst through her. His tongue curled about her own, making her feel as though she might faint from the intimacy of it.

No one had ever kissed her like this. Not that she knew much about kissing. She knew more about cold, hard pain, not pleasure. But surely this was wickedness incarnate.

She breathed in the mysterious scent of cheroots and woody cologne. He smelled of old elegance and permanence. And of sadness hiding behind a thin veneer. But most of all, she sensed a strange stoicism coursing beneath a long tunnel of dark experience.

He drew back and before she could gather her wits

and breathe, let alone think about the magnitude of what had just happened, he opened the door. "After you, Mrs. Baird."

Algernon stood by the bow window in his Sunday finery, only a shred of mourning evident in the form of a scrap of black material tied about one arm.

All the smoldering embers in her body were sucked out to be replaced with the familiar icy dread. Her ability to cover her fears with a cloak of indifference, a skill honed over time, stood her well.

"My dear cousin." Algernon bowed deeply.

"Algernon." Rosamunde dipped a miniscule curtsy.

The duke motioned them both to a settee before the vast fireplace, intricately carved from a single slab of white marble tinged gray from many generations of use. He propped himself against it with casual elegance, rather like a great falcon watching his prey. Or was it a vulture?

"Ah, this is a sad state of affairs is it not, my dear?" Algernon's question was more of a statement.

She sat still and mute.

Algernon darted a glance at the duke. Beads of moisture covered his forehead and the skin above his upper lip. Like his first cousin Alfred, Algernon Baird was always overheated in hot weather and in cold. His hair, a thinning, oily mixture of gray and red was combed forward à la mode Brutus. It was uncanny how much he looked like her late husband with the exception of his greater height.

"Well, enough of the niceties," the duke said dryly.

"You've requested an audience with Mrs. Baird and have proposed to me that she and her sister return to . . ."

"Barton's Cottage," Algernon filled in.

"Right. Barton's Cottage, clearly a place much more appealing than this pile." The duke brushed invisible lint from his coat lapel. "And this is to be done today."

"This afternoon, Your Grace," Algernon insisted. "We shan't burden you further."

"You show a forgiving nature, sir, toward a runaway grieving relation. It warms the heart," the duke said.

Rosamunde could not move or speak for the life of her. Her world was crashing in around her yet again.

Algernon preened before him.

"It's obvious any woman would be *delighted* to accept your charity." The duke examined his pocket watch and clicked it shut. "I, however, find a slight— mind you, very slight—problem with your proposal."

"Your Grace?"

"I've never subscribed to gothic scenarios. You understand me, I am sure. A grieving dependant female or two at the mercy of a"—Rosamunde was sure he was going to say licentious idiot but was mistaken— "*gentleman*," the duke continued after a long pause.

Algernon's face paled. "Are they not in the same situation here? Why, I am family to these two girls."

"Girls?"

Algernon blinked. "Ladies."

"Do we really need to belabor the point, Mr. Baird? I would be willing to endure the tedium of an argument, but only if you could find it within yourself to provide just a bit more entertainment along the way."

Algernon appeared confused. "Are you insulting me?"

"I see you've no gloves with you, would you care for my handkerchief?" He reached for his pocket. "I've always found challenges quite amusing."

The first hint of real panic appeared on Algernon's face. Years of desperation prevented Rosamunde from taking any pleasure in it.

"No?" The duke continued after a short silence, "Well, you can take comfort in knowing there are at least three dozen guests here to save Mrs. Baird from, ahem, me."

A bubble of disbelief tinged with hilarity floated in Rosamunde's throat. Where had all those visitors been moments ago, outside the door?

The duke slowly raised a quizzing glass, dangling from a gold chain about his neck, to his face. It enlarged one of his eyes to ridiculous proportions.

"Have you nothing to say about this, *Mrs. Baird*? We're talking about your fate, after all."

"No," she said quietly.

"No?" He looked at her with indifference and her heart grew smaller. "I keep forgetting females have no say in the matter of their futures. And here you have such a tempting offer on the table from Mr. Baird."

"Offer?" she echoed, barely able to speak. Couldn't he divine that the long years with Alfred had instilled in her the importance of remaining compliant and still?

"Why, yes. Mr. Baird explained to me not one half hour ago that he blames himself for your *hasty* departure, that you had not given him the chance to explain his ideas for your happy future."

What was he talking about? She turned to consider Algernon's frippery and slippery words and the sweaty, earthy awful core of him.

"He has suggested that within a month your year of mourning will be over and he would make you his bride. Or was it the sister you wanted, Mr. Baird? Or perhaps both? Yes, that must have been—"

"No," she interrupted quietly.

"No?" the duke considered her answer for a moment. "No to what? No to marrying Mr. Baird, no to your sister marrying him, or no to both of you marrying him?"

She looked at him but couldn't make the muscles in her mouth work. She hated the person she'd become . . . submissive, acquiescent, obedient.

"Ah, finally we're getting a glimmer of an answer. Personally, I think men should never overtax the female mind by asking them to think. Don't you agree, Mr. Baird?"

"Well, I—" Algernon began.

"Excuse me," Rosamunde forced herself to speak. "I must decline all of my cousin-in-law's proposals. And I know I speak on my sister's behalf as well."

Algernon's delicate chair creaked loudly when he rose. "Well, that's the thanks I get for offering to house you, protect you and your sister? I would think you would show a little more gratitude. My offer is surely the only one you will receive, considering the well-known state of your reputation. Why, it is surprising His Grace has allowed you to stay here and mix with respectable people, *Rosie*."

Oh, how she hated that name. The name of the village tavern maid who dispensed her favors freely. But then, was that not how the two Bairds had treated her for so long?

"Algernon, I thank you for your offer but I cannot accept it." She said it with an enormous effort of will.

"I see. So you think to pass yourself off here as a member of good *ton*, do you? I'm curious about one thing. How ever did you wrangle an invitation to stay here . . . at the family home of the gentleman you seduced and then refused to marry?"

The duke's hand, rubbing the stem of his quizzing glass, stilled for the slightest moment.

Algernon stepped closer. "She didn't tell you, Your Grace? She had relations with your brother, but her fickle nature took over afterward. She must be kept firmly in hand."

The Duke of Helston's bored expression took in everything and gave away nothing in return. "A most accommodating female. I'm more and more intrigued. In my experience a lady will use every feminine wile to clamp a leg shackle on a gentleman. But in this case, it seems Mrs. Baird enjoyed the role of a jilt. How odd."

"How odd indeed," she whispered, sure no one had heard her.

"But it was *your brother*, Your Grace." Algernon tugged at his lacy cravat. "All your neighbors and wedding guests are talking about her being here. And as usual, Rosie is taking pleasure in her bold, reckless ways, leaving a wake of damage wherever she goes."

"And you are so kindly willing to take on this brazen piece of baggage, and her sister too?"

"It's the charitable thing to do."

The duke slowly perused the length of Algernon Baird and then coughed. "How illuminating. Your generosity does you great credit, sir." There was the suggestion of a smile about his lips as he continued casually, "And now that I have the full story, I shall have Mrs. Baird's bags packed and tossed off Amberley's grounds before she taints the happiness of everyone gathered here."

"And her sister?"

His Grace lifted one supercilious brow. "Oh, her sister is equally to blame, obviously."

An icy ball of fear grew in the pit of Rosamunde's stomach, but she resisted the urge to lick her dry lips.

Algernon pursed his mouth, trying to conceal his delight. "With your permission, Your Grace, shall I signal for a maid to begin packing?"

"*Rosie*," the duke said. "This is what you want?"

"Go to the devil."

Luc St. Aubyn, the eighth Duke of Helston, laughed long and loud.

"You see?" Algernon smirked. "Observe the vulgar woman behind the façade."

The duke smiled shrewdly. "Mr. Baird, it pains me greatly, but I fear I must insist on being allowed to take on the reformation of this wayward woman's character.

She's damaged my family in the past and so it's in my purview to exact repayment." The duke crossed the room and gave a swift yank on the bell cord. "I'll satisfy your notions of divine retribution by promising to house both sisters in a cobweb-filled garret without a fire in the grate, where it will be perpetually too hot or too cold. Shall I have them forced to work in the kitchen as well?"

Algernon, flustered beyond measure, allowed his sycophantic nature to take over. "Well, of course, Your Grace. I shall abide by whatever you decide. But really, I hate to burden you with this. I think it is best for her nearest and dearest relation to—"

"Say no more." His Grace turned to indicate something to the able-bodied footman who had slipped into the room. "A man can tolerate only so much sympathy in his lifetime and I fear I shall use up all my supply if you stay another minute longer."

By the look on Algernon's face, it was clear he was utterly confused by the duke's words. Still reeling, Rosamunde was herself unsure which gentleman deserved more pity.

But there was no doubt in Rosamunde's mind what the swarthy footman's mission was as the manservant advanced toward her brother-in-law. Thank goodness for muscle and brawn.

Chapter 4

Guilt, n. *The condition of one who is known to have committed an indiscretion, as distinguished from the state of him who has covered his tracks.*

—The Devil's Dictionary, A. Bierce

Amid a clutter of discarded sheets of precious paper, Rosamunde sat at an escritoire in the ridiculously large apartment in Amberley into which she had been moved. The housekeeper, a robust Cornishwoman with a strong accent, had insisted she remove from her old room, and for a moment Rosamunde had wondered if she was being escorted to the attics. But apparently not—it was simply that new guests were arriving. And then she froze and worried for the hundredth time if her family members had been invited to the wedding and any other festivities. Fate couldn't be so cruel as to force her to face them.

She gazed at the odd bouquet of flowers she had gathered this afternoon. There had been few blooms from which to choose, the gardens having been somewhat neglected with the family from home for so many years. But already, new gardeners had been engaged. Rosamunde had had to stop herself from joining the under gardener in pulling up weeds surrounding the mignonette and phlox in the lower garden.

She would have stayed there all day if she could have, wandering the gardens, which were wonderfully silent save for one large droning bumblebee. It was a bittersweet remembrance of her garden at Barton's Cottage. By herself. Always by herself very early each morning, when she could escape.

But she'd been unable to find solace here. She'd kept turning at every sound, fearful she'd be found and compelled to rejoin the others. She'd managed to avoid everyone after yesterday's horrendous interview with Algernon and the duke. Just thinking about His Grace made her struggle to breathe.

What must he think of her? Surely he considered her a scandalous woman, pushing herself where she was universally despised. And she had refused to defend herself. It would only have made her appear false. He was probably disgusted by her, sure she had withheld her past to gain entrance. Why hadn't he immediately dismissed her from Amberley?

But most of all she wondered why the duke had kissed her. Surely he had done it to divert her. And he had accomplished it.

She had relived his kiss a hundred times in the past

day and a half and each time she was sure she must have dreamed it. She kept picturing those magnetic eyes turning a dark, mysterious blue as they gazed at her and the heat and strength of him as he had leaned into her, his ironlike thighs pressed against her own. He had kept his hands behind his back, giving her the precious chance to back away at any moment.

Her heart raced yet again, and she looked down to see her hands shaking, the ink from the quill spattered across the sheet of parchment. Oh, what was the point? She knew she would never send a letter to her father pleading for him to send a carriage. Begging just wasn't in her nature. She would rather starve to death.

A little voice inside also reminded Rosamunde that if Father refused her supplication, she would know forevermore they could never, ever go home. Not knowing was better.

In her most optimistic moments she liked to dream it was only her wounded pride that stood in the way of reconciling with her father—but really, there was so much more. There was her father's pride, too. Overcoming the mountains she and her father had built between them would require a glacial age to erode them.

The movement of an ant crawling on one of the flowers caught her attention. The bouquet's fragrance wafted in the air. Rosemary, signifying remembrance, joined the symbolic pleasure and pain of dog rose, the grief and despair of marigold all wrapped up in the perseverance of ground laurel and sorrow of purple hyacinth. The bouquet was hideous in its significance, yet beautiful in the last of the day's rays streaming in from the window. Was it not like the last few days had been? Wonderful yet shockingly dreadful.

There was a light tap on the door and Sylvia slipped into the room. "Rosa, you're not ready? The dinner bell shall sound any minute."

"No, my love. I . . ." She had never been any good at lying. "I shall send my regrets."

"Again?" Sylvia picked up their mother's ancient silver-backed hairbrush to arrange Rosamunde's hair. "The duchess said she would send for the apothecary if you hadn't improved by tonight."

When Rosamunde didn't respond, Sylvia continued to dress her high chignon, breaking off small flowers in the bouquet to add to the coiffure. "You don't have a headache, do you?"

"Not really." She twirled a flower that had dropped from Sylvia's hands. "Has His Grace said anything to you?"

"No." Sylvia paused. "He's very strange, don't you think? Several ladies have warned me to stay away from him. They said he's called Lord Fire and Ice because he's a notorious rake with an unpredictable temper. Auggie's friend keeps flirting with him on the sly."

"And does he flirt back?" she asked, not really sure she wanted to hear the answer.

"I think it's gone beyond that, by the way he looks at her."

Rosamunde didn't know if she was more annoyed learning this or more irritated at herself for being annoyed.

"He's even rumored to have killed someone," Sylvia said in a hushed tone.

"That's ridiculous. You know how gossip grows. The man was in the Royal Navy. He probably did kill while fighting the French, but I highly doubt he killed anyone here in England. Lord Fire and Ice indeed," she snorted.

"Well, I'm afraid of him. He's nothing at all like . . ."

Rosamunde swallowed. "You're right, he isn't anything like his brother."

Sylvia fiddled with a flower. "It isn't fair, you know. You're forcing me to face everyone alone again tonight when coming here was your idea."

"Has it been that bad?"

"Worse than you can imagine. The ladies stare at me and whisper. And the gentlemen just gape and sometimes smile ever so slightly"—her gaze dropped—"knowingly."

"I'm so sorry, Sylvia. I had hoped my past wouldn't taint you here. At least the wedding is next week and then they will all leave. In the meantime, we can stay to ourselves and try to figure out our future. You don't have to go down for dinner either, you know."

Rosamunde turned on her stool and took her beloved sister in her arms, not sure who was comforting whom. The balm of sisterly love had been the only thing that had sustained her spirits for so long.

Sylvia's muffled voice floated to her ear. "I'm so glad. I just can't face Auggie Phelps and her circle of friends again."

Rosamunde brushed a limp, ebony lock from her

sister's face. Neither of them had ever been able to force a curl to stay long in their thick straight hair.

"But, Rosa, Her Grace asked me to play her harp as entertainment after dinner. And—"

"And what?"

"And you know how hard it is to disappoint her. I told her I would, but only if you accompanied me with your voice."

"You didn't. You would never—"

A loud rap at the door interrupted her and their gazes flew to it.

"Yes?" Rosamunde called out.

The last person she wanted to see entered first. Then Ata pushed passed His Grace, elbowing him viciously.

"Those should be certified as weapons," he said under his breath.

"Well, if you'd stop gawking, I wouldn't have to use them now, would I?" she said sweetly.

His Grace glanced at the ceiling for help.

This time it appeared the dowager was undecided in her dress. She wore a conservative dark aubergine gown, but a petticoat rustled underneath and Rosamunde was sure she had seen a hint of dark rose lace at the edge.

"My dear, Luc and I thought we must look in on you. I do hope the infusions helped. They must have, since the gardener reports you've been strolling the gardens this afternoon. Shall we all go down for dinner, then?"

She had such an innocent goodness in her expression Rosamunde didn't have the heart to offer an excuse. Funny how Rosamunde's old governess had used the same trick and she'd succumbed every time.

"Well, of course, Your Grace. I would—"

"Ata, please." She'd said it with so much sadness Rosamunde knew she would never err again.

"Ata . . . Sylvia and I are almost ready. We'll descend in an instant."

Luc had decided he wasn't going to let her hide anymore. It hadn't taken his grandmother's incessant questions to make him act.

Standing there in the doorway made him wish he had proceeded sooner. The two sisters, so similar in appearance with their glossy hair and pale complexions but differing eye color, sat at their toilette, a study in Botticellian attitudes. He could barely maintain his careless demeanor looking at the elder.

She was not the beauty of the two, except for those eyes. She was all angles and harsh splendor as opposed to her sister's soft elegance. The pretty blooms in Rosamunde's hair contrasted with the wildness he sometimes spied in her eyes and in her heart.

She had gained some sort of hold on him. A hold that he revolted against with every fiber of his being. He had no desire to become entangled with a lady. A casual joining of bodies for mutual pleasure was one thing, caring about another being's future was another.

In the few times he had interceded in the affairs of the widows in Ata's club, he had done so with impersonal efficiency. It annoyed him intensely that he had wanted to do more than that for this woman. He had wanted to smash Algernon Baird's sweaty, garrulous face in and present it to her on a platter.

He gazed at her firm jaw and remembered the soft sweetness he had discovered beyond those lips that became plush when she let them. With a rush, he cursed himself again for the monumentally stupid impetuous moment outside the door where Algernon Baird had waited.

He had meant to innocently kiss her to shock her out of her fear. Instead he had been struck dumb by an explosion of emotions and unparalleled desire. He exhaled sharply. She had bewitched him—of that there was no question. He could only hope she knew how to play the game, since he had obviously not only forgotten the rules but had lost his mind as well.

"We shall wait outside your door." He glanced at her dull mourning gown. It was as hideous as ever. "Shall we say five minutes, then?"

She bowed her head in acquiescence.

Ata dipped out of the room and he followed, closing the door behind them.

"Luc, why did you order her moved to this suite?"

"I have no idea what you're talking about."

She harrumphed.

"The housekeeper mentioned something about drafts on the third floor," he said. "Or was it mice?"

She shook a wrinkled, pointed finger under his nose. "Ha. You can't fool an old fool. You're up to something. Does she know this room adjoins your own?"

"I certainly hope not."

Ata sniffed. "Highly improper, Luc. I'll not have it. I'll have Phipps install a bolt tonight. Better yet, a bolt on her outer door as well. And, and—"

"Yes?" He rose to his most imposing height.

"And you're to be less obvious with that other chit. She giggles too much when she's around you and it grates on the nerves."

His lips twitched. "Yes, ma'am."

She stomped her cane on his foot. "Don't you dare condescend to me, young man. Now, I really don't like the idea of Rosamunde Ba—"

He grimaced. "Give me that. You've never limped a day in your life."

"I carry it to keep gentlemen away from the ladies in my club. Do I need to remind you that Mrs. Baird is recently bereaved?"

"Bereaved? Don't you mean *relieved*?"

"Luc—" she pleaded.

"It's high time the lady has a bit of fun in her life."

"But it can never lead to anything, Luc, except heartache for her. I know you too well." Ata snatched back the cane, and tried to appear indifferent when she continued. "By the by, I understand your Mr. Brown has come down from town."

"He's not *my* Mr. Brown."

"Well, he certainly isn't *mine*," Ata muttered.

"*Really*?" he asked, hiding a smile.

Ata sputtered. "Why, the very idea—"

"Enough," Luc interrupted. "If I can't escape this end of the world, my man of affairs must join me here."

He shrugged. "I had Phipps put him in Mrs. Baird's room, and no, I see that look. *In her old room*. Couldn't have Brownie in this adjoining room. Why, I'd never have a moment's peace."

Luc glanced at the door and willed it to open.

"Well, I've placed him next to that nasty Miss Phelps during dinner," she said.

"Lucky dog."

Luc knocked on the door. "Come along, Mrs. Baird. Your audience awaits," he said dryly. Damn all females and their machinations. Before the last knock the door swung open and his fist was left hanging in the air. She was wearing the same appalling gown.

She cast down her gaze at his stare.

This demure act was killing him. He could tolerate it in insipid females but deplored it in this woman who had demonstrated there was something hiding under all those layers of ugly false mourning. Especially since he had tasted what lay beneath her cool exterior.

Ata nearly pounced on Rosamunde's arm in her rush to escort her instead of allowing him the honor. He settled for the younger sister and bowed before her. "Lady Sylvia."

Luc led the foursome past the burnished oak railings of the upper staircases. Clearly a former shipbuilder had built this solid wreck. There was something about this manor that was magical and permanent. He had never cared where he had lived before, since he knew it was the people who made a pile of stones a home. It wasn't until the last few years, when he had relinquished his naval command and insisted Ata and his sister join him under the primary ducal roofs, that he had ever called a place home. For now, that was Amberley.

Candlelight reflected off every gleaming crystal and silver surface in the elegant dining room. Rows and rows of candelabra flanked the three long tables covered with lace, slightly yellowed from age. White roses intertwined with ivy graced the tables in honor of the wedding couple.

When Rosamunde dared peruse the flow of guests, she refused to stop at any one face for fear of the looks of disgust she might find. There were at least a hundred guests gathered tonight to celebrate the upcoming nuptials. One thing was obvious. Ata liked a good party. The duke and dowager duchess abruptly disappeared into the masses when the butler claimed their attention.

She felt so underdressed, looking at the colorful fashionable silk and satin surging around her. Her gown wasn't in the current Greek high-waisted style. Instead it was of the last century, the aged muslin nipping her waist and gripping the length of her arms, a remnant of one of Alfred's long dead relations.

Suddenly she realized everyone was in the final stages of searching out their place cards and she was one of the last left standing. Oh, it had been so long since she had attended a formal affair, she had almost forgotten things that should have been second nature. She felt the burn of many eyes watching her make her way to the last open seat at the main table presided over by Ata, the duke, the Countess of Sheffield, a beautiful young lady who was the duke's sister, and the beaming groom. The other ladies of the club had been discreetly sprinkled at the far end of the table.

A short older man rose from his place beside her to help her with her chair. "Allow me to present myself, ma'am," he said and inclined his head, "Mr. John Brown." Before the words were out of his mouth the buzz of general conversation covered the silence.

"Mrs. Baird, sir." There was something about Mr. Brown that was very likeable. Perhaps it was the kindliness she spied in his unremarkable face.

"Well," hissed Auggie Phelps to her rotund fiancé, loud enough so Rosamunde could hear, "I don't know why they were seated at the main table."

Rosamunde hoped she wasn't blushing. Her sister gave her a halfhearted smile and widened her eyes a little at the sight of so many forks, knives, spoons and crystal wineglasses before them.

Rosamunde shrugged slightly, placed a heavy, lace-edged napkin on her lap, and turned to the gentleman, dressed in clerical garb, on her other side.

"Ma'am, I believe you and your sister are the only two people in the neighborhood I haven't had the pleasure of meeting yet. I'm the new vicar, Sir Rawleigh." He offered his left hand to her and it was then she noticed his right sleeve was pinned to his shoulder.

Rosamunde completed the introduction and continued, "Have you been long in Cornwall, sir?" He was a classically handsome gentleman, a blond archangel sent to tempt pious women everywhere.

"Not long at all. Just above a week only." The vicar looked toward Sylvia and his composure faltered. "The captain—or rather, the duke—was kind enough to give me the living when Mr. Fromley died." He looked her fully in the eye. "I'm sorry I wasn't here to preside over your husband's funeral."

Rosamunde nodded and noticed her sister's flustered appearance. She turned to take a peek at the duke but became ill at ease herself when she perceived his attention on her. She doggedly continued, "I assume you made His Grace's acquaintance at sea, then?"

"No. Actually, it was before that. Have you met Peter Mallory, the besotted fiancé?" When she shook her head no, he continued. "I suppose I should use his proper title, Viscount Landry, since he received it for valor and"—he winked—"he likes to lord it over us."

Mr. Brown chuckled.

This vicar certainly didn't behave like other men of the cloth Rosamunde had met.

Sir Rawleigh continued, "The three of us were inseparable at Eton"—he leaned forward with a conspiratorial glance—"and our good friend His Grace would have my head if he knew I would tell you how he fared there."

Before she could try and stop him, he grinned again. "He was abominable in philosophy, kept arguing with the masters, but took firsts in history, English and mathematics. Landry and I followed him to sea when," he paused, "well, when he decided to join the Royal Navy before the last term. Took ten years off Landry and my father's lives, since they'd had other plans for us. But we learned there was something about salt water and French cannon fodder that binds people for life." He stopped short and shrugged. "But that's not a topic for a lady's delicate ears."

Auggie glanced at Rosamunde and snorted.

Mr. Brown cut in before Auggie could say a word, "Ma'am, are you in need of a handkerchief?"

"No, not at all. I was—" Auggie tried to continue but was interrupted again by Grace Sheffey, the rich countess with not a blonde curl out of place, who sat across from Auggie.

"Miss Phelps, will you be married to the baron in town or in the neighborhood?"

Rosamunde's breast swelled with emotion. The last few days had been filled with strangers determined to enforce polite behavior. Silent gratitude filled her.

"Why, in town, at St. George's of course," Auggie simpered, placing her hand possessively on the baron's and smiling at her best friend, Theodora Tandy, who kept giggling and batting her eyelashes at the duke. "Everyone will be invited. Well, almost everyone," she said, eyeing Sylvia and Rosamunde.

"Oh Miss Phelps," called out Ata from the other end of the table. All clatter of silverware paused. "Do pass the salt, will you?" she asked, sweetly.

Rosamunde looked down to confirm what she knew. There were tiny scallop-edged salt and pepper dishes in front of each place setting. The look on Auggie's face was priceless as she wavered between pointing out this fact to a grand duchess or not. Silently, Auggie passed her tiny dish with the miniature spoon up the row of dinner guests. A few grains spilled in front of Sylvia and she discreetly threw them over her shoulder. Rosamunde smiled at the familiar gesture.

The duke leaned forward and said something to his grandmother. Ata muttered, "Well, she hasn't earned her salt. And she's been under our roof for nearly a week. I don't care if she's a cousin twenty times removed from somebody's uncle."

"Magnificent isn't she?" Mr. Brown whispered softly. He clearly didn't expect an answer.

"Mrs. Baird," asked Sir Rawleigh to relieve the tension, "Will you allow me to present you to my sister, Charity?"

"I'd be honored, sir."

Rosamunde smiled at the lady several places opposite her. The young lady's carrot-colored curls were a tangle of corkscrews framing her heart-shaped face. Her vivid green eyes were the only things that proclaimed her to be the vicar's sister.

"So sorry about your recent loss, Mrs. Baird."

Rosamunde's whole heart became engrossed in the banality of the dinner conversation. She had forgotten the simple joy of forming original observations on the age-old topics of the ever-changing Cornish weather, the tides, and events. She pushed back her fears of exposing herself to public condemnation. And surprisingly, she almost enjoyed herself.

Until, that is, she remembered the after-dinner entertainment.

* * *

Compliments for the fine meal rang in his ears as he watched her beyond the other diners moving into the next room. He was sure he could read her mind. He would offer a solution, or rather a proposition she would sure to like . . . only slightly more than singing in front of more than four score guests.

"Mrs. Baird," he said, allowing stragglers to move past and pointedly ignoring Theodora Tandy's winks. "I perceive a distinct lack of enthusiasm on your part in this musical scheme. You dislike providing amusement for your neighbors, am I correct? We are of one mind."

She looked at him mutely.

"My last season in London cured me of every desire to hear another Beethoven sonata murdered beyond redemption by the young ladies trotted out by their tone-deaf, marriage-minded mothers."

She raised her dark eyebrows, which swooped oh-so delicately heavenward.

"Not that I don't think you must sing like an angel, you understand."

She didn't appear to understand at all.

"Well, do you or don't you want to exhibit your-self?" He might have just barked.

"You've already proclaimed I dislike it."

He sighed. Why did he feel like he was winning his object but sinking his ship? "I shall make your excuses if, but only if, you agree to ride with me tomorrow morning." He raised his hand when she opened her mouth to protest. "To Men-An-Tol, where Ata has ar-ranged for an outdoor picnic. I know you told Ata you would prefer to stay here. But she has her heart set on this outing. The West Penwith moors are special to her and I won't have her disappointed." He paused and noticed the tilt of her proud chin. A pulse point was beating erratically on her long neck and he longed to touch it—soothe it. "The others will follow."

She looked up at him. "I will go, but only in a carriage with my sister."

"No. The carriages are all spoken for. And"—he dared her to look away—"your sister tells me you enjoy, or rather, *enjoyed* riding at one time."

"Perhaps."

"Perhaps you enjoyed riding or perhaps you will go?"

"You ask a lot of questions."

"Which you often refuse to answer."

They stared at each other.

"I cannot leave my sister to perform alone."

"You worry a lot about your sister."

"As you do about your grandmother."

He tried hard not to reveal a smile. "So the lady does know how to defend herself."

"I don't need to defend myself. And if you were a gentleman you would stop trying to bargain with me at every opportunity." She took three steps back.

"Ah, but I keep telling you I'm not a gentleman."

"But I keep hoping you're wrong. Perhaps your insistence proves just the opposite."

He chuckled. "Usually everyone takes my word for it." He took one step closer to her. "Now I am forced to confuse you by asking politely if you will do me the honor of riding with me tomorrow."

She narrowed her eyes. "Only because Ata would like it."

Ah, she was a contrarian. He adored contrarians.

He reached to touch her cheek and she looked at his hand as if it might burn her.

At that precise, awful moment Theodora Tandy chose to reenter the dining room. She giggled.

The moment shuddered to a stand still. Rosamunde Baird turned and bolted, Luc's hand still raised in mid-air.

Ata was right about the giggler. But then, wasn't Ata always right, damn her wrinkled hide.

Chapter 5

Lecturer, n. One with his hand in your pocket, his tongue in your ear and his faith in your patience.

—The Devil's Dictionary, A. Bierce

"There's nothing more to be done, Luc. You must sell off one of the unentailed estates or the ship if you insist on buying another cottage for your grandmother." Brownie scratched his tonsured crown. "You can't squeeze another drop from what you've got, even though you've done very well with what was passed on to you at the start."

Luc looked up from the massive green leather-topped desk in his study. Dusty books and naval ornaments were stacked and scattered everywhere, proving he had been successful in scaring the housemaids with his threats of beheadings should anyone touch a particle within his lair.

He uttered not a syllable.

"And you can't expect to dower your sister with thirty thousand pounds and continue on as before. You would have done better to offer half."

"Yes, however, I don't think Madeleine would've been happy with half a husband." He directed a hard stare at his former ship's purser, current steward, and most respected friend. "It was only fair to give Landry a decent start."

Mr. Brown coughed.

"Look, old man, I've yet to hear of a new title with real money behind it. Is there such an animal?" Luc sighed. "And my sister is so particular, she has refused two offers from rich, idle suitors. She has the odd notion that the heirs in town lead nothing but pampered, gilded existences. You know she's had her heart set on marrying a Royal Navy lieutenant since the day she found my bloodied pirate cutlass."

"Don't fool yourself," Mr. Brown muttered. "It's those Royal Navy coats and gold epaulettes that gets them, if you don't mind me saying so."

"As if I could stop you."

His aging friend grinned in his usual fashion, which was so huge and gummy his eyes above were squeezed shut.

"All right, then." Luc paused. "Sell or let the rubble in Yorkshire. It's too damn cold there anyway. Let someone else freeze his tail off. And by the by, that'll be the last time I hear you suggesting we sell off *Caro's Heart*."

Mr. Brown shuffled documents back into the fat

leather portfolio and then placed a money pouch in the middle of the desk. "Here are the funds you requested, and"—he pushed another purse next to it—"the smaller amount."

"All of it?"

"Yes," he paused, "and the dossier on Mrs. Baird's family you requested."

"Very good," Luc replied, accepting the papers.

"Charming lady, by the way."

He gave Brownie his most bored expression and pushed the smaller pouch back toward him. "Find a way to slip the *charming* lady this. I lost a bet. And make sure she doesn't know where it came from. She won't accept it otherwise."

"Lost a bet, eh?"

"You'll not go fishing in those waters if you treasure that shiny scalp of yours."

Mr. Brown cleared his throat, which did little to cover his laughter. "I also thought you should see these." He pushed some newspaper clippings in his direction.

"What are these?"

"Gossip columns. It seems the first few copies of your book"—he paused when Luc glared at him—"that is, *Lucifer's Lexicon*, have made their way into some lordly mitts."

Luc's stomach clenched but he controlled his voice. "And?"

"They particularly admired your, let's see,"—he thumbed through the editions—"'deliciously cynical sense of the absurd.' People are speculating the author is the same mysterious lady who wrote *Pride and Preju-*

dice and that other bit of fluff. Guess it's because you share the same publisher."

"They think I'm a *girl?*" He nearly choked.

Brownie's expression was one of poorly contained glee. The man looked down at one of the newspapers. "It's running ten to one in the betting books at the gentlemen's clubs."

"Are you laughing?"

"Of course not."

Luc rolled his eyes. "There are days I wonder why I ever employed you."

"Because I blackmailed you."

Luc hid his smile. "Right. Well, at least I won't have to worry about remaining anonymous," he muttered. "Taken for a bloody female, no less."

"But you wouldn't have to sell off the land if I placed a few discreet bets and then you revealed yourself."

He stared down at his friend. "There is no way in hell I'll ever admit I wrote that ridiculous book."

"But just think of the quid—"

"I said no, you stubborn Scot." He shuffled the papers. "Dukes do not write idiotic dictionaries or dabble in fusty, academic tomes. Nor should they employ cheeky bastards."

Brownie coughed. "I guess that leaves only one other possibility besides selling off the northerly bits."

"If you suggest I finish that book about Trafalgar one more time, Brownie . . ."

"You can't fool an old fool. I know you're working on it. Actually, I was going to suggest you reconsider the Countess of Sheffield or look over the other rich petticoats down from town for the wedding. You could sell yourself off like Landry." The man had the grace to flinch when he looked at him. "Beggin' your pardon, but I'm sure you could do better than Landry, maybe even fifty thousand quid. That countess's husband left her off pretty grand, I hear tell."

Luc felt the familiar black fury fill him. He restrained his wrath to a whisper. "I would write an epic masterpiece and proclaim it to the world before that, you idiot."

"It would take about three o' those things at this point."

Luc rose from his chair and Mr. Brown made a wise, very swift exit.

Damn his financial troubles. Thoughts of slow ruin, brought about by generations of St. Aubyn pampered living, kept him up more than half the night. No one knew of the never-ending drain he was trying to reverse while secretly helping his grandmother. Ata suspected nothing. Nor his sister. He had sworn to preserve Madeleine's innocence and Ata's hard-won late-in-life happiness. But that was not really what kept his eyes closed yet his mind working all through the night.

His thoughts wandered to what lay beneath layers of ugly black muslin just beyond the adjoining door. He had a very good idea. A wicked idea. It had been enough to leave him in a heated, foolish kind of mood.

And what did he have to look forward to today? Feeding and entertaining yet again masses of fashionable fribble and pretending to be the polite, reasonable man he was not. He would give almost anything to lock himself in his study and write and drink himself into a stupor to try and forget.

Forget the money problems, forget the memories of battleship carnage, but most of all forget the dark anguish of his familial past and his beautiful mother's face the last time he saw her.

Yes, what he needed was a diversion if he was going to have to entertain a herd of silly houseguests. It was not yet dawn and Luc yanked on the cord to request a tray for Mrs. Baird. If he couldn't sleep, neither should she. It made perfect sense.

He dressed with the same economy of motions he had used for so many years in his compact ship's cabin, forgoing his new valet, whose idea of casual dress involved too much lace and too many colors.

A maid soon appeared at his door, tray in hand. He motioned for her to leave it on a table and lifted the top of one of two silver pots. "Chocolate? Not tea for madam's breakfast?"

The garrulous, hefty maid with the weather-beaten face replied in a Cornish sing-song voice, "Yes, Your Grace. The lady said it were 'er favorite. 'Adn't had it forever, Mrs. Simms', she says to me. Fancy her using my proper name. Never wants toast, only chocolate, this one. Lots o' it. But then she needs it, wot wif them bony arms."

Luc contemplated the aroma as he nodded to the servant and tugged on his worn, supple boots. He glanced at the connecting door but dismissed it. He feared she might fly away if she knew a mere door separated them.

He balanced the tray and made his way through the outer door and into the dark hallway, pausing only to knock on her door.

There wasn't a sound.

He knocked again. Nothing.

He looked up and down the hallway and then pounded on the door with his boot.

Silence.

Cursing, he awkwardly opened the door with the edge of his hand only to encounter utter darkness. He placed the tray on the floor and fumbled toward a window in the room that had once been his mother's.

Luc opened one curtain and an early-morning ray of foggy light cut through the room. He turned toward the massive bed, draped in pink and white toile from France, and the wind was knocked out of him.

One long, very long, leg was twined carelessly around the bunched lace coverlet. Her white bed gown had lost its battle with propriety and was wrapped high above the knee. Why an inch or two more and . . .

He staggered forward.

A tangle of black locks lay sprawled on the pillow. He stared at her even profile, all hard planes and soft skin. With each quiet breath her breasts rose beneath the translucent white linen. A hint of one rosy tip peaked between tiny buttons.

His mouth went dry.

She appeared so innocent and young in white. This

was her color—not black, not jewel tones, not anything except pure white. The almost imperceptible pink of her cheeks was visible instead of the wan color when she dressed in that wretched black.

He forced himself to speak. "Mrs. Baird."

He cleared his throat. "Mrs. Baird."

He touched her cheek. "Rosamunde."

Nothing.

He placed both of his hands on her shoulders and shook her with a force that would wake St. Peter from his tomb. "R-o-s-a-m-u-n-d-e Baird, wake up."

"I'm awake," she muttered without batting an eyelash. She sighed and settled deeper under the covers.

He shook his head in disbelief. Relying on the rich scent of hot chocolate, he dipped his finger in one pot and spread a dab of the fragrant liquid on her relaxed lips.

"Mmmmm," she sighed and her delightful tongue curled along her lips.

It took every ounce of control not to pounce on her.

"Remind me never to count on you as a lookout," he said dryly.

Her breathing stilled, and one eye opened.

And within a moment she was scrambling under the covers. "My God, what are you doing in my room?" she screeched.

"Such language, Mrs. Baird." He tsk-tsked.

"If there's no fire, you'd better have a good reason for not knocking."

She looked like a young girl of sixteen, her straight

hair around her shoulders and a fast blush staining her cheeks.

He chuckled and poured a cup of chocolate and brought it to her. "Without knocking? Why my dear, I'll have bruises from the pounding. Do you know you sleep like a drunken sailor on shore leave?"

Her eyes were huge in her face. Smoky blue and green swirled around large black pupils. "I most certainly do not. Why, I always sleep with one eye open."

He bit back a smile. "Perhaps at—what did your brilliant in-law call it—Bastard's Cottage? But not here. Must be the change in scenery or"— he cleared his throat—"perhaps the chocolate?"

She seemed to relax slightly when she realized he wasn't going to touch her. "Why are you here? This is completely inappro—"

He interrupted her. "You've forgotten our engagement."

She gave him a blank stare.

"Our ride to West Penwith," he prompted.

"But we're not to go for hours."

"Correction: Ata and our guests are not to go for hours. We're to go now."

"Why this is everything ridiculous. I didn't promise to go."

He narrowed his eyes.

"Oh, all right," she said. "But I haven't a habit, and I haven't the proper boots, I haven't—"

"My dear, those boots of yours look like they would benefit from a little rest from walking. A long ride will do them quite well, I'm sure."

She muttered something.

"What did you say?"

"Nothing, absolutely nothing."

"It sounded rather blasphemous."

"You are impossible."

"Not that I don't approve of taking the Lord's name in vain, mind you. It adds enjoyment to this life, and may very well improve our accommodations in the next." He smiled. "That is, if you like to be warm."

She shook her head. "If you will please leave, I will meet you in the stables in five minutes."

"Is that similar to the five minutes Ata and I spent waiting outside your room last night, or five minutes according to my pocket watch?" He glanced down at his timepiece.

"It'll be five minutes in dog years if you're not more polite, sir."

He winked at her and left before she could throw her pathetic excuse for a boot at him.

He had plans for rehabilitating the sometimes demure, sometimes not, Mrs. Rosamunde Baird. Delightful plans for tasting the delectable fruits that lay behind that false nature she used when facing the world. He took curious pleasure in forcing her to throw off her reticence.

So far he had only been able to see her more exuberant passionate nature by provoking her. He would give a queen's ransom to see it up close without effort.

And what he would give to possess her in that moment.

It was too bad she had such a sense of humor when

she chose to use it. Humor was serious business and made him want her more than he should.

Rosamunde fumbled with the stirrup, swatting away the duke's offer of a leg up. It was tricky climbing into a sidesaddle. She had always preferred the forbidden pleasures of riding astride when no one was about. The stable boy held firm the girth straps on the other side as she hoisted herself from the mounting block.

She hadn't had time to get nervous, since there was no question she'd be at the stable within five minutes of his leaving her room. She'd gone on a tear, and taken inordinate pleasure at his look of pure disbelief when she appeared, leisurely strolling down the center aisle, gloves casually in hand.

She hoped her hair wouldn't fall from its perch under her netted hat. She'd had time to stick precisely three pins in it, pull a gown over her chemise, and gulp half a pot of chocolate.

The duke took the lead, briskly trotting his beautiful black mare with four white hocks past the small field behind the stables. Rosamunde clucked to her mount, a dark bay gelding, who showed great impatience to follow the mare. Surprisingly, His Grace said not a word. Perhaps this was going to be more pleasant than she'd envisioned.

Rosamunde tried not to take too much delight in riding again. But it had been so many years and this had been her favorite pursuit. She attempted to feel guilty about breaking her vow, but could not call up any sentiment except a well of exultant joy bubbling inside her.

She looked at the beauty of the flowering shrubbery and only then noticed the overcast sky. She smiled to herself. Living in Cornwall taught everyone that if you didn't like the weather, just wait awhile, for it was sure to change.

With horror, she realized there was no groom for propriety's sake. She stopped.

He looked over his shoulder.

"I'm not going without a groom."

"Rosamunde, do you really think I would allow the chance for you to ruin my reputation?"

"*Your* reputation?" His absurdities knew no bounds.

"Yes, you have a history of compromising gentlemen." He cleared his throat. "My brother, to be precise."

"Why, I—"

"Yes, why did you?" His eyes burned into hers.

A deep stab of embarrassment coursed through her. She held firm to her dignity. "I'm going back."

"The groom is on the other side of the hedgerow, pretending to ignore us."

She turned, and indeed the young stable hand who had curried the horses was partly visible beyond the hawthorn and dog-rose leaves.

"Shall we go on?" He motioned for her to precede him under the low branches of a passage. "I shall give you plenty of time to think of an answer to my question, madam."

She pretended not to hear him and trotted past. She couldn't stop herself from speeding up or slowing down each time he attempted to ride beside her. It was childish, but she hated being forced to play a game she didn't know.

The pastures teemed with green blades poking past the shorn brownish winter wheat. Overhead, gulls screeched their displeasure at being disturbed when they reached the coastlands. They turned inland at Penzance, past the ancient stone circles, home to legend and lore of mysterious people long gone.

Out of the corner of her eye, Rosamunde noticed the duke breaking past to lead her away from the track. A quarter hour later they came to an enormous oval pond, at least a mile around, its wavelets making lapping sounds. Hoofprints and a few obstacles abounded the course, its purpose revealed.

He looked at her and raised a single black amused eyebrow, in a silent dare.

"Absolutely not," she said quietly.

"No?"

"No."

"Are you certain?"

"Certain," she replied.

He paused. "You know, my dear, sometimes it's almost as if you're looking for an argument."

"*Almost*?" she countered.

He grinned a most devilish expression, then surveyed the circuit. "Actually I rather like that about you. Usually no one ever dares." He leaned over, murmured something to his horse, and then gathered his reins. "It truly is as amusing as your predictable reaction to every challenge." His mare pranced and balanced on her hindquarters before sprinting forward into a dead run.

Caught unawares, Rosamunde muttered something and had but a moment to collect herself before her horse whinnied his intent and strained against the bit. She was not going to take the bait.

Absolutely not going to.

The gelding was very keen to follow and snorted his annoyance at her tight grip on the reins. She held fast, but coiled desire unfurled in the pit of her stomach.

She longed to let him go.

Longed to feel the wind on her face and the exhilaration of soaring over a split rail fence.

She spied the white tail of a rabbit hopping along the hedge line. A gray fox slinked around the corner and dashed after it. Her horse shied, took the bit between his teeth and bolted.

Afterward, Rosamunde halfheartedly tried to convince herself she hadn't been able to hold him, but in her soul she knew she'd given in to temptation. She might be repentant, but it had truly felt wonderful to fly again, into the teeth of her beloved Cornish salt air.

The wind whined past her ears and the long familiar rush of excitement shot through her as she leaned forward and tried to ignore the brittle sidesaddle. There was no chance she could overtake him. For the only time in her life it didn't matter. The mare, far in front, was kicking up sodden chunks of turf. Rosamunde guided her horse to the extreme inside curve in a daring maneuver to cut the distance.

Once or twice, he looked over his shoulder at her. He was doing it again, crinkling his eyes in an extremely vexing, knowing fashion, when she watched his horse hesitate and falter in front of a wide ditch.

In a remarkable feat, the duke lost his balance and began to fall to one side, almost tumbling into the muddy edge. At the last moment he righted himself.

Rosamunde swallowed a giggle and trotted up, the young groom a few paces behind her.

"Yes, well, that worked out nicely for you," the duke said dryly and came to a halt.

She bit her lip to control a gurgle of laughter.

The groom stopped his small white horse alongside and jumped off, "Beggin' yer pardon, sir, but Boney here's pulled a shoe."

"Boney?" she asked.

"Short and arrogant like Bonaparte," the duke replied, then stared hard at her while addressing the boy. "Tom, lad, take him back."

"Do yer want me to return, sir?"

"Of course," he said coolly. "Come back on old Posey, why don't you."

The boy tipped his cap and grinned, and led the small horse toward home.

"Well, as my sister always reminds me, white horses bring ill fortune."

He threw one leg around the front of the saddle and slid down the side. Without a word he reached for her; his warm hands encircled her waist almost entirely.

She flinched slightly. The strength in his arms and his nearness left her discomfited.

"Your sister is very superstitious."

"Not really. We're both just cautious."

"And yet . . ."

"And yet what?"

"I hesitate to say," he said.

"You've never hesitated before."

He chuckled. "Quite right." He took her horse's reins and led them both to a patch of clover near a small stand of trees.

He stared at her shrewdly.

"You want me to tell you what I should've told you when I arrived the first day," she said quietly.

He had that annoying way of remaining silent, making her feel even more tongue-tied.

She forced herself to say what she most wanted to hide. "You want me to deny that I was with your brother."

She looked down at her hands and saw that she was pulling at one of the knotted threads of her string-backed gloves. She leaned against a small tree, and tried to ignore the rough bark digging into her back.

Not a whisper of a sound could be heard.

"Well, I can't," she said, looking him straight in the eye as she had never done before. "I brazenly offered myself to him."

He took a step closer to her and she could see the muscle in his cheek working. "Henry had talent. Women were always throwing themselves at him. I had to work a bit harder at it."

"Stop. You act as if it was nothing."

"Well, was it?" he asked in that deep baritone voice that licked her insides.

She ignored his question and looked down at her ugly boots. "We were caught."

"I see."

He couldn't possibly see at all.

"And this was where?"

"On the beachhead at Perron Sands."

"That must have been uncomfortable. Never could understand the allure of sand and rotting seaweed. Should kill any desire."

Anger gripped her. "I don't doubt you know nothing about it, locked away in your library day and night. They say . . ." She stopped short, horrified.

His mocking smile appeared. "'They' being of course the razor-sharp intelligent Auggie Phelpses of the world? Tell me what *they* say."

"That you're a rake and a recluse with a notorious past," she said, looking away. "But being somewhat of the same ilk, I don't hold it against you."

He chuckled. "Really? Why that's the nicest thing you've said to me so far, Rosamunde."

"Thank you." She played with a strand of her hair that was starting to come undone. "Pray, what do you do in your study all day? My sister tells me you're almost never at any of the meals or entertainments."

"You're changing the subject quite expertly, my dear. After you were caught, what happened next?"

She looked away. "I refused his offer."

"Why?"

"You may ask all the questions you like. But I might choose not to answer them."

"Why," he demanded.

"You're determined to humiliate me. I've accepted my punishment. It's enough."

He stared at her. "Why?"

"Because he didn't love me," she nearly shouted. "There. Now you know it all, the full humiliation."

He turned his back on her, leaned a hand against another tree and bowed his head.

He obviously found her repugnant in her shameless, ugly ways. She tried to find some comfort in it. At least he wouldn't continue to single her out to amuse himself for some reason she couldn't fathom.

"And did you love him?"

"Oh, not at all," she said wryly. "Haven't you heard? I've no moral fiber whatsoever."

He growled, "You loved him."

She spun away from him and picked at the mottled tree bark.

She heard him come up behind her and sensed his arm casually grasping one of the branches above her.

"And do you still?"

"Of course. How could I not?" She crossed her arms and squeezed the flesh at her elbows so tightly it hurt. "I lured him to ruin me, and he was obliged to reluctantly offer for me. Our fathers dared us to resist. But"—she paused—"as you know, I can never resist a challenge. And so I refused to follow convention." She heard a branch break when she mentioned his father. She turned to see the broken piece in his hand.

"You refused to repair your own reputation out of pride?"

"Pride? Is that what it is when a woman refuses to marry a man who's admitted he loves someone else?"

"Rosamunde," he said softly. "Ah, Rosamunde. Well, at least you were not as blind as most. Only fools think marriage can be anything more than a complete and utter descent into madness."

She glanced quickly at him. "We're of one mind, sir."

"And yet, you've been punishing your good sense ever since."

"Not at all. Every lady who can must marry, unless they want to become a burden on their family. And I got exactly what I wished. A husband who wasn't forced to ask for my hand." There was a long pause. "And now, you're justified in asking me to leave your property. I realize I've no right to mingle with your guests. Your father"—she swallowed—"said no Langdon was ever to set foot on St. Aubyn property again. I've trespassed. My sister and I will leave no later than tomorrow."

She finally had the courage to meet his gaze again and it nearly took her breath away.

"Where do you propose to go?"

"I have friends in London."

"Liar."

A gust of wind rustled the new leaves above them.

He continued, "Immoral I might be, but not stupid. Do you think I don't know you would've never come here unless it was the very last resort?"

"I have money, and I'll start anew in London."

"Hmmm," he murmured doubtfully. "Well, before you go you must pay penance for your deception"— a rush of coldness swept through her—"by allowing me to give you back a portion of the girlhood my *idiotic* family took from you." He put up his hands. "No, you can't refuse me. You've been so long from society you've forgotten dukes aren't to be refused anything for any reason. Actually, it's one of the few privileges that gives me any joy."

He was so odd at times that Rosamunde could not make out his character. Why was he doing this? Gossip implied he was inconsistent in his actions at best. An absolute scoundrel at worst. Well, in her eyes he had only ever been noble, even protective, even if it was sometimes in a high-handed, loutish sort of way.

But if the talk was true, she could not count on him. He went through life on a whim, she suspected, and woe to anyone who dared cross him. The dark blood running in his veins promised a nasty bit of temper. And she had seen enough of that.

But standing in front of his penetrating, heavy-lidded gaze she found it difficult to defy him, especially since it appeared he was trying to be attentive, in his own absurd, distant manner.

He spoke when she didn't respond. "You'll allow me to give you a season full of pleasure, and it will be far away from the dirt and weeds my gardeners tell me you're so all-fired fond of."

"Really, you owe me nothing. If you're looking for

pleasure, *Lord Fire and Ice*, perhaps you should look toward Theodora Tandy."

He chuckled and scratched his head. "Are you jealous?"

"Absolutely not," she said, fearing she sounded flustered. "It's just that you're not playing by your favored rules."

"I wouldn't be too sure of that, my dear. I might be giving the appearance of doing you a good turn, but really, you know my character well enough by now to know that I must certainly have an ulterior motive. If I were you I would consider your answer quite carefully." He leaned in and brushed his fingers near the corner of her lips.

Her eyes widened. "I would prefer you didn't—"

He interrupted, "—remove the chocolate from your face?"

There was something about him that left her vulnerable. Maybe it was the deep baritone burr in his voice, or his eyes as they focused so intently on her, becoming a purer sapphire blue the nearer he got. Whatever it was, she was determined he would not see how he affected her. While he looked nothing like his brother, she wasn't going to make a fool of herself, especially not with another St. Aubyn.

He looked down at her. "My brother was a fool. My father was worse. I must be allowed my own way of making up for your wretched beginning with the St. Aubyn family."

"But, I can't do this. I'm not even certain what you're suggesting," she stammered. What she really meant is that she would never, ever, *ever* trust another man, especially one who kept staring at her lips and talking about pleasures. But she would never be so rude as to say it aloud.

His eyes danced with amusement. "Really? And here I was hoping you'd lead the way."

"Don't mock me."

Luc St. Aubyn looked at the sensuous curve of her lips and had a horrible thought. "Just how many times have you been kissed?"

She blanched, then raised her chin. "Twice. No, three times."

Before he could stop himself, he continued, "And dare I hope your husband didn't insist on exercising his other rights?"

If it was possible, she lost what little amount of color remained in her face. He hated forcing her to speak, but like a perverse voyeur he had to know the full horror of how she'd lived.

"No," she whispered, her eyes full of pain.

With that one small word, he knew. Knew she had suffered more than she would ever reveal. If Alfred Baird was anything at all like the oily lizard of a cousin, then it was a miracle she hadn't jumped off the cliffs above Perran Sands.

It was due, no doubt, to his father, once again. As the ranking member of society in the district, he could have banded with her family to do everything in his power to try and restore a portion of her standing in the parish. Instead he had denounced her entire family and spread vicious rumors to boot. And his father's ham-handed dealings were obviously the reason Henry had changed so much the last years of his life, traveling endlessly on sea and on land always searching for something he couldn't name.

Luc felt like tearing something apart. It was that suffocating, long-ago feeling of being powerless. He had never been able to protect things dear to him.

All those churchgoing fools who pretended to worship good in the world were deluding themselves. Evil always triumphed in the end; the sooner they accepted it, the happier they would be. Hadn't he tried to explain it to his beloved brother? And look where Henry's optimism had left him. At the bottom of the sea.

Well, he would do something to repair the repressed look he saw in Rosamunde Baird's eyes. He might not be able to completely restore her standing in the *ton*, but he could lead her down the path of delicious, unbridled pleasure.

He looked deep into her stormy eyes, the same color of the warm waters off the West Indies, and he forced back the bitterness that pervaded his life. "Well, I've formed a plan. First off, chocolate three times a day. Then, an adventure, like today's, which you shall endeavor to endure. You shall just have to learn to love idleness and leisure, my dear. I assure you it has its merits. But first, I do believe we should correct one deficiency before the adventure begins in earnest."

She stared back at him mutely.

"Kissing. The deficiency in kisses. You know, the thing that separates us from the beasts."

"I had thought that was reason or compassion."

He ignored her. "Good. I didn't hear a 'no.'"

"But this is impossible. I'm in mourning."

He defused her with a steady look.

"And besides, perhaps I don't even like you."

"Me? You don't like, me?" he raised his quizzing glass to his eye.

Her eyes sparkled with laughter. "Your Grace—"

"Luc, if you please, in private."

"I—I just can't afford to risk—"

He interrupted her, "My dear, what have you to lose that you haven't lost already?"

He could see in her eyes that there was something more on her tongue, but wild dogs wouldn't tear it out of her.

She finally sighed. "Only my mind. But, what have you to gain from this . . . this ridiculousness?"

"Why, bragging rights. I shall best you at every turn. Let me show you." He lowered his lips to hers, and she tentatively kissed him back. It was such an innocent, young girl's kiss that it was all the more poignant, and his gut twisted like a sail caught between shifting winds.

He forced himself to hold back, to entice her slowly, gently, with infinite patience, his lips touching hers over and over with the barest of pressure.

She began to relax against him, still unsteady and unsure. And then gloriously he felt the moment of her indecision pass. He deepened the kiss, seeking entrance beyond and almost smiled when he tasted the warm chocolate of her. It almost made him consider forgoing brandy for breakfast on a regular basis. Her light breath feathered the hollow of his cheek, and it inflamed him. When her tongue tentatively touched his, he was swept into a swirling maelstrom of longing.

He pulled back before he drowned in the exquisite sensations, but then couldn't resist trailing a line of kisses down her neck until he encountered the prim and itchy high neckline of her gown. "Isn't there some rule that ladies with revolting husbands don't have to wear mourning for as long as you have? Twelve months should only be reserved for the husbands who deserve it," he murmured against her lips. "This truly is the most hideous rag. I'm sure Ata has a white muslin gown stashed away somewhere. Much more appropriate."

She tilted her forehead to rest against his. "I'm not a young lady anymore."

He leaned back to look down at the thick spray of lashes against her cheeks. "Somehow I can only picture you climbing trees, running races, and generally getting into trouble." He paused. "Especially after watching you ride like a hellion just now."

The sound of light raindrops on leaves came from the branches above. "I can't deny my family despaired of my ever learning to be a lady. I think they gave up when I was sixteen."

"Thank the Lord for small favors."

He watched her lips purse and then she broke out in the widest smile he had ever seen. It transformed her face. "That's exactly what I used to tell them." She laughed with unfeigned enjoyment and he wanted to take her right there. Under the dogwood tree. Kiss her senseless and see her laugh like that again and again.

His arousal was deep and hard, and he instinctively pressed her lightly against the tree. Unerringly, he fit into the juncture of her thighs and an intense jolt of desire burned through the itchy, ink-colored layers of his clothes and hers.

She made a sound and pressed her hands against his lapels.

He instantly released her.

She was gulping air.

"I didn't mean to frighten you." His head spun at the look of panic in her face. He forced back a promise never to hurt her. Words would mean little to a lady with a past littered with broken promises.

He should have never cornered her. It was quite obvious she was terrified of being touched. As just punishment, the heavens loosed the watery goods of one of Cornwall's most oft-heard proverbs: Where there is mist, rain is sure to follow. When there is no mist, it is raining already.

Ata's plans for an outdoor picnic were now ruined. And perhaps, he thought, dashing for the horses, his plans for Rosamunde Baird were as well. But then, he did have the ride back to convince her to accept a season of adventure. Only from now on he would keep his blasted paws off of her.

Conversation was the answer. Although how that would remotely warm his cold Cornish bed at night was the damned question.

Chapter 6

Idleness, n. *A model farm where the devil experiments with seeds of new sins and promotes the growth of staple vices.*

—The Devil's Dictionary, A. Bierce

He had promised to wage a campaign of adventure and he had lived up to his word, Rosamunde thought, four days later.

While she sat sipping divine chocolate, she closed her eyes and remembered every moment of those wicked amusements. He had barraged her each and every morning with his plans of idleness, her favorite being hours on the back of a magnificent horse, while the rest of the vast house party slept. Every muscle in her legs screamed from the time spent in the saddle again.

And he had kept his other promise. The unspoken one.

He hadn't touched her again. Not in greeting, not to

help her onto her horse if they dismounted, not even to escort her from the mansion. And because of this, she had been able to finally relax and enjoy their folly to the fullest.

Rosamunde had been very careful to have a maid wake her well before each invasion, *well before dawn*. It had not been difficult. Years of fear and unhappiness in her last life had always driven her early from bed if she had wanted to grasp at small, quiet moments of peace.

But at Amberley, he would not let her think about anything except the moment. They were to have adventures, even if sometimes he did not seem to be enjoying himself at all. Especially the morning they had ridden to a beach near the ruin of an ancient church, where parishioners of Sundays past were said to haunt the grounds.

On that particularly hot day, he hadn't been able to hide his distaste for her idea of scaling a large rocky ledge to get a better view of the waves pounding the huge boulders.

"Second thoughts?" she had asked, laughing. "You know, you promised me amusements to erase years of—"

"Only a madwoman would enjoy climbing in such heat," he had grumbled before a flurry of stones cascaded down the cliff. "I told you we would have been better off swimming."

She had laughed at the look of disgust on his face.

"I've created a monster," he had muttered.

She could not believe she had been so free with him, so unafraid to speak her mind. It was something she hadn't done in so long. Even with Sylvia, the layers of guilt made it impossible to be lighthearted together. A great lump in her throat formed and she replaced her cup in its saucer.

And yet, when they were in company with others the duke had been cool, his haughty condescension mocking, while she was forced to endure the varying looks of disdain or pity from the houseguests.

The difference between his character when he was alone with her and with others made her wary. Was he just dallying with her in private? She had no experience with these things. When they were among others, he erected a cold barrier making her and almost everyone else hesitant to talk to him. Even Theodora Tandy had stopped giggling around him. It was comical at times, and she almost felt sympathy for the sycophants who tried to curry his favor, only to be shredded by his cynical responses. Some knew not that they had been skewered. Perhaps it was best that way. But most of the time he was locked away in one of his private domains.

She went to pour another cup of chocolate and found the pot empty. Well, that was a first. He apparently wasn't coming to demand an outing today. She started at the light tap on her door before her sister entered, breathless with excitement.

"Her Grace has asked a group of us to go for a day of sailing. You're to come, Rosa."

"Sailing?"

"Yes, the duke has some sort of sailing ship anchored at Penzance."

"Who's joining the party?"

"I'm not certain. The duchess muttered some very strange comments about muffins and early birds, and then a gleam came to her eye and she announced it was a perfect day for a sail. I think it's to be mostly the Widows Club, but Charity was to be invited as was . . . her brother," Sylvia's words trailed off.

Rosamunde tilted her head to try and read the expression on her sister's face. "Sir Rawleigh seemed quite taken with you last evening."

Her sister plunged forward. "You are mistaken, Rosa. I was delighted to form an acquaintance with his sister. Charity is kindness and sweetness itself. I should never say it, but I am glad the old vicar is gone. He brought nothing but division and rancor to the parish."

"Why that's the most unkind thing I've ever heard you say," Rosamunde murmured. She took up one of her sister's hands in her own.

Sylvia could not meet her gaze. "I still shudder to remember the pious look on your husband's face each Sunday before he set off for church, when he reminded you that you weren't allowed to go with him."

Rosamunde took her sister in her arms, and closed her eyes. "Well, at least I had you to comfort me, dearest. Truly, I enjoyed Sunday mornings alone with you better than any other day of the week. It was the only time we could walk about unfettered by anyone else."

Sylvia pulled away and walked to the window to stare out to the sunny day. "Rosa," she said quietly. "You are going to join the boating party, aren't you?"

Rosamunde hesitated. There was something in her

sister's tone that made it obvious this was important to her. It must involve the vicar, and Rosamunde would swim the seven seas if it would bring happiness to her sister. She hadn't the heart to needle her again. It had been so long since Sylvia had shown excitement in anything. "Of course, I will."

One hour later, the dowager duchess bustled a handpicked group to the port before any of the more boorish guests, as she called them, caught wind of the plan.

They approached the crescent bay in an open carriage and Rosa gazed at the beautiful, crumbling edifice on St. Michael's Mount. The spire of the ancient Benedictine monastery pierced the low-lying mist in an obvious effort to rejoin its heavenly inspiration.

The shifting winds of dawn had, indeed, foretold a grand day for sailing. Small clouds scudded in from the west and the coolness of morning sneaked beneath Rosamunde's thin shawl while the morning haze muted the colorful houses flanking the bay. Seaweed lay tangled about the beach and the mount's shingle path, which was revealed only at the vast low tide.

Rosamunde's breath caught in her throat when she spied Luc St. Aubyn high in the knotted rigging of a magnificent cutter, which dwarfed the fishing vessels around it. At least sixty feet of solid English oak floated below him.

His imposing wind-whipped figure was every inch a commander despite the informality of his rolled-up shirtsleeves and long dark hair that the breeze had forced from the confines of his queue.

As she boarded, Rosa noticed *Caro's Heart* in gold lettering on the black stern and she wondered if the lady in question had captured his heart or if he had captured the lady's. Her own heart constricted and she wondered what sort of woman the duke had loved or still loved. She had overhead whispers in the garden yesterday between two married ladies, who spoke of *Lord Fire and Ice* and the wake of broken hearts he had left in town. One of the ladies, the more ravishing one, had not been smiling.

The duke's beautiful sister, Madeleine St. Aubyn, joined Rosamunde at the varnished oak railing while the others converged on the picnic baskets, brought forth since the duchess had hurried everyone through breakfast.

"My grandmother tells me you and your sister will be visiting for the season, Mrs. Baird."

"Yes, she has been very kind to us."

The young lady, who could not yet have reached her twenties, had dark brown hair and the same color eyes as her brother. But that was where the similarity ended. Her expression was everything open and innocent, while his was guarded and shrewd. Discomfiture tumbled inside Rosamunde when she glanced at his handsome profile.

"Grandmamma is only nice to those who deserve it, as I'm sure you're well aware. I'm counting the days before she tosses the baron and Augustine Phelps on their ears. Indeed, it's a wonder it hasn't happened already. I guess she doesn't want any unpleasantness before the wedding."

Well, in one way the St. Aubyns were all alike. They spoke their minds and did not suffer fools lightly. Rosa wished she were in a position to do the same. It seemed a long time ago, those days when she had spoken without a care.

"Have you ever been to London?"

"No, never, Lady Madeleine." She knew it sounded odd, but refused to explain further.

"Please, you must call me Madeleine. And will you allow me the same informality?"

"If you wish," Rosamunde breathed.

The ship shifted portside as they cast off and the wind caught the sails. Three deckhands nearby coiled the docking lines.

"You shall have a lovely time when you go with Ata and the others. You must force my brother to take you to see the sites, especially the Tower, and the theatre. But Vauxhall at night is my absolute favorite. You must do it right, eat strawberries with champagne and dance under the stars and lanterns threading the trees."

"I hadn't thought we would go to town."

"Why, certainly. Luc never stays long in our country estates. It brings back . . . Well, he prefers town. And Ata will not stay anywhere without him for very long," Madeleine continued.

Peter Mallory, Lord Landry, came up behind his fiancée and caught her in his arms and swung her around, oblivious to the impropriety. The young lady giggled and her look of pure happiness caught at Rosamunde's heart.

Lord Landry raked back sweat-streaked hair and re-placed his tarred straw sailor's hat. "Here I am doing all the work, already. Is this how our marriage will be? Tell me now so I'll be forewarned."

Madeleine looked at him coyly. "Why, yes, Mrs. Baird was just explaining the importance of setting ground rules for wedded bliss." Madeleine winked at her. "The first of which is that the man is to do all the work and the lady is to lounge about and act the part of a delicate flower to make the husband feel manly and protective."

Lord Landry hooted with laughter. "So your brother forbade you to climb the rigging again and help with the sails, did he? Don't worry, my dear, I shall always *order* you to do your full share of the work when we're married."

She pouted. "Luc told me the only man I was ever to obey was him. He reminded me for the hundredth time that I am to return home if you ever dare order me to do anything I don't like."

"Well, I like that. The scoundrel still thinks he's my commander. I'll soon put a stop—"

Luc St. Aubyn came out of nowhere and drawled, "You'll never do anything to make her want to come home if you know what's good for you."

Lord Landry rolled his eyes. "God knows I'd rather face the press gang than endure the wrath of an over-protective brother."

"I've always nursed the belief that marriage turns decent men into brutes. I daresay Mrs. Baird would agree with me." He glanced at her sideways for a moment before he turned back to his friend. "Let us hope you prove the exception, Landry."

"Well, since I'm the only one between us who will ever agree to willingly become a beast, I would think you would at least take pity on me."

The duke snorted. "I'll keelhaul you until you drown if you don't keep her insanely happy. You might as well order your headstone now, for I doubt you'll have time to do it later."

Rosamunde bit back a smile. Why was he so cynical about the marriage state? She had every reason to be, but his disgust ran much deeper than her own, if it were possible.

"Power always does breed insanity," Lord Landry replied, shaking his head. "How soon one forgets the bonds of fraternity. Was it not I who willingly and bravely joined you after you decided a lark at sea facing floating gun platforms would be just the thing to thwart your father?"

Rosamunde stood stock-still. She didn't need to look at the duke's face to know that his friend had crossed the line. Perhaps Lord Landry could talk to the duke in this manner in private, but not here, not now, in front of her.

"Actually," Luc said quietly, his voice coated with frost, "you've twisted it as usual to suit you. If you will remember, my father was delighted to see me off to war. He had purchased a pair of colors for me to join the Horse Guards. I don't think he really cared that I chose the sea over the land. If you and Rawleigh hadn't drunk enough Blue Ruin to fell an ox, you wouldn't have been stupid enough to stow away with me on the first ship bound for battle."

Only the sound of the rig cutting through the waves could be heard.

Madeleine's quick thinking broke the silence. "Well, I think both of you had the better lot. I was the one packed off to Miss Doleful's—"

"Miss Dilford's," Luc St. Aubyn gritted out.

"Miss Dilford's School for Young Ladies. It seems that while Father thought you'd learned enough, I was to be improved by a daily dose of Johnson's sermons, embroidery, and horrid lessons on the pianoforte."

"I shudder to think of the waste of money," the duke said dryly.

"I would have much preferred facing the cannonade with you both."

The wind rustled through the duke's hair, a wild halo of black locks surrounded his angular, hard face. He was completely ignoring her presence and Rosamunde felt the self-consciousness of the unwanted. A shout from one of the deckhands interrupted them.

"The devil, Rawleigh's heading us toward the shoals," Luc said, then hurried to the helm.

Madeline spoke softly to her fiancé, seemingly unaware that Rosamunde was still there. "You must be kind to him, Peter. Father always taunted him, said he was weak, and spineless, with his head in the clouds and his nose in a book. I remember it well even though I was but a child when Luc disappeared with you both. Father was determined to take the poet out of him and toughen him up, he reminded us constantly."

"And what did your mother have to say?"

"My mother? Why, I can't remember." Madeleine paled. "My mother was always very quiet."

"Really?" replied Lord Landry, who smiled. "So like you, my love." He kissed the tip of his beloved's nose.

She swatted him playfully and regained her smile.

Rosamunde turned away from the couple, feeling every inch the intruder in a conversation that had become much too personal. The entire outing was leaving her ill at ease. She didn't belong here, didn't belong anywhere. That was the worst part of it. She had taken for granted her place in the world as a young girl, but as a mature woman she knew security was a silly illusion.

Rosamunde crossed the deck and reclined on an empty lounge chair. Luc St. Aubyn stood at the helm just a few yards away, silent and watchful, Mr. Brown at his elbow. She stared into the whitecaps, which sparkled in the bright sunlight.

She had been wrong about him. There had been hints of his real character beneath the layers of biting cynicism. She tried to picture him as a young boy, lost within the pages of a book, and shook her head. Was that what he was doing beyond the door to his study—lurking behind great tomes of poetry? She had always thought he was drinking himself into a stupor. She could picture the latter quite easily.

As if he could hear her thoughts, she heard him mutter, "Mr. Brown, it seems you've forgotten the brandy."

"I never forget anything, Captain."

Rosamunde opened her eyes and turned her head slightly. He was staring at her when he unscrewed Mr. Brown's flask and sloshed back the contents. It was almost as if he was trying to comfort her with the illusion of his black soul. It was much easier to trust in the innate evil of a man. She turned away from him and tried to concentrate on the view in front of her.

Never had she been on a ship like this. Huge sails soared overhead, shadowing the starboard side, where she sat. As the coast became smaller Rosamunde found a peace unlike any she had known.

The expanse of the sea made her realize her own insignificance in the grand scheme of life. And for some reason it calmed her. Oh, there was no doubt there would be more dark days ahead, but facing the horizon, she took courage and realized she would make her way in the world.

She had decided she would ask the duchess to help her find a post somewhere, perhaps as a companion to an older lady, or even a governess. She would have liked to have had children, but it had never happened. God had punished her further by making her barren. In retrospect, perhaps it was for the best.

She had thought to speak to Ata after the wedding, but now wished she had done so sooner. She would not go to London. She could barely tolerate the knowing looks here in Cornwall. And she knew the *haut ton* would only be more harsh in their assessments. The disgraced and disowned daughter of an earl could expect censure to be at its zenith in the capital of Christendom.

But before she found a post for herself, she thought as she watched her sister and a group approach, she would help find a portion of happiness for Sylvia.

"The Cornish have a saying, Sir Rawleigh, that those who will not be ruled by the rudder must be ruled by the rock," Sylvia said shyly.

His open expression looked back at her sister with something more than mere kindness. "And here I thought all men were ruled by their stomachs."

Sylvia laughed, bashfulness and sweetness in her face.

The enticing aromas of hot Cornish pasties, cold asparagus and gooseberry tart wafted in the air when Sylvia handed her a plate with a sampling of each.

"You've not had any of the picnic foods, Rosa." Her sister perched on the end of her long chair.

"And you will catch your death without a shawl, Sylvia."

Charity giggled. "Do you always mother hen each other?"

Sir Rawleigh shrugged out of his black clerical coat and draped it across Sylvia's shoulders. Sylvia blushed and tried to refuse but he stopped her. "No, I insist. You must allow me the pleasure. Besides, it matches your gown." His eyes were so friendly and Rosamunde was struck anew by how handsome and charming he was. He was the perfect complement to her sister.

Sylvia returned the vicar's smile and Rosamunde positively ached for her sister's happiness.

Grace Sheffey set aside her plate and withdrew a small leather-bound book from a hidden pocket. The countess's pale curls danced in the breeze below a fashionable hat made of brown straw and pheasant feathers. She was the picture of dainty English femininity as she turned a page, glanced at the duke, and settled more deeply into her chaise.

Grace was the only one of the widows with whom Rosamunde had been unable to form a certain level of friendship. It was no wonder. The countess rarely mingled with any of the other widows. She was always in the company of Ata and sometimes with the duke. But that was to be expected, since the lady had known the family for many years if what Georgiana Wilde had told her was true. And Rosamunde didn't doubt it.

There was something about the way Grace Sheffey looked at the duke that made Rosamunde know there was something between them. What, she didn't know. Grace always seemed to smile a bit wider and her eyes sparkled just a little brighter whenever he entered the room. And he was unfailingly polite to her in return.

Rosamunde picked at the delicious food and watched the crew at their labors. The tasks were performed with precise movements at the command of the duke. When she dared, Rosamunde snatched glimpses of him each time he barked an order.

While he was not as classically handsome as Sir Rawleigh, his sleek and brutally powerful physique made her feel as gangly as a newborn colt. His hawkish features elicited sensations within her that reminded her of the feelings she had had for his brother long ago. Only this time it was worse. And again it could only lead to disaster. Her heart was barely working, as it was. It had been torn apart and mended with guilt and harsh trials, and it could not take any more strain.

"Mrs. Baird," he called out. "Would you care for a turn at the helm?"

She couldn't maintain a refined and cool response. She simply jumped at the chance. Literally.

She dipped into the breach within his wide stance, then carefully poised her hands on the wheel's spindles below his own strong, scarred hands. His whispered instructions in her ear made her shiver. Holding the power of the ship within her grasp filled her with the same sort of excitement as two tons of horseflesh beneath her during a hunt with the hounds at full cry.

Ata tottered up and almost tripped on her skirts. Mr. Brown caught her at the last moment.

"Your Grace, I've told you. You can't wear those high-heeled boots o' yours on the ship. You'll go right overboard one o' these days, see if you don't."

"Well at least I won't have to worry about your plaguing me to death about my footwear anymore, if I do, you impudent man," she muttered. She refused to look at him and instead spoke to her grandson, "When are you going to do something about him?"

Luc St. Aubyn chuckled. "I don't know what makes you think I can control him. Brownie was capable of holding a ship full of three hundred cutthroats, and starving impressed men from mutiny on the promise of imaginary pork chops and wine for a solid week. I rather think you don't stand a chance, Ata."

"Well!" the duchess huffed.

Mr. Brown grinned. "By the by, Captain, I've never known you to let a lady take the wheel."

"Well, Mrs. Baird seems born to it, don't you think? Not the delicate, refined sort at all."

She didn't know whether to feel insulted or the opposite.

"You've never let *me* take the helm," grumbled his grandmother.

"You'd never be able to see over the wheel," chided Mr. Brown.

"Look who's talking, you old badger."

Rosamunde could feel Luc's chest rumble with pent-up mirth.

"And," Ata continued, "I was addressing my grandson, not someone so far beneath my notice."

Luc cut in. "Are you ever going to forgive him, Ata?"

"Why I've no notion what you're talking about."

"About your mysterious past history."

"If you say another word, my darling, you'll find yourself regretting it."

"Hmmm," he responded.

"Indeed," Ata replied. "I find I have much time on my hands since Madeleine will soon be out of the nest. I might just set my sights on you."

The rumbling from his chest stopped. "I hadn't thought the years in your dish were scrambling your wits, Grandmamma."

Ata harrumphed and teetered to the rail.

Suddenly, Rosamunde noticed that Luc's shadow behind her disappeared. He was walking to the other group. Grace Sheffey moved the ruffled edge of her skirt off the end of her lounging chair and he sat beside her.

The countess's pretty face lit up with pleasure, and his harsh expression eased in response. They perfectly complemented each other—he so dark and she so blonde. He said something to make her laugh. Rosamunde forced herself to watch them.

Grace Sheffey was reading to him and his hand touched hers when the wind blew back a page. And suddenly, Rosamunde could envision it all, the young, serious boy he had been, the way books had probably allowed him to forget any unhappiness life had brought him. And obviously, quite obviously, elegant and refined Grace Sheffey was someone who knew how to make him feel lighthearted, something he needed. She looked away.

"You must keep a steady eye on the horizon, ma'am," Mr. Brown said to her. "It takes some practice."

"Thank you, sir."

"Don't mention it." His gnarled hand, covered in age spots, gripped the spindle above hers and corrected the direction. "You've a talent for this, lass. And I don't doubt Luc sees it too." He sighed deeply. "Your husband leave you much of anything?" he tried to ask casually.

Rosamunde started. What on earth? "Why, not a farthing."

"Pity," he shook his head. "'Tis a great pity. But," she thought she heard him mutter under his breath, "we'll just have to find another way."

The man had apparently consumed more spirits than his master.

"The captain asked me to give you this a while back. Said you won it off him fair and square, something about archery." He placed a leather pouch that jingled in her pocket. "Asked me to give it to you all mysterious-like. But," he said with a small cough, "there's no way this old head of mine can think of passing it off without you figuring it out. I'm thinking you've got too much brains in that pretty head of yours."

His foolish compliment warmed her. "Why, Mr. Brown, His Grace doesn't owe me anything." She tried to reach into her pocket but he stopped her.

"Now, ma'am, the first rule is you can't take your hands off the wheel. These here are treacherous waters. And don't go making my life any harder. Why, he would have my head if you don't take your winnings. And you'll be doing me a favor if you don't tell him I couldn't figure out a way to slip it to you."

"You've known the family a long time, haven't you?" she asked.

"Since that stubborn little duchess was a wee lass of six and ten," he said, his Scottish burr suddenly making an appearance and gliding over his words. "And I was the brawny son of a laird with few coins in my pocket but lots of hair to make up for it. She was the daughter of an earl. Yes, there was a time when I enjoyed her smiles much more often than her frowns." He removed his tarry hat and scratched his balding head. "Och, but it was a long, long time ago." He looked up to the sails and Rosamunde barely heard the words he said under his breath. "Long before she begged me to watch over her bonny grandson."

Rosamunde glanced at Luc St. Aubyn and saw him watching her. A ray of light passed over his face, revealing the shocking blue of his eyes against his bronzed skin. His magnetism was mesmerizing. He was, quite simply, the most purely masculine and enigmatic man she had ever known. And suddenly she knew she wanted him, quite desperately, but in a way that was nearly impossible to explain. It was the most selfish thought she had had in a decade, primal to the bone in nature.

Now what she would do if she ever had him for herself she didn't know, for while she wanted his admiration there was no question she couldn't ever face anything beyond his kiss. She had promised herself after Alfred's death that she would never ever suffer the pain and humiliation of marital relations ever, ever again. Even a life spent in a workhouse was more appealing. And if she had endured such pain with Alfred, a man half the size of the Duke of Helston, she would never be able to tolerate the act with this man. She looked at the sheer size of his physique and shivered. He was so strong. *So male*.

She felt the deck creak beneath her feet, and continued to stare into his compelling eyes.

Chapter 7

Alone, adj. *In bad company.*

> —The Devil's Dictionary, A. Bierce

The wedding morning dawned as fair and bright as the bride's face. There was not a cloud in her veil of happiness, not a seed of doubt to her future well-being.

She was a giddy fool, thought Luc as he kissed Madeleine's cheek and made his promises to return for her in two hours. He closed the door to her chamber and removed to his library.

At least she was marrying a man as irrationally good-hearted as she. They would probably be disgustingly happy for a solid year before all the well-known eccentricities would creep in on stealthy feet, bringing boredom to the marriage, followed closely by quarrels, a slow descent into indifference, and in many cases much worse. His parents were the definitive example.

He sat at his desk and weighed in his palms the sextant from a looted French privateer's ship. The only reason Luc had agreed to allow Landry to marry his sister was because he could keep an eye on them. And Landry knew without a doubt that Luc would make good on his promises to hurry his sorry arse off this world if he was ever stupid enough to cause Madeleine a moment of distress.

Luc glanced down at the manuscript before him and reached for a freshly trimmed quill. His publisher, that shrewd Scot John Murray, intent on milking Luc's abilities—and the voracious new appetite of a fickle public in the process—had asked to see Luc's almost-completed manuscript about Trafalgar. *Just as Brownie had suggested.*

In fact, Luc didn't doubt the two of them had cooked up the idea together. Only now, the publisher wanted him to start each chapter with witty definitions such as the ones in *Lucifer's Lexicon*. Luc also didn't doubt they were plotting to let slip his secret identity in the process. The publisher had hinted he wanted to use the public's curiosity to sell more books. Luc didn't even want to think about how Mr. Murray had managed to whip up such a frenzy.

But like a moth to a flame, Luc couldn't seem to harness the desire to thwart them. He knew exactly what he was doing and where this would end, just as Christ had gone to the cross. And there was no doubt Judas had taken the ridiculous twin forms of Mr. Brown and Mr. Murray.

Well, at least this work on Trafalgar wouldn't be mistaken for the work of a girl.

Luc opened an inkwell and dipped the quill into the hell pot. He wrote at the top of the first chapter, "Captain, *n.* The gentleman onboard who drinks the best wine in exchange for the privilege of leading boarding parties and having his brains blown out first."

He fingered an old scar on the back of his neck and chuckled. This was going to be easier than he thought.

He turned to the second chapter and continued, "Admiral, *n.* A gout-ridden plotter in London who collects full pay whilst other poor bastards carry out the proper action without ever seeing Fatty's orders. Admiral Nelson, of course, being the exception." He bit back a smile and scratched through the words twice, the ink pooling. He'd never be able to face his former commanding officer again if that was in print.

Thoughts of having to offer up his sister's hand were putting him in a black frame of mind, it seemed. It always was easier to write when he was in a mulish, ugly mood.

And thoughts of Rosamunde's exquisite, wind-whipped face from yesterday made him even more blue-deviled. He ramrodded thoughts of her back, but just like a cannon's recoil, the feeling of her body against his, her lips against his own, and even the clean soap scent of her skin kept kicking back into his gut. He'd been rigid in his efforts to keep his distance for the past week. He had succeeded until inexplicably he'd found himself inviting her to take the helm. What had come over him?

It was that look of starkness he saw in her eyes from time to time. The look of wistful longing for excitement. She was made for adventure.

She was the most passionate woman he'd ever known. Oh, she kept it simmering beneath the surface when they were surrounded by others, but she couldn't hide it when she rode his horses, scaled insanely high cliffs, and sailed for the first time.

What it would be like to dance seduction with her dogged his last waking thoughts each night, and left his body aching for release. But sampling more than her kiss was the worst possible idea. And it would take hours to invoke trust, hours to bring mutual pleasure, then many more hours of regret. But above all he could never pay the price to satisfy her resulting guilt.

Marriage.

She was not a female with whom to trifle. She was not like so many ladies in town. He only accepted the invitations of rich, secure, knowing women who welcomed flirtation, sought out seduction, and knew how it would end with him.

For he never had any woman twice.

It would only encourage expectations. And Lord knew he could only be counted on to do the exact opposite of what was expected of him.

His behavior, he knew, had quite perversely worked in his favor. It sealed his fate as a prize for the women who wanted a night of sin. But one night only.

Between the sheets, ladies whispered in his ear the moniker they had for him, Lord Fire and Ice. Fire within his arms, ice the morning after. Some had tried to thaw him, but none had succeeded.

But this spring, the allure of it had waned. It was easy to figure out why. There was no chase. It was too easy. In fact it was worse than that. He had begun to feel like a prize stallion when the ladies slipped notes in his pocket or proposed a secret rendezvous.

And he knew his desire for Rosamunde was precisely due to the fact that she was the first female who presented a puzzle. She had not propositioned him, had not used her feminine wiles. In fact she was more like a young girl who knew less than nothing of seduction, and certainly didn't welcome it.

She was a challenge.

But he knew how to walk away from a challenge. He had learned how to do that when he was seventeen years old, when he had walked away from . . .

He beat back the thought he locked behind every door in his mind. He would pack Rosamunde Baird off to London with the rest of the widows after Madeleine's wedding today. Somehow, like every season before, Ata would find a way to bring peace and happiness to her as well as each of the other widows. And he would do what he knew best. Walk away. It would be the right—

A knock sounded at the door. Who would dare . . . ?

Knocking again.

"Come," he barked.

His groin lurched when the very woman he was thinking about came through the door.

"Yes?" he asked more harshly than he intended.

She glanced at his desk in embarrassment. He swept

the disordered pages into a pile and weighted it with the brass sextant.

"I'm sorry, I was told your grandmother was here with you." She held an exquisite bouquet of flowers, ivy trailing the ground. "These are for your sister."

"They know better than to disturb me here." He narrowed his eyes.

She backed toward the door, and he forced himself to swing off his leather chair and go to her.

"Forgive me, Mrs. Baird." He had deliberately gone back to using her formal name this past week. "You've caught me in the middle of contemplating my sister's future."

She stopped and a flicker of a smile crossed her features. "Ah."

"Well said."

"While I know I am wasting my breath, and presuming too much, I think you needn't fear for your sister's happiness."

"Really. I had thought you a tad more enlightened in the area of female enslavement."

"No. Just more practical. While I would never marry again, your sister appears to have chosen well." She set the bouquet on an end table and closed the distance between them. Clearly she was not going to leave him in peace. "Most women have little choice in the matter of marriage as well you know."

"I'm familiar with most females' point of view on the matter."

She tilted her head and looked like she was pondering her next words. "Women know men have altogether different thoughts. Your sex grumbles about taxes and marriage, but in the end both are seldom avoided."

He chuckled. "You have a certain flair for words."

"As do you."

He stopped short. "Who told you that?"

"No one had to." She looked beyond his shoulder to his desk. "What do you do in here all day? You can't be reading." Her arm swept past the meager number of books on the shelves and he quickly covered his ink-stained thumb and forefinger with his other hand.

A crystal shot glass beckoned along with a decanter of brandy inside the side desk drawer. He filled it and threw it back. Anything to keep him from taking three long strides toward her and taking those beautiful lips and crushing himself against them.

"Ah, yes, of course," she murmured.

"And here I'd thought you were quite intelligent when in fact you're remarkably slow, my dear," he drawled. He poured another drink.

"Perhaps." She took several steps to his desk and ran the edge of her index finger along his desktop. "But perhaps not. For some reason you seem to enjoy giving the illusion you are Lucifer himself, but I know you are anything but."

He sputtered. "Have you forgotten my name?"

"What has that—"

He stared down at her, her eyes just inches from his own. She was one of the tallest ladies he had ever encountered. "My given name happens to be Lucifer

Judas Ambrose St. Aubyn, or Helston to my more intimate friends."

Her eyes glittered with emotion. "For some reason, you want everyone to think you a scoundrel. But I believe the first truth: Actions speak louder than words. And I've never seen you act unkindly to anyone less fortunate. You are just the opposite. And I know many who speak kindly but act horridly. Your words are often harsh, but there is nothing behind them."

He felt heat claw at his belly. "You think me a good man, do you?" he whispered.

"I do."

"Then you're a fool."

"Oh, there's no doubt of that. I've had eight years to learn the price of being a fool. But I think I've learned how to judge the measure of a man."

"You know nothing about me."

"I know enough." She glanced at the whiskey. "And I know a prop when I see one."

His laughter began as a chuckle, but grew loud and cynical to his own ears. "And what else do you know?"

He watched her throat convulse in a swallow. "I know you were once a boy who loved books and learning. And I knew your father. I can only imagine how a boy such as you fared under his thumb."

"My dear, you really must do better. Your deduction skills are not as refined as you think." He stared into the depths of her ethereal eyes.

She refused to blink or look away.

He wanted to see the look of revulsion fill her eyes.

Wanted her to be afraid of him. Wanted the truth to be bared once and for all.

He finally spoke, so quietly she had to lean in to hear him. "My father loved me in the only way he knew how, with moderation and at a distance. And he might have been severe but he had my best interest at heart. As the second son, I was groomed to become an officer, and a bookish boy would not do."

"But you were too young to go. Most are allowed to finish university. Why did your father force you away?"

He rubbed his temples. "For many reasons." He was silent.

"Tell me," she said.

"Perhaps because my success overshadowed my brother's, and that wouldn't do. The heir must be the more intelligent one. Perhaps it was the only way he could force me to become the man he wanted me to be."

"My father always encouraged my brothers to pursue their different interests," she whispered.

The intensity of the moment was such that Luc could have sworn he could feel heat radiating from every pore of his body. "Your father wasn't like mine."

She shook her head. "You're right. But then in other ways he was worse. Because I thought his love was everlasting, impervious to anything that might happen in my life. And I was very wrong." She looked at her hands. "But we were talking about you."

He would tell her. If only to make her take a deep and abiding disgust of him, and never tempt him again.

"Did you never meet my mother?"

"Your mother?" She was thinking. "Why, yes I did. She was quite beautiful, I remember."

"She was more than beautiful. She was goodness, sweetness, and the mother every child dreams of having. And my father made her miserable. Oh, she tried very hard not to show it, she was very good at acting. She always smiled and did everything my father asked and more. She was the glue that bound our family together, making it seem almost normal. But I could see beyond her false smiles. The only time she was truly happy, as were we all, was when Father was gone to town and we were alone with her—just Henry, and me, and later Madeleine. But I . . ."

"Yes?" she prompted when he stopped speaking.

"I was her favorite. And I loved her more than anyone or anything."

"And?" she prompted again.

"And, ultimately, I couldn't save her."

"From what?" she whispered.

"From my father and from unhappiness."

There was a long pause.

"What do you mean?" she asked softly.

"I was a coward. I wouldn't do the one and only thing she ever asked of me."

"What did she ask?"

His eyes focused on a point above her shoulder, and his vision blurred.

"To take her away from him."

"What?" She asked so loudly it brought him back to his senses.

He walked to the door and opened it. "Mrs. Baird, forgive me. I don't know what I've been thinking. Please, I must ask you to leave."

She walked to him and forced the door closed before he could stop her. She twisted the key in the lock.

He uttered a growl but she interrupted. "Tell me." She shook her head vehemently. "You must. You and your grandmother have done so much for us. You need to tell someone. And it cannot hurt me. It is only fair, you forced me to tell you about your brother. Now it is your turn."

"Dukes don't have to take turns," he said dryly.

"This duke should, this one time," she insisted.

He swallowed and walked to the window. He couldn't bear to look into her eyes.

"She never told me what happened to her behind closed doors. I'll never know. I don't know if he hurt her as he did us from time to time, or just used words to kill her spirit. He was remarkably effective with words alone, as you well know. But with each passing year, my mother lost a little bit of her inherent joy. For seventeen years, I watched her struggle a little harder with each passing season. I think I was the only one who really saw it because we were like two souls tied together. She loved me like no mother has ever loved a son."

Luc took comfort in the silence Rosamunde offered and paused. Memories of his mother washed over him and he forced the tightness from his throat. "My sister was partly correct yesterday. My father arranged for a commission. But it was because he felt Henry needed bolstering. And in a way, he was probably right. And of course I wanted to please my father. He had always made light of my scholarly pursuits." He flexed his hands and added slowly, "Henry never really wanted the responsibilities of the dukedom. I had always been the more capable one, and he had always been the more lighthearted blade. But I was the younger and there could not be two dukes."

"But why did you thwart your father's plans to join Wellington's divisions?"

"I disappeared not to thwart him, but rather my . . . mother."

"*What*?"

He rested his forehead on the cool windowpane. He wished it would rain to match his mood. "My mother begged me to take her away. Said she had held back for so long. Said she couldn't pretend any longer. Said that ever since Father had sent Madeleine away as well as me and Henry, she had no reason to stay. That I was old enough to finally understand. Old enough for her to confide in me."

"But where did she want to go?"

"It was madness. First she suggested Scotland, where she had sisters. Then when I said Father would find her, she suggested following me into the battlefield. And I knew she would do it. That was the hell of it. And I knew he would find her. And I knew . . ."

"Knew what?"

"What he would do to her. I knew he would make her life even more of a living hell for making him look like a weak fool. And so I left. I left her behind. I thought of the only way she couldn't follow me . . . on a ship.

"I left my mother, the person I loved most on this godforsaken earth, behind. I left her to die, in abject misery, alone with my father. The man who had tormented her for twenty years."

"How did she die?"

"She apparently became ill, and perished before I could see her again. My father died soon after. He was on his way to London and his carriage's wheel caught a rut and careened off the side of the road and rolled down a deep ravine. The driver jumped to safety, but my father was trapped inside and broke his neck."

"But he didn't hurt your mother."

"I've always known there was something more to her death than Ata's story."

"And you've never spoken again to your grandmother about this?"

"It brought her such distress, two deaths in as many months, then Henry's death so soon after. I won't add to her pain, not when she has finally become happy again."

"But you must ask her. You'll never know peace until—"

"No," he raked a hand through his hair, loosening the queue. "It won't bring her back."

"But your mother's death isn't your fault."

"I should have taken her away."

"You just said he would have found you, and it would have only made things worse."

"You of all people can imagine her situation. I should have given her a chance at happiness."

"You're wrong. And this regret will only eat away at your spirit. That I can promise you from experience. Besides," Rosamunde continued, "she wouldn't have had any real happiness. She would have been sick with worry from anticipating your father's arrival. Hiding is never the best choice. You did the right thing. The only thing you could do. You were but seventeen . . ."

"I left her to die with the man she feared while the person she loved was lost to her." Funny, he felt so very cold telling her this. Like he was not in his own body, but a spectator watching from above. Or below, more like it.

"Luc," she whispered.

The intimacy of hearing his given name on her lips for the first time made him shudder with repressed emotion.

She shook his shoulder. "Imagination is always worse than the truth. If she loved you as much as you say she did, and I have not one doubt of it, she probably took great comfort in the idea you were finally free of your father, even if she could not be. It was desperation that drove her to ask you to do the impossible. And if anything, she probably regretted it every day of her remaining life."

He felt her head on the back of his shoulder.

She whispered, "I know of these things. I regret the selfishness I showed by not insisting Sylvia return to my father's house. You want a better life for the ones you love. And a better life for yourself is the gift you gave your mother. I'm sure she took great pride in knowing of your heroism and rise through the ranks."

He turned and found himself pulling her into his arms. He closed his eyes and breathed in the early morning dewy scent of the garden on her. "The hell of it," he whispered, "is that I had finally planned to come back to her, to steal her away, once I was given the captaincy of a French ship we had captured. I had arranged for a cottage for her where he would never find her, far from any place he would look. And I would have visited her there when I could. Or I would have—"

A tap sounded at the door. His eyes burned from exhaustion. His emotions had been charred to cinders. He wrenched himself away from the comfort of her arms and brushed past her to his desk.

The door opened and his pretty sister's excited face appeared. Ata's voice sallied forth behind her, "Luc, the carriage is waiting. Ah, I've found you, too." Ata's face peered around Madeleine. The old lady's expression was suffused with happiness, peaches blooming in her wrinkled cheeks as she held her granddaughter about the waist.

Rosamunde retrieved the flowers and handed them to his sister. "From your hothouse and gardens, as promised."

"Why, this is the most beautiful bouquet I've ever beheld," his sister breathed. "You said each flower would have significance. But not that it would be so breathtaking. Pray tell us about the bouquet."

Rosamunde touched each bloom in turn. "Lemon blossoms for fidelity, lilies for your sweet disposition, white roses for love, heliotrope for devotion, blue hyacinth for constancy, and ivy for friendship in your marriage."

Luc shook his head. "You really should have something in there for foolishness, courage, and fortitude."

She gave him a look.

"Or at least something to guard against boredom and rows."

All three women now gave him a look.

"I see my opinion is the minority." At least he had forced levity back into the room. His heart felt anything but light. He couldn't bear to look at Rosamunde.

He had bared his soul to her and it was a god-awful sensation. He was not a man who ever allowed a morsel of vulnerability to show its cowardly face. Every fiber of his being revolted against it.

"I gather it's time to go. Has everyone else left?"

"Of course. And if we don't leave this minute, Peter will think I've had a change of heart," Madeleine said.

"I say we leave him dangling. Wouldn't do for him to think you're too eager."

"Luc!" Ata and Madeleine shrieked simultaneously.

"Oh, for the love of—" he stopped short at the sight of Ata's mutinous glare. Oh, it felt good to be back into his comfortable, devilish skin again. Whoever said it was cleansing to open the soul was a pathetic, pussyfooted sentimentalist.

"For that you'll carry the flowers." Madeleine thrust the bouquet in his face and he sneezed violently.

Chapter 8

Wedding, n. A ceremony at which two persons undertake to become one, one undertakes to become nothing, and nothing undertakes to become supportable.

—The Devil's Dictionary, A. Bierce

They set off in the elegant ducal coach and everyone played their roles becomingly. The bride was a vision of innocent happiness, her grandmother even more so.

When Rosamunde dared to peek at Luc St. Aubyn, she saw he had firmly put back into place the bored look he wore so well. Only an erratic tic in his jaw gave any indication something was wrong.

The breadth of his shoulders was such that Rosamunde couldn't avoid feeling the heat emanating from him. And each jostle and sway of the padded carriage brought the length of his legs in contact with hers.

She was still reeling from the intimacy of what he had told her. It took every ounce of her acting abilities to pretend nothing had passed between them.

Oh, but what he had revealed to her.

She ached with the knowledge. She wanted desperately to be alone with him. To comfort him, to wash away the years of guilt he had carried in his breast. Guilt his mother probably had felt tenfold.

She swallowed as she looked down at the solidly corded leg muscles outlined in his black breeches. Evidently Ata hadn't been able to persuade him to discard his usual deathly garb. The dowager had compensated by dressing like the bluebird of happiness, in every shade of cerulean imaginable, including an ostrich feathered hat that was almost as tall as the lady herself.

Rosamunde noticed a tear in her own dull gown, probably from the rose thorns in the garden. Not that it mattered. She would not enter the church. No one would notice her while she discreetly waited outside the nave.

Her breathing quickened when she saw the old church come into view. She hadn't seen it in eight years. Even if the former vicar was gone, the penance for her sins was not.

A sudden pressure on her hand forced her to look down. The side of his gloved hand was resting next to hers on the padded bench. It was no accident. She watched as he moved his last digit to cover hers, and a swirl of warmth surrounded her heart.

Ata and Madeleine were bubbling with laughter as the carriage drew to an abrupt halt and they fell forward. The duke ignored the iron step and jumped down to aid the ladies within.

Rosamunde hung back, arranging the lace at the back of Madeleine's soft blue-and-white lace gown. Every step toward the church felt like an extra stone had been added to her boots. They stopped beneath the moss-covered eaves, and Luc bent toward his sister and kissed her cheek, his face impenetrable and grave.

Rosamunde swallowed hard against the emotion rising in her throat. There were times when she missed her own brothers, especially Phinn, with an ache that threatened to overwhelm her defenses.

And her family was probably assembled inside. Ata had warned her they would likely be here. She wondered if Sylvia was sitting with the widows.

Beautiful organ and trumpet music wafted from behind the ancient oak door in front of them.

"Ata, you must go in with Mrs. Baird. We'll proceed once I can get Madeleine to wipe that silly grin off her face," Luc said dryly.

"Please"—Rosamunde looked at the dowager—"please go in without me."

They all stared at her.

"But you can't stay here," Madeleine insisted.

"No. I shall wait for you here. I—I want to lay flowers on my mother's grave." She brought forth a small nosegay. It had been so long since she had seen her mother's grave. She would not miss the opportunity.

Luc stepped forward. "What is this nonsense?"

"Luc," Ata said quietly.

They would never stop until they knew. Rosa took a deep breath and blurted out the reason. "The former vicar cast me out publicly before the entire parish and told them to shun me. I was never to force myself on his God-fearing congregation again." She didn't dare raise her eyes from the nosegay.

She heard the old door creak open and looked up to see the duke marching down the marble church floor, his boots clicking loudly. A great hush came over the church, filled to capacity. Rosamunde stepped further into the shadows, and felt Ata's hand find one of hers, and Madeleine's curled into her other.

Ata patted her hand, "'Tis nonsense, is what it is. Luc will put a stop to this. Wait and see."

He was whispering something to Sir Rawleigh, who stood before the congregation in his clerical garb. Lord Landry had joined them from his position in front.

"But, I don't want . . ." She stopped when she saw the three men leave the pulpit, walking toward . . . her. *Of course.* Oh, she shouldn't have said a word. She should have left the bouquet in the care of Madeleine's maid and gone on a long walk instead. She should have never gotten in the carriage.

"Mrs. Baird," Sir Rawleigh said, offering her his arm, "please allow me to escort you to your seat." His sky-blue eyes were so warm and kindly in his blatantly handsome face.

"No, really. It's unnecessary. I'll—"

"You're holding up the show, Mrs. Baird," the duke drawled.

"But really, I'm perfectly hap—"

"You're ruining the bride's moment," he interrupted again.

"No, Luc," Madeleine chimed in, "she's not. But, Rosamunde, I suppose I should tell you now that I won't go in if you don't."

"Well, I like that," Lord Landry cut in. "Are you saying you won't marry me?"

"Say yes, Madeleine. Here's your last chance," Luc St. Aubyn advised.

"Peter," Madeleine sighed, "you have it all wrong. I'll marry you once Mrs. Baird goes in the church. And besides, what are you doing out here? Don't you know it's bad luck to see me before the vows?"

"Oh for the love of Christ," Luc St. Aubyn said, his hand on his brow, "Rawleigh, take Mrs. Baird's arm and drag her to a seat. In front. Landry, take your paws off my sister and escort my grandmother. And Madeleine, if you insist on tying yourself to my former idiotic, lovesick lieutenant, then straighten your veil and keep those damn flowers out of my face."

No one dared disobey him.

Out of the corner of her eye, Rosamunde saw the shocked stares of the entire congregation. There were the Miss Smithams, the original members of the community who had seen her on Perran Sands. The two old ladies shared looks of pure outrage in their every feature and began whispering to their neighbors. Rosamunde forced herself to confront the looks of disgust and worse as she walked down the aisle.

With each step she remembered. Remembered the horror of the first days of the old scandal when seventeen people had cut her acquaintance on a single journey to the village, including three shopkeeps. It had been the first time in her life that her courage had failed her.

Now they were doing it again, turning their faces away from her glance. And she realized that with each successive failure of her courage she had hid from the world by retreating into herself, her own world.

The vicar cleared his throat to gain her attention. His look of caring concern bolstered her and she focused her gaze on the faces of her newfound friends in the front pew of the church. All the members of the Widows Club—Grace, Georgiana, Elizabeth, and Sarah—were there, encouraging her with their expressions. Sir Rawleigh's rock-steady arm was her anchor.

She was about to slip onto the front bench when her gaze faltered and she glanced at the pew behind hers, and looked straight into the mirrored eyes of her *father*.

Dear God.

Oh dear God.

She couldn't breathe, couldn't move. There was a roaring in her ears. And suddenly Ata was at her other side.

"Thank you for coming to share in my granddaughter's happiness today, my lord." Ata's voice rang in Rosamunde's consciousness. "I look forward to seeing you and your family at the breakfast at Amberley after."

Her father's nod was almost imperceptible, his eyes only on her. Rosamunde blinked and found herself ushered further down the pew. Her heart was in her throat, her mind churning a thousand thoughts.

Sir Rawleigh and Lord Landry reassumed their positions and the duke ushered in his sister to the bridal music. At the last moment, Luc St. Aubyn nodded to the vicar, who raised his one arm to the congregation.

"Before we begin, I would like to welcome everyone today. We are all God's creatures, and as such we must remember the Lord's Prayer. The part about trespasses and such is very . . ." he trailed off.

The duke leaned forward and whispered loudly, "Just tell them to forgive and forget, you nodcock."

The congregation murmured and a few titters broke the silence.

"Quite right," the vicar continued with a smile. "On this joyous occasion when God shall unite these two humble servants before us, let us forgive and forget one another's trespasses."

There was a long silence.

A lone person began to clap slowly. Rosamunde closed her eyes. Ata squeezed her hand and Rosamunde looked to find Luc St. Aubyn had turned and was staring at parishioners, daring them not to join him. One by one, the congregation began to clap with him.

Ata shifted her eyes to indicate the pew behind them, the one where Rosamunde's family sat. She turned to see her brother, Phinn, clapping his hands, as were Fitz, Miles, and James. All except her father, who sat like a stone, his eyes focused forward, unseeing.

Rosamunde swiftly trained her eyes on the vicar.

Oh please, let him get on with it. She felt the white-hot discomfort of being the center of attention and loathed every moment the pricks of mortification trickled down her spine.

A light pressure rested on her shoulder and she glanced down to see a gloved masculine hand, *Phinn's hand*. She leaned her head against the back of the pew and against his fingers, as much as she dared, and tried to swallow the great lump in her throat. It was a good thing weddings required handkerchiefs.

The marriage vows proceeded with Rosamunde unable to concentrate on the words. She was too overcome with being in church again, her brothers and father behind her, and a gentleman who made her feel more emotion than she had thought possible. If she had been prone to fainting, she would have lost her head many times over. Unfortunately, the hot blood running in her veins made for sturdy stock and she was incapable of fainting. Never had, never would.

Each time she glanced at the solid, tall physique of the duke, her heart, parched from long years of deprivation, seemed to swell within her chest.

There was another moment of drama during the ceremony when the vicar asked Madeleine to "love, honor, and obey," her soon-to-be husband. Luc St. Aubyn cleared his throat, annoyed enough to interrupt the proceedings.

Madeleine turned to him and whispered quite loudly, "I shall love, honor, and *obey*, but only because he must promise to die for me, Luc, and I won't do that."

The people gathered in the front rows burst out

laughing and the duke finally nodded his acquiescence.

Luc St. Aubyn also growled loudly when the groom took it upon himself to seal the union with a kiss, a shockingly modern and outrageous display.

Guests flocked to the aisles and she turned to find her family. Phinn was closest to her and he reached out to grab her hand for a moment. It seemed no words were necessary. His expression said it all. She ruthlessly squeezed back tears behind clenched lids before the crowd pushed them apart. Rosamunde and Ata were the last to leave the church, along with Sir Rawleigh.

From the top of the stone steps, Rosamunde searched for her father. She saw him near her mother's grave in the small cemetery. He stared back at her. She was gathering her nerve, swallowing her great ball of pride, and about to force her feet to move toward him when he turned his back on her and walked to the carriage emblazoned with the achingly familiar Twenlyne coat of arms.

He had given her the cut direct.

Just like so many years ago.

Her own father.

The one who had told her he loved her nearly every day. Had told her he loved her more than himself. More than anything on earth. That he would never let a cloud enter her bubble of happiness. Her friends had always been amazed by her father, the earl of Twenlyne, and the way he doted on her.

And then she knew she had the answer she had tried to avoid for so long.

He would never forgive her. He would never allow her

back into his arms and into his life. She was dead to him as far as he was concerned. Hadn't Alfred told her that? She was more alone than she had ever felt in her life.

The tiny spark of hope she had nursed with potent memories from childhood was snuffed out. And surprisingly, instead of anger at her father's actions as she had always had in the past, she now felt strangely detached and numb. Her arms felt like lead pipes at her sides and she couldn't move her feet. It was too bad the same could not be said for her eyes.

She noticed many of the people at the bottom of the church stairs looking at her, whispering to each other. Phinn, on the edge of the crowd, was arguing quietly with their three brothers. In the end, one by one, her brothers trooped past the ancient gravestones, the edges of the Celtic crosses worn away, toward the open door of her family's carriage, where the shadowed profile of her father was silhouetted against the light entering the window from the other side.

"But I don't care what the vicar said," came a familiar feminine whisper from the crowd.

Rosamunde refused to search for Augustine Phelps's face among the throngs of people.

"If her father won't acknowledge her, why should we?" whispered another voice.

"She's trying to worm her way into the good graces of the St. Aubyns. Residing at Amberley, indeed," continued another.

Rosamunde stood as still as the statue of St. Peter in the courtyard.

A man snickered. "Probably trying to warm a St.

Aubyn's bed like the last time, if you were to ask me."
A few masculine guffaws followed.

The air whooshed out of her and she could feel
the blood draining from the back of her head where
it tingled. She worried she might trip down the stairs
if she tried to advance, so she stood there feeling very
exposed. But really, what more could they say?

Oh, how she wished to run down the stairs and
keep on running past the cemetery, past the fields, past
everything she had ever known. It was the same exact
feeling she had had when the vicar had refused her
entrance here so long ago.

She had given in to her cowardice then.

But now she was older, perhaps not wiser, but she
knew heartbreak and humiliation could not kill you.
It only taught you how to stand a little straighter, and
smile a little wider, and pretend you're slightly deaf or
perfectly unconcerned with what life drags into your
dish.

A line of ladies dressed in mourning snaked through
the crowd and mounted the stairs, Luc St. Aubyn escorting the countess at the tail end.

Grace Sheffey's pale, regal splendor radiated from
her expression. "Rosamunde, do join us. Her Grace has
asked us to perform an impromptu short concert during the breakfast. And since we cannot find your sister,
we've nominated you as the primary performer."

They had taken pity on her. But compassion, especially *his* pity, was worse than the crowd's loathing.
She must pretend she was unaffected by it all. She
must turn the moment.

Rosamunde forced her mouth to work and whispered, "For the love of Christ . . ." She stopped and looked at the duke, trying desperately to form a smile but failing.

His expression held a question.

"Isn't that what you really wanted to say? Don't you loathe music?" she asked quietly without a hint of humor.

Elizabeth Ashburton, holding Georgiana Wilde's arm, burst out laughing.

His mouth twitched. "Why, Mrs. Baird, I actually like music, when it is played well. But you know I never, *ever*, blaspheme"—he cleared his throat—"without good reason."

"Luc," Ata said, "you always blaspheme. Who knows where you learned to take the Lord's name in vain."

"It's not always in vain. I always ask with great hope, actually. Although it is rarely answered the way I like."

Ata's cough failed to hide her giggle. "By the by, you're standing on my gown."

"No, it's your gown that has a nasty habit of attaching itself to my boot," he said, lifting his Hessian, tasseled with black ribbons instead of the usual white ones.

They were good at dissembling, all of them. Rosamunde clenched her fingers so tightly she thought her nails would perforate the tips of her old gloves. She did it to stop herself from melting into tears of gratitude. She was very beholden to each and every one of them.

She bowed her head.

Ata came around behind her and whispered in her ear, "No, no, you mustn't look down. Look up and stare at them like before. Shame them all. Now then," she said louder so most of the crowd could hear, "I do declare, there are some people here who I distinctly don't remember inviting to the wedding breakfast."

The crowd's babble of wagging tongues stopped abruptly.

"Luc, dear, you do have a copy of the list, don't you?"

"No, but I've no doubt we'll be in possession of an interesting version of it by the time we arrive at Amberley," he rumbled loudly.

"Have I ever told you how much I appreciate how well prepared you always are, dearest?" Ata said, smiling up at her tall, darkly handsome grandson.

"That's what all the ladies say, Ata."

"Oh! For the love of . . ." Ata stopped when the widows began to giggle. "Now see here, it's perfectly obvious he taught me this oath, not the other way around. Why, it's scandalous what I must endure at my age," she harrumphed through her thinly disguised smile.

"And that age would be?" he asked without a hint of a smile.

"Old enough to cross your name off the list too, you insolent puppy."

They returned to Amberley in separate carriages and Rosamunde was glad. Sarah Winters, the eldest and wisest widow in the club, held her hand after the door closed.

"You know, Rosamunde, it is said that those who must endure the most early in life will enjoy even more the earthly joys to be found in later years."

"And has that happened for you?"

The beginning of a few very faint lines edged the paper-thin skin surrounding the widow's eyes, suggesting she was nearing her fourth decade. "Why, no." She paused. "But there is still time, I think."

Rosamunde squeezed her hand. "I am sure of it." And she believed it, for the goodness of this lady was palpable. If anyone deserved never-ending joy it was Sarah, a lady whose husband had never returned from Wellington's war with France.

Elizabeth Ashburton and Georgiana Wilde sat opposite them. "Where is your sister?" asked Georgiana. "I thought she was coming with you."

Rosamunde shook her head. "I don't know. I thought she had gone with all of you. I"—she looked at her hands—"I had not meant to come."

Georgiana patted her knee. "You showed great courage. I couldn't have done it."

Rosamunde ignored the compliment. Her stomach was still so tightly clenched she felt ill. But she could appear normal for as long as it took. "I hope Sylvia didn't go out walking to look for me. I told her I wasn't to go."

"Well, there is one other person who was disappointed when she didn't appear," Elizabeth said, not even trying to hide her grin.

Sarah cast a sharp look at Elizabeth. "Now don't stir up hopes."

"Why it's as plain as the love on the groom's face that Sir Rawleigh is besotted with Lady Sylvia."

Rosamunde quickly looked from one lady to the other. "I do hope you're right. I hope it with all my heart."

"We all do, my dear, we all do. She's not the only one I'm kneeling down for every night," Sarah finished with a wink.

The dip and sway of the carriage signaled the last bridge before the turn into Amberley's vast drive, lined with stately oaks whose roots were crowned with thick periwinkle. The sight of Amberley never failed to awe Rosamunde. It was simply the most beautiful place she had ever seen. It was as if the architects had had divine inspiration in creating such perfection of symmetry and design.

What she would give to jump from this elegant carriage and run behind the mansion to the kitchen door and beyond to the lovely bedchamber she occupied. Her head ached and her eyes burned from the effort to remain composed. She just wasn't sure she could keep up this façade of collected behavior much longer. And she was certain she could not face her father again if he chose to honor the duchess's invitation.

But escape was not in the cards. A horde of guests buzzed about the entrance when they arrived, their carriage being one of the last to do so.

Chastity Clarendon took up her arm and her brother the vicar took up her other. Wedged between the two of them as she was, no one dared utter a word against her. Oh, but it all felt so false. And planned.

The duke had surely designed this tactic during his return in another carriage. As if she could not stand up to the humiliation by herself. Hadn't she been doing that alone for eight years? He obviously thought her a complete weakling.

But then, wasn't she? She'd avoided situations like this at every opportunity.

A tide of guests swept forward into the mansion, pulling everyone with it. She was forced to pretend to nibble ham and slivered eggs on toast while she endured inane triviality. Mrs. Simpson simpered about the new inn at Land's End. Mr. Canberry moaned about rain and haymaking. Agatha Fitzsimmons complained about the price of tea, and then, well, then *it* happened.

Auggie Phelps's fiancé, Baron von Olteda, from Hanover, cornered her near the ladies' withdrawing room. Of course no one was about, and of course he took advantage of the fact, sweeping her into a small morning room with a request for her help. He stood before her, falsely modest in his puffed-out Hussar uniform of latterly overalls and dark blue coat with scarlet facings and yellow lace.

"Mrs. Baird," his eyes appraised her shrewdly, "I understand you might be searching for protection."

"Protection?" she whispered in disbelief.

"Uh, or I think the Brits call it 'a protector.' Da?"

She could feel the blood drain from her face and moved toward the door. "I have no idea what you are talking about, sir."

His iron arm appeared in front of her before she

reached the door. "But Mrs. Baird, you cannot wish to be here. I can offer you protection"—he winked—"and seclusion."

"Allow me to pass, sir." It was not a question, but a demand. She tried to keep the wobble from her voice.

"Don't you want to hear the terms? I promise to hide you away in great luxury. No one will insult or pity you."

She had always thought him a great lummox. But she had underestimated him. He knew just what to say to completely demoralize her. She looked down at his hands and noticed they were just like her husband's— sausagelike fingers with thick hair sprouting on the backs, the nails bitten down to the quick. Revulsion swept through her.

"Mrs. Baird, or may I call you *my Rosebud*? I will pamper you, and dress you in the finest London can offer and you will . . . well, *you will pamper me*."

His sly innuendo sent a shudder straight down her spine. She thought she really might be ill. She pushed away his arm and continued another step. "No, sir," she said, more firmly than she felt. She was lost, floating in a sea of panic.

He grabbed her at the last moment and pushed her against the wall, his barrel-shaped chest grounding into hers. His hands roughly grabbed at her breasts, and she fought against him, against an unbearably familiar sense of violation and horror. She had thought she would never ever have to feel or see hands like that touching her again. Grabbing her everywhere with complete disregard to her wishes, her words, her pain.

She hated the touch of a man's naked, moist hands. Hated it with a passion. She had wordlessly endured it out of duty, hiding her pain, holding back tears and her wishes for many years. But for the first time she was allowed to fight back.

She bit him. Sunk her teeth into one of his fat fingers as hard as she could and then jerked her knee to his unmentionables.

He howled. "Why you little—"

He was cut off by a hideous bone-crunching sound, and suddenly, his body was lying half sprawled by the door.

The duke, wearing the most murderously angry expression imaginable, stood in the baron's place, his stance wide and his hands fisted.

He glared at her, then grabbed the baron by his facings and hauled him to his feet. The man appeared barely conscious. "You," the duke said in ominous low tones, "are an insult to humanity. I shall give you one minute to get the hell out of here and take your deserving bride with you. If I ever see you again, I will stuff that unearned gold braid down your throat to your aching ballocks."

She couldn't deny the tiny thrill she felt at his words until he turned to look at her. The glittering anger in his face would scare the soul from the devil.

"Would you like to kick him before I throw him out?" he asked softly.

"No," she whispered.

"Then I shall do it for you."

"No, please, no."

It was as if he couldn't hear her. With vicious kicks to the stout man's knees, he brought the man down again. And he would have continued if Rosamunde hadn't used all her strength to pull him toward the door. He was like a wild animal with a taste of blood. She had no doubt that he was capable of beating the man past the floorboards into an early grave.

As they were about to pass over the threshold, the baron had the bad sense to utter one last parting shot. "Your husband told everyone about you, *Rosie*. You'll be sorry you didn't accept my offer. Others might not be so appealing."

The duke swore violently and went back to deliver a *coup de grâce*, rendering the stout man insensible and a whisker away from something altogether closer to his final resting place.

But he couldn't erase the words the man had dared utter. His words were engraved on her mind, swirling amid the other harsh reality of her father's refusal to acknowledge her. She could not maintain her charade any longer.

She stared into the floating dust particles in the ray of light from the window and knew that if she moved or said a word she would break down—something she had never, ever dared to do. She might not be able to reverse a descent into madness.

He took two long strides toward her and gently grasped both her arms. "Come. Come with me."

She couldn't move or she would turn into dust. And so with one long movement, he swept her up into his arms and carried her from the room.

Chapter 9

Intimacy, n. *A relation into which fools are providentially drawn for their mutual destruction.*

—The Devil's Dictionary, A. Bierce

If there was one thing Luc knew how to do, it was how to accomplish an action in the most direct, precise manner possible without wasted motion or time. Within moments of leaving the disastrous scene, he had her bundled inside a closed carriage with Brownie driving them to the port. He had to get her away from Amberley and all these damn people.

She hadn't said a word as they crisscrossed through the sandy lanes. She had stared out the window, her eyes dry and unseeing. She hadn't even seemed curious to know where they were going.

For him, there had been no thought to the matter. Like a homing pigeon, he had ordered the direction to his cutter. A place that would promise protection. A place he could completely control.

He thought he would have to carry her again when she took so long to descend from the carriage. But, suddenly, ignoring his hand, she stepped down. Before he could say a word, she walked past him, past the smaller docked boats, and onto *Caro's Heart* without looking back.

He nodded to Brownie, who was arranging for stabling and then boarded the only place that held any balance for him. Perhaps it was because there was no equilibrium here, the scenery and the situation changed each time he set out.

"Cap'n." His three deckhands greeted him simultaneously.

"Set a course for St. Clement's Isle. We'll anchor there till . . ." he did the timetable quickly in his head, "three o'clock and then return to port. We sail immediately."

The deckhands didn't ask questions, and he didn't have to wonder about supplies or readiness. Their fidelity, proven in bloodshed and in deathly storms, was the reason they worked for him.

He shaded his brow from the sun and watched her on the opposite railing, staring westward. What was he going to do about her? She wasn't like the other widows Ata had taken into her protection. The others had been easily led to new lives, either remarrying or finding employment, reuniting with family or settling in obscure cottages Brownie arranged. But Rosamunde? He couldn't envision a happy future for her.

She would never remarry, had vehemently said so a dozen times, had no acceptable family, and was an obvious target for men like the baron. And like a sleek falcon, she would be miserable if her wings were clipped. She would wither away as a governess or companion hidden on the edge of nowhere. She was meant for adventure, to soar with excitement.

She was a hopeless case. A first. He shook his head and went to her, wondering what on earth he would say.

"You've discovered my weaknesses," he said quietly just behind her. "Ladies who do not cry when they are supposed to and wounded young midshipmen who do."

He continued when she didn't respond. "And then, of course, there's the matter of my deplorable *temper*." He looked down the slope of her delicate neck and shoulders held ramrod straight. "Like father, like son, everyone says. There was a reason my father christened me Lucifer, after the devil himself."

She twisted her head to glance at him. "You are truly the best man I have ever known."

He laughed harshly. "That says little for your circle of acquaintances."

She faced the horizon again and he could see her hands gripping the railing so tightly her knuckles were white.

"Shall I tell you the difference between your temper and my husband's serene nature?"

He froze, not quite sure he wanted to hear what she had to say.

"I've seen your infamous anger precisely one time, when I forced you to stop pounding a man I wished to thrash myself."

He watched her swallow convulsively.

"A collected nature is when a man controls your every movement during the day and then takes pleasure in his right to enter your bedchamber at night, stare at your body, and touch . . ." She bit her lower lip and closed her eyes. ". . . and touch you with his hands. And all the while he knows, without you saying a word, that this . . . this invasion is his to command, his to insist upon while you must lie there violated to the depths of your soul by his hushed insults and of course the painful union. Yet he never raises his voice, nor does he beat you. He just kills your will one night at a time. And after he leaves you, you are faced with the knowledge that every night for the rest of your life you will listen for that awful pause in his step outside your door. The pause that means he is coming again to use what the law insists is his to take." She hesitated. "I vastly prefer the man who claims he is evil but acts like an archangel instead of the man who appears everything good but in fact is an instrument of humiliation and worse."

He felt like slamming his fist through the railing. The hammering in his brain almost drowned out her final words. He would kill him all over again. He would dig up Alfred Baird's body and have it drawn and quartered.

She turned to face him, her hair half fallen about her shoulders from the earlier struggle. Raven strands whipped across the fragile features of her face. Her complexion had lost most of its color, making her smoky aqua eyes appear huge in her face.

He was using every ounce of control not to take her in his arms. But she hated a man's hands.

And then one of her delicate palms found its way to his lapel. Porcelain white femininity on pitch-black fabric. She feathered her fingers back and forth lightly as if she were trying to remove dust. But when she should have removed her fingers, her hand strayed over his heart, unmoving.

"I have a favor to ask," she whispered.

"Yes?"

She looked away and a ray of sunlight poured onto her face as the yacht came about and the shade from the sails disappeared. "I would like to lie down."

What? Oh, Christ above, what was she asking? She couldn't—

"With you." He had to lean down to catch the words before the wind whisked them away.

She couldn't possibly mean—

"I know it won't wash away the horrible memories. But—"

He tilted her chin with the crook of his hand to better see her expression. She closed her eyes and refused to continue.

"But what, Rosamunde? Tell me why you desire something that has only ever been ugly to you."

"Because it would be my choice. *My choice*. For once, I would be the one . . ." She was stuck.

"Asking, not obeying?" he finished.

"Yes."

This was a disaster in the making. Of gargantuan proportions. A better man would walk away.

A better man would be a fool.

But it might very well not happen. She would cry off when all was said and done. Hell, he knew he would cry off at the first sign of her fright or pain. This was a fine beginning. He swallowed. There were a thousand reasons to refuse her. And yet, when he looked into her eyes he saw such pain—the haunted look of a person who had too long endured rejection and uniform disapproval at every turn—that he couldn't deny her.

He slowly offered his arm to her.

She placed the length of her forearm above his and allowed him to lead her to his quarters below deck. The last thing he saw before stepping into the darkness was Brownie manning the wheel, his eyes boring into his with a completely blank expression. Damn the old man.

His cabin was dark and a step closer to hell. He watched her swing her gaze around the burnished wood features of the compact quarters, from the nailed-down table and bench to the double-wide bunk.

"Second thoughts?" he murmured behind her. The air had become thick with tension.

"I'm not changing my mind," she whispered.

"I've found that women are often wrong but never in doubt."

"That's where you're wrong. I know what I want is wrong, and I'm filled with doubt. But I hate living in fear, hate being bound to memories. Even if this is a mistake, I would rather remember this moment in this place than everything before." She trembled slightly but her voice never wavered. "There will be no question of expectations after. I will be going with Ata to London, where she has said she would help me find a position as a lady's companion somewhere in the North Country." She turned to face him and dared to raise her eyes to his. "Please . . ."

She had released the veil from her eyes at last and the anguish he found there was shattering.

"Am I likely to get you with child?"

"No. I never conceived. It was my fault, as Alfred's first wife and child died during the birthing."

His mind poured over every objection and rationalized it all away, a little too easily, he thought guiltily. His hand strayed to her hair and drew out a pin tangled in the ebony locks.

Her gaze darted to his fingers and he spied a look of fear before she shuttered her gaze.

He dropped his hands immediately. "This will never work."

She grasped his palms in hers and replaced them in her hair.

"No," he said, "you fear a man's touch. And I have a very good idea what other things might terrify you as well," he said dryly.

"Luc," she begged. Tension flowed through the silence broken only by the sound of the waves hitting the masthead.

Hearing his given name on her lips, he knew he would do it. He knew he would find a way to erase some of her memories of the revolting episodes with her husband. He would do it if it took all day and night, all week, all month. He would give her pleasure, make her find her pleasure. And he knew, quite thoroughly, that he had enough arrogance and experience to do it.

"I think we'll have to borrow some simple rules of navigation," he said, gesturing for her to precede him to the bench. "The first is that you are captain of this"—he forced his lips into a smile—"*maiden voyage*. The second is that you must guide me through every channel by telling me what you like and what you don't like. And you must tell me to stop immediately at any point along the way. And lastly, I shall not use my hands until you guide them to where *you* want them."

Her eyes widened. "I'm not sure I understand the last part."

Finally he was on familiar territory. "You'll know soon enough."

She opened her mouth, then closed it.

He crouched in front of her seated form, waiting. The muscles in his thighs burned from the strain, and his arousal, which had been upon him since she had asked him to make love to her, was painful in its intensity.

He looked at her, his eyes half shuttered.

Very slowly she leaned forward and hesitated like a bird longing to peck seeds in front of a cat. She closed her eyes and kissed him, swerving to his cheek at the last second.

He felt rather like crying.

He relieved the strain on his thighs by changing his position, kneeling, waiting for her true benediction to proceed with this sinful seduction.

She might think she was in command, but the hard edge of his practiced arts in matters of the flesh meant there was no doubt who was really in charge.

And there was no doubt she was dying for guidance. "Touch me, Rosamunde."

Her hands tentatively smoothed the crown of his head down to the black silk that bound his hair. She unknotted the ribbon and drew his long hair forward until he felt it cover his shoulders.

A smile flooded her every feature. It transformed her face into that of an innocent schoolgirl. He knew it was going to be all right, now. "And what, pray tell, is so amusing?"

"Your hair."

His eyebrows rose. "If you say I look like a girl, I may have to kill you."

Her eyes crinkled and she almost laughed. "You are about as far from looking like a lady as I can imagine. A pirate is more like it. It's just," she paused and fingered his locks, "I've always longed for beautiful waves like these."

"Ah."

"You never cut it?" she asked.

"I only ever allowed one person to cut it." As he said it, a poignant childhood memory of his mother clouded his mind. It was something he never permitted himself to think about.

"And who was Samson's Delilah?"

He fought to return amusement to his voice. "I've often found that a little mystery in a man keeps a woman's cursed curiosity whetted," he said slowly, trying to mesmerize her. "But I will tell you about a game Brownie encouraged while we were at sea. He promised king's rations for the duration of our missions to anyone who could get me to cut it."

"And no one ever did," she stated.

"No one was fool enough to try," he murmured. "May I take the rest of the pins from your hair?"

She nodded.

He kept his hands by his sides and leaned in to grasp the remaining pins with his teeth and deposited them in her upturned palm. He glanced sideways up to her. "May I?" he whispered.

She nodded again.

He kissed her wrist, a delicate band of skin with a thin blue vein pumping frantically below. He soothed it with his lips then continued to kiss her draped arm up to her neck.

"My beard is chafing you."

"That's all right," she said a little breathlessly.

"What next?" He breathed in the clean soap and lavender scent of her hair and the hollow of her neck.

"I know you said I was to lead, but really, I'm beginning to think I don't know the proper order of things," she mumbled. "My husband never—"

"Shhhh," he interrupted. "Then I shall make suggestions and you shall tell me if they are acceptable to you."

Rosamunde pressed her face into his neckcloth, her

hands against his shoulders. It seemed she couldn't
watch him as he told her these things, but he would
bet his last farthing she was aching to hear them.

He rumbled against her hands, "I propose to kiss
you, and taste you. All of you. And then, if you like
that, we'll see."

"And what am I to do?" she whispered.

"Whatever you like. Assume control, and never ever
doubt yourself." It would do no good to tell her he'd
broken that rule a thousand times or more.

Neither of them moved a muscle and once more he
found himself exerting iron control over his desire to
bring his arms around her and crush her to him.

She turned her head and kissed his cheek again. He
smoothly drew his mouth to hers and gently prolonged
the kiss, nibbling her lower lip, seeking entrance until
she opened to him. His tongue curled against hers, ex-
ploring and tasting her while he clamped his hands on
the bench on either side of her.

He rained kisses along her temple, forehead, eyes
and the tip of her nose before drifting back to her long
neck. Her modest mourning gown could not hide the
faint evidence of the baron's desecration. He brushed
his cheek and lips over the fading red marks before
he reached the bow hidden under the gathered front
edges of her bodice. He closed his eyes and took the
ribbon between his teeth and pulled.

Her breath caught as her breasts were exposed.
His eyes opened to find perfection. Perfectly rounded
breasts with tiny nipples, the color of pink coral, resting high. He roughly exhaled a hair's breadth above

one and the tip grew taut and even smaller, anticipating his lips.

God have mercy on him, how was he to go slowly when every nerve in his body screamed to take her?

And suddenly he felt her hands weaving through his hair and he bent to worship her breast with his mouth, offering it all the tenderness and wickedness he knew how to give.

"Dear Lord," she moaned, shock lacing the sound.

He built up slowly, first licking then tugging her gently until he heard her breathing grow erratic. Luc took it as permission to nip and suckle her tightly ruched bud so deeply she cried out.

He stopped immediately and glanced at her, desire raging in every pore of his body. Her eyes were dilated with passion and so he flicked his tongue along the other nipple, teasing it gently before drawing it as intensely as he dared into the depths of his mouth.

The air seemed to rush from her body in the reverse manner that his blood seemed to rush to his groin.

"Rosamunde," he said quietly, "it's warm in here. Perhaps you would like to remove your gown?"

"I'm fine, really, fine," she said, her voice wobbling a bit.

"Would you mind removing your gown . . . ?" He left the question hanging in the air.

"Why?"

He felt like cursing. Had she never even been undressed with her husband? "Because I would like you to."

He was sure she was going to refuse, but at the last

moment she rose up and turned, offering a small row of black buttons to undo. "I'll need your help."

He made sure not to touch her skin while making short work of it, wishing he could tear this damn mourning gown into bits and toss it into the sea, it was so hideous in its representation.

Her back to him, she drew the gown over her head and waited for him to loosen her stays. He was certain she would be too timid to remove her chemise, but it seemed he was mistaken when she slipped the garment off after he had untied her corset.

He exhaled raggedly.

She was a siren. He marveled at the supple arch of her beautiful back, her tiny waist, tapering to a heart-shaped derrière.

His hands itched to touch, but instead he kissed the length of her spine, and sneaked his head around the curve of her hip to the soft, secret skin of her taut stomach. He rose up to feather kisses on her ribs and breasts back to her ear.

"Rosamunde," he murmured softly, "if you would like to continue, perhaps we should move to the bed."

She shivered and he looked into her eyes.

"Are you all right?"

"Yes, just nervous, and achy in a strange sort of way."

A flush of heat pounded his loins. "I know precisely what you mean." His hands were gripped tightly behind his back.

She looked at him shyly, took the few steps to the low bunk, and lay down, her hands rigid at her sides.

Against the white sheets she looked like a bride awaiting torture, er, her duty.

"You're beautiful, Rosamunde."

She looked at him with disbelief. "There's no need to flatter me."

For long moments he stared at her. His arousal was painful in its intensity. "I never flatter. You should know that by now."

He joined her and patiently regained the ground he had lost, tasting, laving, urging her to relax to his mouth. Her nipples were constricted to pebbles and she was breathing unevenly, but she made not a sound and her hands gripped the sheets. He had to take a chance.

"Rosamunde, would you like to open yourself to me?"

Her eyes flew open, and she immediately complied by spreading her tightly clenched limbs open. If only he could use his hands to show her, but he dared not.

He moved lower between her legs, all the while watching her. She raised her face, distress and mortification etched on every feature.

"You're not going to . . ." she said.

"Actually, yes. It's what I promised."

"But, you can't really want—"

"Yes, I do. Very much."

Desire and shyness warred in her expression, and he prayed the devil was on his side. He leaned down and took a long loving taste of her.

She made a strangled cry of pleasure and Luc wondered how he was going to hold off. He was aching to sink himself inside her, and yet he hadn't even progressed to removing a stitch of his clothes. But that had been part of his makeshift plan. He knew that the sight of him would probably make her flee.

He used his lips and then his tongue and finally the edges of his teeth to arouse her until she was unconsciously signaling her readiness with small, uncontrolled movements of her hips. And still his hands clenched the bed covering. Her eyes were squeezed closed and she was making small sounds that were testing his endurance.

"Rosamunde, keep your eyes shut and listen to me now. If you ever trusted me, let me touch you with my hands. I promise not to hurt you, and I'll stop at any time."

She leaned on one elbow and reached for his hand. "I'm sorry I was such a fool."

He placed his hand in her delicate one, and she kissed it.

"*Your* hands are beautiful," she whispered.

He kissed her briefly, then urged her back and entered her as gently as he dared with one finger. She was almost as tight as an untried girl, and his body flexed in response.

A rush of dampness drenched his finger and she moaned, "Oh, I'm so sorry."

"No, no. It's just your body preparing itself." He gently spread her knees. "But I must open you wider. Don't be embarrassed, Rosamunde. You are exquisite to me. There now, just a little more."

He hadn't thought she'd have the courage, but she did, and it tested his control. He was determined to bring her to the pinnacle of ecstasy, but not beyond. For he knew that to breach her final fear she would have to be fully inflamed with desire. And she would then ask him to take her, for it would be the only way to ease her pain of passion. And so he teased her with his lips and his tongue and his fingers, stretching her, preparing her to take as much of him as she would be able to bear.

It almost broke him to feel how small she was, barely able to take two of his fingers after many, many long minutes.

And finally he heard the words he had been waiting to hear, "Luc, I can't bear it any more. Please . . ."

He quickly unbuttoned the flap of his trousers and wished he could undress further. He paused. "Rosamunde, close your eyes again," he ordered. He stripped off everything, knowing the feel of his skin on hers would heighten her pleasure and his.

Her eyes flew open when he covered her moments later. Her expression was filled with apprehension. His feet were braced flat against the cabin wall for leverage.

He looked down and saw his hair splashed into hers, the black locks melding together, hers soft and fine, his course and thick.

"Are you sure?" He knew his voice was hoarse, and if he hadn't distrusted God so much, he would have prayed at that moment.

"Yes," she whispered.

He never knew one word could be quite so wonderful.

He gently placed the large, blunt end of himself against her slickness, gently sliding along her folds several long strokes before coming to rest at her juncture. He pushed hard enough to finally wedge just the tip inside her. She was impossibly tense and unyielding.

Her eyes spoke volumes as she looked down to see what he was doing. It was obvious she was trying to mask her fear—and doing a poor job of it. He clenched his jaw and forced himself to speak words that promised a cold bath in short order.

"Are you all right?" he ground out.

Her breath, pent up in anxiety, shuddered from her in one long sigh. "I feel . . . well, I feel very full. But this is so different from before."

He felt himself throb with each of her words, and swallowed back a reflexive urge to flex his hips. He pursed his lips. "Shall I go on?"

He would have to swim all the way back to Penzance if she said no, to cool his aching groin.

"Yes, Luc, please. I want this. Even . . ." her voice broke off. "Even if it hurts. I don't care. At least I will know that I asked. This one time."

The depth of her emotion shook him. He stared hard at her.

"The tightness, perhaps, is just your fear." He touched her beautiful breasts and glided his dark skin over the creamy valley of her warm flesh. He gently pinched the rosy nipple and felt her body give to allow the swelled tip of him to enter a little more.

She was so warm, and so plush, so impossibly taut, but he dared not force any more of himself within her. It was too much. He dared not hurt her, not when she had been so courageous and had opened herself to him.

The effort to hold back made his arms shake. He ran his hands down the slender sides of her body and slipped them beneath her bottom, gliding his last finger along the sensitive folds where he could almost feel himself in her.

"Rosamunde, look at me," he commanded. "You must do as I say now."

"Anything."

"Relax and open yourself further to me."

Her legs opened fully wide like a butterfly's wings on a spring morning, and he tilted her hips to receive him more deeply. The movement caused her to accept a few more inches of his length, and her eyes widened.

He began long, shallow strokes, encouraging her to take a little more of him.

"If you like," he said between gritted teeth, "put your arms around me."

She said quietly, "I didn't know if I should." And he felt her delicate arms tentatively surround him as he kept working her passage.

Dear God, this was sweet agony. He lowered one forearm beside her head; the other hand he used to tease the tip of her breast to new levels of desire.

Her breath was coming in short gasps, and when he

looked at her face, tipped back into the pillow, he saw before him a woman in the throes of full-blown passion. Her cheeks had bloomed with pink color, and her dark lashes were splayed against her cheeks.

His hand drifted to the jointure of her body and he found the small swollen bud. She moaned in response, slightly arching toward his hand.

Desire took on a fine, sharp edge. He longed to thrust himself all the way inside of her, but did not. Instead he constrained himself to small, slow movements.

Rosamunde's eyes opened. "I can't. Oh, I can't stand this."

He abruptly stopped. "Am I hurting you?" He was surprised to find his voice sounded calm to his own ears when his own need had built to an agonizing crescendo.

"No. It's just that I feel . . . It's all so wonderful, and agonizing at the same time."

"The feeling is entirely mutual." He attempted to smile.

"It's just that . . ."

"Yes?" he encouraged her.

"Oh, this is extremely embarrassing."

He was ready to explode. His body was revolting against this exquisite agony of a pause with every muscle.

"I'd hoped you would've forgotten to be embarrassed." He leisurely leaned down and took her tiny rosy nipple between his lips and suckled her, and then bit gently.

She bucked against him. "Well, I'm not embarrassed about what we're doing. It's just that . . ."

"Yes?" he growled.

"I want you closer."

He nearly lost all control. "Rosamunde, you don't know what you ask." He dared not scare her when she had come so far.

"Well, I guess I can wait."

God was punishing him. Surely, he would be allowed at least one rung higher from the fires of hell for his self-restraint. He laughed at the irony.

He rested his forehead against hers and suddenly felt himself sink a little further inside of her.

"I think I understand how it works now," she whispered in his ear.

He began a slow push and pull with her, never daring to strain deeper than the clenched walls within her, always pleasuring her mouth, her breasts, her cheeks and neck with his lips and fingers. He felt so snug, cradled between her limbs.

But she kept twisting up to meet him, until finally he could take it no more. With a curse he snatched a pillow. "Clasp me with your legs."

She obeyed instantly and he placed the large cushion beneath her. His desire, which had been on the pinnacle for so long, rose another notch, and for long minutes he thrust into her, using his arms to draw her body tightly against his own, his teeth to nip her.

"Oh please." A moan rippled through her. "Don't stop."

Her eyes were dark cobalt, so infused with passion

were they. Passion he knew she had never given any other man.

"Luc, you're driving me to madness."

"I was striving for pleasure," he said hoarsely. He slowed his movements, trying to grasp a measure of control.

"Well, it's a lovely sort of madness."

He lowered his mouth to her breast again, this time suckling her more deeply than before.

"Make that a horribly lovely sort of insanity," she gasped.

He released her breast. "Shhhh, less talking and more insanity."

He was losing his grip, forgetting to hold back, forgetting to be gentle. Forgetting everything—his past, his present, his future. There was only this woman in front of him.

Loving him.

Dear God, *she loved him.*

It was the only reason she would ever allow any man to do this to her again. She was the bravest female he had ever known. And while the thought of her love should scare his body down into the deepest circle of Satan's lair, it did not.

He looked at her as his thickness stroked long and deep within her, a mere whisper from being fully sheathed, and he knew as starkly clear as a crisp autumn morning that she had weaved herself closer to his soul than anything or anyone else in all of Christendom and beyond.

The tightness within her began to clench and throb

along the length of him, and it nearly sent him over the edge. Her mouth was open in full rapture and in his desire to please her he thrust until her entire body moved higher up the bed.

And suddenly as he drove in past the wild tremors, the last channel unlocked deep within her and he found himself fully surrounded by her need and her surrender.

She moaned his name, "Luc, oh Luc, Luc . . ." over and over until the clenching eased. He strained and stopped, completely embedded in her to the hilt. His mind reeled with the sensation.

Her unforgettable eyes locked on his, beckoning him to find a fulfillment unlike he had ever known.

"Luc, I never knew. Never knew . . ."

She strained to kiss him tenderly. A kiss so giving and so trusting it broke him.

He closed his eyes and thrust himself fully into her again, reveling in the pure pleasure of it. She responded by urging him closer, pulling him nearer still until every inch of his skin touched hers in this erotic dance.

He felt the tremors begin deep inside of her again and he raised himself above her once more, notched himself just the barest way inside her, and slid slowly, inexorably down this valley of pure rapture. He exploded, his long pulses matching the rhythm of her heartbeat.

Pushing aside the last barriers, they tumbled headlong into passion's grip, allowing themselves to meld into one heart, one soul, one instant in time.

Exhausted from holding back for so long, he eased his considerable weight on top of her before rising on his forearms.

He brushed a few locks of black hair from her flushed cheeks and kissed her forehead gently as they both struggled to regain their breath.

She brought a palm to his rough cheek, soft wonder filling her eyes. "Was that . . . was that how it usually goes?"

Amusement filled him. "Not exactly," he drawled.

"Oh Luc, it was so very wonderful for me. You must show me how to make it wonderful for you too." She paused. "I didn't know exactly what I should do to please you. I wish you had shown me where to touch you."

He growled and felt himself pulse and harden slightly inside her again.

Her eyes flew to his, uncomprehending.

He wedged himself deeper within her. "Rosamunde, does this tell you anything? I shall have to tie your hands behind your back if you dare touch me. I'll have no control whatsoever."

"Well, I guess it's only fair to warn you"—she smoothed her hands down the deep muscles of his shoulders, down his spine, to pull him closer—"I memorized how to tie and untie every knot in my brother's sailing manual when I was ten."

He stifled a laugh. Before him was a woman who could face down her worst fears and then laugh about it. Well, one thing was certain, he wasn't going to allow her to regret it. "Rosamunde, I'm going to withdraw from you. You might feel bold now, but you shall be sorry for it if we continue. You'll be very sore."

He lifted an inch from her and she pulled him back down with her clasped legs and clenched his length. "It's a lovely sort of soreness. Rather like an itch on my back I can't quite reach."

He rumbled and she gripped him again. "God woman, you'll be the death of me."

"But it will be a lovely sort of death, don't you think?"

With that he swept her into a slow rapture as glorious and fulfilling as the last. He had lost his mind by the end of it. He could barely say his own name if his life had depended on it. But she had imprinted herself on his very soul, black as it was.

As afternoon light overtook the day and his eyes grew heavy watching the sky through the porthole, he untangled her legs from his and pulled her back snuggly against his chest, his heart constricting.

What was he going to do with her?

Perhaps, just perhaps—

Chapter 10

Motive, n. A mental wolf in moral wool.

—The Devil's Dictionary, A. Bierce

He could figure out a way to entice her to stay . . . at least for a little longer.

She would never accept the marriage proposal he was honor-bound to offer. She would refuse to marry any man, especially a man who had likened marriage to the bonds of hell. All the riches and titles in the world would not tempt her. Hadn't she told him that at least a dozen times?

Even if he had awakened her to the selfish beast of desire, during more rational moments she was sure to resist capture. She had said she wouldn't allow another man to own her if her life depended on it.

And she was right. He knew what a mistake marriage was. Knew it more than she. He knew not of a single happy couple married above a year or two.

Even though he could say with a fair degree of confidence that he would never, ever hurt her, there was always that tiny fear hidden deep within the recesses of his being. In the heat of the moment, would his actions supersede his convictions? His father had been cool and restrained for the most part, except on those rare yet memorable occasions when rage had overtaken him and threatened everyone in his path. Luc's spine twitched in remembrance.

Who was he to say he wasn't exactly like his sire? They had both had the advantage of being surrounded by kindhearted, loving women. All saints gracing God's green earth. What had made his father unleash his temper in the face of such goodness? And hadn't Luc felt that same fury overtake him on occasion? Why he'd killed more French sailors and pirates than any of the men who served him. In the heat of battle, he could coldly conjure up enough rage to destroy a fleet.

No. He would keep Rosamunde safe from the innate, baser ugliness lurking somewhere deep within him and all men. He would arrange an annuity, and settle on her the last of Ata's purportedly *inherited* cottages he had secretly purchased.

A cottage would bring Rosamunde the peace and happiness she deserved. And they could, on occasion, indulge in their mutual passion for as long as she desired. It was the least he could do for this courageous woman who had been sent to hell and back courtesy of the St. Aubyn family.

He heard a shout and rose from the bunk, putting on his breeches and shirt in one fluid motion.

"Rosamunde . . ." He shook her twice, but she refused to budge. He had to go. Had to find out what was wrong on deck. He cursed through a smile. She slept like a child after too much Christmas candy.

Rosamunde crashed awake, and found herself sprawled on the floorboards of Luc's cabin. The entire vessel seemed to have tipped sideways.

She struggled into her chemise and gown, not bothering with the stays. For all she knew they were about to sink to the bottom of the sea, and heaven knew she didn't need a cinched waist to meet her Maker. She fumbled with her hairpins and crawled through the door.

She swayed while trying to make her way up the ladder and prayed for more strength. Two strong hands hooked under her arms to haul her to the deck.

Luc's eyes locked with hers. "Stay with Brown, and for God's sake lash yourself to the mast if necessary." With that he was gone to join the three deckhands aft.

From the shouting it became clear the men had set the sails before pulling up anchor, and now the anchor had snagged onto something and could not be pried loose. The wind in the sails was making the boat list to one side.

Luc yelled at the men to tie back the sails while he tugged off his shirt. In the fading sunlight, he looked like a wild Greek god, his skin kissed by the sun, his hair whipping about his face. His strength was palpable, the lines slung round his torso as he lowered a sail. He was far from the polished, jaded aristocrat she had first met, appearing more like a hardened privateer with gold on his mind.

And she had lain with him.

There was no doubt about that, and she had the uncomfortable impression that everyone on the yacht knew it too.

She was sore where he had been inside her. Just the thought of the wicked things he had done brought heat to her cheeks. Nothing that pleasurable could be anything but sinful. She had lain with a gentleman without benefit of marriage. And she should be repentant.

But she was not.

She would do it all over again given the chance. Only she would be less fearful and more determined to take part in his pleasure. She would keep her eyes open and explore every inch of him. And ask him how he had gotten the long scar she could see carved from his shoulder to his waist.

She was afraid she would never be pure in thought again after today.

A sail billowed at Luc's feet and he cursed. Rosamunde released her pent-up breath when the ship righted itself and went dead in the water. She watched the play of his muscles as they bunched and hardened while he worked to furl the sail. An ache filled her.

How was she to leave him now when she had tasted such forbidden pleasures? But leave him she must. She couldn't stay anywhere near him, for the temptation to be with him again would be too great. And where would that lead them?

She couldn't face Ata or anyone else for that matter

if there was even the remote possibility of a longer-term affair. She already felt guilty about what had transpired. She would destroy a little bit of herself and the hard-won inner peace she had built if she ever gave in to these new base desires.

She was not cut out for casual affairs. But she also knew she had never been good at resisting temptation.

And so she must leave. *As soon as possible.*

To London she would go, with Ata and Sylvia and the other widows. And she would find employment far, far away from him. It would be her chance at a new life with a slate wiped clean.

And she would be happy. Yes, she would force herself to be happy. And she would be grateful.

The deckhands monkeyed down the rigging. Her reflections scattered in the wind when Luc took a long look toward her before diving over the side.

"What is he doing?" She rushed to the rail.

Mr. Brown appeared at her side. "Loosening the anchor if he can. Otherwise we'll be stuck here."

Luc swam to the chain and jackknifed beneath the waves.

"Cap'n ne'er fails us," a deckhand said with patent false cheer.

"Except that one time," said another, peering over the edge.

Mr. Brown coshed him on the side of his head. "Remember your manners. There's a lady onboard, scallywag."

They looked at her respectfully. She felt a blast of self-consciousness again.

Surely more than two minutes had passed.

"He's been under for so long," she said.

"Don't worry, yer ladyship, they float when's they drown."

Brown took the sailor by the ear and wagged a finger. "No grog for you."

"Aren't any of you going to help him?"

They looked at her aghast. Mr. Brown muttered, "He's never needed help in the past."

But he had been under for at least three minutes now. He was probably caught on something, struggling. No one could hold their breath this long.

Not taking time to think it through, she jumped overboard before anyone could stop her. She prayed her skirts wouldn't hamper her. She had always been the strongest swimmer of her family. Three strokes later she felt the gown's back and arm seams give way.

They were yelling at her from the deck, but she couldn't make out anything, so focused was she on finding him, saving him. He was trapped below. He must already be gasping for air, drinking salt water.

She dove down, eyes burning. It was so murky she couldn't see much other than shadows. She followed the anchor's chain and kept going deeper, the pressure on her eardrums building.

Something rammed her stomach and she felt herself floating to the surface.

Luc gasped for air and she grasped his arm, pulling him close to the chain.

"What . . . what are you doing?" he sputtered.

"Saving you," she replied, spitting out seawater.

"Really?" He glared above. "They let you—"

A wave crashed over them and she coughed. A strong arm clamped about her waist and he shouted for a line. "Now who's saving whom?"

A rope slapped her back and within moments he had fashioned a loop for a seat. She felt herself being reeled in like an overgrown fish. The final insult was the sound of her lower gown ripping from the bodice.

"Well, at least we've a noble end to that hideous thing." Luc had appeared beside her and ordered the deckhands away. The sound of a jaunty tune being whistled revealed the hands' pretending to ignore the scene while working to restore the sails.

"Yes, well, I've no way to return with any sort of respectability now, do I?" she replied, then muttered, "Not that I consider myself respectable in any way, after today."

His eyes twinkled. "Thank God for that, Mrs. Baird."

"Yes, well, you would say that."

He looked both ways and pulled her close. "We have a two-hour sail back. Are we to spend it making sure I warm up every disreputable bone in your body, or are we to read Fordice's Sermons and ponder my future residence in hell?"

"Neither." Her teeth were definitely chattering now, and she wasn't sure if it was due to his arms or the wet clothing.

He rubbed her shivering arms. "Come. We have to get you out of these clothes. You're freezing. I'll find something below."

She knew without doubt then that he wouldn't try to entice her into his bed again. There was just the smallest degree of strain in their conversation. But she had to tell him what she was determined to say before she lost her nerve. She touched his arm before he turned. "Luc . . . thank you," she whispered, "for everything. For not chastising me when I foolishly jumped in after you, and more importantly, for everything *before*."

He chuckled and his eyes glinted with amusement. "It is I who should thank you. I've never had anyone try to save me . . . in more ways than one." He fingered a lock of her hair and placed it behind her ear. "It was a novel experience."

The sail and subsequent carriage ride back to Amberley was accomplished with nary a hitch nor another private word. It was all about staying alone behind the closed door of his cabin, and staying warm.

Mr. Brown had knocked on her door, urging her to eat part of the wedding feast he had surreptitiously smuggled before their hasty departure. "But lass, you really should try some of the Captain's salted snapper from the West Indies. It's a rarity in these parts."

She refused, having neither the appetite nor the courage to face any of them.

The final indignity was being bundled into the carriage before the duke joined Mr. Brown on the driver's bench. He didn't want to be inside with her. It was a serious blow to the small amount of vanity she possessed. It was very clear that he, at least, was regretting their actions, while she was not.

He was obviously not interested in another tryst. But then, why should that matter to her? It made it all easier. She had said to herself that she wouldn't prolong the agony of their eventual parting. And she would hate to have to rebuff him. But the tiny spark in her ridiculous female mind perversely knew it would feel better for her to have to rebuff him than for him not to seek her out again. Oh botheration . . .

She should show more compassion. This was the man who had so successfully shown her how blindingly surreal and passionate intimacy could be after all.

A quarter of an hour after their return he tossed a gown inside the carriage. She paused at the color, a deep crimson. There was no possible way—

"Make haste, Rosamunde," he said quietly from outside. "Ata is ill if the dim-witted apothecary has the right of it."

She prayed there was no one else in the stables, and inched open the carriage door to peek around it before descending. He did up the back of the gown and barked at someone to see to the horses.

"I didn't know whether to kiss the pretentious fool for scaring away the houseguests," he said while she struggled to keep up with his long strides, "or kill the idiot for urging most of the servants to leave as well."

"What does he think it is?"

"The self-righteous witchdoctor had the audacity to suggest a return of the plague before I ushered him to the door with a promise of a true *black death* unless he sent a reputable physician in his stead."

The older housemaid, Mrs. Simms, met them on the

threshold and spoke as she huffed her large frame up the wide staircase behind them.

"This ain't the plague if you was to arsk me. But," she wheezed, "it looks like some sort of putrid infection. There were other guests who took ill, too. And the undercook."

They wended their way through the maze of halls while the maid babbled on. "They've all gone, except me and the cook, who 'ates the apothecary. Calls him the grim reaper, she does. The widows refused to leave. And"—she turned to Rosamunde—"your sister. That pretty Miss Clarendon and the 'andsome vicar are tryin' to drag 'er off to stay with them."

Luc put up a staying hand in front of the door. Hushed whispers greeted them inside the darkened room. The unmistakably elegant profile of Grace Sheffey shadowed most of Ata's tiny form on the bed. The dowager was making pitiful little sounds while the countess wiped her brow. It struck Rosamunde right through the heart.

"Stop, please. The water's too hot," Ata whispered. She turned her head and it seemed like his grandmother's eye sockets were too large for her small face. "Oh Luc, you're here. This is ridiculous. I'm certain it's just the food . . . perhaps it was the sausage pie."

Luc's large hand half covered his grandmother's head. "You've not a fever. Perhaps you're right. Did anyone ask the others who were ill what they had eaten?" He grasped her good hand in his.

But his expression. Frozen, despite the cool and collected words he uttered.

"I don't know," answered Grace. "It makes no sense, as we all ate the same things."

Rosamunde hadn't eaten anything since early morning. Between the events and her nerves, she had completely lost any desire for food.

Luc dipped the cloth in the water and smoothed it over Ata's brow again.

"Luc, stop. Please, it's too hot. I keep telling everyone."

"The water's ice cold, Ata," he said quietly.

She pushed his hand away and sighed. "I don't need it. I don't have a fever."

Rosamunde looked at Ata's withered hand, which the lady had forgotten to hide under the covers. She rushed forward and gained Luc's attention by glancing pointedly at his grandmother's hand.

A blistering rash covered it.

Luc turned his grandmother's good hand in his palm and saw the same condition. It could be so many things, most of them infectious and deadly serious.

"Ata," he said urgently, "does anything pain you?"

She smiled weakly. "Yes. The fact you're all looking at me as if angels are circling to come in for the kill."

"Ata . . ." he said.

"Don't you 'Ata' me. Everything in this old body pains me. Make them go away, will you, Luc?" She continued in a low tone, "Looking at everyone in mourning is giving me the most awful premonition."

Rosamunde edged away until Ata's hand caught at her. "Not you. Why, you're wearing my favorite color. It cheers the soul. I'm so glad you discarded the other."

She didn't have the heart to disabuse Ata of her notions. The dowager seemed on the verge of delirium.

Sylvia tugged her sleeve. "Rosa," she whispered, "Charity has invited us to stay at the vicarage. What would you like to do?"

Rosamunde looked at the three of them—her sister, Charity, and her brother, Sir Rawleigh.

"The apothecary said it would be best if everyone removed from here," said the handsome vicar, his eyes searching Sylvia's with concern.

"And it will be easier if there are fewer house-guests," seconded Charity.

Rosamunde glanced at Luc to find his half-shuttered eyes studying her before she addressed her sister. "You go, dearest. Sir Rawleigh is right."

"I'm staying if you are."

"No. Sylvia, for once in your life, do as I say." She spoke with such harshness it was hard to say who was more surprised, Sylvia or herself.

Her sister bowed her head. "Of course."

Rosamunde was instantly stricken with remorse.

"Perhaps you should consider a retreat as well," Luc said, his voice low and gravelly.

"I've the constitution of an ox. I wish I were more delicate, but my family always said it was the mixture of so many generations of ornery natures."

He picked up her thin wrist in his large palm. "Really?"

"You'll need someone to help you," she pointed out.

He said not a word, turning his attention back to

his grandmother. Gone was the devil-may-care rakish expression that was his second skin. Only the tick of the mantel clock marked the silence.

"Luc," the wizened dowager whispered, "something is very wrong. I don't want to worry you, but I must settle a few matters. Private matters." There was desperation in the depths of Ata's eyes that Rosamunde had never seen before, and given Luc's expression, he hadn't either.

Luc glanced at Rosamunde and with a tilt of his head she understood. She shooed everyone to the doorway. With one foot in the room and one out, she gave hushed instructions to Mrs. Simms to prepare tea and broth, and a few other requests to the others. But between her words, she couldn't help hearing snatches of conversation between Ata and Luc. It was then that the delicate beginnings of a wish she had barely had the courage to consider were effectively destroyed.

"Luc," Ata pleaded, "no more ignoring the future. Listen to me and if you love me as I think you do, you'll not interrupt or . . . or brush this off. If I die, I want you to promise me something. No, I see your look. I've never asked for you to promise anything. I'm asking now and I require your assent."

Rosamunde glanced over her shoulder to see a quick nod from him and then asked Mrs. Simms to bring an extra blanket.

"Say it," Ata insisted.

"I will do whatever you ask." He was so gruff Rosamunde could barely make out the words.

"Luc, you must marry and produce an heir. If you

do not, then what I endured for nearly fifty years will be for naught. I've never pressured you because I'd hoped, well—" Ata burst into tears and glanced toward the doorway where Grace Sheffey stood, talking with the other widows. The sound of Ata weeping was so wretched that Rosamunde edged away from the door and would have retired to her room if Mrs. Simms had not handed her the requested blanket.

Produce an heir . . . produce an heir . . . Ata's glance at the countess and the painful words echoed inside her mind. She tamped down the pain weaving through her chest. If there was ever a time she wished she could run outside and keep running until she could blank out the pain and misery and dashed dreams, it was now. Instead, she did what she had learned to do—she forced herself to stay and be useful. If there was one person on this earth who had always been kind to her, it was this wonderful, generous dowager.

Luc was whispering to Ata and holding her hand when Rosamunde reentered the room and placed the extra blanket on the bed. She held on to the edges of her composure with the dregs of her inner resources.

He kissed his grandmother's forehead. "You look very tired. Perhaps you should try to sleep a little."

"I don't want to sleep," she replied, her voice childlike. "I fear I might not wake up."

Rosamunde was sure that whatever remained of her courage was down in her toes, and she imagined how Luc must feel.

"I shall sit here with you"—he pulled the pins out of the dowager's gray hair and allowed the long thin braid to rest on her shoulder—"and watch your breathing. I'll wake you if there is any unsteadiness."

A lump formed in Rosamunde's throat. Most people would have made light of the dowager's worries. But he had instead told her the one thing she needed to hear to allow her to rest. And Ata was so sure of his word she didn't even require him to swear he wouldn't leave her.

Rosamunde was thankful Ata's eyes were now closed, for the dowager wouldn't have been able to take the sight of her grandson on his knees, his thumb and forefinger clenching the bridge of his nose to stave off emotion. Within moments Ata's long, slow breaths signaled her surrender to sleep.

The soft crinkle of the crimson silk gown followed Rosamunde as she stepped toward him. She rested her hand on his shoulder and felt the contracted muscles beneath her palm.

"Luc," she whispered, "don't give in to despair. We don't even know what this is. It could very well be some passing illness, gone in a day or two. Give it time."

He was silent. "Are you suggesting I practice patience?"

"Yes."

"I've never had much patience for saintly virtues." He looked back at his grandmother and a hollow look crossed his features.

She held her breath. She didn't know what she would do if he yielded to torment now.

"She can't die," he said raggedly.

There was something so painful about seeing someone so strong break down. She shivered and remembered those exact words from long ago.

It was what Sylvia had said to her when she had appeared at Barton's Cottage. That was the reason Sylvia gave for coming to live with her. The thought had woven into her subconscious. She had never understood Sylvia's words. Even at her darkest hour, Rosamunde had always felt she could withstand almost anything.

Except this, now. It would be unbearable to witness this man's catharsis if the worst came to pass.

With considerable effort, she struggled to pull him off his knees and wound her arms around the rock-hard breadth of his massive shoulders. The elemental beat of his heart thudded through his wrinkled coat and damp shirt.

She couldn't think of a single thing to say to comfort him. And so she reached up and stroked his coarse hair, which was still in wild disarray about his shoulders. Small grains of salt had crystallized in it, giving him an untamed, primal look.

"Thank you," he said gruffly.

"For what?"

"For not arguing with me."

She nodded without replying.

"I know it required great forbearance, considering your contrary nature."

He was trying to hold back his emotions by provoking her with a touch of humor. It had been her father and brothers' favorite way of deflating a possible display of sentiment. And she could do nothing but play along. For she hadn't the heart to watch him reel with misery.

"Well, if you're going to provoke me," she said softly.

"It's in my nature."

"Then I shall have to retaliate." And she did the one thing he least expected. She leaned in and kissed his scratchy cheek and breathed in the heady masculine scent of well-worked brawn and the sea. She whispered into his ear, "I know you're imagining the worst. But tell yourself not to think about it until an hour from now. It's the secret to withstanding the worst life tosses our way. But if a good row would take your mind off of Ata, I'm happy to oblige."

It worked.

A glimmer of amusement flickered in his eyes. "You've a wicked streak in you."

"I've been surrounded by males, with the exception of my sister, my entire life. I know how to deflect almost every argument, especially when I am right about something, which is, of course, quite frequently as I'm sure you of all people have noticed." She was rambling, digging herself in deeper while he refused to rise to the bait. "Humor is something I hadn't realized I missed so much, until coming here." She turned to the petite dowager and stroked her gray hair.

The abrupt recollection of her first meeting with Ata and the duke flared in her mind, when they had vocally jousted with practiced ease, and now it was Rosamunde who suddenly found herself floundering helplessly and fighting back tears.

She bit down hard on the side of her tongue and forced her mind to more practical matters. "I don't think this is the plague. I remember hearing a rash is only part of it. The main signs are fever and swelling of the neck and such, and she has neither. Look, why don't we take turns? We must bathe and such."

"Amusing and sensible too," he said shrewdly. "Except when judging how long someone can hold their breath underwater."

"I thought we'd discussed that. And how much I appreciated your not holding it against me."

"You didn't really think I'd let you forget that bit of foolishness, did you?" He glanced at Ata's form.

"Foolishness and courage are in truth one and the same," she asserted. "Only dumb luck separates them."

"Or reality." His smile twisted.

"Or reality," she echoed. "Now who has the courage to trust what we know? Ata does not have the plague. I'm certain it's a passing illness. One of us should bathe and then relieve the other. I think I should take the first turn."

"Your memory is deplorable. I've already told you I don't take turns. Now go and order your bath before I carry you out of here."

She looked at him for a long moment. "Brute."

"Brat," he responded and raised a single dark supercilious eyebrow.

That was the last witty repartee Rosamunde engaged in for a while. And in the end she won her point.

But not in any way she could have envisioned or wished. It was those cursed devil's rules at play.

Chapter 11

Friendship, n. *A ship big enough to carry two in fair weather, but only one in foul.*

—The Devil's Dictionary, A. Bierce

The water in the bath was tepid at best and in short supply. But with so many servants gone it was to be expected. A knock sounded at the door and Rosamunde peered around the demi-screen when Sylvia entered without waiting for her reply. She was dressed for travel, bandbox in hand.

"Oh, I didn't know you were—" Sylvia said.

"No, don't go." Rosamunde continued to lather her hair with the rosemary and lemon soap. "I'm so glad you're still here. I was hoping for the chance to talk to you before you go."

Sylvia put down her bag, her face a mask of impassive stone. "I don't think there is anything left to say. I'm going with Charity to be out of everyone's way. You can send a note when you would like me to return."

Rosamunde knew that tone all too well. Her sister's feelings were hurt, and her reaction was predictable. Sylvia's middle name should have been Jeanne D'Arc, for she was as much a martyr as the famous saint. With sudden clarity Rosamunde saw the lighthearted girl she had once known and the morose spinster Sylvia had become. When had she lost her happiness? Rosamunde wondered with a sigh. But then, she knew, she had changed as well.

"Sylvia, when did we stop laughing with each other?"

"What?" her sister said woodenly. "Whatever are you talking about?"

"Us. Do you remember how we used to spend hours laughing and gossiping and having fun together?"

"Sometimes you say the most ridiculous things, Rosamunde. We put away our childish ways when you married. As a lady should."

"But there's no rule that says we shouldn't try to find pleasure. Promise me you'll try, or else I'll feel as guilty as ever." Rosamunde stopped scrubbing for a moment and looked at her sister. "I begged you to go home for so many years, and you insisted on staying. I kept telling myself I was selfish not to force your departure. Living with me brought you such misery. Why did you stay?" With each word she spoke slower and slower, as if she were thinking aloud.

The color had drained from Sylvia's cheeks and her gaze rested on the floorboards. "I couldn't let you suffer alone. I thought you wanted me to be with you. You're my sister and I love you, and will always love you no matter what happens."

"As I will always love you, dearest." Rosamunde brooded for another moment. "You don't really mind staying with Charity and her brother, do you?"

"No," Sylvia replied and finally relaxed enough for her face to gain color. "They're very kind. But I wouldn't want any expectations to"—she stumbled—"arise."

"You're referring to Sir Rawleigh?" she asked quietly.

"Yes." Sylvia looked away.

"But why in heavens not? You must know it would be my fondest wish come true. This could be your great chance to embrace happiness."

Sylvia picked at a tiny hole in her glove. "I'm not at all certain he will offer for me anyway. And even if he did I couldn't accept. It wouldn't be right for the *vicar* to marry one of the two notorious cast-out sisters, and well you know it, Rosa."

"This is where your argument has always baffled me. I was the notorious sister. You are not infamous, only loyal—overly loyal—and everyone knows it. There is no reason for you not to find contentment apart from me. As I said, for every moment you play the pitying, steadfast sister, I suffer more. You must see that."

"I'm sorry if I pain you," she murmured. "But I beg you to stop tormenting me about this. I have thought it through. Many times. Marriage to him would be insupportable."

"Do you love him?" she asked softly.

Sylvia sucked in her breath sharply.

"I have my answer," Rosamunde said knowingly.

"No," Sylvia cut in, "you only have the question."

"Yes is the answer."

"Only if the question is whether I truly want to strangle you at times." Sylvia raised one perfectly shaped brow, just as she had used to do a long time ago, and laughed. Her sister was truly the most beautiful woman alive when she dared to show her old spark.

"Ah," Rosamunde murmured, "she remembers how to dodge and smile."

"Lean forward," Sylvia commanded.

Rosamunde obeyed. An icy blast of cold water gushed over her soapy head and she sputtered and shrieked. "You . . . you witch!"

"You deserved it." Sylvia replaced the pitcher of cool drinking water next to the pitcher of warm water.

Rosamunde laughed. "You're probably right." She shivered and emerged from the bath to accept the toweling from Sylvia. "I'm sorry I snapped at you earlier in front of everyone. I shouldn't have." Rosamunde yanked on a clean chemise and turned around so Sylvia could help her with her stays.

"It's all right." Sylvia jerked enough to take her breath away.

"If pulling on those strings makes you feel better, go ahead." Rosamunde was relieved and delighted. Her sister had shown more spirit in the last few minutes than in the last half decade.

Sylvia jerked her again.

"What are you doing?" Rosamunde asked breathlessly.

"No, what have *you* been doing?"

"I haven't the faintest idea what you're talking about."

"I'm not loosening these until you tell me where you went with the duke. Auggie Phelps's betrothed made a point of mentioning to everyone before he left that you and His Grace had been seen leaving in a carriage."

"You're a fine one to talk." Rosamunde tried to loosen her stays, but her sister slapped her hands away. "Will you please let me breathe? Thank you. Where were you during the wedding? You missed Father and our brothers."

Sylvia released the ties and Rosamunde gulped in air. "Father was there?" Sylvia asked faintly.

"Through the ceremony. But he said not a word to me and left directly after. Did he come to the wedding breakfast?"

"I don't think so," responded her sister. "I didn't see him, nor did anyone mention our family. And you're changing the subject. Where is your mourning gown?"

Rosamunde pulled the crimson silk gown over her head and fastened the two buttons of the bodice. It was the first gown she had ever worn in the Greek style and her bosom felt very bare. "I went for a sail with the duke." She paused. "And Mr. Brown."

She stopped Sylvia, who opened her mouth to speak. "Between Father giving me the cut direct, and

Auggie's despicable fiancé trying to, well, to paw me, His Grace was kind enough to give me a reprieve from facing the rest of the wedding celebrations. Sylvia, it was the culmination of everything happening this month . . . and actually for much longer. I'm sorry if I've disappointed you."

Rosamunde prayed her sister wouldn't have the audacity to question her further. She just couldn't lie to her own sister, but she wanted to preserve in secret the memory of her interlude with Luc St. Aubyn. There was something about sharing those moments, truly the most glorious of her life, that would cast a shadow of guilt and sadness on it. And she could never explain to Sylvia why she had done it. She had never told her sister how painful and degrading her marriage bed had been.

"Well"—Sylvia spread the damp toweling on the screen—"I'm sorry about leaving you to fend for yourself at the wedding. I just couldn't go and watch everyone staring at us, and I had a premonition Father would be there, what with all the signs of bad luck yesterday. I saw an owl during daylight and I heard you singing before breakfast—although perhaps it was only humming."

Rosamunde resisted the urge to throttle every last superstition from her sister's head. It was the most annoying trait Sylvia possessed. "Well, I'm sorry to force you away from here. But I do think it will be good for you. You deserve to spend some time with your new friends, and no, I see your look. I won't utter another word about Sir Rawleigh other than to say he seems the kindest gentleman in the west county—and the handsomest man I've ever seen."

"Please don't say anything more, Rosa."

"I won't. But here, take this small bouquet I picked yesterday."

Sylvia accepted the tiny bouquet of pearl-colored spikes. "White heather . . ."—her sister smiled radiantly—"is good luck."

"I know, dearest." Rosamunde eased onto the slipper chair in front of the toilette table and Sylvia pinned back her hair into a ruthless topknot. "But I doubt you'll need it . . . not with the way Sir Rawleigh looks at you. If he's not dirtying one knee of his breeches in a fortnight, I'll—"

Sylvia's image in the mirror facing Rosamunde appeared stricken. "You promised not to say another word."

"I shan't as long as you promise to consider what you would prefer, either returning to Father and begging him to take you back, marrying Sir Rawleigh *when* he asks, or finding some hideous post as a lady's companion or governess. Sadly, not one option will allow us to live together unless you would like to add returning to Barton Cottage and playing run around the table with Algernon." Rosamunde stood and slipped on her old boots. "There is only so much charity and pity I will be able to accept from Ata and her grandson."

She handed Sylvia her worn leather and cord bag and embraced her with more feeling than she ever had before and whispered into her ear, "Please, please, for my sake, try to take some pleasure from this stay with Charity and her brother."

Sylvia avoided her eyes and passed through the door. "I shall if you promise to take *less* pleasure from your stay here with the duke. It's guaranteed to lead to more gossip."

Sylvia was right. If there was ever a time to step cautiously, it was now. Hurrying down the darkened corridor of the east wing of Amberley, she stopped at one of the windows to peer at the yellow waxing moon breaking through a rush of clouds in the night. A few raindrops spattered against the old, irregular glass panes.

The weather was changing. The heat of a string of calm summer days promised a spectacular electrical storm. Rosamunde adored the sound and the fury of jagged lightning bolts and booming thunder.

A burst of wind whistled from the cracks around the window and a shiver wended its way down her spine. She was taking too long to return to Ata's chambers and she knew why. She needed more time to fortify herself against the yearnings Luc St. Aubyn stirred in her breast each time she was with him. She was beginning to be afraid of him or of what he made her feel. Perhaps he really was the devil sent to tempt her again.

And this time it was so much more powerful than the sensibilities his brother had conjured up so many years ago. She had worked so hard to change. Desire and reckless pursuits had only ever led to a lifetime of trouble and regrets. And here she was riding, climbing, sailing, and discovering something so much more dangerous—passion.

She forced herself toward the whispers she heard behind the door. Before she could knock, the door opened and the perfectly composed figure of Grace Sheffey emerged.

"Oh," the countess said, "I'm so glad you've come. We were worried you had taken ill as well."

Looking above Grace's slim shoulder, Rosamunde saw Luc near Ata's form, his hair glistening wet and his dress very informal. Patches of his fine white linen shirt clung to his damp torso. The room was illuminated by a single beeswax candle that left eerie, moving shadows from the vast canopy of Ata's bed all the way to a gleaming hipbath half hidden in a room beyond. Pools of water and toweling surrounded it.

"He . . ." Rosamunde gulped. "He bathed while you were here?"

"Of course not. Whatever are you inferring?" The countess didn't wait for an answer. "He refused to leave her so he ordered a bath in the adjoining room."

"How is she?" Rosamunde whispered to Grace.

"About the same, I think. She keeps moaning in her sleep, as if she's in pain."

"Has a doctor come?"

"Yes. He was mystified, yet certain it could spread to others. I'm glad his sister and Lord Landry left before so many took ill. Luc asked me to arrange for the other widows to return to Helston House in London. All except you and me, that is."

He had asked the countess to stay, then. Perhaps he was already granting Ata's final wishes.

"I'll see to some tea. Try to get him to rest, will you? He doesn't look well."

Rosamunde nodded mutely and closed the door behind the beautiful widow.

She came up beside him and spied lines of worry etched on his brow. "You look exhausted. Will you rest a bit?" She didn't dare command it since it seemed he often did the very opposite of what was asked.

"Perhaps," he said to her surprise.

A flash of lightning illuminated the entire room for a second. And in the blackness that followed they both remained silent, counting the seconds and miles before the sound of the rolling thunder. Five miles away, at least. It was coming from St. Ives.

She hurried around the room, securing the windows and closing drapery, but taking care to keep her distance from Luc when she went to Ata. The dowager was moving restlessly whilst humming and talking nonsensically about a harp.

"Does she want for anything?"

He appeared so lost in thought he didn't answer her. The storm increased in intensity, the leaves and tree branches heaving and roaring in the wild wind, which shook the windows in their frames.

"Lucifer, please don't. I beg of you!" Ata moaned and struggled.

Luc instantly freed her arms from the covers. "Ata," he whispered, "I'm right here."

"No! Please don't touch me. No!"

It was as if a bolt from the night sky had scorched his hands. He looked at Rosamunde with such anguish. "Help her." His face, shrouded in unbelievable pain, appeared bluish gray in the dark room.

Ata garbled her speech, then quivered. "Not my hand, please not my hand. I promise I won't play anymore. I promise I won't ever play again. Lucifer, no!"

Rosamunde shook Ata's frail shoulder. "Ata, Ata! Wake up. Come now. Open your eyes and look at me. No one is hurting you here."

Ata's dazed eyes opened and were unfocused, unseeing. "No, you must get out of here. He'll hurt you. But you mustn't tell anyone. He punishes and we deserve it. Mustn't tell, promise, mustn't tell."

"Shhh . . ." Rosamunde urged. "I won't tell."

And then Ata's eyes suddenly focused on Rosamunde's face. "He hurts. Mustn't tell. Mustn't tell Luc he looks just like him . . ." She wailed and her eyes rolled up and she closed her lids again and whimpered. Ata's withered hand twitched on the covers.

Oh God, someone had broken Ata's hand. Not for a moment did she think it was Luc. It wasn't even remotely possible. "Who was Lucifer?" she whispered, not daring to meet his eyes.

"I am," he said it in a tone which defied her to refute him.

The rain beat hard against the panes, water sluiced through the eaves in a rushing noise. "Don't be ridiculous. Was that your father's name, too?"

"Barbas Henry St. Aubyn," he replied.

"And your grandfather's name?"

"One guess, and I'll think you a simpleton if you're wrong," he said, an odd glint in his eye.

Anger pooled in her fingertips. "Did you know? Did you know he did this to her?"

"Henry and I deduced the truth, although we weren't fool enough to discuss it with anyone else. It wouldn't have changed anything if we had, as our dear grandfather possessed the good sense to die before either of us was born."

"But why . . ." She tried to think.

"Haven't you guessed? Generations of St. Aubyn barbarians killed their neighbors for their property, raped the land, hurt their women, and generally enjoyed themselves immensely in the process. There was a reason they were given the title Helston." The storm was on top of them and it was as if God was warning her to take seriously the namesake of the fallen archangel.

"Are you trying to scare me?"

"You're a fool if you're not. I'm trying to warn you. Helston is the infamous stone covering the gateway to the underworld right here in Cornwall, although in my opinion we were ever and always in the devil's inner circle rather than hovering above it."

"You *are* trying to scare me." She shook her head. "You know, I've never believed in superstitions. Perhaps it's because I tired of Sylvia's proverbs. But more so because I always accumulated misfortune no matter how much good luck I practiced. Your stories don't frighten me. The only question is why you feel it necessary to warn me of the evil Helston past."

"Because the past has a remarkable ability to color the present, as well you know."

"Perhaps."

"And because man is too stupid, for the most part, to deviate from what he knows."

"There, you're utterly wrong."

He crossed his arms and offered her his blackest expression. "I had thought living with the delightful Baird cousins would've cured your more ardent romantic notions."

"You're the most cynical gentleman of my acquaintance, and yet probably the finest man I have ever—"

Rosamunde rushed forward when she saw him sway. Even in the dim light she could see he was pale, despite his bronzed features. "Whatever is the matter?" She didn't wait for an answer, instead forcing him to sit on Ata's bed.

"Wait," he said between clenched teeth. "It'll pass."

Panic crept in on silent feet and clutched at her hands. "Luc, I suppose I should warn you I'm not a very good nurse."

"So now you tell me." He swallowed. "Not very sporting of you, as I've just sent the others away."

"Devil's rules." She licked her dry lips nervously. "You taught me well. So perhaps you'd better not take ill. You're just fatigued. I'm certain." She hoped she sounded more confident than she was.

He flexed his fingers and they stared at the redness radiating on the backs of his hands. "It's the damnedest thing. Like pins and needles, only different." He shivered and then looked pained. "It always amazes me how a great many things can go wrong in the shortest span of time. But then, a wedding always brings disaster in its wake."

He stood up and swayed again.

"I think you'd better lie down."

"Advice from the wretched nurse?" he mumbled.

"Advice from someone who is fairly certain she won't be able to lift you if you faint."

He gripped his head. "Ata—"

"Ata will be watched," she interrupted. "I'll stay with her."

"Or perhaps Grace. She's an exceptional caregiver."

Rosamunde tried not to feel slighted.

She reached under his broad shoulder and he suddenly slumped against her, his weight staggering. Were there any footmen left? With stark clarity she remembered Mrs. Simms's dragging in the copper hipbath and making Cornish oaths about cowardly male servants afraid of a silly cold.

She looked up into his eyes and he attempted a lopsided version of his devilish grin but failed miserably, his face sagging. "'Fraid my—my legs aren't working properly. Can't—"

"Shhh . . . just tell me where your apartments are." Rosamunde half dragged Luc out the door, until he pointed at the chamber next to her own.

What? "Don't tell me you've been next door all this time?"

"You're not going to warm my ears now, are you?" He mumbled, nearly unintelligible.

"Your timing has always been impeccable," she said under her breath. "You had better not be faking . . ."

He shuttered his eyes.

"You're faking, aren't you?"

"I have renewed appreciation for your dear husband. I—I think I'd better—"

And then his head lolled back and Rosamunde was forced to use every last ounce of strength she possessed to kick open the door and stumble toward his massive dark mahogany bed. When she fell onto the goose-down coverlet carrying him, the enormity of the situation hit her.

He might die.

She looked at her hands and they were trembling. She would think about the possibility in one hour. That's what she would do. Never let it be said she couldn't follow her own excellent advice.

But he could die. She almost wailed.

She tried to collect her thoughts. She would call for cold water and compresses. She sprang up toward the rope pull, and then remembered Ata hadn't had a fever and had hated the compresses. She sat back down and touched his forehead. It was as dry and cool as her own. She used the last of her strength to pull back the thick eider-down duvet, lift his legs onto the bed, and push him toward the center.

His lids moved. "Ata . . ." he groaned.

She jumped. "Right. I'll get help."

As she rushed down the myriad staircases to the bowels of the house, forgetting all about bell cords and such instruments of modernity, a black feeling of dread coursed through her. It wasn't the first time she had felt alone, but it was the first time it scared her all the way down to her toes and back.

The refined splendor of Grace Sheffey waited at the kitchen door, a silver tea service in her capable hands. Never had Rosamunde felt so grateful or so incompetent.

Chapter 12

Weaknesses, n. pl. Certain primal powers of Tyrant Woman wherewith she holds dominion over the male of her species, binding him to the service of her will and paralyzing his rebellious energies.

—The Devil's Dictionary, A. Bierce

It was the worst feeling in the world, trying to hang on to consciousness when the blissful threads of sleep or something else wound themselves in and around the edges of Luc's vision. It would be so easy to let go . . . to a place that promised peace.

But something nagged at the corners of his mind, and he couldn't give in to stupor. A new small, agonized voice whispered in his psyche . . . *"He hurts. Mustn't tell. Mustn't tell Luc . . ."* He jerked back into his skin. It felt like a battalion of ants was performing marching drills on his extremities. He shivered and he could have sworn that even his teeth wobbled. He was sicker than a green recruit in his first storm and a hell of a lot more uneasy.

For Ata. For Rosamunde. Hell, for all the widows.

He groaned as he remembered the insane promise Ata had forced from him—marriage and an heir. Damnation, he would never be able to accomplish it. Perhaps one but not the other. The one woman who was a remote possibility clearly could not fulfill Ata's fondest wish.

A low melodic voice floated into his brain. *Her voice.* The voice of reason—and goodness. Must hold on to it . . .

The vision of Rodger St. Aubyn drifted through his thoughts. His blasé fourth cousin thrice removed stood next in line to wrest the duchy from his shoulders. He'd never considered the chance of dying before Ata. He'd be damned if he'd allow that effeminate wastrel to take control and consign Ata to some pathetic dowager's ruin on the edge of nowhere with a ha'penny quarterly allowance. Why, the last time he'd seen his cousin, at the ripe old age of fifteen, the young fop had been beggaring his addlepated father into an early grave.

Just before one of the longest days and nights of his life gave up the ghost, Luc wondered at the cursed absurdity of his last thoughts on this green earth being of his feckless relation instead of the winsome Rosamunde Baird in the throes of newfound passion. God certainly had more of the sense of the ridiculous than he had previously thought. Perhaps there was some hope for his tarnished soul after all.

The soft oblivion of helplessness enveloped him despite his desperate grab for more time.

He awoke, simmering in uncertainty and confusion. He had no idea if he had slept for several hours or a fortnight. The ill ease of not knowing exactly where he was prickled down his spine and he wished for a candle since he couldn't see a blasted thing in the pitch of night. With a curse he fumbled for the nightstand as he slid his feet to the side of the bed and attempted to stand. A dizzying wave reeled through his head and he sat back down quickly.

"Luc," a woman's hoarse voice whispered nearby.

He felt about with his hands. Nothing. "Rosamunde?" he croaked.

"Thank God," came her reverent whisper. He felt the side of the bed sag under her weight and a cool hand found his.

"How long have I been—"

"About two days."

"Ata . . ." he said suddenly, his heart pounding.

"Is much, much better," she finished. "I just left her. It's you we've been worried about. The doctor has been here several times. You keep shivering but have no fever."

"You've been with me all this time." It was a statement for he knew the answer. Another wave of dizziness swept through his frame and he sank deep into the bedcovers.

She touched his brow.

"I thought you said you were a wretched nurse."

"I am. My only other patient died."

Her miserable husband. He would have laughed if he had had the strength. Right now he felt rather like the fires of hell had left their mark on every inch of his hide. He groped for the glass of water that was always within reach on his bedside table.

"Here you go," she said softly.

His hands clutched at the glass and he drank long and deep, emptying it. "Light a candle, would you?" he asked and sighed.

A dark silence descended, the kind of stillness that claws at the brain. "Rosamunde?" Why wasn't she fumbling about, scratching at the tinderbox, illuminating the heavy veil of night?

A flutter of air fanned his face and he instinctively reached and grasped her wrist. "Rosamunde?" he asked more harshly.

"Luc, close your eyes. I'd forgotten." An edge of panic laced her fragmented speech. "The doctor. He said to wrap cloth about your head, that your eyes would be sensitive to light."

"You're lying. Light a candle."

"Luc, let me put this—"

A band of fabric touched his face and he pushed it away roughly. "*Don't you ever . . .* Light a candle, I say." He reached for his nightstand, glad to feel the familiar edges of the table in his room.

"But it's full day." Her voice cracked awkwardly. "There's no need."

Vicious, evil torment snaked through him and curdled his senses. A deep chill welled in the pit of his stomach. "I can't see a damn thing." And then the truth needled him as painfully as the burning on his hands and feet.

He was blind.

"Tell me—precisely," he ground out, "what the doctor told you. And if you've a notion to dissemble, think again."

She rushed on, "He doesn't know what this illness is. It seems to have affected everyone similarly but with a few variations."

"And?" he nearly shouted, the blood pounding in his head.

"And Ata is weak, but improving. She still has tingling in her hands. She said her teeth felt loose. No one has had a fever. It's definitely not the plague. The undercook is almost on her feet."

"And is anyone else *blind*?" he roared.

"No," she whispered so softly it almost sounded like a sigh.

"Damn you, Rosamunde. If I can't see, the least you could do is speak up."

"No," she said louder. "Although I haven't any reports from the neighbors who took ill. I'll send someone or ride out as soon as you say."

"Go." He turned his head away. "No, wait. Have Grace write a letter, and Brownie—is he still here?"

"Yes," she assured him.

Tell him to carry a letter to Dr. Davis at the Royal College of Physicians in town. Tell him to come. To . . ." He couldn't force another word from his lips. Thank

God Rosamunde didn't touch him, didn't try to comfort him. He might very well do bodily harm to anyone who would dare, except his bones felt like they had turned to jelly.

"I'm going. I promise Mr. Brown will find the doctor and I'll bring news from the neighbors myself." Her voice came from afar, her steps on the floorboards echoing behind.

The door shut and with it went any sanity he still possessed. He ground his fists into his eye sockets until shards of light should have appeared. Nothing.

Bloody nothing.

It had always been his greatest fear. The memories of his father's method of punishment had played on that terror. And now it all vividly filtered through his mind. His father, calling him a damned weakling, taking away his books, blindfolding him, forbidding him to remove the cloth for a full day. For two days the next time he was caught, and then three days the last time. He had begun to take heed when his father started burning the books each time he was caught spending more than an hour a day with his nose between the pages. And so he had learned.

He had learned to carry a pair of spurs or a light sword with him, always pretending to be on the hunt for his brother to ride or fence should his father come upon him. And he had learned all the blood sports from his brother for good measure, in exchange for writing Henry's papers at Eton.

He was paralyzed.

Fear rooted around in his brain and trickled down

cold to the base of his skull. The inability to see the words on a page, the inability to dip a quill in the black sap of civilization. It was the very thing that brought light to the world. There was nothing that could compare to reading or writing a combination of words that formed the perfect thought. He had brought the mountains and valleys of the world into his small yacht cabin or the tragedies of the kings of lost centuries into his study. And he could create them.

But now.

But now. . .

Now he was lost.

He would rather be—

A barely audible knock sounded at the door. It was too soon for her return.

"Go away," he shouted.

She rode like a gypsy, not bothering to put on a hat or a cloak. She had ordered saddled the largest, strongest animal in the stable, a stallion that had apparently bolted from his owner's paddock and had appeared yesterday at Amberley, trying to tear down one of the stall doors in an effort to get at the mare behind it. The horse's mood suited her perfectly.

The young stable hand's eyes bugged out as Rosamunde gathered her skirts and mounted astride, showing more leg than the boy had probably seen in his lifetime. The animal reared slightly, then broke into a dead run down the estate's wide tree-lined lane, which spilled into the main cart path toward the village. He skidded around the curve and bucked his displeasure, sending a spray of muddy gravel into the hedgerow.

She leaned forward as the massive shoulders of the animal collected beneath her to jump a largish puddle of water from the rains that had flooded the countryside for the past two days. It was the first time she'd been outside, and the crisp clean Cornish air filled her lungs, forcing out the bitter smells of the sickroom.

Each time her mind dared touch upon the man who lay helpless in the growing distance behind her, she spurred the horse forward.

God couldn't, wouldn't be so cruel.

Oh, but he could. *He would.*

She forced her mind to map out the fastest circuit to the village green and the three nearest neighboring estates who had reported the illness within their confines. The blurred edges of the whitewashed houses of the town came into her line of vision, and she pulled the horse back into a trot as she made her way to the smithy.

Within half an hour, Rosamunde had gone 'round to all the cottages occupied by the people who had attended the wedding. There was not a single report of blindness. For once in her life, she had held her head up high on her quest for answers despite the whispers plaguing her back at every encounter. She knew she should care. She always had in the past. But really, truly for once, she didn't care what these people thought of her.

Mrs. Murch and her sister, two village spinsters, had averted their eyes before one said to their only servant, "We don't know this person. Please have them leave."

The spineless creature had cringed when Rosamunde had shaken an answer about the illness from her.

And so it went. Rosamunde galloped between the far-flung estates, crossing the patchwork of fields filled with bare-armed laborers reassembling storm-tossed haycocks. The stallion's flanks became lathered while her own mouth became dry and her confidence shriveled as she became less and less sure there would be any positive news. She traveled over hills she knew from her girlhood, not seen for almost a decade, and she felt heavyhearted yet free, like the falcons soaring on an updraft over Kynance Cove.

And she felt like crying for the years she had wasted as a cowardly recluse, digging—constantly digging in her garden as if she could crawl away to the other side of the world to get away from the hurt of her father's abandonment and the horrid life she had made. And now just when she was making new memories and on the precipice of a different life for herself, she was forced to witness the new hellish cage of the very person who had freed her.

Tears coursed down her cheeks. She would not cry in his presence. She would not show an ounce of pity for him. Receiving sympathy was the most detestable feeling on earth. It carved chasms. She should know.

In a burst of courage, she grappled the reins and turned toward her first home. *Edgecumbe.* The home of her heart, her blood, her very spirit.

He would know what to do. "Father," she pushed the word into the wind rushing past her face. It was the word she had thought she would never be able to utter in his presence again. Today, she would taste it once more. "Father, help me," she moaned again while she nudged the horse beyond the ancient Celtic stones flanking the entrance to Edgecumbe.

She didn't care if he didn't love her anymore. She didn't care if he tried to refuse to see her. She didn't care if he humiliated her. But he would help her. She would make him help her. For him. *For Luc.*

The audacity of her action became very real when she jumped off the horse and faced a stable hand she didn't recognize. She handed him the reins and brushed her cheeks with the backs of her bare hands. She could only guess how hoydenish she must appear.

The normally imperturbable family butler, Mr. Shepherd, opened the door and Rosamunde's nerve faltered when she encountered his expression.

"Good day, Shepherd. Is my fa—my brother receiving?" Oh, she wasn't making any sense. No one would ever ask if their own brother was receiving. It sounded so very ridiculous.

"Which one?" he responded before quickly glancing behind him and rushing on. "Lady Rosamunde, may I be permitted to say how very glad I am to see you? Do come in." He grabbed her arm and nearly dragged her inside as if he was afraid she would run away. He began muttering as he always had in the past. "I told him . . . you must want tea . . . I'll return in a trice."

She was almost flung into the library. Truly, it was amazing old Mr. Shepherd had this kind of strength at his age. She took a deep breath and her sensibilities reeled from the scents of the past. Her father's pipe tobacco, the heather and sage eau de toilette, even the same slight tinge of lemon wax hung in the air. She very nearly gave in to her panic until she spied a young girl peeking at her from the crack in the doorway.

"And who might you be?"

The little girl widened her eyes but stood her ground. "You first."

Rosamunde stifled a nervous snort. "Rosamunde Baird."

"Oh my." The girl's eyes rounded even further. "You're her."

"You're *she*."

"What? I am not her."

"No. I mean you should have said 'she.' 'You're she.'"

The girl almost wailed. "I am not."

"No. Of course not," Rosamunde said, her stomach unclenching with the silly exchange.

"Wha'da ya want?" the chubby little nymph asked baldly.

God love children and all their brutal honesty. "My brother Phinn. Is he here?"

"Ohhh, Lord Barton, the handsomerest of them."

"The handsomest."

"That's wha' I said, silly."

Rosamunde pursed her lips to keep from laughing. "Is he here?"

"No."

Rosamunde's heart plummeted.

"I wouldn't be allowed to get into trouble upstairs, as me mam says, if Lord Barton weren't shooting grouse."

Her heart climbed back on its perch. She had to ask. "My father?"

"He's in Lon'on town with some of yer brothers. I wish I had a brother. Or maybe even a sister if she didn't take my doll."

"Yes, well, brothers can be a menace too. They have a penchant for drowning dolls. Take my word for—"

A tall figure rounded the doorway. *Phinn*. She drank in the sight of his laughing brown eyes and burnished gold hair that had darkened with age.

He looked at the little girl. "They only drown them when a sister melts their tin soldiers."

"Phinn," she breathed.

He squatted. "Emma, tell your mother"—he mouthed 'Cook' to her—"the lady who loves her poppyseed cakes more than anyone is here, and I'll bet she gives you some too."

The little girl disappeared and Phinn took two long strides and stood before her, looking at her.

They had always been the closest of all the siblings. Her father had said she was the male version of Phinn in reverse colors. Her black hair to his blond. Her pale blue green eyes to his brown. But they had the same heart, the same love of adventure, the same love for each other.

He grabbed her in his arms and she squeezed back her tears while basking in the comfort of his love. He smelled of plucked bird feathers and old leather, just like heaven.

"I've missed you," he whispered into her hair. "I don't think I knew how much until I saw you in church. I'm sorry I never tried to see you. I would've if I hadn't thought it might just kill Father."

She nodded her understanding. The back of her throat choked with emotion and she couldn't force any words past the constriction.

"Are you well?" he asked, refusing to let her leave his arms. "What's wrong?"

She swallowed hard. "I think you know I wouldn't have come unless I was desperate. It's Luc. Luc St. Aubyn. The duke," she stuttered. "He's been unwell, like the others who took ill after the wedding. Did the sickness spread here, too?"

"No. We were fortunate. But our neighbors weren't so luck—"

She interrupted. "Phinn, have you heard of any blindness?"

He paused to think. "Yes, maybe"—his hand tightened on hers—"What? Has he gone blind, then? The Duke of Helston?"

"You mustn't tell anyone. But, Phinn, I need your help. I've got to go back to him. I'm begging you to help me find anyone else who's been afflicted and find out if the blindness goes away."

Only someone with relentless determination matching her own would immediately agree without further questions. He steered her toward the French doors in the adjacent morning room. She gave him a questioning look.

"You don't really think I can take you out the front

door, do you? Why, I'm certain Shepherd is guarding the gates with his life. The old man actually *smiled* when he found me. Didn't even know the old grouch had any teeth left. He'd flay my hide if he knew I was letting you escape."

They sprinted across the wet grass and Phinn ordered fresh horses. They mounted and each turned from the raised block before Phinn promised to come to her by nightfall.

"Rosa," he said from his gray gelding, "You called him *Luc*."

He had never dared to question her eight years ago, and she was surprised he dared to question her now. She held up her chin. "And I call you Phinn."

He smiled broadly. "So you do." He patted the horse's neck to calm the animal. "You know one day, you're going to have to tell me what really happened. I never did—"

She interrupted. "And you never shall."

He was staring at the horizon, and his nod was almost imperceptible. "You're as hardheaded as Father, you know." He turned to her then, his warm whiskey-colored eyes trying to cover the pain of losing the sibling he loved most.

She looked away. "Please don't speak of it. I can't bear it. He shan't ever forgive me for going against his will. And I shan't forgive him for turning away from me. For making a mockery of all those years I thought he loved me."

"He's never stopped loving you, Rosa. He's just as stubborn as you are. And you never wanted forgiveness. You've certainly never made an attempt at reconciliation."

"Because Father would never meet me halfway, you blockhead."

"I've never known you not to try for something you wanted, Rosamunde. What has happened to you? You're not the strong-minded female I once knew."

"Or perhaps I've learned the futility of attempting the impossible. I'm not willing to fight for something I cannot win. A body can only stand so much rejection in one lifetime."

He snorted. "And yet you were willing to come here, to face him, to ask Father's help just now."

She tried to stare down her brother and failed. She looked away, flustered.

"You never were any good at hiding anything from me," he continued. "Does *he* love you?"

The very question had burned a path in her mind these last two days. "Why should I bore us both with an answer since you can read minds?"

He chuckled. "Poor man."

"Remind me why I like you."

"Because of my good looks and charm. And because of my humility, of course."

"You're about as modest as a prized peacock. And by the by, are you losing your hair?"

He sputtered. "I am *not* losing my hair. Why, I—"

"Got you," she shouted. And before he could muster a retort, she galloped down the drive, cutting across the vast lawn like the old days, Phinn blistering her back with a plethora of pithy names. It was wonderfully comforting.

There was no question he would scour the rest of the countryside for her. For that was what family did for one another. She had nearly forgotten the sense of security familial love brought. It made her throat ache with repressed emotion.

The sensation did not cease until five o'clock in the afternoon, when a note arrived from Phinn. She had kept herself busy organizing the household staff, who were trickling back into Amberley as threats of the plague proved false. And she had bathed, gone to the garden, and arranged flowers for Ata and Luc, anything to avoid his room before she had an answer.

Rosamunde picked up the vase for his room and rushed up the stairs while reading the note, nearly tripping the two footmen who were easing a copper hipbath from his room. She stumbled inside, only to find Grace reading aloud, sitting arched and elegant, a book in one hand, Luc's hand in her other. Rosamunde nearly dropped the vase.

Chapter 13

Forgiveness, n. A stratagem to throw an offender off his guard and catch him red-handed in his next offense.

—The Devil's Dictionary, A. Bierce

The beautiful widow paused in mid-sentence and searched her face. "Rosamunde, we have been waiting for you."

We. How she loathed the word. She had had no idea how exclusionary it was until this very moment. "Yes, well, I didn't want to intrude until I had something to relate."

Both of them turned and again she noticed how handsome they were together. His barely contained raw power and her petite prettiness. She swallowed.

"And?" they asked simultaneously.

"I've a note from my brother." She forced her eyes back to the paper. "He mentions Auggie Phelps's friend, Theodora Tandy, who apparently became blind and is recovering." She emphasized. "Her sight is improving."

"He has seen her? He knows this is certain?" His voice was hoarse with strain.

Rosamunde stared at Grace's staying hand on his chest. He was like a caged panther, trying to escape the confines of his comfortable prison.

Grace's calming voice floated in the air, "Wait, let her finish."

"He's on his way to see her himself. He says he'll send an express as soon as possible."

Luc sank into the pillows at his back. He was at least acting like the black devil he had been in the past. She glanced at his hands and noticed the redness had lessened.

Grace looked from Luc to Rosamunde with a pained expression and stood up before straightening his pillows. "If you don't mind, I think I'll look in on Ata and then rest."

He grasped toward Grace and she placed her hand in his. "Thank you," he said warmly.

"It was my pleasure," she murmured and then brushed by Rosamunde's skirts on her way out the door.

Rosamunde felt like a gawky scarecrow, all angles and elbows to Grace's petite soft curves and blonde curls. Oh, what was wrong with her? Was she to always fall in love with someone who favored another? This was everything ridiculous.

Grace Sheffey could give him an heir. In a sudden

rush she could see them hosting enormous, elegant garden parties and picnics, with two or three perfectly dressed children following a prim governess. Her cursed imagination even conjured up a small spaniel gamboling behind, biting at sticks that would be thrown and retrieved.

Rosamunde could only drive him to distraction. She could not deliver Ata's wish in swaddling clothing. She could not be the proper duchess of legendary popularity Ata would like.

Rosamunde would vastly prefer to walk the rocky beaches of Kenneggy and Praa Sands, or follow hounds on a scent, or climb mountains, swim lakes—anything but the tedium of hosting fashionable events and becoming a *tonnish* patroness. It was impossible. Why, no one would even come to any events with her name on the invitation.

And to make it thoroughly worse, she had had the audacity to beg him to make love to her. And he had taken pity on her and then condescended to do precisely what she asked. It had only made her realize all the more how much she had gone ahead and foolishly fallen in love with him. Now she would be forced to walk away from the only man who had ever shown her joy.

He flung his arm over his eyes.

"Can you see anything yet?" she whispered, her feet still glued just inside the doorway.

"No, not even a shadow. Come here," he commanded.

She crossed to his side, and placed the bouquet on the bedside table.

"What have you brought?" His nose twitched. "A funereal arrangement?"

"Come, there is hope," she urged. "Remember my brother's note. And you must show—"

"If you say 'patience,' I may have to kill you."

There was something about the horrid urge to laugh that was similar to the urge to cry uncontrollably. "No. I was about to say that you must show a bit more tolerance toward your visitors or they might think you want to kill them." His lips pursed in annoyance or humor, she dared not guess which one.

"Is there anything taciturn in that bouquet of yours?"

"No, the teasel wasn't in bloom. But," she wondered if she dared, "there's a bit of fumitory for spleen."

His lips twisted. "I suppose I deserved that. What else?"

"Laurel for perseverance—"

He interrupted, "Another deadly boring trait, except perhaps when facing privateers or the French."

"And gloxinia signifying a proud spirit." She dared not tell him the rest.

"And what is that familiar sweetness?"

"The tuberoses, perhaps?"

"And you chose those for . . ." His question hung in the air painfully.

"Um, for your pleasure."

"My pleasure? What in hell does that mean? What sort of pleasure?"

"Oh all right, *dangerous* pleasure."

"Ah, vastly more entertaining," he drawled.

She thanked the Lord the rare hothouse red tulip, which was a declaration of love, had no scent.

"Any more?"

She blanched. "I'll be forced to add hemlock and nightshade if you ask me any more questions."

"It's such a comfort to have you so near."

"I try," she replied archly.

"Rosamunde, you've never said why you love"—her heart lurched—"flowers so."

"Because they don't plague me with demands and questions, I suppose. And," she hesitated, "they're a gift of peace and beauty in a sometimes ugly world. They're a reminder of the possibility of rebirth each spring. And they can sometimes thrive in harsh conditions with little care."

He kept silent.

"Would you like me to read to you?" she asked. "Grace left the book here."

He pursed his lips. His blank immobile gaze toward the ceiling left her discomforted. She opened the book to the marked page and uttered a line or two of prose. He leaned over and fumbled before gripping her arm.

"No," he said harshly.

"I had thought you would like . . . Grace read to—"

"That was different," he interrupted her.

"I see," she said, not seeing at all. Or perhaps, she saw very well. A bubble of hurt arose within her.

"No, you don't see."

"No, I think I do," she countered.

"Look, Rosamunde, I won't have your pity. No, don't say a word. I can hear your sympathy in every syllable."

"That's absurd," she raised her voice. "I of all people do not pity you. It's just the reverse. Don't you think I see and hear it? 'Poor Rosamunde, she only has her flowers, she only has her sister, and a ghastly dead husband who left her without a farthing and a father who refuses to acknowledge her. Oh, and yes, she even had to beg me to touch her.'" She stopped and felt lightheaded. There, she had said it. Everything that should not be said.

"Beg me again," he said so quietly she wondered if she had imagined it.

"What?"

"You heard me." He turned away.

"But I—"

"For Christ sakes, Rosamunde, I can't ask you to give yourself to me."

"Can't or won't?"

"Both. Either. Whichever it takes to get you to climb into this bed." He ground both fists into his eye sockets. "God, I can't stand this."

He was begging her—imploring her to help him forget the bleak helplessness he felt, if only for a moment. He, the man who had probably never begged anyone to do anything in his life. And there was nothing she could say that would make him understand that she would take more comfort from his arms than he ever would from hers.

A plume of longing curled through her breast. He

was giving her the chance for one last taste of heaven before she would have to leave.

She had the presence of mind to cross the room and lock the door.

"Rosamunde?" His arm rested over his eyes again.

"I'm still here."

She removed her gown and stays, then hesitated before removing her stockings and even her shift. She would never have been so brazen if he had been able to see her. She shivered in the cool, still air. "Shall I help you?"

He growled. "I can manage."

She watched with unabashed curiosity as he yanked the nightshirt over his head, still damp from his bath. She hadn't had the nerve to look at his naked form when they had been in his boat cabin. She had had to clamp her eyes closed through most of it to gain courage. But now, oh now, she could drink in the beauty of his physique without fear or embarrassment.

He was simply the most starkly beautiful man she had ever seen. And he wanted her. She could die from the tension and exquisite feelings coursing through her.

Her eyes drank their fill of the breadth of his impossibly wide shoulders and the corded muscles along his rib cage and below. Her eyes widened at the narrow trail of dark hair that led to his groin still hidden under the covers. She stared until apprehension seemed to swirl around them both like the static before a storm.

She held her breath and slipped beneath the layers of soft bed coverings, his body suffusing the sheets with delicious warmth.

He lay back, his head and chest propped up by large pillows. His pure blue eyes stared beyond her shoulder, unseeing.

The expanse of his bronzed chest fascinated her. She dared to shyly raise her finger to trace the scar that slashed from his shoulder to his waist.

He exhaled sharply and grasped her wrist.

"No," she said. "Let me touch you, as you touched me."

He released her arm and shuddered as the pads of her fingers brushed his skin and encountered one of his perfectly symmetrical crests. When it contracted slightly under her touch, she felt her own constrict to tight points. Mesmerized, she leaned in and tentatively swirled the sensitive place with the tip of her tongue.

"Oh God," he choked out an exhalation.

Emboldened by his response, she instinctively nibbled on the tiny nub and tweaked the other with her fingers.

His hands flew to her hair and dislodged half the hairpins as he ran his fingers through her locks.

"Come here," he rumbled and hooked his hands under her arms to pull her to his lips, stopping short of kissing her. He seemed to understand that she wanted—needed—to take her time.

In the shadows of the approaching gloaming hour, she stared at the firm contours of his full lips, which were every female's dream and every father and husband's nightmare. She shifted and brushed her mouth against his with gossamer-light kisses endlessly, until he groaned and took full possession of her mouth. She shyly opened at the touch of his tongue against the seam of her lips. Pure heat swept through every pore of her body as he deepened the kiss and she felt herself drugged by the raw, protective power of him.

Tremors of desire licked her insides as his broad arms gripped her frame fiercely to his chest. She pushed away breathlessly. "Wait," she implored.

"What is it?" he murmured in her ear.

"Let me touch you . . ."

"And?" he whispered. "I sense an 'and.'"

"*And* . . . look at you," she choked out, embarrassed beyond measure.

His hands stilled and the pupils of his eyes dilated, making the irises almost disappear into the dark mystery of his being.

His large hand swallowed her wrist in his grasp and he slowly moved her fingers to the corner of the covers that were bunched around them. In heartbreaking tension, she drew down the sheets, exposing his hard sculpted physique to her curious eyes.

She froze.

She'd never had the opportunity or courage to actually look at this part of any man. Her breathing quickened and he blindly grasped the sheet to recover himself.

"No," she blurted out, pushing his hand aside.

"Rosamunde," he said harshly, "now you are frightened again."

"I'm not," she whispered. She tentatively touched him, and felt him pulse and surge forward, now no longer resting on his muscled thigh. He felt rather like an iron bar covered with satin and as she traced the length of him, he groaned and his hands flexed, then tightly fisted.

"Am I hurting you?" she asked, her mouth dry.

"No, but you're killing me."

A rush of delight bolstered her courage and she joined her palms together to span his width and caress him before coming to a rest when he gasped and stayed her hands.

His breath was labored and she could see a faint sheen on his brow. She streamed a light path of kisses down his chest using the faint trail of hair as a guide. He smelled of soap and the achingly familiar cologne that she had come to know as his signature. She stared hard at the length of blatant masculinity before her and wondered if he would like her to . . .

"Should I—" she whispered very quietly.

"Only if you like," he gritted out.

What she would like to do was kiss every inch of this man who had shown her the beauty in what had always been an act of degradation. The man who had made her truly understand longing and love and almost forgiveness for everything in her past that had gone wrong. If she had to endure the last eight years to arrive at this moment in time with him, then it had been worth it.

She kissed the tip and then paused, unsure. He grasped her shoulders and pulled her up. "I don't know what I was thinking," he said in a strangled voice. "This is madness."

His chest rose up and he moved to cover her before he paused. His large hands spanned her waist and lifted her to straddle his great hulk before she could utter a word.

His hands were everywhere then, stroking her hair, her shoulders, her breasts, until he reached her most intimate place of all and she trembled with longing. A surge of dampness rushed between her limbs and she felt anew her embarrassment.

But he seemed so happy. For the first time since the illness had descended, his lips were curled at the edges.

His voice rumbled with pleasure, and his hands moved to grasp her hips firmly to raise her in a position above him. She watched with nearly unbearable yearning as he teased her until she was sure she would die from the pleasure. She wanted him so badly.

"Easy," he ground out as she attempted to take him inside of her.

She felt so hesitant and inexperienced.

"Relax your muscles," he murmured, his hands easing her up and down just the slightest bit. "That's it. Now just a little more."

For long moments he touched her, guided her knees to open wider, encouraged her to take more of him inside her, and all the while the heat of their passion whirled around them, cocooning them together in the silken strands of pleasure as he patiently helped her.

He must have sensed her growing frustration, for all at once he held her tight and rolled to switch positions. His weight sunk into her, heightening the sensations to overwhelming proportions. His hands hooked her knees, opening her wider still as he plunged into her in one thick, heavy slide, surging deeper and deeper until he was fully seated within her. And finally her body tightened, and in that pulsing, exquisite second she let go of the edge and fell helplessly into a molten spiral of release as a bolt of liquid pleasure shot from his body into hers. She heard him gasp, "Rosamunde. Oh Rosamunde."

He collapsed on her and she reveled in the immense weight of him. Caressing his long black hair, still infused with dampness from his bath, she turned her face to kiss his jaw. She tried to memorize the feel of him against her, the scent of him, the very essence of this man who made her heart nearly burst with longing.

He rose to his elbows and his eyes were filled with sightless emotion. It took nearly every ounce of self-discipline not to whisper her great love for him. For there was not a shadow of doubt that he would construe it as pity or worse. And so she remained silent.

And so did he.

It was better that way.

He moved his mouth to speak, but she forced herself to turn the moment in the most painful way she could imagine. "Why are you known as Lord Fire and Ice?" she whispered, her heart breaking.

"Rosamunde . . ." He rubbed his temple.

She continued doggedly, "It's something I've overheard several times since the day I first met you."

He pulled her into his embrace and kissed her until her toes curled from the heat and power of his need.

"Don't change the subject. I wish to tell you some—"

She interrupted. "Is it because of the way you make a woman feel or the way you fought while commissioned in the Royal Navy?" She strained to blather on when she saw his troubled expression. "You never speak of the battles you fought. How, for example, did you receive this impressive scar?" She tried to inch away from beneath him with little success.

He remained blessedly silent for long moments. "I'll answer your questions, but then you shall answer my own."

She swallowed and murmured her assent. "Your scar?" she prompted him.

"God knows why women find scars romantic. I assure you there is nothing good about being sliced like a ham."

"It's a badge of courage," she answered. "So how did you get this one?"

He paused. "Would you like the story I usually tell, or the truth?"

"Oh, both. Definitely both."

"You would. Let's see. The one with valor first, I think. It was during the battle of Trafalgar. I dispatched twenty-seven French soldiers aboard the *Redoutable* before being cut down by the captain."

"Oh, very good. Perhaps a *bit* overdone, but women love heroes, even braggarts."

"Yes, well," he said dryly, "I found that version reeled them in quite well."

"That explains the Lord Fire part, but not the Ice," she said. "And the truth?"

"That was the truth. Except the scratch I received courtesy of *Capitaine* Jean Lucas is here." He touched the scar on the back of his neck. "That particular frog was the best in the French navy, I always thought."

She examined the scar and he continued when she didn't answer. "Now this other scar you admire so much was given to me by my dear brother. He was teaching me how to fence but lost his sword's leather button during the exercise. I did learn an important truth that day."

"Yes?"

"When fencing you should remember the lie your parents tell you at Christmas. . ." He captured her face between his beautiful strong hands and kissed her gently. "It's always better to give than to receive."

She shook her head and laughed.

"Although," he said, "at a time like this, there is something to be said about the joy of receiving."

She felt a surge of hardness within her.

She squeezed her eyes shut. She wasn't sure she could do this again. Each time he spoke to her, touched her, she fell deeper in love with him. She couldn't bear the agony of maintaining a façade of lightheartedness when what she really wanted to do was give him her heart and receive his in return. But her conscience forbade it.

Ata was right. He needed a wife. A wife who would give him an heir. A quiet, elegant wife admired and respected by all the peers of the realm. In short, the perfect duchess. Certainly not a barren widow past the first blush of youth with a hideously blemished reputation. A woman not received in any respectable drawing room.

Rosamunde was about as far removed from qualities of a suitable duchess as she could imagine.

"Rosamunde," he whispered, "let me love you."

She almost cried out with agony. She wasn't strong enough to resist this.

"Please . . ." he said when she didn't move.

As she wrapped her arms about his shoulders, accepting the inevitable pleasure and pain that was to follow, she was at least grateful he wouldn't be able to see the tears already threatening to spill onto her hot cheeks.

With his kiss, her heart splintered into a desperate maelstrom of unspoken dreams that would never be fulfilled.

Luc kissed her, pouring all his undeclared feelings into his embrace. He knew with crystal clarity that he was taking her in fear now. *His own.*

His sight gone, his other senses drowned in Rosamunde's essence. Her unique sweet scents, the softness of her sleek skin, the crooning of her low whispers. It was unbearably intoxicating. He couldn't get enough of her. And now he knew he never would.

Despite the curse of blindness it seemed momentarily a blessing, for he suddenly realized, sight or no sight, he had been living in darkness. Only when he was with her did he experience . . . light.

But she didn't want his declarations, didn't want him to tie up her emotions with his own. In short, she didn't want him. And he knew why. Yet, she was too good to refuse him because of this illness and blindness.

He had thought she might regain her courageous former spirit and let the repressed horrors dissolve, leaving her open to the possibility of love and marriage once again. But it was obvious she could never come to trust another man. And how could he, blind and with a ruthless temper, hope to bring lasting happiness to any woman? He hadn't even been able to give his beloved mother the only thing she had ever asked for in desperation. And wasn't he disregarding his grandmother's sickbed wish?

He could not be counted on. *By anyone*.

Rosamunde's arms brought him closer to her and he felt the moment when she gave herself up to him again. This would have to be the last time. The very last time he would allow himself the illusion of a happy future with her.

He pressed a kiss on her forehead and slowly thrust into her, expertly prolonging the sensations with every stroke. He knew how to bring her to the agonizing pinnacle and he thought at the darkest moment of his longing for her that he might just sweep her there and leave her hanging repeatedly, until he would force her to listen to his avowals and drag out a promise to stay with him.

If he thought he had hated himself in the past, he was wrong. He now knew there was the potential for a new low in self-loathing.

In the unseen twilight hours he almost succumbed

to his sinful object, forcing them both to mind-numbing heights of desire and passion until she was mute with fulfillment. He breathed her name. "Rosamunde, I—" He was on the verge of spilling himself and his declarations all over her soft body when he felt a single tear splash onto his cheek.

It sizzled through all the taut layers of his face and lodged itself next to his self-respect. In the end he could not force her to love a blackhearted devil. Her tears were proof of her sadness and regret. In agony he released his seed and his dreams into her barren body. He closed his lips, closed his heart, and opened his eyes only to notice . . . *an elusive shadow.*

Chapter 14

Quill, n. *An implement of torture yielded by a goose and commonly wielded by an ass.*

— The Devil's Dictionary, A. Bierce

The almost imperceptible scent of parchment and India ink met his senses as Luc awoke sprawled over his massive desk in his lair. He rubbed his hands over his whiskered face and stretched back. He felt like hell. But it was a good sort of feeling. There was nothing like accomplishing something, anything after inactivity. And work was also balm for a wounded heart.

The lure of his writing and books had been too much to resist last night after Rosamunde had left his chamber in a rush to find the doctor down the hall. Even though he knew she had left to get the doctor, it had also felt as if she was running away from him. And the pain had been vicious.

The doctor had echoed the cautious advice Rosamunde's brother had offered in an express received earlier. It seemed Miss Tandy had recovered her sight three days after becoming afflicted. All doctors advised bed rest. Little did they know that he would have showered them with gold guineas if just once they would exclaim, "Yes, Your Grace, carry on, exhaust yourself. That's the answer!" He almost chuckled to himself.

He had always recuperated much faster than any physician advised, and no one was going to keep him away from the page now that he had regained his strength and the beginnings of his sight. Especially if he had a chance of meeting the deadline Mr. Murray had suggested. And he could still do it. With every passing hour the darkness receded and he could focus better, although his handwriting, never precise to begin with, now suffered from his blurred vision. He doubted many could read such chicken scratch.

He had already finished the chapter headings and the first seventeen chapters. Now he was at the climax, when Nelson, mortally wounded, uttered the words every midshipman knew by heart: "Thank God I have done my duty."

He looked down at the heavy black scrawl and shook his head. That draught he had accepted from Ata to stop her coddling last night had been laced with something that fogged the mind. He screwed his eyes shut and rubbed his face.

He looked up to see the devil's handmaiden herself, Ata, open his door without warning. And Rosamunde, looking embarrassed and flustered, appeared behind her, carrying a tray. His heart constricted at the sight of her. He felt the same rush of joy and longing he experienced last eve when she was the first thing he saw . . . He had almost forgotten, taken for granted, the beauty of her ethereal eyes and the milky translucence of her skin against her lush black hair. She was quite simply an angel.

He clenched his jaws and hoped he wasn't going to make a fool of himself like every other lovesick idiot. He would get over this. He would have done with it.

Luc glanced at Ata. "If you are daring to bring me more of that vile concoction from last night, I shall pinch your secret reserve of Armagnac. Oh, what? You thought I wouldn't find it?"

"Well!" Ata huffed and looked toward Rosamunde. "This is the thanks one gets for bringing him tea."

He always knew he was in for it when Ata began to pretend he wasn't in her presence.

"Ata . . ."

She addressed Rosamunde. "I suppose he doesn't even want to know about the awful visit by that revolting . . . well, by your cousin Mr. Baird."

"Ata, tell me right—"

"Or the things I said to the toad. Or how I have ordered the servants to prepare for our removal to London. Or how the doctor from town is certain it was the salted fish or the ham that made everyone so ill . . ."

He stopped listening to all the things he wasn't supposed to want to know when Ata drew nearer. Perhaps it was the clear morning light, or perhaps his vision had improved dramatically. Whatever it was, he was left reeling from the sight of his grandmother's face.

She had aged almost overnight.

With his perfect streak of ill fortune, he was given back his sight only to see his dearest relation look more haggard and closer to the grave than ever before.

"I'm so sorry, Ata," he said gruffly. "Are you feeling better?"

That stopped her.

"Well, this is a first. What, pray tell, is going on now? You've never, ever seen fit to apologize before. I'll have the reason now, if you please. And even if you don't, please."

"Forget I said a word," he said dryly.

"Dukes," said Ata with a huff. "Can't count on any degree of correct manners from them, or any sort of refined deference."

"You should know," said Luc.

"Well!" she said much annoyed. "Luc, we have a serious problem. Enough of this tittle-tattle. I have my ideas but I need your help in convincing Rosamunde."

"Yes?"

"That nasty Algernon Baird came 'round, or rather paraded into our house with six other neighboring lummoxes."

"To what did we owe the pleasure of the lummoxes' calls?"

"Well, they suggested that . . ." Ata cleared her throat. "They suggested that . . ."

"I'm a *whore* twice over," Rosamunde said quietly, not quite meeting his eyes. The light had left her expression, leaving her vacant and disengaged.

Luc's head snapped up. "What? The bloody fool used that word here?"

Ata was so distraught she didn't bother to chide him on his language.

"Why wasn't I summoned?"

"You were, Luc," Ata said. "But the footman returned and said you weren't in your bedchamber."

"You, of course, told Baird to take his sorry—"

"Luc, you were seen escorting Rosamunde onboard *Caro's Heart* with nary a single female accompanying her."

"And don't forget," Rosamunde said with a smile that did not cover the pain in her eyes, "my dramatic return many hours later. Why, three of the witnesses in the port were delighted to describe the colored stripes of the blanket I wore. Of course I did have to correct them on the background. Cream, not white."

She appeared on the edge of shock.

Was her shame by the hands of the St. Aubyns ever to end?

"And the purpose of the visit?" he asked. His low voice belied the seething rage he felt to his core.

"To inform that everyone has been warned of my indecent actions. That while some had truly hoped I had reformed my character given my long seclusion after my marriage, that it was now obvious I was nothing more than a—a . . . well, they fear my seductive wiles could contaminate the God-fearing people of Cornwall. They asked me to leave the parish."

"The hell you will," he shouted. He stared at the devil-headed ink blotter in his hand and it was all he could do not to hurl it into the cold grate behind him.

In the silence, the sound of the brass clock's tick echoed loudly.

"You shall marry me. Then let them dare to say a single pious thing."

"What?" Rosamunde said. Or was it Ata? Luc looked up from the ink blotter at the pair of them. For a moment, he saw hollow despair in Ata's eyes before she covered her face with a blank mask.

Rosamunde whispered, "I'm so sorry." She cleared her throat. "I appreciate the honor you do me by your suggestion, but I am certain you understand I could never, ever accede to your suggestion." She walked to stand beside his desk. "You and Her Grace have been so kind to me, and I would never repay your generosity and compassion by doing something so foolish. I have lived with—well, I am used to living in the shadows of society, and I don't mind it. I actually prefer it if you must know. I. . ." She paused and turned to address Ata in a rush. "I would be very much obliged if you would help me find a position as a lady's companion. I am, or soon will be, too notorious to find employment here or in London, but perhaps I could find something in Scotland or in Europe. I do speak French and Italian adequately."

Ata sighed and settled into one of the huge leather armchairs that dwarfed her. "I'm certain I can help you, my dear. But Luc, you must make her see reason. Tell her about the town houses and cottages I inherited. I've decided I want Rosamunde, her sister, and

Sarah Winters to take possession of one of them. You did say I had one in Wales, right?"

He became queasy.

Ata continued on without waiting for an answer, blissfully unaware of the financial anxiety that churned in his belly each time she graciously offered up one of her so-called *inherited* cottages. But then it was his fault he was in this conundrum, as Brownie was happy to point out to him on every occasion.

Rosamunde interrupted. "Ata, I'm humbled by your generosity, but honestly, every fiber of my being forbids it. Your family owes me nothing. It pains me to even ask your help in finding a position. But I couldn't live an idle life, accepting the sort of generosity you are suggesting. It is too much."

"Luc," Ata begged, "you must talk to her. I can understand if she won't allow you to marry her, but I refuse to permit her to languish under the thumb of some demanding mistress."

"Yes, I've found all your friends to be demanding, screeching spinsters, if you must know."

"Luc," Ata almost moaned in annoyance. "You must take this seriously."

Silence filled the room. It was hard to force his mouth open. He was hurt by Rosamunde's prompt rejection of his suit although he would crawl in a pit of vipers before admitting to it. Oh, he knew she would not agree, but it wounded him nonetheless that she hadn't even looked the tiniest bit tempted. He pushed back any remnant of pain from his voice. "I do think we are forgetting the obvious."

They both stared at him.

"Rosamunde has every quality needed to recapture the heart of the *ton*. She is the daughter of an earl, for Christ sake. True, her reputation must be mended. But if a duke and a duchess cannot accomplish that, whoever else can? And after, she will be befriended by ladies because of her kind heart, and"—he felt his hands ball into fists—"gentlemen will be taken by her wit and vitality. She will be an Incomparable. No red- or blue-blooded Englishman will be able to take his . . ." He stopped and cursed softly under his breath. "Rosamunde, I can assure that you will have several options before you, not including servitude to an ancient crone." The question was whether or not he would strangle any man who came within an inch of her. He would purchase a whole damn block of town houses for her before he would allow another man to . . .

"I think you are both being overly kind and optimistic," Rosamunde said softly.

Ata cupped her face with one small hand. "No, my dear. You must allow us to help you."

"Ata is correct. We should leave for town at once. We were to go after my sister's wedding, in any case. It was only this illness that forced a change in plans."

Ata took over the conversation. "The other widows are waiting for us in Portman Square. Georgiana, Elizabeth, and Sarah are very anxious to see us. And—"

"And Rosamunde must brazen this out," Luc interrupted. "She has the manner, figure, and face to do it. And she's a widow. These backcountry yokels breathing fire and brimstone have no notion how most widows carry on in town."

"Well, you would know," grumbled Ata. "But Luc is right, my dear. This is the very reason I began the Widows Club. Each season for the last two years I've been very successful in finding lasting happiness for the ladies I've chosen to help. Most remarry. The few who do not reside in the country cottages or London town houses I inherited from my cousin, the Earl of Carmady."

Ata rose from her chair and forced Rosamunde to take her good hand and sit with her on a small loveseat in the corner of the room before continuing. "But it makes me furious these people are assuming anything happened a'tall." She turned to Luc. "I told them Mr. Brown is a pillar of propriety. And they saw him board the ship with her. I told them they were a pack of sinful gossips."

Luc didn't dare encounter Rosamunde's expression. He prayed she would not utter a word.

"Ata," Rosamunde said quietly, "I am begging you not to force me to do this. I have no desire to go to London, no desire to have the St. Aubyn family once again mired in my scandal. And I cannot accept anything from you other than your help in securing a position. In short, I want to leave Cornwall and find a new place to live, far from everything and everyone that I have ever known."

"My dear," Ata continued, "as I said to you in my letter inviting you to join the Widows Club, you mustn't let pride stand in your way."

"I'm not. I'm asking for your help. And I hate to do even that. But I will not be able to find a position without it. You are my last hope. But I cannot . . . cannot possibly accept anything else. Nor can I go to London."

Luc hoped his gamble would pay off. "Rosamunde, you have two choices, you will come to London and allow us to try and restore your standing, until we have found an appropriate, happy future for you, or you will immediately accept some obscure cottage my grandmother has offered you, where you will live in isolation and we will assume your living expenses for the duration of your life. This would of course be the coward's way out. But we will not hear any more nonsense about you working as a slave to some haranguing old nag like my dear grandmother."

"Luc!" Ata and Rosamunde shrieked simultaneously.

A knock sounded at the door and Luc thanked some distant lucky star. "Come," he commanded.

"Your Grace," a footman said, pretending he hadn't heard the shouting behind the door, "A note from the vicarage. Said it was to be delivered to you immediately."

Luc accepted the missive and scanned the contents. Hmmm, a letter from Charity Clarendon. *What the devil?* He pushed back his chair abruptly.

"Ladies, I think enough has been said." He looked pointedly at Rosamunde. "You're too practical to behave like some gothic heroine and run off. We've time to form a methodical assault on the *ton* on the way to town. We'll leave at first light." He strode off leaving his heart but not his pride behind him. He had never thought he would have the nerve to offer marriage to anyone. Worse, he had never thought to be refused. He wasn't sure if he was more hurt or insulted. He was furious he wasn't relieved.

Leaning against the warm leather squabs of the closed carriage a short while later, Luc pushed away thoughts of what had just transpired. And failed.

She had done him a favor. Who would have thought he could be so magnanimous in the cold, clear light of morning. Weren't proposals of marriage typically rendered in the solitary splendor of the black of night? Well, certainly not in front of one's grandmother.

Thank God she had refused him. The look on Ata's face when he had suggested marrying her had been enough to break an ogre's heart. It wasn't until that moment and listening to her premature deathbed plea that Luc realized how much his grandmother wanted an heir from him. How was he going to ever explain to her that he would never be able to give her one? He held his temple in his hand. He was going to disappoint Ata. It was quite fitting, actually. Rosamunde would be allowed to disappoint him as penance.

He would be damned if he would take a wife as a broodmare. He'd seen enough of that in his lifetime to know how disastrous that could be.

He steepled his fingers and looked beyond the smudged windows of the closed carriage. A figure was walking along the lane. He rapped the lacquered roof with a walking stick and the cabriolet lurched to a stop. Without waiting for the steps to be let down, he wrenched open the door and leapt to the ground.

"Lady Sylvia," he called out.

She stopped in her tracks and dropped her bag. Lady Sylvia almost crumpled before him.

Luc rushed to her side and half carried her to the carriage, motioning away one of the drivers. He tossed in her bag and lifted her inside before commanding his man to take the longer route on the return to Amberley. *Propriety be damned.*

Seating himself opposite her, he took a good look at her. It was remarkable, really. At first glance, Lady Sylvia appeared extraordinarily like her sister, with the same raven hair, same profile and height. Well, she was a tad more delicate-looking with that air of restrained refinement about her. She was the sort that inspired a protective instinct in men to shield her from the ugliness of life.

But her eyes were very different from her sister's. Those sad, doelike brown eyes held none of the sparkle or intensity of Rosamunde's. A man could melt in Lady Sylvia's elegant eyes if he was a proper, poetry-loving Englishman. To a coldhearted demon, she only inspired pity tinged with exasperation.

"I received the note from Miss Clarendon."

She nodded, her head bowed.

He really didn't want to hear a single syllable about whatever had occurred. He was up to his teeth in female problems. Perhaps there had been a reason he chose to lose himself in the Royal Navy, where cannons and cutlasses solved almost every problem quite easily. But then hadn't he always tried to turn away from the messy problems females seemed to inspire? He sighed and felt the bone-deep guilt of his mother wash over him.

"Perhaps you would like to tell me about it?"

She looked toward the window and he could see a flood of tears delicately balancing on her lower lid. "I'm sorry, Your Grace, that you had to bother yourself. But I'm very happy to see you are much improved."

Silence. Not another blasted word. Lord, he was going to have to force her. "I am guessing you had a row with Charity, or was it with Rawleigh? Why he ever thought he could dress like a vicar and parade about like an angel is beyond me. He has a countenance that might look cherubic, but I assure you he is as sinful as the rest of us. He's not to be taken seriously."

She swallowed and finally faced him. "You're wrong. He is the perfect man for the clergy. He's very attentive and forgiving—"

"Well, he'd better be forgiving, knowing how often he has sinned," he interrupted. "And I'm certain this is his fault. Why—"

"No. You are not to say a word against him."

And then of course, the dam broke and tears spilled down her cheeks and Luc kicked himself.

"It's my fault. All of it. But no one ever blames . . ." her voice trailed off.

"Just because you refused Rawleigh . . . That's what this is about, is it not?"

She nodded almost imperceptibly to his query. "Well it's his fault then. He obviously didn't go about it in the proper manner. Knowing Rawleigh, he probably botched the entire affair, telling you about how little he could offer, and how hard your life as the wife of a parish vicar would be, and how little he could give you, and how you'd never have pretty bonnets or seasons in town and the like. I hope you threw a slipper at him and told him to take his sorry, er, face from your sight." He had no idea what inane things he was offering up. It was all said to give her time to try and stop crying, collect herself, and maybe even laugh. But it wasn't working.

She was still soaking her scrap of a handkerchief and Luc didn't want to have to give up his own. It was the last one he possessed. It was amazing the number of handkerchiefs one could lose track of when surrounded by a gaggle of widows.

With a sigh, he offered his last square of linen. "Come, come, my dear. No one is worth this."

"You're quite wrong. Sir Rawleigh is everything good and kind."

Females. He would never understand them. "Well, if that's the case, why won't you have him?"

Sylvia stared at him. "It wouldn't do for me to marry him. Please don't argue the point as he did. You will never understand how ostracized my sister and I have been for almost a decade. You've only known us a few weeks. People have acknowledged us while we've stayed with you and your grandmother, if only because they think we've managed to ingratiate ourselves under your roof. But now . . . now, with this new scandal . . ." There was a question in her eyes.

"Yes, yes, I know all about that nonsense," he said quickly.

"Well, we cannot stay here."

He ignored her. "You aren't actually going to be that noble, are you? Rawleigh could give a hoot about scandal. Why, in a fortnight something new will take its place. We're removing to London, but you would do better to stay here and marry Rawleigh, since it's painfully obvious to everyone that you love each other given these overblown ideas you've both conceived. No," he held up a hand, "don't defend him. I've seen the calf's eyes he makes at you. And by the by, he's never made such a sap of himself before. So he does love you, if you were in any doubt. My dear, don't play the martyr. That went out of style during the Crusades."

Luc noticed they were rounding the last turn to Amberley's lane, canopied with high arching branches of majestic oaks, and inwardly cursed the efficacy of his driver.

Lady Sylvia looked at him with haunted eyes. "Please Your Grace," she gulped, "don't force me to accept him. I cannot." She resolutely looked away as the footman opened the carriage door.

And Luc had always thought men to be the more obstinate sex. Clearly the Earl of Twenlyne's daughters had invented the word.

Chapter 15

Witch, n. 1. An ugly and repulsive old woman, in a wicked league with the devil. 2. A beautiful and attractive young woman, in wickedness a league beyond the devil.

—The Devil's Dictionary, A. Bierce

London, Helston House

Luc took pleasure in trimming this particular quill for the last time. He had begun writing the book in Helston House library with this quill and he would end the draft with this one. There had been many others in between. Sprawled before his desk in town, he dipped the translucent goose-feather nib into the crystal inkwell and wrote, *Finis*. Certainly "The End" was the most beautiful sentiment, in Latin or English.

Then he paused and added one last quote: "War, n. A crimson arena painted by the best and worst of mankind." He shuffled the leaves of paper and allowed himself to ponder the dilemma for which he had only himself to blame. What was he—

A knock sounded.

"Come," he growled and pulled at his fob to glance at his pocket watch. Damn, most of the day was gone. "Yes?"

"Your Grace, the landau has been ordered from the mews. Her Grace asked me to inform you that . . ."

"Well, out with it."

The face of the Helston House footman turned a deep burgundy, rather like the Chateau de La Chaize wine Luc had gotten for a bargain from his favorite importer, er, smuggler.

"She said that if you leave her waiting for longer than a quarter hour she will take the ribbons herself."

He pursed his lips to smother a smile. "You may inform Her Grace that I shall be there shortly. And by the by, Toby, you may remind Her Grace that we are down to the last acceptable carriage, due to the last time she decided to take the reins."

Toby had a hard time keeping a straight face. "Yes, Your Grace." He bowed and shut the door quietly.

Luc flexed his ink-stained fingers and examined his hands. In the past fortnight, the tingling sensation had lessened as had his grandmother's symptoms. His sight had improved steadily, thank God, with only a slight problem focusing when he was tired.

Luc steepled his fingers and closed his eyes in thought. Even work couldn't erase her from his thoughts. He had tried to steer clear of her at every op-

portunity to avoid pain, but had redoubled his efforts
to ease her back into society. The tension of knowing
she was under his roof sleeping in a bedchamber not
fifty yards from his own was killing him. He must help
her regain her footing in the polite world and then settle her with her sister and the eldest widow of the club
in a pied-à-terre.

So far his idea of Rosamunde brazening it out in
town had met with little success. And Luc hated to be
proven wrong. It seemed the *ton* had changed their
feathers. He had always known most peers of the
realm to cold-shoulder minor infractions within their
ranks with a holier-than-thou attitude. But being human, the members of the *beau monde* had never been
able to ignore the fascination of the more notorious
characters.

And that is what he had counted on. And what had
failed. *So far*.

Oh, as soon as the Duke and Dowager Duchess of
Helston had put up their knocker on Number Twelve
Portman Square in Mayfair, the invitations had arrived
in stacks that would have made a wallflower weep
with envy.

All the cream vellum cards were "charmed to include the Mesdames Wilde, Ashburton, Sheffield, and
Winters" for a dizzying array of balls, dinners, musi-
cals, private theatricals, and routs. Three quarters of
the more daring mentioned Lady Sylvia. But not one
invitation included the name "Mrs. Alfred Baird."

The Upper Ten Thousand had pronounced judgment. Silently and lethally.

Rosamunde didn't know. Ata had simply refused every invitation. With any luck Rosamunde, having never been to London or experienced the whirl of a season, would never learn the truth.

However, he would have to force the issue. And there was only one person who could help him. The Countess of Sheffield. Luc hated to ask her. Hated to ask a woman who was charming and engaging and who had been besotted with him since the day he had first met her, at the age of ten.

Grace Sheffey's grandmother had shared a bed-chamber with Ata when they had been allowed a year or three at Miss Dilford's School for Young Ladies more than a half century ago. Luc was certain the two old birds had cooked up an eventual joining of their families in that nursery for ninnies. It was just very un-fortunate it was going to fall to Luc to have to break the two grannies' hearts.

After his brother had died, Ata had turned to him, as her last remaining relative save for Madeleine. He had ignored Ata's obvious desire for so long that it had become second nature, although to be truthful, he had probably assuaged his guilt by attending to every need of the Widows Club and then some.

He foresaw disaster on so many fronts by asking Grace to help the lady he loved in secret, but there was nothing to be done. He would do whatever it took to effectuate Rosamunde's reentry into society, and at least see her settled in comfortable circumstances. It would have to be soon.

As long as she was permitted entry into a respectable number of homes, she would find a modicum of happiness.

And at that point Luc would be able to resume his old life. Alone, but at least not plagued by this awful sensation that seized his heart whenever he was around her.

Then he would have to make a decision about Grace Sheffey. She was everything Ata wanted, everything he was supposed to want, and everything he did not want. Deep down he doubted he would be able to do it. Besides, why ruin a perfect streak of breaking the heart of every woman he knew?

And so as he walked to the front hall precisely fourteen minutes after Toby had knocked on his library door Luc reformed his plan to thaw the doors frozen to Mrs. Rosamunde Baird, widow extraordinaire. This first event would put a crack in the ice, and subsequent entrées would effect little chips until an ice floe was achieved.

"Ata, Grace, your servant." Luc made a perfunctory bow, and belatedly saw Grace pull back her proffered gloved hand discreetly. Thoughts of Rosamunde were clouding his mind and his manners.

Ata harrumphed.

He reached for Grace's fingers, letting his hand hang in the air until she slowly offered her own. Luc leaned down and kissed the air a fraction of an inch from her fingers and looked up at Grace's hopeful, pert face.

"Ladies, Hyde Park awaits."

"Don't forget, Luc, we're to stop for the others at Gunther's."

He nodded and handed them into the open landau that was to carry the Helston flock to Hyde Park to preen during the fashionable five-o'clock ritual. He had a quarter hour to charm Grace Sheffey.

"Grace, you're looking uncommonly fetching today. It's good to see you out of mourning. Lavender suits you."

Ata snorted.

Luc raised his brows and looked at his grandmother. "You, stay out of this."

"She's been out of mourning for three months," Ata muttered.

Grace laughed and the sound was slightly irritating, a little nervous and a lot like a titter. "Thank you, Luc. What do you need?"

She might titter, but Grace had never been a fool. So much for his legendary charm. "A favor, if you must know," he muttered.

"Well, I think I will need to know if you want me to help."

"Yes, well . . ."

"Out with it," said Grace, smiling. "I'm honored you would ask for my help. It's surely a first."

"I would be very beholden if you would host a ball."

Both ladies' eyes widened. They exclaimed, "A ball?" together.

"A ball."

"For whom?"

"Wait. It must be an event so mysterious and spectacular no one would ever dare give it a miss."

"And?" Grace prompted.

"And I will, of course, insist that the bills be sent to me."

"And . . ." Both ladies were exasperated.

"And the official hosts must be you, Ata, at least one of Almack's patronesses and Rosamunde Baird."

Only the clip-clop of the horse's hooves on the cobblestones could be heard in the silence that followed.

"Luc . . ." Ata whispered.

Grace, to her credit, kept her eyes unwaveringly on Luc's own.

"This is your club, Ata," he said to his grandmother. "And you would like to settle her, wouldn't you? I think it fair to go the extra distance considering our family's devastating influence on her head."

Ata appeared to consider his words, then turned to Grace. "It's true. What do you think?"

"I think Luc is right. The only way to do it is if the event is at Sheffield House. We must give the appearance that people outside the Helston family are willing to accept her. And Lady Cowper owes me a favor involving Lord Palmerston, her lov . . . ummm. Well, suffice it to say it's a rather large favor."

"You are a lady to be admired, Grace," Luc murmured. "I shall not forget this."

"Oh," Grace purred, "I shall not let you."

Luc looked into Grace's demure eyes and saw a witchlike hunger that would strike fear in the heart of many a lesser bachelor. Undoubtedly there would be a price to pay and it would not be met with jewelry unless, of course, it was that strangling circlet of gold most unmarried females seemed to crave.

Ata glanced rapidly at one and then the other, hope in her eyes.

Luc longed to squeeze his own eyes shut. Instead he returned Grace's gaze and nodded slightly.

The landau lurched to a stop, the carriage driver cursing a cockney blue streak at a rider who had cut him off. Gunther's Ice Shoppe was a half block away. Grateful for the interruption, Luc called to the driver to "circle 'round" whilst he retrieved the other ladies.

The street teemed with foppish dandies and ladies wearing bonnets displaying far too much fake fruit and real feathers. This was to be expected with the annual return to town after a lazy summer spent planning the seasonal assault. Within a week, the milliner's windows would be stripped bare of even the most hideous fashions, due to the voracious appetite for anything new no matter how atrocious. For the mothers were in full force in the fall. It was time to nudge their female ducklings from under their breasts into the well-feathered nest of an endowed drake, er, rake.

Luc ushered Rosamunde, Georgiana Wilde, Elizabeth Ashburton, and Sarah Winters into the now cramped landau.

"Really, Luc, I'm not certain we'll all fit," Ata said.

"And whose fault is that?"

"I beg your pardon?"

"The phaeton was so damaged it will be a fortnight before the smithy is done replacing the tiger's stand."

"I've told you it wasn't my fault. And besides, what

has that to do with anything? That little toy of yours could barely fit three."

"It has everything to do with it since I could have driven two of you in it today," he replied.

"Well, you did say I was to amuse myself," muttered his grandmother.

"Very amusing indeed."

All the ladies were giggling now. He wouldn't be able to stand an hour of this insanity. "I think I'll share a bench with Mr. Jones," he said, nodding to the driver.

Ata smiled widely. "What a wonderful idea. Besides, we ladies have a ball to plan."

He had been watching Rosamunde from the moment he had ushered the group to the landau. At the mention of a ball, her eyes had darted to him and then looked away, her lips pressed into a thin line. It did not bode well. Just wait until she found out she was one of the hostesses. The driver's bench looked inviting indeed.

Rosamunde tiptoed past the breathtaking frescoed upstairs gallery of Helston House. She had been in awe since the moment she had set foot on the pavement two weeks ago and stared at the imposing Corinthian columns fronting the Mayfair mansion. Inside, severe Greco-Roman simplicity was echoed in every detail. While she walked through the upper floor's wide halls, she again glanced in wonder at the exquisite combination of exotic fabrics and elegant shapes of furniture made of precious rosewood and marquetry ornamentation.

She quickened her steps toward the boldly curved

staircase to the front hall. She had learned the only way she could chance a morning walk alone was if she went at dawn and bypassed the other inhabitants of the house and the servants as well.

But there was one person whom she hadn't had to worry about running into during the last fortnight. Luc St. Aubyn had assiduously avoided her. Or perhaps it was she who had guarded her own movements. It was just too painful to endure his casual disinterest. Mealtimes were the worst. Each time she found herself in the same room with him, she feared she would say or do something that would make her fragile façade crumble. She loved him with such fierce longing it made it nearly impossible to speak. In the privacy of her room she relived every moment she had spent with him. The rides together, scaling the cliffs, the laughter, his blue eyes looking at her, and the way they darkened with mystery when he . . .

She squeezed her eyes shut for a moment. She had tried so hard to stop the thoughts.

She hated the situation. And hated herself even more. She was now in a position even worse than before. One afternoon spent on the Bay of St. Michael with Luc St. Aubyn had ruined her first true chance in eight years to rejoin reputable society. She, of all people, should have known a lady's reputation was as fragile as a butterfly's wings. A single whisper dismantled freedom irrevocably.

There was only one reason she was still here. Two or maybe three reasons, actually. The first was Sylvia. Rosamunde still held on to a slender branch of hope that the dowager duchess would arrange a union. Why? Because Ata was a force of nature. She had witnessed firsthand the power of the tiny lady's persuasion. Ata had extracted a promise from Sylvia and Rosamunde to stay with her through the season and help her plan a ball. And while no one said it, it was obvious it was all being done for Rosamunde.

She was horrified. Horrified by the expense and by the potential for disaster. But she had agreed, for no one dared refuse Ata.

The last reason she remained ensconced in the charming little room at Helston House—which, ironically, had once belonged to Luc's brother, Henry—was because she had nowhere else to go and little money. But she was placing her hopes on Phinn. She had written to her brother begging him to help her find a position by the end of the season. And Phinn, who had said the entire family was in town for the season, would do it. She was certain.

She rounded the turn toward the front stair and peered over the banister. Two footmen in casual conversation flanked the door. She would have to go around to the back stair. She hesitated, hearing the conversation below.

"The nerve o' tha' bloke, comin' after dark yester-eve."

The other footman replied, "'Spect 'e was a-thinkin' 'e'd catch the master a' home, 'e did."

"An' when 'as that ever meant 'e'll pay 'em? Why I've 'ad to shut the door in the faces of more 'an a dozen since the cap'n came back."

The other footman shook his head.

"But why 'e owes every dressmaker in town, and the coalman in west Lon'un, and—"

"It's a lady bird, if you were to arsk me," the be-wigged footman replied.

"Or three's more like it. D'yer think one o' them is that fancy piece, the Countess o' Sheffield?"

"I wouldn't care if 'twere the queen 'erself. I 'aven't had me wages the last two quarters, I 'aven't," the other grumbled. "If it weren't for wot he done fer me at Trafalgar—"

The other man squinted up toward her and Rosamunde ducked out of sight.

One of the men cleared his throat and Rosamunde crept on all fours back to the upper hallway toward the bedchambers.

He had a mistress? She thought she might be ill. She tried to regulate her breathing. It just couldn't be Grace Sheffey.

She bit her lips. Perhaps she had been a silly, gauche, countrified fool all this time.

Of course, it was the countess. And probably there were more. He was not called Lord Fire and Ice without reason. The man had more dark, mesmerizing charm than the devil himself.

She stood up and turned only to bump face-first into a shadowed, solid wall. Two strong hands gripped her. She looked up into the hard planes of . . . his face. *His face.*

"Can't sleep?" Luc St. Aubyn murmured in the warm baritone that made her want to weep.

She shook her head.

"It's the ball next week, isn't it?"

"Partially, I suppose," she whispered.

"Come, let's—"

"No," she interrupted.

He paused. "Of course. Didn't mean——"

"No, I'm sorry." She looked up to see the corner of his mouth curve.

"Are you ever going to let me finish a sentence?"

"Perhaps," she said.

"Where were you going, crawling around like that?" Despite the dark hall, she could see the crinkles on the side of his eyes. "Chasing mice?"

"Rats, more like it," she said, remembering he probably had a mistress.

"Ah yes, plenty to be found here," he said with a chuckle.

"I've only seen one, actually. *A large black one.*"

He smiled hugely. "How appropriate."

"Exactly," she replied, folding her arms.

"Are you going to tell me where you were going or not? I hope you're not thinking about going out alone. Ata should have warned you to take a maid at all times."

"I know very well the importance of giving illusions. But I hate to wake someone just so I can walk two minutes to Hyde Park. The only people I shock are milkmaids and people of trade."

He gawked at her. "Why ever are you going to the park at"—he checked his pocket watch and scratched his head—"six o'clock in the morning? There's not a lady out of bed in London before half ten. And that's on the early side."

"That's why I go now." She had a sudden notion of why he was up so early. He had probably spent the night at Number Thirty-four Portman Square and taken the rear stairs. The Countess of Sheffield's town house was directly across the square's garden from Helston House. "As I told you, I like gardens and flowers. They're *silent*."

He took her arm and ushered her down the back stair. "I'm not sure why you're looking at me as if I've committed murder, but I won't let you walk outside alone. If you're determined to take the air, I'll accompany you."

"Really?" she asked more haughtily than she thought she knew how to do.

"Really." He doffed the beaver hat he'd been carrying. "But not without a maid." He called down to the kitchen and an aproned young girl flew up the stairs. With a word or two they were off, the beleaguered kitchen maid in tow.

The cool, fresh air revived Rosamunde's spirit. She walked in long strides as she had always done, quite aware that other ladies preferred a most delicate strolling gait.

"What precise route would you like to take?" Luc asked after they crossed into the park a few minutes later.

"I like to start by the stand of trees on the north side. That's where you can see a duel if you're lucky and early enough. And then—"

Luc skidded to a stop, the kitchen maid almost bumping into them. "For God's sake, Rosamunde. Are you out of your mind?" He shook his head. "I'd give you a litany of reasons why you shouldn't put yourself in such danger, but if you haven't figured it out at your advanced age, you're a hopeless case, I'm afraid."

Her eyes widened. "Advanced age?" she said outraged. "Why—"

He interrupted. "Seriously, why do you watch?"

"It's just that . . ."

"What? It's just what?"

"Well, it's always interesting to see physical evidence that there are those having a worse go of it than yourself."

Luc burst out laughing. "Rosamunde. You can't be serious . . ."

"Well," she said, "it is diverting."

"You do like living dangerously. I could've used you in battle."

"Hmmm. No duels today, I think," she said, peering through the birch trees. "All right now, let's cross toward Tattersalls and into Green Park." She stooped to pick a few wildflowers along the way.

"And what is so interesting in Green Park? You'll notice I don't have to ask why you want to trot past Tats. Could we please slow down? You'll be the death of Sally."

She stopped abruptly. "This is why I hate to ask anyone to accompany me. Your poor maids have too much work to do as it is." They admired the stream of horses being led from the famous stables for morning exercise. The sleek horses' muzzles sent swirls of heated breath through the early morning. They set off again when Sally caught up. "In truth, I don't spend much time in Green Park. No formal flower gardens, you know."

"No I didn't know. Why not?"

"The lepers."

"The *what*?"

"St. James' Hospital buried them in unmarked graves there, and supposedly it's kept somber out of respect for the dead."

He shook his head. "How do you know these things?"

"You have a phenomenal library. And I've had little else to do other than help plan the ball and stay away from the windows." They entered the northwest corner of the smaller park and Rosamunde dropped the wildflowers haphazardly along the way.

"Those I suppose are for the dead?"

"Of course," she murmured, feeling more than a little foolish. "If I were a leper I would want flowers, not just dirt and tufts of grass."

He cleared his throat uneasily. "I'm sorry you've been forced to remain at Helston House each day. It's just that if we've any chance of restoring your—"

"I know, you don't have to say it. I'm very willing to do whatever it takes to help everyone help me. It's the least I can do after everything you and Ata have arranged. I'm only sorry I cannot repay you. Even though I don't say it, I'm extremely grateful," she said softly. "I'm sorry I haven't shown it."

"I think you know I prefer anything to gratitude. *Gratitude is the kissing cousin of pity.* Now, shall we discuss that hellish black rat you've been watching?"

She forced a smile. "Of course. And what a perfect spot to do so, don't you think?" Green Park ended at the northern corner of St. James Park.

"Go ahead," he said, revealing the slightly crooked tooth that made his rare smiles all that more heartstopping. "I know you're dying to tell me why."

"It's because King Charles the Second always liked to parade his mistress around Rosamond's Pond."

"And that has what to do with a black rat?" His eyes were sparkling as he shook his head in mock despair.

"Wicked peer, parading mistress, *Rosamond's* Pond? I never thought you thickheaded."

He barked with laughter. "I am this early in the morning. Now why don't you tell me more about this delightful rodent?"

"I've said more than enough."

He looked at her shrewdly. "Well then, shall we walk back? Or better yet, let me hail a hack or I shall have a very tired kitchen maid and an angry cook."

The hack's worn leather seats were slightly damp from the leather soap the driver had used at the start of his day. And the air was decidedly quieter given the kitchen maid's presence. But Rosamunde was glad. She had made her point and he had understood she knew what he was about.

Rosamunde couldn't have done it better if she had had time to rehearse a hundred times in her chamber. She had wanted him to think she was unaffected by his obvious affair with the countess. And she had learned a very long time ago that it was always preferable to pretend indifference than to express emotion. Alfred had been her teacher. But then, she thought suddenly, wasn't Luc St. Aubyn the master of them all?

She wasn't sure she could maintain this cheerful façade much longer. She clutched her hands when she glanced at the mesmerizing blue of his eyes and prayed a letter from Phinn would be waiting for her upon their return.

Chapter 16

Fortune-hunter, n. *A man without wealth whom a rich woman catches and marries within an inch of his life.*

—The Devil's Dictionary, A. Bierce

Luc allowed his valet, or rather his former cabin boy, to tie his cravat. The young man was in raptures as he glanced back and forth between a drawing of some ridiculously complicated affair and Luc's neck. His own patience was wearing thin.

"Corky, you have precisely three more minutes before I tie you to a chair using those perfectly good neckcloths you ruined."

"I'm sorry, Cap'n, er, Your Grace."

"'Captain' will do in private." He vastly preferred his old Royal Navy designation. He'd never gotten used to the other. Reminded him too much of his father, or worse, the loss of his brother, who should've held the title far longer.

"Right, Captain." Corky stressed the "t."

Luc hid a smile. Corky was trying so hard to become a proper gentleman's man and Luc had given him so little chance to practice his arts.

"There. Now hold still, Cap'n. Her Grace gave me this."

He looked down to see a single gleaming ruby on a neckcloth pin.

"Not if you treasure your life," he said dryly.

"Her Grace said you have to wear red, for 'fire.'"

Ata, Grace, and Rosamunde were impossible when they put their heads together. They'd gone ahead and ordered the invitations without consulting him. "Fire and Ice Ball" indeed. He muttered something not fit for anyone's ears and Corky raised his impish brows. Well, he had to concede they had been somewhat brilliant. Not one of the four hundred invitations had been declined. Seemed the *ton* had a fascination for humorous secret references and scandal after all.

Luc fended off most of Corky's final touches and made his way across Portman Square to Number Thirty-four. Inside, a chorus of feminine voices assaulted his ears.

"Luc," Ata moaned, "what are we to do?"

"Drink and frolic with pretentious toadies?"

"Oh, not now," Ata pleaded. "You've *got* to help us."

"Half of the orchestra," Grace Sheffey said, "all the strings, have yet to arrive. The conductor says they were engaged to play this afternoon at Lady Iveagh's garden party on the edge of Hampstead Heath."

"Well," he replied, looking at the bevy of hopeful faces. Where were Rosamunde and her sister? "We'll have to double the champagne or we're wrecked."

At that moment the door to the ballroom opened and Rosamunde entered the hall. Her sister and a beleaguered-looking man carrying sheet music followed her. And suddenly Luc couldn't hear Ata's babbling, or anything else for that matter.

She was stunning.

Absolutely, breathtakingly, achingly ravishing. She looked like a bride. *His bride.*

Dressed in white with red and white rosebuds threading her ebony hair, she glided forward, her expression remarkably filled with relaxed good humor. She should be terrified. Instead, it was the sister who looked ready to expire.

Rosamunde stepped forward and curtsied. "Your Grace."

He bowed and forced himself not to sweep her into his arms.

"Ata and Grace, I hope you don't mind," Rosamunde said, "but I've taken the liberty of asking Mr. Brown to arrange for two carriages to go to Lady Iveagh's. Perhaps there was an accident. And Sylvia has agreed to play the harp until the strings arrive and the dancing begins."

"And if they don't arrive?" He tried not to stare too intently at her beautiful face.

"Well, I do have an idea, but let's not talk about that

yet. Ah, thank you, Mr. Wynn," she said, dismissing the conductor. She leaned forward and whispered to the intimate group, "Mr. Brown asked me to suggest bribing several of the violinists playing at the countess of Home's house at Number Twenty in this square. Seems she's having a musicale tonight. Not that I'm recommending this course, you understand."

Ata pounced on the idea like a mouse on cheese. "Oh yes, let's do. How many violinists does she really need anyway? No one likes musicales. Don't you agree, Luc?"

"I would like to hear your last resort," he said, turning to Rosamunde.

When her sister remained mute, Lady Sylvia cleared her throat and said softly, "I told Rosamunde she should sing."

Silence greeted this news.

"You're not serious?" he drawled, then paused when Rosamunde's eyes narrowed. "You're serious."

Her eyes dared him to say another word.

"I'll go get the bribe," he said before the countess grabbed his arm.

"Wait, Luc, I like Sylvia's idea better," Grace Sheffey said.

And for the first time Luc wondered how much Grace was willing to show of her heretofore-unseen perfectly manicured little claws.

Rosamunde could barely breathe, let alone enjoy the beauty of the Countess of Sheffield's mansion furnished "in the first stare." But then she had had two days to see every square inch of one of the most stylish town houses in Mayfair while she oversaw the formidable floral decorations.

Rosamunde stood with the countess, Luc, and Ata on the second-story landing, staring down at the magnificent marble stairway. Swags of greenery topped with petite bouquets of red and white flowers twined the railings. Only Rosamunde knew their significance, which gave her comfort for some odd reason.

She glanced at Luc out of the corner of her eye. He was resplendent in the harsh black of his knee breeches and dress coat with long tails. She knew why he had chosen to stand next to her. It was to dare the *haut ton* to utter a single affront.

Below, the butler opened the heavily lacquered front door and Rosamunde clenched her hands together. Good Lord, the guests were already arriving.

A lovely lady entered with all the splendor and stature of a queen. A dull-looking fellow was beside her.

Ata's hands flew to her wrinkled cheeks. "Oh thank heaven," she whispered to the countess. "I don't know how you managed it."

"It's Lady Cowper, one of Almack's patronesses," Luc confided to Rosamunde. "And of course her lackwit husband—although, stupidity is a trait to cherish if you're going to cuckold your husband, don't you think?" His eyes danced with laughter.

"You're abominable," Rosamunde whispered, watching the regal lady surrender her wrap and mount the stair.

"Oh no. I adore Emily. Her mother, Lady Melbourne, was one of the cleverest women alive. On her deathbed, she told her daughter to be true to her lover instead of her husband." He cleared his throat and stepped forward to accept Lady Cowper's proffered hand. "Lady Cowper," he bent to kiss her glove.

"Helston," she replied. "Delighted to see you back in town. It's been an age."

"Thank you for standing up with us tonight," he said warmly and greeted Lord Cowper.

"Oh pish. Hold on to your appreciation, Luc," Lady Cowper said. "Haven't you heard? *'Gratitude is the kissing cousin of pity.'*"

Rosamunde glanced at him. It was a moment of déjà vu.

He blanched. "I had no idea," he said faintly.

"Well, you would if you'd read *Lucifer's Lexicon*. Fabulous, simply fabulous. Even if you haven't a moment to read in your rakish existence, you must find a copy. Everyone is talking about it."

"Indeed," he said quietly.

Lady Cowper turned an assessing glance in Rosamunde's direction.

"Well, it's always a pleasure to help launch a deserving lady." Lady Cowper nodded, the crimson ostrich feathers in her turban trembling. The grande dame winked coyly. "You must be Rosamunde Baird. I told your father long ago he should have managed that earlier nonsense much better than he did. I've been longing to meet you."

Rosamunde felt a warm glow around her heart and she curtsied. "You do me a great honor, Lady Cowper."

"Pish, it's nothing."

But they both knew it was everything.

"Now," Lady Cowper said, linking her arm with her own, "I shall stand on one side of you and Luc shall take your other side. Oh, and look, just in time. Get ready now, chin up. Now let's see who dares . . . Lady and Lord Hardwick, how good of you to join us. May I present the Earl of Twenlyne's daughter, Lady Rosamunde?"

Oh, her confidence almost deserting her, she was being presented as her father's daughter. Rosamunde had refused to use her former title since the fateful day she had gotten into Alfred's shabby carriage and left her father's house, bound for Scotland.

In the next hour, Rosamunde greeted almost four hundred guests. From time to time, she looked down the stair, hoping to see her brother Phinn's fair head. An ache in her heart and in her limbs made her weary. She had been forced to curtsy so many times, she felt her knees begin to wobble with the effort.

"Don't wear yourself out," Luc whispered in her ear. "You'll have to dance soon."

Ata leaned in. "But the strings haven't arrived yet," she moaned.

And then it happened. Someone gave her the cut direct. Lady Cowper had turned away to greet someone while Luc placated Ata. A very plump matron glanced at her and turned away with a harrumph as she tugged on her husband's elbow.

"Did you say something, Lady Skiffington?" Luc said, sharply turning around and almost barring her entrance to the ballroom beyond. "I do believe you haven't had the pleasure of meeting Lady Rosamunde."

The older lady sputtered, "I've met everyone I need to, young man."

Luc smiled shrewdly as he stepped sideways at the same moment the lady tried to move around him. "I think not."

Rosamunde wanted to crawl under the side table but she stood very still and very tall.

"Amanda Barnstable," Ata said quietly, "you should be ashamed of yourself. But then at Miss Dilford's School you never could balance a book on your head to save your life. Now if you would just follow the example of Lady Rosamunde."

"Well!" Lady Skiffington huffed, "I never thought—"

"And you never do, my dear," Lady Cowper interrupted.

Rosamunde felt a hysterical giggle tickling her throat amid the tension. She wondered if Lady Cowper had taken lessons from Ata. Evidently, intimidation by way of interruption was something of an art form taught at Miss Dilford's. It was too bad Lady Skiffington hadn't been an adept pupil. Rosamunde almost felt sorry for her.

The older woman nodded a fraction of an inch, and Rosamunde curtsied politely. "Delighted you could come, Lady Skiffington," she murmured, while Luc bowed and extended his arm toward the ballroom.

"The trick," Lady Cowper said to her, "is to know when to stand firm. The Duke of Helston has always known how to do it perfectly. You are lucky to have him in your corner, my dear. You'll be the envy of half the ladies here tonight."

"But, he's not—" she whispered before being interrupted by an expert.

"A lover to give up without a fight," Lady Cowper said quietly yet firmly while smiling at the last guest to enter the ballroom. She turned to Luc and continued smoothly, "Now what is this I hear about Rosamunde singing for us tonight? Grace tells me we've a shortage of strings, unless you've managed to snare a few from under the Countess of Home's nose."

Luc sighed. "It appears she doubled my incentive."

"Well, I don't blame her. She's been in a temper ever since she heard you picked the same date as her little musicale. I say 'little' because almost everyone but her most stalwart circle chose to attend this ball over her amusement."

Rosamunde heard the faint sound of a harp coming from the ballroom, and her heart plummeted. When she'd agreed to this mad scheme, she'd been sure Mr. Brown would be able to secure the musicians from the garden party. She hadn't really thought about how impossible it would be to stand up in front of four hundred members of the *ton*, some of whom would be only too delighted to witness her mortification.

"Feeling like you might have bitten off more than you can chew?" Luc asked, looking down from hooded eyes.

"Not at all," she muttered. "I've always enjoyed

large portions of humiliation with intense mortification on the side."

Lady Cowper laughed. "Me too. Good for the soul, don't you think? Come along, my dear, I shall introduce you."

The ballroom was awash with the magnificent splendor of hundreds of vividly attired members of the *beau monde*. It seemed they took their entertainment very seriously, and loved dressing the part.

Rosamunde and Lady Cowper ascended the three stairs to the musicians' small stage and stood near Sylvia, who was furiously blushing behind a harp. The conductor tapped his stand and Lady Cowper raised her hand to quiet the crowd.

"I do hope you've all been enjoying yourselves. You've been immensely patient. But we promised mystery and more during this Fire and Ice Ball, and so without further ado, I give you Lady Rosamunde Langdon, daughter of the Earl of Twenlyne, who shall perform an enchanting song to welcome you tonight." Lady Cowper, winked and nodded to her with encouragement.

She faced the huge crowd and thought she might just very well faint. Her body felt stiff and her breath had completely deserted her. A faint buzzing in her ears began, which threatened to overtake the opening measures of Sylvia's harp, joined by a flute and pianoforte. She glanced down and saw Luc standing directly in front of her. He shook his head ever so slightly and directed her gaze to his eyes with *V*'d fingers of one hand. If she had had her wits about her she would have taken perverse humor in the fact that he appeared more anxious than she.

Slowly, ever so slowly as she focused on the depths of his eyes, the rest of the crowd seemed to melt away, leaving her alone with him and the music.

The lyrical Welsh notes soared and at the highest point, Rosamunde joined her voice to one endlessly long melancholy note. Rosamunde closed her eyes against the bittersweet memories of the song.

It was her father's favorite, one she hadn't dared sing since leaving Edgecumbe. She sang of love and loss, of hope and sorrow, and of a passion that never died.

She sang the story of life. Of her own life. And during the last phrases of the song, she opened her eyes and scanned the room, no longer afraid to meet the faces staring back at her. With the greenery edging them, the many guests wearing red and white and black looked like a glorious field of scarlet poppies swaying in the wind.

Suddenly she realized why she had turned to nature and flowers in her misery. It was because her husband had denied her music. Her soul and her senses had craved beauty and the garden was the only place she had been able to find it.

Coming almost full circle, her gaze rested on Luc St. Aubyn, the Duke of Helston, where intelligence and complete awe warred with the harsh kindness radiating from his face. His was a different kind of raw beauty she craved now more than any other thing in the world.

A face beyond his shoulder, beside the ballroom doors, came into focus and her voice almost faltered.

Her father . . . and beside him Phinn, Fitz, Miles, and even James. Oh, it was just like outside the church on Madeleine St. Aubyn's wedding morning. He was going to turn and walk away from her. Pain radiated through her chest until she saw the sheen on her father's cheeks. He was crying.

And in that moment her voice grew stronger and she held an impossibly long, rich note, all the while staring back at her father, his image growing blurry through her own tears. At the end she reached one arm toward him. The song begged him to find the love they had lost. The music abruptly ended; flute, harp, and song echoed through the dead-silent ballroom.

Rosamunde closed her eyes and bowed her head. A thick fog of loud whispers grew and enveloped her. She finally opened her eyes, tears spilling over wet lashes, and saw Luc, very pale, staring at her, shocked admiration on every feature. He seemed frozen, his hands locked behind his back.

With every emotion yearning for acceptance, she glanced to the edge of the vast ballroom but couldn't find her father as the crowd surged and roared its approval, the flames of all the hundreds of candles flickering with the movement.

Luc seemed to wake from his trance as he escorted her down the three steps. Mr. Brown led six harried musicians, their wigs askew, to the stage.

Rosamunde fought the crush of people, each trying to say a word. She had to get to her father. Had to tell him she was sorry for disappointing him, had to hear his voice. Oh, how she longed to hear his voice.

"Luc," she said. "Please help me. I have to get to the door."

His eyes questioned her words.

"My father . . ." she begged.

He understood and forced a path through the waves of people like the masthead of a warship. In their wake, Rosamunde barely heard the words of wonder and praise.

It seemed forever before they reached the spot where her father had been standing. Now only Fitz and James stood by the double doors. James crushed her to his chest as only a brother could do, before she pulled away. "But, where is Fa—"

"He's gone. Forced Phinn to go with him." Fitz hurried with an explanation. "You know how he detests scenes, Rosamunde. He always has. Can't bear the attention, the strain of everyone staring at him. But he was determined to come, Rosa. And he's determined to see you tomorrow."

She turned to Luc. "Oh please. I must see him now."

James stopped her. "No, Rosamunde. You mustn't. It isn't what he wanted. He expects you to stay. Told me so himself."

"Come, it's the opening set"—Luc grasped her hand—"and you must dance it with me."

"But, I can't. I must . . ."

"No, you mustn't." He shook his head slightly. "But that doesn't mean you can't see him at some ungodly early hour tomorrow morning." He looked at the two fair-haired brothers. "You must dance with your sister too. With more than half the peers in Christendom at her feet, now is the time to show the fickle-hearted aristocracy that Rosamunde is at ease with her family."

Unbearable longing dragged at her heart.

"Your voice has already entranced most of them. Now let your grace and elegance speak to the rest."

"I shall claim the second set," James said.

"And the third shall be mine," added Fitz.

Their cinnamon-colored eyes were so very dear to her, so like her sister's.

"And you'll all dance with Sylvia?"

"Of course," they chorused.

James took her aside. "Don't be such a ninny. Go with His Grace before he changes his mind. He does you an enormous favor."

Once a brother always a brother, it seemed. "Your confidence in me always was extraordinary," she said dryly, then turned to place her gloved hand on the top of Luc's ironlike arm.

He led her through the press of people to the top of the set. Just when the opening sounds of a minuet should have been struck, Luc tipped his head toward the conductor and the flowing measures of a waltz filled the air. Even Rosamunde knew it was audacious and improper. She glanced at him and he raised a single winged brow, daring her to question him.

The lady next to her giggled and said, loud enough for the people around her to hear, "What was the definition for waltzing?"

Her partner laughed and replied, "The thing that separates us from the beasts?"

"No, no, no," chided another lady, "that's *kissing*."

Rosamunde was absolutely certain she'd heard *that* quip before. She whipped her head around to stare at Luc.

A sly young man nudged her and leaned in to confide to Luc, "The waltz is one hundred forty-five steps closer to hell. Isn't that what *Lucifer's Lexicon* suggests, Your Grace?"

"I wouldn't know," he bit out, then grasped her hand and pulled her inelegantly toward the French doors. "Damn fools."

He had a strange look in his eye, and it was hard for Rosamunde to keep up with his large strides. What was this *Lucifer's Lexicon* everyone seemed to know by heart? Luc's profile was grim and he mumbled something about "imbeciles who can't count."

Several of the ladies murmured compliments to her about her singing as they wound their way through the crowded room, growing more merry with each successive pass of the trays filled with champagne and spirits. Ata had insisted that there should be no lemonade, "Makes for a watered-down affair." And she had been right. It even allowed for the two of them to duck through the throng and slip past one of the many sets of doors leading to the terrace.

The moon was a perfectly round dark yellow orb, mysterious valleys etched upon its face.

Rosamunde set her heels on the empty patio when he would have gone into the garden. "What did you mean when you said the idiots couldn't count?"

"I didn't say that. I said *imbeciles*. Everyone knows the waltz has three beats to a measure."

"I beg your pardon? What has that to do—"

"Simple mathematics. It couldn't be one hundred forty-five steps. It must be one hundred forty-four."

Like the dominos she used to set up on the nursery-room floor at Edgecumbe, his last utterance tipped off a cascade of understanding. "You . . . you . . ." she stammered. "Why do you become so annoyed each time someone quotes from this strange dictionary? It's as if you, well, as if . . ."

"As if what?" he asked, his lips in a thin line.

"As if it means something to you. As if you're connected to it somehow. As if . . ." She finished the thought in her mind. All those cynical witticisms were precisely the sort of clever remarks she heard him utter time and again.

"Rosamunde . . ." he warned.

"You wrote it, didn't you?" she said with wonder. "Why is it such a secret? Why didn't you tell me?"

"Why didn't you tell me you could sing?" he asked dryly.

"Did you know you're very good at changing the subject?"

"We'll discuss it later." He took her in his arms and danced through the double set of doors. "Come, we must dance in public unless you want more scandal."

She realized he might never tell her. Since they'd come to London she'd felt a gulf rending them apart. She'd thought she understood his demons, but evi-

dently she did not if he had kept this momentous secret from her.

For long moments she kept her gaze focused above
his right shoulder as she pondered this revelation,
fully aware that the inquisitive eyes of society were
upon them. She had wondered what it would be like
to dance with him, but she'd been afraid to be on display. Afraid that everyone would be able to tell that
she cared for him more than she should. She had never
been to a ball, never had her season, never understood
the heady aura of wit and beauty and old-world elegance found only in a London ballroom. It was where
dukes rubbed shoulders with marquises who rubbed
elbows with counts who rubbed fingers with barons
while mere misters looked for a title to marry.

She could not relax until she noticed the guests were
no longer staring at them and the flow of idle conversation had resumed. Oh, but then. She let her heart
soar in sheer happiness as Luc's warm hands held her
while they circled the floor. She had known he would
be a magnificent, powerful partner in dance, just as he
would be in life. As she lost herself to the notes swirling around them, the music beats matching the pulse
of her heart, she finally allowed herself to gaze into his
glittering eyes. What she found there made her almost
weep with longing.

"You've been avoiding me," he said quietly.

"Whatever are you—?"

"No," he said, interrupting her, "lying, while a virtue, is never a good idea when facing me."

"But we went walking just last week."

"And I haven't had a moment with you since." His hand gripped hers and he hugged her to his breast momentarily to avoid a near collision with another couple.

She must get him to stop talking; her nerves were near to breaking.

"Please, Luc . . ." she said in a tone that sounded miserably begging to her own ears.

"Why didn't you tell me you could sing?" He repeated.

"Why did you assume I couldn't?"

"Because I always assume the worst in everyone. That way I'm rarely surprised. Devil's rules, don't you know."

She shook her head and almost had the courage to smile. "Gentlemen such as you never like surprises."

"Precisely."

She wondered if there was another soul on this earth who could make her feel more comfortable in her own skin. "Well, I'm glad I surprised you, as hard as that might have been for you. But I think you shouldn't hold on so tightly to your devil's rules."

"Trying to snatch the very coattails off the devil, are you?" He rolled his eyes. "I see you've forgotten the condescension due my rank."

She laughed, and with a burst of bittersweet joy she marveled how he never failed to fascinate and thrill her with his magnetism and wit. "Nevertheless, I shall make you rethink several of your rules before I leave."

He sobered instantly. "You cannot leave."

"But I think I can now. Don't you feel the change in the air? I know I'll find a place for myself. That was the plan, wasn't it?"

For a moment, a haunted look appeared in the depths of his mysterious eyes before he shuttered them, "Rosamunde . . ." he said, letting her name hang in the last notes of the waltz as they drifted into the night.

Their days were numbered. Of that there could be no doubt.

Looking into his eyes with such miserable sadness pounding her soul, she knew with every fiber of her being that they would be pulled away from each other. And both of them would allow it.

For him. For her. For Ata. For everyone.

Chapter 17

Cynic, n. *A blackguard whose faulty vision
sees things as they are, not as they should be.*

— The Devil's Dictionary, A. Bierce

She dozed fitfully through the first part of the night
and consequently fell into a deep slumber just
before the first rays of dawn appeared. She was having nightmares again, something she hadn't had once
since coming to stay with the St. Aubyn family.

Alfred was coming up the stair, his step heavy and
growing louder as he came closer to her door. And
then there was the awful pause as he stood there, his
shadow evident beneath her door. She could almost
hear his heavy breathing. But instead of waiting silently and motionless, she ran to the door to confront
him only to find Luc standing there with Grace Sheffey, both of them dressed for the ball, arm in arm, looking as if they were made for each other.

In the dream, Luc smiled benevolently and the hallway was transformed into a Cornish meadow filled with wildflowers and Celtic stones in an ancient circle. Someone was walking toward them through the mist. It was Father, her brothers behind him, reaching out his arms. Only Sylvia was missing. Then the mist grew dense, swirling up their bodies until she couldn't see, couldn't breathe, and at last woke up panting as if she had run all the way from Cornwall to London.

She arose early, too early, and sat at the escritoire in her chamber. There was no ladies' toilette table since she was still ensconced in the room that had once been Henry St. Aubyn's. It was ironic. She was in the very room that she had longed to occupy as his wife all those years ago.

She reached for the drawer where a maid had placed the silver-backed brush that had been her mother's, along with the matching looking glass and her hairpins. The drawer was stuck. Rosamunde jiggled it by reaching with her fingers under the edge, trying to ease the tall pin case away from the top.

Her hands brushed against something soft as the drawer eased open a little. Feeling blindly, she again reached under the space and came away with a thick note, yellowed with age. A lock of pale gold hair peeked out from one of the corners. Her breath caught as she fingered the strands and instinctively brought her other hand to her oval mourning locket where her mother's pale hair was interwoven with her own. The outside of the note read, "For Luc, my beloved son."

Rosamunde turned it over, and the crimson sealing wax bore the intertwined initials *CSA*.

CSA. . .

St. Aubyn. C. St. Aubyn. Her heart raced. *Caro's Heart*. Caroline St. Aubyn, *his mother*.

She must give this to him. Right away. Her hand stilled while her mind raced. And then she hesitated, uncertain which of the two ideas forming in her mind would be the right thing to do.

Perhaps she could carry out both. Carefully, she eased a few of his mother's strands of hair from the fold, leaving the rest undisturbed. She would place it in his hands this very morning.

After quickly splashing herself with cold water and donning the crimson gown, she made her way to the breakfast room.

Sitting around the breakfast table with the rest of the Widows Club, she fought the twin desires to find Luc or to run all the way to her father's house.

It was only her deep gratitude to Ata that kept her in her seat, picking at toast, barely able to drink one cup of chocolate, while listening to the ladies talking about the magnitude of the events of the last evening.

"And where, pray tell, is my grandson?" Ata asked a footman.

The liveried servant leaned forward. "He left early this morning on an errand, Your Grace."

"Hmmm, he's a sly devil. Methinks he has gone to buy pretty posies for someone," Ata said, winking at Grace Sheffey. "So good of you to come share breakfast with us this morning, Grace."

"I wouldn't miss it for the world. I admit my house in town seems very empty since living with you this past summer, Ata."

"Oh, my dear," Ata said, her eyes slightly misty. "I really don't think you shall remain alone in your lovely house for long. I don't have to hide my sentiments from my dearest confidants at this table. No one could miss how beautiful you and Luc looked dancing last night. And"—she winked again—"he asked you to dance *two* sets."

The countess looked exquisite in a pink walking dress, her pale hair artfully arranged with a spray of curls over one shoulder, and pink and white pearls displayed on her décolleté. She looked like a woman on the verge of a marriage proposal.

Another footman entered and bowed. "Your Grace."

"Yes?"

"Where would you like us to put the rest of the flowers?"

"Oh, it's been such an age since we've had morning-after-a-ball posies. But, surely you know they should be placed in the sitting rooms, Gordon."

"We've filled every table to overflowing, Your Grace."

"What?" Ata said, astonishment flooding her face.

The widows began chattering. "Surely they must be for Rosamunde," Georgiana said quietly, turning to her. "You sang so beautifully. I've never heard anything like it."

Rosamunde could feel the heat of a blush overtake

her. "No, you must be mistaken. They must be for Ata, and from all of your dance partners."

Elizabeth laughed, "Well, I for one can't stand the suspense. I cannot eat another bite until I see this for myself."

"Oh yes," Ata breathed, "do let's go see."

Ata teetered on her high-heeled boots out the door, the rest of the ladies in her wake. Rosamunde was the last to leave, behind the Countess of Sheffield.

"Grace," Rosamunde said softly, "I know words are not adequate, but I wanted to thank you again for opening your house to host the ball. Until this summer, I had not had the opportunity to enjoy the friendship of many ladies. I shall always treasure this summer, and most especially your extraordinary generosity. I'm sorry I haven't the means to give you a proper gift, but I did want to offer a token of my gratitude . . ." Rosamunde withdrew from her pocket a little package wrapped in tissue.

"Oh," exclaimed Grace, "I shan't say 'you shouldn't have,' because that takes away from the sentiment of your gift. May I open it, then?"

"Please," she said, watching the petite countess unfold the tissue. "I had hoped you might like this since you enjoy reading so much, just like His Grace."

The countess held up a small book. "Oh," she breathed.

"It's a collection of Welsh poetry my father gave to me when I was sixteen."

"Oh, it is very dear to you, which shall make it all the more dear to me. I shall treasure it always and think of you when I read it. Rosamunde . . . I am so glad I could help you. And I just know you will find happiness now with your family. It was the one thing I was determined to do before I consider fulfilling the wish of Ata and my grandmother, lost to me now."

Rosamunde felt her heart pounding in her breast. She nodded.

"You are going to see your father this morning, aren't you?"

"Yes. As soon as I can politely extricate myself."

The countess smiled at her warmly and embraced her. "I understand. Come. I'll aid your escape. Let's find the butler and I'll order a carriage for you myself. Ata won't mind in the least."

The note for Luc would have to wait then, until later in the day.

Grace arranged for a maid and a carriage to be brought from the mews before they entered the drawing room filled with an overwhelming number of bouquets. There were sweet peas and violets, larkspur, and lilies. But most of all there were roses, her namesake, in every color imaginable. The widows were glancing and laughing at the cards, some of which contained phenomenally unoriginal poetry.

"Look, here is the fourth 'A Rosamunde by any other name would smell as sweet,'" Elizabeth said, giggling.

"I daresay half the florists in town are giving a prayer of thanks to Rosamunde as they pat their plump pockets," Ata said, a wide smile on her withered face. "It was a grand success after all, thanks to your exquisite voice and Grace's unparalleled hospitality."

Rosamunde was speechless. The widows surrounded her, hugging her senseless. "Oh, this is everything ridiculous," Rosamunde said, but couldn't stop the smile spreading across her features. "Now look, here is one for Georgiana," she said. "Hmmm, it is from a Lord Horton. Did you not dance with him?"

Not waiting for an answer she looked at another card and said, "And this one is for . . . yes, here is one for Elizabeth. Let's see. It says, 'To Eliza who is no pariah.' Oh dear, I think that one takes the prize." They dissolved into laughter.

The housekeeper entered carrying another bouquet.

"And this is for. . . ?" Ata asked, without any curiosity lacing her laughter.

"Lady Sylvia, Your Grace," the housekeeper replied primly. "And there was a very unpleasant man who just delivered something altogether larger in the foyer."

Sylvia stepped forward to accept the white rosebud posy and brought it to her nose. She averted her face to read the note.

The ladies drifted into the foyer and were astonished to find wrapped in soft coverings a beautiful inlaid wood harp in the Welsh style. There was no question who had sent the grand gift.

No one heard Sylvia's slippered feet behind them. "It's from Sir Rawleigh," she said in awe. "Oh, I cannot accept . . ." She looked longingly at the harp, touched the gleaming wood once before pulling away her hand as if she had been burned. She then rushed past the assembled widows to the hall beyond.

Rosamunde found her in the first chamber, Luc's dark Egyptian-inspired library, where a large, book-laden desk was supported by golden entwined serpents. Sphinxes decorated the immense floor-to-ceiling bookcases, giving the entire room a dangerous aura.

Dwarfed within the seat of a leather armchair, Sylvia lay huddled and rocking slightly. Rosamunde rushed to cradle her in her arms, whispering endearments of sisterly love. "Dearest, you mustn't do this to yourself," she pleaded. "You mustn't. He loves you so. Can't you find it within your heart to accept him?"

Afterward, Rosamunde could not recall the gentle persuasive arguments she used on Sylvia for the next quarter hour. All she could remember was the rush of emotions that washed over her when the library door opened and she found herself face to face with her father. Luc stood behind him.

Her sister and Luc seemed to fade into the background as she stood very still before her father. He was so close she could see him swallow against the tension in his throat as she fought to calm her nerves. He was staring at her, drinking in the sight of her.

Slowly she raised a hand toward him and took a tentative step forward, equal parts hope and anticipation beating in her breast. Only this time there was no fear. Even if he rejected her, said something unkind, she now knew she would survive it. She had somehow changed, gathered a bit of courage during the last season, and had learned in hindsight that she could withstand the worst trials fate tossed her way. And she took comfort in knowing this. Perhaps, just perhaps, she thought, maturity could indeed be better than the sweet bloom of girlhood.

"Rose . . ." her father's dearly familiar voice whispered to her.

At that one utterance, she ran into his arms. The bouquet of scents from him sprang to life as she buried her nose in his worsted-wool riding coat. Smoke from his cheroots and his woody cologne mingled together, the essence of him.

"My impetuous, beautiful, headstrong girl . . ." he said so quietly and wistfully.

"Father . . ." she choked out, "I've missed you so."

The touch of his trembling hand on her head made her eyes ache with unshed tears. She forced herself to straighten and looked at her father's face, which had aged since she'd last seen him. Streaks of gray had appeared at his temples.

"Why did you have to leave," he whispered, "run away from Edgecumbe? I know you were angry . . . at me, angry with Helston, angry with us all. You never liked to be forced to do anything. But why did you have to leave . . . me?"

She breathed deeply and shuddered before she told the unvarnished truth of it. "Because you cared more about propriety than you did about me, Father. Because I disappointed you and you no longer respected or loved me. And I couldn't spend the rest of my life with a husband who would be wishing he were with someone else. But it seemed you only cared about our name and how I had sullied it."

His aged eyes took on a bit of the old hardened metal to them. "Propriety *is* everything, girl. Certainly you know that now," her father insisted gruffly. "I acted in your best interest. I knew what would happen to you if you didn't marry His Grace's brother. No one of good name would have you then. You would remain a spinster, hiding in Edgecumbe's shadows, and bearing an unspeakable label like a millstone for the rest of your life. I also did it for your sister. Your stain would hamper her chances. And . . ."

"And?" she asked, hope for his love fading.

"And I did it because I knew you loved him. Everyone did. You had been moon-faced about him for over two years." He covered his face with one hand and added quietly, "Ah, Rose, I did it because *I love you*, not because of propriety."

Rosamunde raised her head to stare more fully into her father's poignant Welsh eyes, so like her own. She could feel him trembling with repressed emotion.

Her father continued, "Henry St. Aubyn would've come to love you and he wouldn't have dared ruin you without knowing the consequences."

Luc cleared his throat.

Rosamunde had almost completely forgotten there were others witnessing the intense intimacy of the moment. Her mortification was complete.

"You are correct, of course, sir." Luc stood gripping the ornate edge of the desk in front of him, tapping one finger against it. "And that is why I kept asking myself why my brother did not force the issue. I, of course, would've been quite capable of walking away from a female in need. But not Henry. He was a gentleman in every sense of the word. He would've charmed Rosamunde and insisted he loved only her even if it meant lying through his teeth once he ruined her. But there is one thing for certain. He would've gotten her in front of a vicar no matter what it took. Clearly there was an impediment. An impediment no gentleman should speak of . . ." His voice trailed off while he walked around his desk to settle on the corner. "But then, I am no gentleman. And perhaps the answer is very simple. A carriage ride with a lady who possesses startlingly similar hair and form to her sister left me wondering if there had been some sort of confusion . . ."

The silence was such that it drew attention to Sylvia's huddled form. Only now she was weeping steadily, her face hunched down. "Oh no, please . . ." she started in a strangled, tiny voice. She darted an anxious glance at her father, who seemed to only now realize Sylvia was in the room too.

Before he could utter a word, Luc cleared his throat. "Lady Sylvia, the last time you chose a certain course. Don't you think, my dear, you might now try another?" he asked in a surprisingly soft tone, his eyes hooded.

Rosamunde rushed to intervene, hating to see her sister look so forlorn, "Leave her be. What has a carriage ride to do with anything?"

"Wait." He raised a staying hand. "Let your sister speak."

Keeping her eyes on her fingers, Sylvia traced the

intricate Egyptian pattern on the chair's arm. "Henry told me he loved me. Promised he would do whatever I chose. I chose poorly."

Numbness moved up Rosamunde's clenched fists to her arms.

"I'm a coward," Sylvia said softly and looked up at the group, a haunted expression in her eyes. "I couldn't admit it was me those horrid gossips saw on the beach at Perron Sands. I didn't have the nerve to face down everyone or tell Rosamunde. When she roundly refused him, I insisted Henry wait a little, to see if our scandalous actions had caused a chi . . . a child to take root. To wait a month to give us more time to determine the best course. To take the coward's way out by doing nothing." She bowed her head. "But then," she turned to Rosamunde, "you solved the problem by running off to Scotland to marry someone who turned out to be . . . an abomination. After, Henry told his father he wanted to marry me. The duke threatened to cut him off and never see him again if he dared marry a girl from a family of such ill-bred females." Sylvia shot a glance at Luc. "And you, sir, are sadly mistaken. Your brother was quite capable of walking away. He didn't like the idea of living in poverty or at my family's whim until he inherited."

Rosamunde's head felt very cold and she wondered if she was going to faint. "You loved Henry." She had to say it to believe it.

"I don't know anymore," Sylvia said, not daring to look at Rosamunde this time. "I was almost sixteen . . . excited by the attentions and protestations of love from the most charming, handsome gentleman I'd ever known. We first chanced upon each other while I was taking the air one fine day. He gave me the consideration and admiration I craved. It was thrilling. And I"—she finally looked at her sister and paused after searching her face—"Oh, Rosamunde. I'm so very sorry. I—"

"Sorry? You're sorry?" All the breath seemed to have left Rosamunde's lungs and she felt she might suffocate. Anger trickled faster and faster in her veins until it heated her fingertips. "You—you deceived me . . . your own sister. You allowed me to feel guilty for almost a decade. Were you ever going to tell me?" Her voice rose a notch with each stinging word. Rosamunde shook her head. "You're not the person I thought you were."

"Oh, Rosa," Sylvia said, a tear trickling down her face. "You always had such high expectations. I could never be as good as you, and I couldn't bear to let you down. Before the duke put a stop to Henry's intentions, I originally refused him because you are my sister and I love you. Doesn't that count for anything?"

Blood was pounding at Rosamunde's temples and her head ached in the worst way. "But surely you must see that if you had just admitted the truth we would have both been better off. You should have gone to Scotland with him immediately. We both would have been spared such persecution and my horrible marriage."

"Yes, well, the wrong course always becomes blindingly obvious upon retrospection. I'm sorry I behaved in such a disgraceful fashion. I know there is little I can say that will make any of you think better of me. And I hate giving excuses for something so inexcusable."

"Bravo, Lady Sylvia," Luc said softly, with a twisted sort of smile. "It's not often one gets to witness an act of bravery."

"It's easy to be honest when you've nothing to lose or gain. And I'm tired of hiding behind all the lies," she replied.

"And I must thank you for rectifying my opinion," Luc continued. "I had always wondered how Henry had managed to evade inheriting the more charming Helston attributes. Now I can rest easy knowing he was following in the family tradition," he finished dryly.

Her father had staggered forward during the proceedings. Luc had gripped his arm and led him to a chair on the other side of the fireplace, across from Sylvia.

"Oh God," their father said. "I was so harsh, neither of you would confide in me, allow me to help you. You feared I would—"

"No," Sylvia interrupted. "I did something very shameful and couldn't stand the thought of losing everyone's good opinion and a public humiliation. So I waited and allowed others to act. Someone who was much stronger than I . . . my sister."

Rosamunde kneeled beside her sister's chair and forced herself to take one thin hand in her own stronger one while she held fast to the first threads of clear thought. She tried very hard to hold in check the bitter taste of resentment. "I suppose we've each of us some share of blame. I was a spurned, overly proud girl who acted impetuously, to my own detriment and to the everlasting shame of my family."

"And I," her father inserted, "allowed another man to ruin the happiness of my two daughters. His Grace, at my insistence, shed light on your lives with Baird. I daresay I will never forgive myself for not trying harder to find out how you lived."

"You tried to . . ." Rosamunde began, the first shade of joy tempering her hot feelings.

Her father continued. "I wrote to you once, hoping for reconciliation. I never received an answer. And then—"

"But I never got a letter," she interrupted.

"Obviously. And then your husband paid a call and said you both felt my sentiments were too late and you wanted to sever all ties. He said you were very happy as mistress of your own home and no longer wanted any memories of the past.

"And Baird handed me a note from the Duke of Helston, who gave me to understand that as magistrate he would uphold Baird's insistence to leave all of you in peace. His Grace reminded me of the marriage laws and a husband's right to see to his wife's welfare and insisted I not set foot on Baird's bit of land. On every level I was made to feel my entreaties were unwelcome. I swear to you both, I would have come, would have killed the miserable bastard if I had but known . . ."

Rosamunde took comfort in her father's raw fury. "Alfred told us he had visited you to try and effect a reconciliation. He said he was rebuffed and informed we were now formally disowned, barred forever from entering Edgecumbe or addressing anyone in our family should we chance upon any of you. Sylvia and I were so hurt we didn't dare set foot in the village or anywhere we might see you."

Luc said stiffly, "Truly, your Mr. Baird missed his calling. He should've been born a Helston. Surely there must have been some good to the man. No one is so purely evil."

Rosamunde chuckled. "Well, he did have a good appetite. And he didn't force me to improve my needlework, unlike others." She hid a smile as she glanced at her father.

Sylvia brushed at her tear-stained lashes. "And he always took my superstitions to heart, unlike everyone else."

There was a knock and Ata poked her head around the door. "Sorry to intrude, but Grace ordered a carriage for Rosamunde, which of course is now not necessary, I'm happy to see," Ata said before addressing Luc. "Don't forget you promised Grace last night that you would escort us to the library before the Countess of Home's breakfast today."

"And here I'd hoped you'd already breakfasted," he said, the suggestion of a smile about his lips.

"Luc, you know breakfasts never start before two o'clock. And you must go to smooth the ruffled feathers of our neighbor. I daresay she won't forgive you very soon for that bribery business you insisted upon last night."

"The question, Grandmamma, is whether I can forgive you for dragging me there to do the dirty work for you. No"—he held up his hands—"don't say a word if you want to be allowed to drive the carriage yourself this morning."

Ata raised her chin. "Grace and I will be waiting." And with that the tiny dowager was gone, shutting the door a little too loudly. Her grandson masked all traces of humor with his usual haughty demeanor.

"Your Grace," their father said, "I'll never be able to repay the goodwill you've shown my daughters despite the history between our two families. You're a man of great integrity and compassion and I'm entirely indebted."

Luc assumed a shrewd expression. "I would think you would have learned that appearances can be deceiving, my lord. That said, I'm glad we could resolve this matter. Lady Rosamunde and her sister belong in your care, under your roof, instead of mine."

At his bald words, Rosamunde's heart plummeted into her slippers.

Her father bowed his agreement. "It is as we agreed during the carriage ride, then? I shall send 'round my carriage to collect my daughters and their affairs tomorrow afternoon. That should permit adequate time. I do hope you and Her Grace will accept an invitation to dine with us at your earliest convenience. Perhaps next Saturday?"

Luc bowed stiffly and left without another word.

Rosamunde wasn't allowed a moment to dwell on the agonizing mixture of sadness, relief, and newfound joy vying for dominance in her mind. The three left in the room looked at one another, unsure of what to say or do next. And then all of them spoke at once. Words of relief, love, and sorrow stumbled over each other in an effort to heal past wounds. Of all of them, it was Sylvia perhaps who was most affected. Rosamunde thought her sister completely transformed by their acceptance despite her ruinous encounter with Henry St. Aubyn. Her father beamed with happiness. There was only Rosamunde, whose joy was tempered by a despair that could not be voiced.

Her father left after two rounds of tea, with promises of plans for the morrow. As they waved good-bye to him at the top of the steps leading to his carriage, Rosamunde realized with horror that with the excitement she had neglected to give Luc the letter she had discovered. But she had not forgotten her idea.

A gift from the heart.

If his mother's letter proved a disappointment, perhaps this would soften the blow.

"Sylvia, if you're not too exhausted, would you mind very much showing me where the best shops are in town? I know you've been with the other ladies and I need to buy a few things before we leave tomorrow."

Sylvia's brown eyes sparkled with merriment. "Shopping? You want to go shopping? Now, after one of the single most important mornings of our lives?"

"Yes," she muttered.

"I never thought I would see the day. You hate shopping. Avoiding the village stores was the only part of our exile you relished."

"You're not going to start making fun of me again now that I've forgiven you, are you? If you do I might have to change my mind." Oh, it felt wonderful to banter like sisters again. "What is shopping for silly ribbons and ugly hats to chasing foxes and climbing hills and vales?"

Sylvia raised a single sweeping brow. "Ah, but you haven't seen Bond Street yet . . ."

Chapter 18

Male, n. *A member of the unconsidered, or negligible sex. The male of the human race is commonly known (to the female) as Mere Man. The genus has two varieties: good providers and bad providers.*

—The Devil's Dictionary, A. Bierce

Luc sat in the shadow of the Helston second-tier box in the rebuilt Drury Lane Theatre. Rosamunde sat in front of him and slightly to one side. The angle afforded him a discreet but excellent view of her youthful excitement at attending the theatre for the first time. Ata had decided at the last moment they should all go. His grandmother had done him a great service by her suggestion.

He was in no mood for conversation. He was, however, in an excellent mood for a tragedy. The ingenious Mr. Elliston was performing Hamlet to record crowds.

There was nothing like a little poison, murder, and revenge sprinkled with glimpses of the devil to remind you of real life. However, Luc saw not an inch of the stage, nor did he listen to a word of the play. His eyes were focused on the beauty of her profile, the arch of her back, and the curve of her cheek as she smiled with unabashed enthusiasm.

And he had the luxury of being able to be alone with his thoughts. For the first time in a long time, he had not a single goal in front of him. John Murray had called on him today, Brownie tripping at his heels, to discuss the Trafalgar manuscript and its looming publication. The man had been barely able to contain his glee, and if Luc had not been in such a black fog of a mood, he would have been almost happy. The only thing that raised Luc's spirits was the advance monies. But it was not enough to forestall for more than a few months the eventual shipwreck of his financial crisis.

Beyond Rosamunde's shoulder, he spied Grace's elegant form while she used a jeweled lorgnette to view the actors on stage. Illumination from the glittering chandeliers reflected off her lovely gold hair. Ata sat beside her, whispering delightedly from time to time, while the other widows had been paired with gentlemen Ata had deemed worthy of the honor.

They were all of them like fish in a barrel, he thought in his usual black humor. He, most of all. When Ata had made up her mind, nothing could stop her. And now, she had set her sights on him and on Grace.

Well.

There were worse fates, although he wasn't sure

what they were. He was on the verge of breaking a long-held tenet . . . that of avoiding marriage. But perhaps he could do it and still hold on to the shreds of his sanity. With Rosamunde happily settled in the bosom of her family, exactly where she wanted to be, he could marry Grace and father an heir. Grace knew how to conduct a marriage of convenience. Theirs would be one based on longstanding friendship, not love. She would gain a higher standing in society, something she craved, and he would benefit from the material wealth to be gained from the marriage. And Ata and Grace would have an heir or two to dote on while they sorted out the lives of various widows in the club. It was a perfect arrangement. And Luc liked order in his life.

Why then, did he feel like hell? He watched the Lieutenant Colonel seated beside Rosamunde glance at her with obvious interest in his eye. *Sexual interest.* It was all Luc could do not to stand up, haul the officer to his toes, and thrash the redcoat's knowing half smile off his face. Luc turned away.

He would get past this. He was just going to have to—

A roar of applause intruded on his thoughts, and all the occupants of the box save him were standing and going in search of refreshments and the chance to gossip with acquaintances in other boxes during the intermission. Tonight he couldn't call forth the effort to play the host. He had wrought enough goodness in the world today. And enough agony for himself.

"No, Ata, I will not go fetch ratafia and lemonade

for the ladies. There are gentlemen enough to escort everyone. I shall remain here."

Grace Sheffey gave him an odd look, then laughed. "That's what I like about you, Luc. Always able to speak your mind without worrying about giving offense."

"I encourage you to do the same, Grace. It frees the soul," he replied, and bowed to everyone as they exited.

He regained his seat and cradled his forehead in his fingertips as he rested his elbows on his knees. His head ached with a vengeance.

The gentle rustling of the velvet curtains behind him signaled someone's return. "Yes?" he said without looking up.

"Your Grace?" said Rosamunde.

He instantly straightened. "You'll spare me the honor of using my title when we're in private."

"Luc, I'm not here to thank you for what you did today, or for everything else you've done for me and for Sylvia," she said quietly. "I know your dislike of gratitude. I came back to ask you something."

He lowered his lids to hide a tiny flicker of hope.

"I would like you to give me a lock of your hair."

This was rich. He should have known better than to hope at his advanced age. But he did know how to bargain. "Really? Hmmm. Well, that could be arranged . . . in exchange for a lock of yours."

"No," she said without emotion. "You know I cannot. It wouldn't be fair to Grace."

"Dare I ask why you want it?"

"I'd hoped you wouldn't ask," she replied softly.

He stared at her, unable to think of a single retort.

"You used to at least trouble yourself to find the humor in any situation. Please try to do so now."

"Actually, I find there is so much humor in this set of circumstances that it has almost ceased to be funny." He looked away from her.

"Please, Luc?"

It took every ounce of self-control not to jump up and shake her and then kiss her senseless. "Why not? I assume you've brought your gardening sheers," he said archly. "Or some other suitable lethal weapon appropriate for attending the theatre."

"Of course," she said, the sound of relief and a smile coming through the words. "Thank you."

He closed his eyes again when he felt her touching the tight queue he always wore. Before he could think, he said in a rush, "Cut it all."

"What? Everyone would notice and ask questions. Besides, I just can't. I . . ."

"If you want your blasted lock of hair, then cut it all." He seethed. "Don't worry, I shall leave. You may tell the others I've left to attend to a blasted headache."

"All right," she whispered. "If you're sure."

"Do it."

He immediately heard the blades sheering off his queue, and his head felt a stone lighter.

"Lean back, please," she said.

He felt her soft hands smoothing his hair as she made a few more snips on the sides of his head. She again ran her hands through his hair and he could not stop the involuntary tremor that raced through his body. He gripped her hands as she moved to touch his head again. "Rosamunde, for the love of God, stop. I must go."

He abruptly stood, knocking back the chair in his haste. With three long strides he was past the curtain, down the crowded corridor filled with returning box holders, and into the vestibule. The air on Woburn Street was cold and clean, and suddenly he realized his headache was gone.

Rosamunde placed his black satin-twined hair in her reticule. It had felt like a punishment. For what, she did not know. She wasn't even sure if he had insisted she cut it all as punishment for her or for him. But, despite the strain of the moment, perhaps it would help usher in a new chapter of his life and her own.

She was certain that within the year he would marry and learn joy as a father to a child that a union with the countess would bring. From her window at Amberley one afternoon, she had observed him with the children of the houseguests who had come for Lady Madeleine's wedding. He had overseen a game of cricket. It had been the one time when he had seemed completely at ease and in his element, organizing the boys, encouraging the girls, and mollifying the youngest. Yes, he would finally find the happiness he refused to acknowledge that he deserved more than anyone.

And for the first time in a long time, wistful longing clouded her judgment. She fought it the rest of the evening . . . on into the early morning hours as she wove a minute section of Luc's glossy black hair with his mother's golden strands, mimicking the pattern within her own locket. All the while, she softly sang the melancholy Welsh song she had performed while she had looked into the eyes of the man she loved and must leave.

The morning dawned bright, the weather forever refusing to match the state of Luc's mind. As he spurred his dark bay gelding down the last stretch of Rotten Row's sandy track, he realized the futility of his outing. He had hoped it would allow an hour's respite from the machinations of his mind, but it had not.

Today *she* was leaving and Grace Sheffey was coming to visit Ata to take tea, the favored brew of matrimonial-minded females intent on going in for the kill. At least Rawleigh could be depended upon to provide diversion. His former second in command's letter had said he would arrive this afternoon. No doubt to blubber about Lady Sylvia. It was enough to make a man long to rejoin the fleet.

Luc rode back toward Portman Square, past the morning bustle of chimney sweeps and servants. A young girl stood on the corner, selling violets for tuppence per bunch. He pulled up and bought a handful.

A footman stopped him at his door. His presence was requested in the garden.

Rosamunde sat alone on a wrought-iron bench, dappled sunlight filtering through a cluster of birch trees. Her old straw hat dangled down her back from its black ribbons. She wore Madeleine's crimson dress, having refused every offer of new gowns from Ata save the one for the ball. Here in this glorious garden, Luc could almost imagine being back in Cornwall.

Luc crossed to her and bowed. "Your servant."

"Oh, we've been waiting for you."

"We?"

"Ata should return in a trice, but I suppose I shouldn't wait." She paused and looked up at him.

"Waiting is for people with patience, Rosamunde."

"I asked for a lock of your hair last night because I wanted to give you something before I take my leave." She appeared nervous. "It was done out of a desire to remind you there was once a woman who loved you very much."

He blinked and stood stock still.

"A mother's love never dies. It lives on in the heart of the child left behind. But sometimes a tangible symbol gives comfort where memories do not." She reached toward one of his tightly fisted hands, and uncurled it to offer a locket on a gold chain.

"What is this?" He strained to keep his voice calm.

"I bought it yesterday using some gold guineas that found their way into my pockets." Her small smile twisted.

Brownie had obviously botched the ruse. Lying had never been Rosamunde's forte.

"Open it," she said, interrupting his thoughts.

He worked the clasp and found glass encasing black and blonde hair woven together in an intricate pattern.

"By stoke of luck I found a lock of your mother's hair and I wove it with your own."

His mind reeled in shock. He had nothing from his mother. His father had purged the house of every reminder of her.

"I have an almost identical mourning locket to remember the mother I barely knew. Luc, I"—her mouth twisted again—"Oh, where is Ata?" She brought forward an old, slightly crushed letter. "This is from your mother, I think. I found it wedged in the top drawer of an escritoire in my room . . . in Henry's old room here."

Luc, all this time standing, sunk onto the opposite end of the bench. His vision tunneled inward and without a word he cracked the seal bearing his mother's initials. A lock of hair fell into his hand and he devoured the words on the page.

He could barely comprehend it. A few phrases here and there blazed in his consciousness: . . . *beg your forgiveness, I should never have, so proud to call you my son . . . I love you, know I love you always. When I look at the stars at night I take great comfort in knowing you are looking at them too and probably thinking of me as I think of you with such overwhelming love in my heart. A love that will never die.*

The last line echoed Rosamunde's very words to him minutes ago.

A slow warmth spread from his fingers holding the edges of the note while he read the lines a second time, slowly. Rosamunde had moved closer to him and had placed her hand on his sleeve. He cleared his throat.

"Rosamunde, forgive me, I . . ." His voice broke. He desperately tried to hold his emotions in check.

"It's all right, Luc. Would you like your privacy?"

He shook his head no.

Rosamunde looked up and he followed her gaze to find Ata wandering across the lawn in her guarded, tiny steps, attempting not to trip over a ridiculously long white gown more appropriate for a girl in her first season.

"Luc—" Ata trundled up out of breath, her hands on her cheeks. "Do tell us what it says. I'm sorry I was detained."

He doubted his mother had ever confided in Ata and refused to tell his grandmother something that would only cause her suffering. "Rosamunde has done me a great service in finding this." He shuttered his eyes.

"No, Luc," Ata said quietly. "You must tell me what it says. For so long after you came back I thought it was because of the war—because of seeing death and bloodshed—that you had changed. And I thought if I just gave you time and diversions you would revert to the optimistic, idealistic young man I used to know. But, recently, I've thought that perhaps I was wrong. That there was something else . . . I don't want to always have to pretend to be cheerful while my heart is sad and yearns for your happiness."

"Tell her, Luc," Rosamunde said quietly.

And so in the briefest way possible he explained his mother's desperate request, his denial, and the letter that had asked for his forgiveness.

Ata's face was bleak. "It was my fault, you know. I should have taken a stand from the moment my 'spectacular' marriage to a duke was arranged by my well-intentioned parents. But, there was a price to pay for reaching so high. I learned I was chosen because of my bloodlines and docility so that I would breed a proper heir. I don't know if you remember, but your grandfather was a remarkably ill-humored man. And he taught by example." Ata glanced wistfully at her withered hand. "I was the example and your father was the pupil. And when your father married your mother, I was forced to watch it unfold once again. But there was one difference . . . for many years your mother was not as compliant as I had been. It was only later, when you had fully grown that she became weary."

"I cannot forgive myself for not taking her away."

"Luc, your mother came to you in a moment of weakness. Her letter shows she regretted it terribly. Think how unhappy she would be to know that a half hour's madness has plagued you for so long. You must stop punishing yourself and let it go. It's what she would have wanted."

"She should have had joy before the end. Instead she died brokenhearted."

"You're mistaken, Luc. Caro died of an illness, not a broken heart. She was forever catching cold and never had the patience to sit still long enough to recover. The doctor said her lungs were filled with fluid when she died the very day after she had given a huge dinner party here.

"And she had joy. Until you have a child yourself

you cannot understand. Henry, you, and Madeleine *were* her joy and mine. Both of us would have chosen to live our lives over again the same way if only to have you and Henry and Madeleine in our lives. She was not as fragile as you think. Caro might have had moments of sadness, but don't you remember? She was like a ray of sunshine, so optimistic, so devilishly witty, and always with her nose in a book when she could. So much like you *used* to be."

Luc took Ata's wasted hand in his own and stroked it. "Are you suggesting I'm nothing but an irritating bore now, Ata?" He turned to Rosamunde, who had remained so still and silent. "She did suggest that, didn't she?'

"If you think for one moment I will take sides, you are completely mistaken," Rosamunde said, her lips holding in a smile. "May I?" She took the locket and held it up to clasp around his neck.

He slid it beneath the folds of his neckcloth. A shock of his newly shorn hair fell into his eyes. He hadn't gotten used to being freed from the weight. "Thank you, Rosamunde," he said simply, hoping he didn't sound like a sheepish idiot. There was certainly nothing pleasant about baring one's soul no matter what sort of relief it brought.

"And for Ata," she said. She looked at Luc and raised her chin, handing his grandmother a book. "A token of my appreciation for your extraordinary invitation to join the Widows Club. I've never met a better or a kinder lady, and certainly no one as generous with her heart."

The she-devil had had the nerve to give his grand-mother a copy of *Lucifer's Lexicon*. "Why, Lady Rosamunde, *how very kind and thoughtful*," he commented.

"I thought so," Rosamunde said under her breath.

Ata embraced Rosamunde and murmured her delight before she brought her hand to her mouth. "Oh dear, I completely forgot to tell you both. Sir Rawleigh is just arrived. Rosamunde"—she winked at her—"I do hope you don't mind, but I took the liberty of conspiring a bit. My thinking is that if your sister and the vicar are left to their own devices they might just make good use of the opportunity, don't you agree? Just think, there might be *two* weddings to plan this fall"—*now* she was winking at him for God's sake—"and with any luck *two* christenings next summer! I just adore weddings and babies."

He had to put a stop to this. "I do hope you plan to interrupt the pair before they bypass the first part of your idea and proceed directly to the second," he said dryly.

"Lady Sylvia?"

She inadvertently plucked an awkward set of strings on the harp and looked up quickly at the sound of the masculine voice. Oh . . . it was *he*. Could she feel more ill at ease? She rose quickly and curtsied. "Sir Rawleigh."

He walked toward her, his heels clicking on the marquetry floor of the music room. His usual dancing eyes were now serious and his brow etched with anger. "What is this?" he asked, his voice strained. He gripped a letter in his hand, which was shaking.

Lord, he was holding the note she had sent to Charity. The one in which she had very properly thanked them *both* for the beautiful harp but insisted she could not accept it. "My note?" she said faintly.

"Yes, it's your letter. A letter you sent to my sister. *My sister* . . . not to me, the man who took the trouble to go to Wales to select the most beautiful harp he could find, in an effort to show a lady he had not forgotten her, that his feelings would not change, his heart was truly engaged. And this note . . . addressed to my sister, is all I am allowed in return?"

She looked down at the tips of her toes, unable to meet the intensity sparking from his green eyes. "But, it isn't proper for an unmarried lady to carry on a correspondence with a gentleman. Especially a vicar."

"I am just a man. I've never been an angel. Lord knows it'll take years of prayer to make up for . . ." He stopped until she raised her eyes to meet his hard gaze. "And to hell with decorum. I'm fed up to here with notions of propriety. I'm the man who loves you. There, I've said it. Now do me the honor of refusing me with as much honesty. Don't hide behind etiquette and a set of mysterious rules I never quite learned."

Her heart plummeted. She couldn't tell him. She could not tell him the truth. It would require exposing her past to the man who meant everything to her. It would mean having to watch a look of disgust invade his handsome features.

It would mean watching him walk away from her. Her gaze faltered.

He grabbed her chin and forced her to meet his gaze again. "Is it my injury? Are you disgusted by the idea of spending your life with an impoverished one-armed vicar?"

"No," she said with a burst of emotion. "Of course not. There is not a single thing about you that is not perfect," she whispered. "Your wife will be the luckiest woman alive."

The silence was deafening.

His stormy eyes softened. "Sylvia, I'm a long way from being perfect. My two best friends would have much to say on the subject if you asked them."

He inched closer. "Will you do something for me?" When she didn't respond immediately he continued. "Lay your head on my shoulder and let me hold you for just a few moments. And you have my word I won't try to kiss you again as I did in Cornwall. I should not have presumed—"

His words were interrupted when she did what he asked. She just could not bring herself to refuse a moment of comfort and bittersweet happiness. She felt his one arm come about her body like a band of iron. His warm breath teased the tendrils on the side of her head.

"Now you will tell me what this is about. Because I am not an honorable man and I will not let you go until you tell me. You see, now you have tangible proof that I am as sinful as the next man."

Sylvia felt the warmth of his body penetrate the layers of black vestments he wore and she squeezed her eyes shut. "I could not come to you as a bride should," she whispered so softly he had to bend his ear closer to her lips. "And I have no one to blame for my loss of innocence but myself."

He stiffened.

Well, she had said it, and now she would finish the job, making sure to twist the knife as firmly as possible. She told him every embarrassing detail, and the misery she had caused her entire family. And suddenly at the very end she noticed he was kissing the top of her head. She ceased her confession.

"Does your heart still belong to him?" he asked, still holding her.

"Now I realize I probably wasn't in love with him. That's what makes my actions all the more reprehensible."

"Allow me to tell you that you're entirely wrong. Sylvia, you were in love with him. No one with a sensitive heart and conscience such as your own would have ever given herself without being in love and having him love you in return. You've chosen to further punish yourself by imagining wrongdoing in every direction. But the question I asked was if you *still* love him."

"No," she said, not daring to hope.

"Well then, do you think you could find it in your heart to forgive me too? For I am very sorry to say I would not come to our marriage as pure as—ah—well, I was not quite as bad as Luc St. Aubyn, but I will admit I was considerably worse than Lord Landry. That is to say—"

"No," she interrupted with a hint of a smile. "I don't think I want to know anything about the trail of broken hearts you left at every port."

"Well then," he said, the old glint of amusement in his eyes returning, "dare I offer my heart to you again? You're not going to send a letter of refusal to my sister if I do?"

"Oh, but Sir Rawleigh—"

"Philip."

"Philip, I . . ." Staring into his mesmerizing eyes, she knew what she should do, what she ought to do, what the noble thing to do was. In a sudden rush, she threw all the *should haves*, *would haves*, and *could haves* over her left shoulder quite properly and kissed him within an inch of his life.

Chapter 19

Future, n. *That period of time in which our affairs prosper, our friends are true and our happiness is assured.*

—The Devil's Dictionary, A. Bierce

Rosamunde untied the ribbon holding the violets Luc had handed to her when she had stepped into her father's carriage a fortnight ago. She wondered if he knew the significance . . . *faithfulness.*

Oh, there was no question on her side. She would be faithful to her memories of him for the rest of her life.

She carefully laid the tiny purple flowers between the sheaves of waxed paper and weighted them with several tomes in her father's library. She glanced about in wonder at the quiet elegance surrounding her while she sat on the rose-and-beige Aubusson carpet. Her mother's portrait hung above the ornate gray marble mantel, above the crackling fire that illuminated the wide bookshelves much like Luc's study at Helston House. She forced her mind away from the comparison.

She had been here for almost a fortnight and she still did not feel as if she was truly at home. Oh, the anxiety had evaporated. But she felt more like a very well loved guest than the daughter and sister she was. Everyone was on their best behavior, refusing to let any irritations fly in the way of newfound happiness. Even Phinn had refrained from . . .

Her father interrupted her thoughts with his entrance. "Ah, daughter, I've the invitation from the dowager duchess that she mentioned during dinner here last week. We must respond and"—he crossed the room to help her to her feet—"well, I sensed some hesitation on your part." He did not relinquish her hand but drew her to the warmth of the fire.

"No, not at all. Ata has been so kind to us. I cannot refuse."

Her father searched her face. "We do not have to attend, you know. I'm looking for any excuse to return to Edgecumbe. We could send out regrets and be walking or riding the cliffs three days from now. Away from the dirt of town."

Rosamunde shifted her gaze to her mother's portrait. "Do you miss her?" she asked softly. "You never spoke of Mother."

He smiled. "Hmmm. I suppose I never spoke of her aloud because I have conversations with her in my mind every day."

"You loved her very much . . ."

"Yes," he said simply.

"And you never thought about finding another love, another wife?"

He studied the portrait, and a warm glow of happiness radiated from his face. "Never, Rosamunde. I know I always told you and your siblings it was because I didn't want to inflict an evil stepmother on you, but that was not it, you see. I was too discomfited to tell you the truth. Some people never find the love I shared with your mother. I was lucky. We were given sixteen years to build memories. Those are all I want, along with you and your brothers and sister. Now, I am fully content with you and Sylvia returned to me."

Rosamunde stepped into her father's embrace. "As am I, Father."

"Are you, my sweet Rose?"

She reined in her emotion. "How can you doubt it?"

"Because you're no longer my dangerous beauty, ready to do anything to gain your heart's desire."

She pulled away, shocked at his words. "My heart's desire is here with you and Phinn and . . ." She glanced at her father's expression and stopped.

"Is it really, Rosamunde?" He perused her face. "I can't bear the thought of giving you up again now that you're here with me. It's like a dream. But my darling, I want for you what I once had."

There was no use continuing to pretend. She fiddled with a button on his waistcoat. "Ata told me there's to be some sort of important announcement at her ball. I'm certain she will announce the duke's engagement to the Countess of Sheffey."

There was a long silence.

"I find it hard to believe the man who handed you into our carriage not two weeks ago would consider such a monumentally stupid idea. He loves you, Rosamunde. I knew it within a quarter of an hour of our acquaintance. The only question is whether you love him. You've learned how to hide your feelings to the point that I have to ask to be certain. Do you—"

"I can't give him a child," she interrupted in a whisper. "An heir."

"You do love him." A light flickered in his eyes.

"Father, he must have a child. For himself, for Ata, to bring new life and love. You have just said your happiness stems from being surrounded by all of us, and that you can live without a wife's love."

"No, you're twisting my words. I believe I would've married your mother even if she'd been known to be barren. But to be truthful, it would have been a difficult decision for I longed for a large family." He sighed. "Perhaps the duke is willing to forego a child. Perhaps his heir is competent."

"But—" she started.

"My darling," he interrupted, "you're on the brink of surpassing the very trait you deplored in your sister. A sister who I'm quite delighted to watch happily purchasing half the gowns here in town for her trousseau."

Rosamunde smiled wistfully.

Her father kissed her forehead and whispered, "Sometimes selfishness is a virtue."

* * *

A quarter of a mile away, Luc sat in his own library wondering who, indeed, was the employer and who was the employee. For the thousandth time.

"Enough, Brownie," he said impatiently. "I see your point. Send them down to Amberley then if we cannot manage a town house for this season's widows."

"And you will finally tell your grandmother the state of affairs. There can be no more balls after this one, no more mysteriously inherited cottages, no more—"

"No more what?" Ata asked, gliding silently into the room, something she had never managed before given her propensity for high heels.

Luc jumped up, praying she hadn't heard a word. His grandmother looked more petite than ever before. He tried to turn the conversation. "You're not wearing your usual . . ." He wafted his hand in the direction of her feet, not wanting to embarrass her.

Ata stuck her nose in the air. "Grace insisted I buy these slippers, and I would not disappoint her for the world. And you're changing the subject. I distinctly heard Mr. Brown suggest you will finally tell your grandmother the state of affairs. There can be no more balls after this one, no more mysteriously inherited cottages, no more . . . something."

Damn her hearing. Why hadn't she lost that sense like the rest of her contemporaries? Well, what did it matter? His marriage to Grace Sheffey would change everything. There was no danger in telling Ata the state of their precarious finances.

And so he did.

Ata sagged into the leather chair opposite Brownie

while Luc paced and explained that Ata's mysterious relation had never left her any cottages, and that he had barely managed to finance her dreams for the widows in the club each season. He came to rest at the mantel, his arms crossed. "Ata, you are not to worry. Soon everything will be set to rights again. Everyone knows the cycle of an aristocratic family. The first generation makes it, the second generation spends it, the third generation marries it, and the cycle repeats again. I had planned to beg Grace's hand in marriage this very afternoon."

Ata beamed. "Oh Luc, you will be so happy. Grace adores you and is so charming and kindhearted, and will make you the perfect wife and duchess, and—"

"He doesn't love her, you blind termagant," growled Brownie.

Luc bit back a smile. He would give anything to know what was behind the long-held antagonism between the pair. "Now Brownie, I fear your memory is slipping. Wasn't it you who suggested I reel in a dowry fatter than the one I parceled out to my sister?" Luc drawled.

Brownie pounced. "That was before you fell in love with the dark-haired lass."

Luc shuttered his eyes.

"Besides," the older man mumbled, "I'm certain her father would dower her adequately. And you also refuse to consider the one brilliant idea I've suggested repeatedly."

"Brownie," Luc growled, "If you treasure your—"

"To hell with my position here. I've tired of it

lately. My bit of land in Scotland has shown a tidy profit, and I've saved every penny I've earned the last forty years." Brownie took a breath. "You forgot a step in the cycle, Luc. Or perhaps it's just for the Scottish landed gentry. It's the generation who *saves* it."

Ata narrowed her eyes. "Well, I for one didn't forget it. Scotsmen always save it, because their pride refuses to allow them to marry it."

Ata and Brownie glared at each other like a cat and canine on the verge of warfare, each eyeing the other's vulnerabilities and assets. Luc hadn't been so entertained in a decade. He eased out of sight within a bow window's frame.

"If you pester your grandson into marrying a woman he doesn't love, *Merceditas*, you will come to regret it to your dying day."

Merceditas indeed, thought Luc with amusement.

"Luc has cared deeply for Grace many years. Love will grow," Ata insisted.

"Did it grow in your marriage?" When Ata didn't answer, Brownie barked at her, "You're asking him to chain himself to a pretty bauble who likes parties. And he will spend the rest of his life wishing he was in bed with Rosamunde Baird." The last was said under his breath.

"Well!" Ata said, shocked from silence. "Your vulgarity knows no bounds. And I suppose your mysterious, brilliant idea will solve everything."

Luc stepped out of the bow window, determined to put an end to—

"He should reveal himself as the—"

"Don't say another word, Mr. Brown," Luc interrupted.

" . . . as the author of *Lucifer's Lexicon*. He should trust the publisher's instincts. Doing so will increase demand for the book as well as assure the success of the one to be released next week. And"—Brown's voice rose in pitch—"he should marry the bonny widow who likes to sail."

Luc dragged his hands down his face, determined to haul Brownie to his feet and thrash the audacity out of him.

"You wrote a book?" Ata asked in wonder. She rose from her chair and took a few tentative steps until she faced him and reached to place her good hand on his lapel.

Luc looked down into her impish expression. For a moment he saw beyond the wrinkles, into the face of a petite, vivacious young girl. "I think between the two of us we can take him, don't you?" Luc drawled, nodding toward the loquacious Mr. Brown.

"Oh, Luc. Why didn't you tell me?" Ata asked softly. Understanding bloomed on her withered face. "And it's the one several people mentioned at Grace's ball. The one Rosamunde gave me."

"Perhaps," he admitted gruffly.

"Why are you ashamed?"

"This should be rich." Brownie said, under his breath.

"Shush, you old badger," Ata huffed.

"Ata, I refuse to sully the Helston duchy," Luc said.

"I'll not be taken for a sniveling literary bore and let our name become synonymous with fusty, knock-kneed weaklings."

"Actually, they think he's a bluestockinged spinster," Brownie said, owl-eyed.

"What?" Ata said completely confused.

"They think he's a girl."

"Say your prayers, old man," said Luc, coming toward him.

"No wait," Ata pleaded. "Why would you . . . Oh Lord, it's your father again, isn't it? He hated seeing you and your mother reading because he earned remarkably poor notes at Eton and was sent down from Oxford. Books represented failure to him."

Luc regarded his tiny grandmother intently.

"Surely you knew that," Ata said. "Oh, Luc, I can't wait to tell everyone my grandson wrote that witty lexicon." She ignored Brownie, who had cleared his throat loudly. "And there is another book?"

Her words hung in the air. Both of them turned expectant faces toward him . . .

He was living in a madhouse. Surely he deserved some sort of medal for enduring these two pint-sized editions of so-called good intentions.

And suddenly he realized his fatal error. He had been brought to these agonizing crossroads because he had failed to act. Decisively. *About everything*.

It wasn't like him. Living on land was making him soft. He had been reading too much philosophy and it showed. What he needed was a bit of debauchery. Just a touch of dissolution and wickedness mixed with

Ata's Armagnac and a visit to Letty's House of Love-
lies lest he lose his moniker forever.

Then he would be able to think very, very clearly.

He turned and stalked through the door, a chorus of
voices floating at his heels.

At some point between the last half of the first bottle
of brandy or the first half of the second bottle, Luc accepted the fact that no amount of alcohol was going
to bring the much-desired oblivion he sought. And at
some point between the first layer of clothing Letty's
loveliest removed and the last layer, he made a similar
decision before pressing an absurd amount of coin in
the disappointed lady-bird's palm and departing with
a string of curses under his breath.

Nothing was going according to plan. At least he
instinctively knew when to retreat as all good com-
manders do.

In the cold clear light of dawn he rode through the
streets of London, and he took his decision. There
had never been any doubt. But like the condemned
throughout the ages, he had attempted a final meal before succumbing to the fate of all proper English aris-
tocrats.

Twelve hours later he found himself weaving those
same streets high atop his phaeton, Grace Sheffey beside him as pretty as a picture and nodding graciously
to occupants in each carriage they passed. It was the
fashionable time of day to see and be seen in Hyde
Park, and this was surely where Grace would most like
to receive a proposal of marriage.

Luc tooled toward a thicket of trees and set the brake. There in the dappled afternoon sun, Luc offered himself up on the platter of matrimonial sacrifice to insure the continuation of the Helston duchy.

"Well then, Grace, when would you like to set the date?" he asked.

She raised a single perfectly styled eyebrow. "Come now, Luc, you can do better than that."

So she was insisting on her pound of flesh. "You are perfectly right, my dear. Shall I get down on one knee? I think I can manage it, although you'll have to move your feet outside the carriage."

"No, you'll ruin your pantaloons. Proceed."

He clasped one of her hands. "Grace Sheffey, will you do me the immense honor of consenting to become my wife?"

"Why?" She searched his expression, and for a moment Luc saw the barest hint of sadness.

"Because . . . because I have taken the decision to marry. And we will suit. You know I care for you and will always see to your happiness."

"Why?" she asked softer this time.

"Grace, enough of this foolishness. We have always been meant to marry and I will see it through."

A rush of wind rustled the autumn leaves above them, sending several into the carriage. Grace twirled one of the stems between her fingers. "Did you know I received eight proposals two years ago before I married the Earl of Sheffield?"

Luc did not respond.

"And after he died three months later, I received

three proposals within a week of the one-year anniversary of his death."

Luc scratched his head. He had a very bad feeling about all of this attention to detail. Details were never a good sign.

"And can you imagine, Luc? Out of eleven proposals, not one of them sported your spectacularly unoriginal turn of phrase." She looked away.

"Lord, Grace, you're not going to insist on a lot of romantic drivel, are you? We've known each other far too long for that nonsense. However, if you insist . . ."

"No," she interrupted. She crushed the dried leaf in her spotless white glove and watched the remnants flutter into the wind. "I decided against you long ago—during the ball at my town house, actually. But I felt I deserved the enjoyment of watching you squirm through a proposal." She turned her head, but not fast enough to hide the tears in her eyes.

"Grace," he began gently.

"Don't," she said vehemently before placing a veil in front of her emotions. "I'm sorry I cannot return your affections. I do *not* love you, Luc St. Aubyn."

Luc came closer to loving Grace Sheffey at that moment than at any time during all the decades he had known her. If it had not felt condescending he would have even said he was proud of her. He brushed a lock of her hair from her face and bent his head to encounter her expression. "I do love you, you know."

"Hmmm," she said. "May I suggest that perhaps there are other ladies, or rather a particular lady, who might be more receptive to your *eccentric* charms?"

Luc smiled and swept her into the most wicked kiss he could muster for his lifelong friend. He looked at her startled pale eyes when he released her. "Eccentric, eh?"

"Let go of me, you big oaf. I see Lady Cowper over there," she nodded toward the grand allée. "Let me down if you please, I find this phaeton remarkably ill sprung and I would prefer to go about with Emily. Her fourth cousin, next in line to the king of Bavaria, made me an offer last week, and"—she sighed—"I cannot quite decide if it would be more correct to refuse him on a Saturday or a Sunday. She will give me the best advice, I think."

"Of course," he said, handing her out of the carriage and escorting her to the patroness. "You will still honor us with your presence at Ata's ball tonight, won't you, my dear? I won't take no for an answer this time."

She sent him an arch smile. "Wouldn't miss it for the world."

Rosamunde had forced herself to accept the dowager duchess's request to see to the final floral arrangements at Helston House the afternoon of the ball. Ata and she had been working for at least an hour attaching long strands of ivy to the last of the bouquets gracing the side tables in the ballroom. She was painfully aware each moment that the heart of the man she loved was beating nearby. She could feel his very essence, could feel his powerful presence. She was grateful to Ata for maintaining a steady stream of conversation.

Rosamunde had never thought she would tire of

the London whirl, but she had been wrong. More than anything else she longed for the wild beauty of home . . . Cornwall. She wanted to walk the Boscawen cliffs, where the hollows were scented with heather and yellow gorse, and the salt air braced the skin and the panoramas of the sea nurtured the soul.

Her father had promised a remove to Edgecumbe Monday, the day after tomorrow. If she could just withstand the unbearable finality of the betrothal announcement tonight, she would then be able to take some comfort in knowing she would be soon home.

"Rosamunde," Ata said, "I do believe we are short a bouquet. I can't imagine how we overlooked the table by the French doors. How odd."

Rosamunde looked at the dowager. She had missed Ata very much when she had left to go to her father's house a few blocks away. She had come to love the older lady like the grandmother she had never had. "I'm certain no one will notice. Let's move the palm in front of it."

Ata tapped her finger to her lips. "Hmmm. I know. There's a bouquet of lilies in my chamber. Do you mind very much if I ask you to fetch them for me?"

She saw the glimmer of something in the dowager's intelligent dark eyes. Rosamunde crossed her arms. "I'm certain the housekeeper knows your room better than I. And I'm not quite finished here."

Ata's lips twitched. "Are you arguing with me?"

Rosamunde burst out laughing. "Heavens no, Ata. I wouldn't presume. It's just I don't want to invade your home, your privacy."

Ata lifted her chin and lowered her lids. "I rather think you did that a long time ago, dear child, at my invitation. Allow me to renew the invitation."

Rosamunde's heart was pounding in her breast. And yet, she felt so weary. She just wasn't up to the game anymore.

"Rosamunde . . ." Ata said very sweetly, "I promise this will be the very last time I ask you to do anything for me. Will you please go up to my chamber and bring me the lilies?"

"Of course," she replied, quite sure there was more involved.

Rosamunde climbed the familiar curved marble front staircase with a heavy heart. In the portrait gallery the austere faces of the first six Dukes of Helston glared down at her and she almost smiled. The portrait of her great-grandmother, the disapproving countess Edwina, put them all to shame. The Earls of Twenlyne had held their countesses in great esteem and had honored them with portraits, unlike these puffed-up heathens. A certain sense of pride grew in Rosamunde and she lengthened her stride toward the bedchambers.

Along the corridor, darkening with late afternoon shadows, the unmistakable aroma of lilies permeated the air. Not the overly sweet tang of the larger, showy blooms. This was the intoxicating scent of Lilies of the Valley, which always reminded her of the promise of spring.

Rosamunde crossed the threshold into Ata's rooms. A canary in a gilded cage trilled a welcome to a suite filled with mementos and lace of the last century. Now the scent of the flowers whirled about her, the source still a mystery. Until . . .

Rosamunde spied a scattering of the tiny bell-shaped flowers leading toward an inner door. She paused and closed her eyes.

A return to happiness . . . Few knew the language of flowers. She mustn't jump to—

A ragged sound stole from her lips and she darted to the half-open door, pushing into the beyond.

Her vision telescoped to an armchair, Luc's large frame sprawled inelegantly and disheveled across it, his head resting against the frame. His black hair was slicked back and his eyes stared at her, harshly inviting. A small bowl of the fragrant white blossoms stood on a table at his elbow.

For perhaps a full half minute they gazed at each other before he spoke. "A lady once told me she favored flowers because they were silent."

She watched him take hold of the delicate crystal bowl and study it intently before raising his eyes to her own. The turbulent longing she found in the sea-blue depths made her faint with hope.

"If silence is what you truly want, Rosamunde, relieve me of these and be on your way."

She wasn't aware of her steps toward him, only of the unconscious need to find the perfect combination of words to express herself. But looking into his face, the face that haunted her dreams and every waking moment, she couldn't seem to form a single coherent sentence.

Time seemed suspended as she gazed at the bowl of

lilies he held between them. "Luc . . ." She swallowed the rest of the words. With a rush she knocked the crystal from his grasp. Water and flowers sprayed through the air as the heavy bowl thudded to the carpet.

"I hate flowers," she whispered. "I hate silence."

Tension spun about them, eddying around their forms.

He slowly offered her his hand, the calloused palm exposed and waiting for hers.

She slipped her hand into his and felt the beat of his heart she had sensed so poignantly. Slowly, inexorably, he pulled her onto his lap, where his lips found hers and she tasted a little bit of heaven.

She couldn't seem to stop herself, so lost was she. Such a welling of the rightness of it flooded her, making it nearly impossible to say the things that must be said.

"Luc," she said finally, closing her eyes and resting her forehead against his.

He put his finger against her lips. "No, there is something I must tell you." He moved his hands to cup her face and brush her lips with his thumbs. "I have gone 'round and 'round in my mind searching for a way I could promise to bring you nothing but peace and happiness, but I find I cannot. You deserve these things, Rosamunde, after living so wretchedly. And a Helston is the worst possible man to take a chance on. We are all of us a totally unreliable, domineering, selfish lot. But you see, the thing is, I can't let you go without telling you I love you . . ."

She opened her mouth to speak but he silenced her

again before continuing, "No, I see the reservations already lining up in your mind. Just answer one question if you please. Do I dare hope you might feel the same? That you—"

"But I . . . a child. I can't—"

"Hush," he interrupted in a whisper. "I hate children. Complete barbarians, the lot of them."

"That's not true." She could barely breathe from wanting. "And Ata . . ."

"You're not very good at following directions are you?" He kissed her forehead. "And here I was hoping for an obedient wife. Now answer my question."

The words were stuck in her throat behind all the other reasons. She looked down at the opening in his white shirt. His wrinkled cravat was carelessly draped over the edge of the chair. The locket she had given him gleamed against his bronzed skin. She closed her eyes tightly. "I love you." She took a deep breath. "I've loved you, I think from the first day, when you told me about your devil's rules." She shook her head. "No, I think it was the next day, when you confounded Algernon Baird . . . Well, I am certain I loved you when you bashed in the baron's head."

"You're a bloodthirsty wench, aren't you?" He leaned back and smiled the achingly familiar devilish smile that made her weak at the knees. "Dare I hope you're an impatient one as well? Name the day you will be my bride."

"Luc, what about Grace?" she asked softly.

"She turned me down flat."

Rosamunde pursed her lips to fight the bubble of

mirth before arching a brow. "Ah, I see. So I'm your second choice?"

"Precisely."

"Clearly you're interested only in my dowry."

"What a lovely word that is, *dowry*. Hmmm. Are you good for fifty thousand? It would make Mr. Brown supremely happy if you are."

"And you?"

"Me? Well let's see . . . supremely happy? I think I should require a scrap of your embroidery," he said, lips twitching.."

"Well then, I suppose I shall have to settle for pleasing Mr. Brown instead."

He kissed her then with such exquisite thoroughness that Rosamunde wondered if one could expire from such delirious happiness. "Name the day," he said insistently. "And if it's not by Special License within a week, I'll not be held responsible for any scandal in the interim."

Rosamunde looked into the loving expression behind his hooded eyes and shook her head. "Luc, what about an heir? You haven't satisfied the question."

"Rosamunde, if you dare let the matter of a squalling infant come between us, I daresay I will never forgive you. For—"

"But . . ." she insisted.

"I love you," he nearly shouted, "and I don't give a bloody damn who is next in line. In fact, my heir is particularly unappealing. But I've purchased half the cottages in England currently occupied by half the widows in England. When I die you will sell these unentailed parcels, build a castle, and start a nunnery. Or you will sail across the sea on *Caro's Heart* along with Ata, who is certain to outlive me, and never look back. But what you must promise me is that you will not regret anything."

Rosamunde ran her fingers through the damp strands of his hair. "I regret cutting your hair."

"I shall grow it back."

"I regret not having had the chance to sail more."

"I shall take you on a long sailing expedition after our wedding. By the by, you're allowed only one more regret tonight."

"I regret"—she nuzzled his neck—"not having enough time to make love to you before the ball."

He growled and there was no more talk of regrets or balls or sailing or heirs or duty. There was only talk of needing and giving.

At half past ten o'clock that same evening, Luc St. Aubyn escorted Rosamunde's father from the Helston library to rejoin the glitter that could only be found at a London ball. He saw the older gentleman to his daughter and then mounted the steps to the musicians' stage. There was no need to draw attention to the fact. The elegant crowd had been waiting for the betrothal announcement with curiosity and impatience. Not once had they seen him dance with the Countess of Sheffield. In fact, he had not danced at all, having missed the start of the ball by a good one hour. He took immense pleasure in defying convention and the half-hearted dressing-down by his grandmother. But perhaps he took the most pleasure from the apoplectic back-slapping and I told you so's from Brownie.

As he looked about the silent, assembled guests before him, there was only one face he sought, the dangerous beauty surrounded by Ata and her family.

"Ladies and gentlemen, thank you for honoring me with your presence tonight. As many of you know this event is to celebrate an important announcement. Actually, there are two announcements, if you will allow." He had thought of the best way to cause the least embarrassment to Grace, who was standing between Lady Cowper and her princely relation. "I must say, I've been vastly disappointed lately by all the slowtops residing in town these days . . ."

A trickle of hushed, questioning sounds emanated about the room.

Luc spoke louder. "I've always said gossip and dissipation were food for the soul, but truly I think you've all overimbibed."

The sounds were interrupted by a few hoots of laughter.

"But then none of you have been following my advice very well. If you had but adopted my rules and drunk more brandy, I assure you that you would have guessed by now the name of the true author of *Lucifer's Lexicon*. And by the by, Mr. Quigley, a waltz is one hundred forty-*four* steps closer to hell, not one hundred forty-five steps, you imbecile. You, sir, might not be able to count, but I assure you the Devil of Helston can."

The crowd erupted in a frenzy, each of them vying

for attention. Luc spied the two Scotsmen, his publisher, John Murray, and Brownie, in the corner dancing their own version of a celebratory waltz, which looked remarkably like a Scottish jig. Luc held out his hands for silence.

"And so can the future Duchess of Helston. Lady Rosamunde?"

Luc watched Rosamunde's family and Ata weave a path to the front of the crowd, still roiling with the answer to the number-one question in the betting books of London, the burning topic which had occupied the hearts and minds of the *ton* for the last two seasons. Nary a one of them was looking at Grace Sheffey, who was smiling at him.

Rosamunde's father handed her up to him and he gazed into the depths of her ethereal eyes and well-kissed lips. "I give you Lady Rosamunde, who has consented to become my bride."

"Heaven help you now, Lady Rosamunde," called out Mr. Quigley, and the ballroom exploded with mirth.

Luc bowed to her. "Care for a dance with the devil?"

"Surely you can be more original," she chided. "I fear you're slipping."

He glanced at the rapt audience out of the corner of his eye. "Well, now that the courtship is over, surely I won't have to try so hard."

"Really?" She arched a brow. "I don't see a ring on my finger yet, do you?"

He growled something suitably devilish. The first

notes of a waltz sounded and he grasped her scandalously close.

The crowd roared their approval.

"Bully," she whispered.

"Witch."

She stared into his sparkling, hooded eyes and laughed. "My darling."

"My love," he whispered back.

And then he kissed her in an outrageously possessive manner that left all the ladies in the crowd sighing and thoroughly put out that Lord Fire and Ice was obviously hanging up his forked tail.

All the gentlemen breathed a sigh of relief for the same reason.

Epilogue

*Baby, n. A misshapen creature of no particular
age, sex or condition, chiefly remarkable for
the violence of the sympathies and antipathies
it excites in others, itself without sentiment or
emotion.*

— The Devil's Dictionary, A. Bierce

Dear Mr. Brown,

*I am condescending to write to you solely at the
request of my grandson. I am to inform that the
duchess was safely delivered of not one but two
infants last evening. Luc tasked me to relate that
Henry Horatio Philip Brown Rawleigh St. Aubyn,
and Caroline Merceditas Sylvia Edwina St. Aubyn
are both raven-haired and bonny like their mother.
Rosamunde insists they take after Luc. Lady Sylvia,
who we have just learned is increasing herself, in-*

sists the son takes after Rosamunde and the daughter after Luc.

But, well, if any of them had eyes in their head they would know that both babies look exactly like me. I know what you are thinking, sir. But if you have the temerity to suggest it is because they are wrinkled and toothless, I shall be forced to rescind the invitation Luc feels compelled to extend to you for the coming season. You are to come in a fortnight.

The current members of the Widows Club—Georgiana Wilde, Elizabeth Ashburton, and Sarah Winters—are still in residence here; however, Georgiana Wilde has been spending a lot more time at her deceased husband's estate in anticipation of the heir's eminent arrival. If you ask me, which I know you won't, there is something she's been hiding from all of us. Why anyone would choose to hide something from me when I am sure to find it out is beyond me. I'm determined to sort it out next season. By that time the Countess of Sheffield should be returned from her tour of Italy. I hope to entice her down here too.

And by the by, there will be no more talk of who was right last fall. If you were a gentleman you would know that a lady is always right, sir, even when she is wrong.

Pax,
Merceditas St. Aubyn
Dowager Duchess of Helston

Avon Romantic Treasures

Unforgettable, enthralling love stories, sparkling with passion and adventure from Romance's bestselling authors

Avon Romances

the best in exceptional authors and unforgettable novels!